Edward Faulkener

The Book of Psalms of David the King and Prophet

Edward Faulkener

The Book of Psalms of David the King and Prophet

Reprint of the original, first published in 1875.

1st Edition 2024 | ISBN: 978-3-38538-637-2

Verlag (Publisher): Outlook Verlag GmbH, Zeilweg 44, 60439 Frankfurt, Deutschland
Vertretungsberechtigt (Authorized to represent): E. Roepke, Zeilweg 44, 60439 Frankfurt, Deutschland
Druck (Print): Books on Demand GmbH, In de Tarpen 42, 22848 Norderstedt, Deutschland

THE BOOK OF PSALMS

"OF DAVID THE KING AND PROPHET"

ܕܟܬܒ ܕܬܫܒܚܬܐ ܕܕܘܝܕ ܡܠܟܐ ܘܢܒܝܐ

DISPOSED ACCORDING TO THE

RHYTHMICAL STRUCTURE

OF THE

ORIGINAL.

WITH THREE ESSAYS:

I.— The Psalms of David Restored to David.
II.— The External Form of Hebrew Poetry.
III. The Zion of David Restored to David.

WITH MAP AND ILLUSTRATIONS.

By E. F.

LONDON:
LONGMANS, GREEN, AND CO.
1875.

INTRODUCTION.

I N the following attempt to arrange the Psalms of David accord
ing to the structure of the poetry of the Hebrew original, the reader
will observe that the old translation, or that in our Prayer-books.
has been retained, partly because the language is more simple and
Saxon, and therefore more rhythmical ; partly because it is more
deeply impressed upon our memory by the constant reading of the
Psalter in our daily services ; and partly because in many instances
it will be found that King James's Translation, being more literally
exact, is for that very reason, like all literal translations, sometimes
harsh, or even obscure ; whereas the old translation of 1539. by a
greater licence of translation, sometimes apparently guessing at the
sense, as in the Seventy-eighth Psalm—" their maidens were not
given in marriage," where the original is " their maidens were not
praised "—is not only more accordant to our English idiom, but
frequently more accordant also to the real meaning. One example
will suffice. In Ps. lxix. 27 we have in the Bible translation—

Add iniquity unto their iniquity.

But the word here translated "add" is in the Hebrew נתן ; the
primitive meaning of which is *to give*, but which in Ps. xvi. 10,
and cxxi. 3, signifies to suffer, to allow, or to permit—" Thou wilt
not *suffer* Thy Holy One to see corruption ; " " He will not suffer
thy foot to be moved : " as in Ex. xii. 23, " The Lord will not
suffer the destroyer to come in : " so again in Esther ix. 13, " Let
it be *granted* to the Jews." It is in this sense that the word has

B

been taken by our old translators—Suffer them to go from one
iniquity unto another, or as they have given it—

> " Let them fall from one wickedness to another,"

a translation which, though it looks like a mere paraphrase, is in
fact a more accurate rendering than the Bible translation ; and,
considered theologically, *true*, while the latter is *false :* for this
appears to make God the author of evil : while that expresses the
mere act of *sufferance*. Hammond says—" For so it is ordinary
with God, as a punishment of some former great sin or sins, *though
not to infuse any malignity, yet by withdrawing His grace*, and
delivering them up to themselves, to *permit* more sins to follow,
one on the heels of the other." Words which seem to be copied
from Augustine, " *Adde, non vulnerando, sed non sanando*."

For the same reason, as few alterations have been made as possible, and care has been taken to endeavour to express these alterations in as rhythmical language as the original translation, and in
every case to examine them with the context, before adopting them.
These alterations are—

i. Where the signification was missed by our translators, as in
Ps. lxxxiv., where sparrows and swallows are supposed to
build nests in God's house ! or where, as in Ps. xx. in
the Biblical version, we pray—Let the King hear us when
we call ; instead of praying that God would hear our prayers
for the king.

ii. Where it was necessary to restore the tautology of the original,
which our translators have striven so much to do away with,
thinking that they thus gave greater richness to the style ;
being unaware that they thereby destroyed one great ele-
ment of the Hebrew poetry.

iii. Where it was necessary to cast out any superfluous words
which have been added by our translators, where such words
made the line too long.

iv. Where it was necessary to alter the construction of the
sentence, if we wished to bring out the parallelism of the
original.

But although the chief object of this work is to point out the parallelism of the original ; it has been found desirable in many instances, in order to avoid unnecessary departure from our authorized translation, not to insist too strictly upon the particular kind of parallelism there exhibited. In many instances where an inverted parallelism of the original has been rendered by our translators as a direct one, it would not only interfere too greatly with the familiar phraseology of our recognized translation to change it back to the inverted form, but the alteration would appear harsh, and unconformable to the structure of our own language. Thus we should make no improvement upon—

Let us come before His presence with thanksgiving,
Let us show ourselves glad in Him with psalms :

by changing it back to the inverted form, as in the original :—

Let us come before His presence with thanksgiving,
And with psalms let us sing unto Him.

For the same reason we must be content to let even the direct parallelism remain as we find it in our translation, where not exactly the same as the original : for we should gain nothing by altering it, while we should lose greatly by a useless unsettling of a translation which is so justly endeared to the hearts of so large a portion of God's children. The following example will be sufficient to illustrate this :—

Show me Thy ways, O Lord ;
And teach me Thy paths :

sufficiently exhibits the parallelism, without putting it in the original form—

Thy ways, O Lord, show me :
And Thy paths teach me.

From what we have said it will, we think, be found that the careful study of the ancient parallelism cannot fail to make more clear and more emphatic the poetical portions of Holy Scripture.

Next to parallelism, we should direct our attention to the division of paragraphs : and here again we cannot be too careful : for the proper appreciation of the Psalms of David depends very much upon the assistance given to the eye and voice by the careful divisions of the several parts. As Hebrew poetry was at one time believed to be subject to the laws of Greek and Latin verse, so these paragraphs have been thought by some German writers, as Hengstenberg, Kurz, and Delitzsch, to assimilate to strophes or stanzas, and to be subject to a rule of numbers. Our attention is drawn to the supposed fact that the paragraphs in a particular Psalm consist of a certain number of verses, or that there is some certain number of such stanzas, as though there were in this some particular motive. This with Delitzsch is merely a poetical arrangement; but Hengstenberg attributes a cabalistic meaning to these numbers. The natural result of such preconceived theories is to cut up the poem into disjointed paragraphs, and so to do away with the use and meaning of a paragraph.[1]

[1] In some few instances, however, Delitzsch attaches a symbolical meaning to the stanza. Thus in his commentary on Ps. xcii. we read—"Certainly the unmistakeable (!) strophe-schema, 6, 6, 7, 6, 6, is not without signification. The middle of the Psalm bears the stamp of the sabbatic number." And in Ps. xcix. —"The first two sanctuses are two hexastichs; and two hexastichs form the third, according to the very same law by which the third and the sixth days of creation each consists of two creative works." And in Ps. cx. —"The Psalm therefore bears the threefold impress of the number seven, which is the number of an oath and of a covenant. Its impress then is thoroughly prophetic." But such expressions occur in every page of Hengstenberg. There is, however, no authority for a strophical arrangement. As we shall see presently, parallelism in Hebrew poetry is not confined to the two hemistichs of a verse, but it is frequently alternate, the first hemistich of one verse being parallel to the first of the next verse; and the second of the first to the second of the next. This naturally gives us four lines, which would constitute a stanza: and if this were general throughout the Psalms, there would be no doubt of their being written in stanzas of four lines each. But the contrary is the case: and thus all those who have adopted the stanza-system have been obliged to divide their stanzas into different numbers of lines, thus bearing a strong improbability on their very front. Let us, however, take Delitzsch's valuable and learned work, it being moreover one of the latest and therefore most perfect expositions of the system, and see how it works out: it being premised that this is done in no captious spirit against the work of this distinguished author. Thus in order to carry out the strophe-system he is obliged to divide such passages as the following :—

The Lord Himself is the portion of mine inheritance and my cup,
 Thou shalt maintain my lot.
 The lot is fallen unto me in a fair ground,
Yea, I have a goodly heritage. (Ps. xvi.)   [He

The last thing that should engage our attention is the frequent occurrence of the antiphon. This is so marked in many of the Psalms

He bowed the heavens, and came down,
And there was darkness under His feet.
He rode upon the cherubim and did fly :
He soared upon the wings of the wind. (Ps. xviii.)

At the brightness of His presence
There issued from His thick clouds
    Hailstones and coals of fire.
The Lord thundered out of heaven,
And the Highest gave His thunder,
    Hailstones and coals of fire. (Ps. xviii.)

The Lord looketh down from heaven ;
    He beholdeth all the children of men :
From the habitation of His dwelling
    He considereth all them that dwell on the earth.   (Ps. xxxiii.)

Let them fall from one wickedness to another,
    And let them not come into Thy righteousness :
Let them be blotted out of the book of life,
    And let them not be written among the righteous.   (Ps. lxix.)

He gave them their own desire,
They were not disappointed of their desire.   (Ps. lxxviii.)

He turned their rivers into blood,
    And their waters they could not drink :
He sent swarms of flies to devour them,
    And frogs to destroy them :
He, etc. etc. (Ps. lxxviii.)

While passages like the following are united, where one part refers with all
the previous portion of the Psalm to the king ; and the other, with all the
concluding portion of the Psalm, refers to God's enemies :—

For the king putteth his trust in the Lord :
And in the mercy of the Most High he shall not be moved.

All Thine enemies shall feel Thy hand :
Thy right hand shall find out them that hate Thee.   (Ps. xxi.)

Hengstenberg, whose commentary is otherwise so valuable, endeavours to
show that these strophes have a mystical meaning, the verses of which they
are composed bearing some sacred numerical value. His favourite numbers
are seven ; four and three ; and ten. This hypothesis, elaborately instanced
in every Psalm, is unproved, mystical, and unsatisfactory. He also attaches
great weight to the name of God appearing so many times : which was one of
the conceits of the Talmudists. But while we repudiate the strophe-system,
with its evident inconsistencies, and its fanciful symbolism, we shall see that
there are some few occasional instances in which the Psalm does resolve itself
into stanzas.

that it would be unwise not to seek for it in others. The antiphon gives life and spirit to the psalm ; and there can be no doubt that what is called antiphonal singing in our churches, where the two sides of the choir sing alternately, would be much more effective and full of meaning if the alternate song were by paragraph, instead of verse ; and would be still more so, as well as much more in accordance with ancient practice, if the antiphon proper, or response, only, were sung as a chorus by the whole choir or congregation, as in ancient times.[1] The alternate recitation by the *people*, instead of by the two sides of the choir, has sprung out of the congregational worship of our Protestant Church : before the discovery of printing the people were not sufficiently educated to take such part.

We shall find numerous indications of this antiphon in different parts of Scripture. The word to which we give this interpretation, עָנָה *Onoh*, signifies to *sing in answer*. This is the meaning attributed to the word in the Septuagint, the Vulgate, by Hammond, Bishop Lowth,[2] Street, Jebb, Dathe, Rogers, Phillips, De Burgh, and Hengstenberg.[3] This *answering* was by the whole congregation, and corresponded with our *chorus*, and was a hearty acquiescence by the people in the subject of the song, taking up and emphasizing the most striking verse or sentiment. Thus, when Moses and Joshua came down from Mount Sinai, Aaron and the people had been sacrificing to the golden calf, and Joshua exclaimed, as they heard the voices of the people in the distance, "There is a noise of war in the camp:" but Moses replied—"It is not the voice of them that shout for mastery, neither is it the voice of them that cry for being overcome, but the noise of them that *sing in answer* do I hear." (Ex. xxxii. 18.) On the building of the second temple, after the return from Babylon, we read that the priests and the Levites the

---

[1] "The Psalm should be distributed between the Levites and the congregation, the lines containing the refrains being probably sung antiphonally by the latter." (Perowne, ii. 328.) The only Psalms which are adapted for alternate recitation are the hundred and thirty-sixth, (but here it is not every other verse which should be read alternately, but every other line,) the twenty-ninth, and the sixty-seventh, which are in alternate stanzas.

[2] *Præl.* xix.   [3] In Ps. cxlvii., but not in Ps. lxxxviii. *Tit.*

sons of Asaph praised "the Lord, after the ordinance of David king of Israel, and they sang together by course in praising and giving thanks unto the Lord:" and then follows the antiphon which they sang—

"For He is good :
For His mercy endureth for ever toward Israel ;"

"and *all the people shouted with a great shout* when they praised the Lord." (Ezra iii. 10, 11.) And a few years later on the occasion of rebuilding the walls, "The singers sang loud, with Jezrahiah their overseer, and rejoiced, for God had made them rejoice with great joy. The *wives also and the children rejoiced :* so that the joy of Jerusalem was heard even afar off." (Nehem. xii. 42, 43.) Thus we see that the solemn feasts were attended not only with the harmony and music of the Levites, but with *the hosannas and acclamations of the people.* Hence Jeremiah compares the military clamours of the victorious Chaldeans in the temple, to those that were formerly made there in the day of a solemn feast :—"They have made a noise in the house of the Lord, as in a day of a solemn feast." (Lam. ii. 7.) David says—"Blessed are they that hear the joyful sound." (Ps. lxxxix. 15.)

In most cases we are not only told that they *sang in answer*, but we have the words of the answer or antiphon. Thus, when "Moses and the children of Israel sang a song unto the Lord" on the occasion of passing through the Red Sea, it was the principal verse of the song, or the antiphon, or refrain, only, which "Miriam the prophetess, the sister of Aaron, with a timbrel in her hand, *and all the women* with timbrels and with dances, *answered*—

'Sing ye to the Lord, for He hath triumphed gloriously ;
The horse and his rider hath He cast into the sea.'" (Ex. xv. 21.)

Here is a long song of some forty lines, and yet it is only one verse which is taken up as a refrain. Other instances of the antiphon occur in Num. xxi. 17, where we read that "Israel *sang in answer* this song—

'Spring up, O wells.'"

In Is. xxvii. 2, the Prophet says—" In that day *sing ye in answer* to her—

'A vineyard of red wine.'"

On the occasion of David's victory over Goliath " the women came out of all the cities of Israel, singing and dancing, to meet King Saul, with tabrets, with joy, and with instruments of music; and the women *answered* as they played, and said—

'Saul hath slain his thousands,
And David his ten thousands;'"   (1 Sam. xviii. 6, 7.)

words which, like the antiphon in general, were so terse, concise, and yet expressive, that they were easily remembered, and were repeated afterwards on two occasions by the Philistines. (1 Sam. xxi. 11 ; xxix. 5.)

From these instances in other parts of Scripture, we may expect to meet with antiphons in the Book of Psalms; for it was in psalms and songs such as those of which this book is composed that the antiphon occurred. That antiphons do occur, and occur most frequently, so frequently indeed as to be almost universal, this work will, it is hoped, prove : but what we have now to show is that these antiphons are referred to as such. We naturally begin with Ps. lxxxviii., which bears the title of "Leannoth," a responsive or antiphonal song; a title justified by the Psalm, which we find divided into three parts, the second and third of which are, as it were, echoes of the first, each part beginning with an antiphon—

O Lord God of my salvation !
In the day-time have I cried, and in the night, before Thee.   (Ver. 1.)

I have called daily, O Lord, unto Thee,
I have stretched forth my hands unto Thee.   (Ver. 9.)

Unto Thee have I cried, O Lord !
And early shall my prayer come before Thee.   (Ver. 13.)

The next instance we will notice is in Ps. cxlvii. where we find the following antiphons—

> Praise ye the Lord !
> For it is a good thing to sing psalms unto our God,
> For it is a joyful and pleasant thing to sing praises. (Ver. 1.)

> Praise the Lord, O Jerusalem :
> Praise thy God, O Sion ! (Ver. 12.)

> O raise the antiphon unto the Lord, with thanksgiving :
> Sing praises upon the harp unto our God ; (Ver. 7.)

or, as it is more literally, "*O sing in answer* unto the Lord." In all these cases the *singing* was the song itself, and the chorus or *antiphon* followed, accompanied by loud noise. So in the Psalms we have—" The singers go before ; the minstrels follow after ;" [1] and in another Psalm—" The singers also and minstrels' (shall sing) ; and in each case there follows the antiphon which they sang : in the former instance—

> " Bless ye God in the congregations :
> Even the Lord, ye that are of the fountain of Israel ; "

and in the latter—

> " All my fountains[2] are in thee." (Ps. lxxxvii. 7.)

---

[1] " Proportoinable to this was the ancient Greek custom, poetically expressed by Apollo and the Muses, Apollo singing, and they following ἐν ἀμοιβαίῳ, *answering* with musical instruments to the tune which he began. So in Homer (Il. ω, 720), in a funeral, there are first θρήνων ἔξαρχοι, *the beginners or precentors of the lamentations,* and then κλαίων ἀμφίστατ' ὅμιλος, *the company stood about wailing,* and ἐπὶ δὲ στενάχοντο γυναῖκες, *the women came after,* or *answered in their morning,* this *wailing* bearing their proportion with the music which was often used in their funerals."—(HAMMOND, *in* Ps. lxxxviii. *Tit.*)

[2] This text has puzzled commentators, but it is easily explained by the context. God is represented as saying—Some of those who become my children come from Egypt and Babylon, from Philistia, Tyre and Ethiopia, and other strange lands : but the great bulk of those who become my children spring from thee, O Sion. It is curious that the word "fountain" should be connected with "singers and minstrels" in two passages, here, and in Ps. lxviii. 25, 26. That it has the signification above given is evident from Deut. xxxiii. 28, "Israel then shall dwell in safety alone. The fountain of Jacob shall be upon a land of corn and wine : all his heavens shall drop down dew." And Is. xlviii. 1, "Hear ye this, O house of Jacob, which are called by the name of Israel, and are come forth out of the waters of Judah."

The "singers and minstrels," though relating to the annual "goings-up" to Jerusalem, refer especially to the first entrance of the ark into the holy city, (2 Sam. vi.,) on which occasion a psalm was composed by David, (1 Chron. xvi. 7—36,) which begins— "Give thanks unto the Lord," and at the end of it it is stated that "all the people said, Amen, and praised the Lord." The words of their praise were probably what we read immediately before, and which constituted their antiphon—

"Blessed be the Lord God of Israel, for ever and ever;"

the subject of which agrees with the beginning of the Psalm, and with its title, as it does also with the antiphon of Ps. lxviii. in which this entrance to Mount Sion is referred to; the singers going before, and the minstrels following after, singing—

"Bless ye God in the congregations :
Even the Lord, ye that are of the fountain of Israel."

Ps. lxxxix. exhibits an instance where the antiphon comes first—

"Righteousness and equity are the habitation of Thy seat,
Mercy and truth shall go before Thy face."

Immediately after which we have—

"Blessed are the people who know the shouting :"

thereby indicating that the preceding antiphon had been sung with shouting.

This antiphon, as we have seen, was sung by the whole congregation, and with loud voice; so loud as to be heard from a great distance. That *shouting* is the proper word to be used in all such passages is evident from an examination of Ex. xxxii. 17, 18; Josh. vi. 20; 1 Sam. iv. 5; 2 Sam. vi. 15; 1 Chron. xv. 28; 2 Chron. v. 13, xv. 14, xxix. 27; Ez. iii. 11—13. Such shouting having its institution in the command of God—"Sing ye for joy unto God our strength; shout aloud unto the God of Jacob . . . . For this was made a statute for Israel, and a law of the God of Jacob." Ps. lxxxi. 1—5; see also Num. x. 10. We have several indications of this in the Psalms, where the people are called upon to sing with all their strength.

Sing with joy unto the Lord, O ye righteous!
For it becometh well the just to be thankful.
Praise the Lord with the harp,
Sing psalms unto Him with the ten-stringed psaltery.
Sing unto Him a new song,
Strike the chords skilfully, with shouting.   (Ps. xxxiii.)

O clap your hands together, all ye people!
Shout unto God with the song of rejoicing!

God is gone up with a shout,
And the Lord with the sound of a trumpet.   (Ps. xlvii.)

Sing ye joyfully unto God our strength!
Shout aloud unto the God of Jacob!
Take the psalm, bring hither the tabret,
The pleasant harp, with the lute.
Blow ye the trumpet in the new moon,
At the time appointed, and upon our solemn feast-day.   (Ps. lxxxi.)

O come, let us sing with joy unto the Lord,
Let us shout aloud unto the Rock of our salvation.
Let us come before His presence with thanksgiving,
Let us shout aloud unto Him with psalms.   (Ps. xcv.)

Shout aloud unto the Lord, all ye lands,
    Break forth, sing joyfully, and sing psalms.
    Sing psalms unto the Lord upon the harp,
    With harp, and with melody of praise.
    With trumpet also, and with melody of cornet;
Shout aloud unto the Lord the King!   (Ps. xcviii.)

Shout aloud unto the Lord, all ye lands!
Serve the Lord with gladness,
And come before His presence with a song of rejoicing!   (Ps. c.)

Arise, O Lord, into Thy resting-place,
Thou and the ark of Thy strength!
Let Thy priests be clothed with righteousness,
And let Thy saints shout with joyfulness.

I will clothe her priests with salvation,
And her saints shall shout for joy, and rejoice with shouting.   (Ps. cxxxii.)

In all these instances the words themselves appear to constitute the antiphon : but the antiphonal shouting is referred to in other instances—

> I will sacrifice in His tabernacle sacrifices with shouting :
> I will sing ; I will sing psalms unto the Lord.   (Ps. xxvii.)

> That they would sacrifice unto Him the sacrifices of thanksgiving,
> And tell out His works with shouting.   (Ps. cvii.)

This responsive song, or antiphon, sung by the whole congregation to the accompaniment of loud music, was a striking feature of the Jewish worship, and accordingly we find the Psalmist exclaiming—

> Blessed is the people who know the shouting :
> They shall walk in the light of Thy countenance.   (Ps. lxxxix. 15.)

In the same manner we find the Prophet Hosea (ii. 15), when foretelling the punishment of God's people for their sins, holding out a promise of reconciliation, and telling them—" I will give her the valley of Achor for a door of hope, and she shall *sing in answer* there, as in the days of her youth, and as in the day when she came up out of the land of Egypt," when she sang—

> "Sing ye to the Lord, for He hath triumphed gloriously ;
> The horse and his rider hath He thrown into the sea."

Some of these antiphons were doubtless great favourites among the people, such as that which we have twice noticed[1] as referring to themselves as the "fountain of Israel," but that which was most common was—

> "O give thanks unto the Lord : for He is good,
> For His mercy endureth for ever."

This was the antiphon composed by David, and which he instructed his choir to sing, when he established the tabernacle service—

> O give thanks unto the Lord !
> Because His mercy endureth for ever !   (1 Chron. xvi. 41.)

---

[1] See *ante*, note, p. 9.

This it was which Solomon adopted when he arranged the temple service—

> O praise the Lord !
> Because His mercy endureth for ever !   (2 Chron. vii. 6.)

and which he directed to be sung when the ark was brought into the temple—

> O praise the Lord : for He is good !
> For His mercy endureth for ever !   (2 Chron. v. 13.)

This it was which Jehoshaphat directed to be sung when he marched out against the Moabites and the Ammonites—

> O praise the Lord !
> For His mercy endureth for ever !   (2 Chron. xx. 21.)

And this antiphon was sung, not by the priests and Levites only, but by all the people.   For at the consecration of the temple we read—" And when *all the children of Israel* saw how the fire came down, and the glory of the Lord upon the house, they bowed themselves with their faces to the ground upon the pavement, and worshipped, and praised the Lord, saying—

> ' For He is good !
> For His mercy endureth for ever ! ' "   (2 Chron. vii. 3.)

And this is the antiphon which David incorporated into so many of his Psalms ; the hundred and sixth, the hundred and seventh, the hundred and eighteenth, and the hundred and thirty-sixth, beginning—

> O give thanks unto the Lord,
> For the Lord is good !
> For His mercy endureth for ever !

the last verse of the hundred and eighteenth being the same, while three other verses of this Psalm, and every verse of the hundred and thirty-sixth, terminate with—

> For His mercy endureth for ever !

And only two years before the Babylonian captivity and the destruction of the city, Jeremiah, in delivering his final prophecy

against the city, announced God's gracious promises of reconciliation, saying—" Again there shall be heard in this place . . . . the
voice of joy, and the voice of gladness, the voice of the bridegroom,
and the voice of the bride, and the voice of them that shall say—

> ' Praise the Lord of hosts !
> For the Lord is good !
> For His mercy endureth for ever !' "   (Jer. xxxiii. 11.)

If we turn again to the Book of Psalms we shall find, that
though in general the antiphon springs out of its particular Psalm,
as in Ps. lviii., where we have—

> And thus shall it be said—
> Verily, there is a reward for the righteous :
> Verily, there is a God that judgeth the earth :

in many cases the antiphon is of a more general character, and is
common to several Psalms.   The most common would naturally be
the ascription of praise to the Lord God of Israel who liveth for
ever and ever, which is more or less full in different instances.

> Blessed be the Lord God, even the God of Israel,
> Which only doeth wondrous things.
> And blessed be the name of His majesty for ever
> And let all the earth be filled with His majesty.
>   Amen and Amen.   (Ps. lxxii.)

> Blessed be the Lord God of Israel,
> From everlasting to everlasting !
> And let all the people say—
> Amen : Praise ye the Lord.   (Ps. cvi.)

> Blessed be the Lord God of Israel,
> From everlasting to everlasting !
>   Amen, and Amen.   (Ps. xli.)

> Blessed be the Lord for evermore !
>   Amen, and Amen.   (Ps. lxxxix.)

Other antiphons in the Psalms are—" The Lord shall reign for
ever and ever," (Ps. x. 18, and cxlvi. 10,) taken from the song of
Moses, Ex. xv. 18.—" The Lord is merciful and gracious, long-
suffering, abundant in goodness, and truth," (Ps. ciii. 8 ; cxlv. 8,)

taken from God's description of Himself on Mount Sinai. (Ex. xxxiv. 6.)—"Bless the Lord, O my soul." (Ps. ciii. 1, 22 ; civ. 1, 35 ; cxlvi. 1.)—"Let them be ashamed and confounded together, that seek after my soul to destroy it. Let them be driven backward, and put to rebuke, that wish me evil. Let them be desolate, and rewarded with shame, that say unto me, Fie upon thee, fie upon thee !" (Ps. xxxv. 4, 26 ; xl. 17, 18 ; lxx. 2, 3.)—"Give unto the Lord the honour due unto His name: worship the Lord with holy worship." (Ps. xxix. 2 ; xcvi. 9.)—"Rejoice in the Lord, ye righteous ; and give thanks for a remembrance of His holiness." (Ps. xxx. 4 ; xcvii. 12.)—"Be glad, O ye righteous, and rejoice in the Lord : and be joyful, all ye that are true of heart." (Ps. xxxii. 12 ; lxiv. 10.)—"Set up Thyself, O God, above the heavens : and Thy glory above all the earth." (Ps. lvii. 6, 12 ; cviii. 5.)— "Our help standeth in the name of the Lord ; who made heaven and earth." (Ps. cxxi. 2 ; cxxiv. 7.)—"O Israel, trust in the Lord !" (Ps. cxxx. 7 ; cxxxi. 4.)—"O praise the Lord ! For it is a good thing to sing praises unto our God : yea, a joyful and pleasant thing it is to be thankful." (Ps. cxlvii. 1 ; xcii. 1.)

Many excellent works on the Psalms of David, as those by Hammond, Hengstenberg, De Burgh, and Wordsworth, are simple Commentaries, with critical notes on the authorized version, and therefore, although of most essential use in enabling us to ascertain the true meaning of Scripture, are only of secondary assistance in giving to the text itself its original character. It is only in new translations that we may hope to effect this ; but here also we fail in arriving at any satisfactory result. The reason is that each man sits down to write a new translation, according to his own critical and philological training ; without sufficiently examining the labours of others, without accepting the work which they have achieved, and consequently without the hope or intention of arriving at any generally accepted standard. Surely with such an admirable translation as we possess in our old version, based upon the Hebrew, the Septuagint, and Jerome's translation, and resembling, more than any other translation, the easy flow and rhythm of the original, we should endeavour to correct and perfect this translation, instead of setting up another; so that the reader, in recognizing the general form of words to which he is accustomed, should be better able to estimate and value the alterations which are made. Instead of this, we find each man proposing some new form, even when that new form brings out no new meaning, but merely substitutes other words and other idioms, in the place of those which are so hallowed to us. Let us take, as an instance in illustration, a passage in which we have the same word עֲנָה, which we have met with before, but differently pointed. In Ps. xviii. 35, we have in our Prayer-book translation, "Thy *loving correction* shall make me great," which is founded on the reading of the Seventy, the Vulgate, the Syriac, and the Arabic, Thy *discipline*, or *teaching*, or *correction;* and which is followed by Phillips, Thy *chastening*, and by French and Skinner, Thy *afflicting hand*. The Bible version, both here and in 2 Sam. xxii., has *gentleness*—which is followed by Jebb—and the margin *meekness :* Hammond has *care ;* Horsley and De Burgh *humiliation :* Bagster *humility ;* Tholuck, Weiss, Alexander, and Kay *condescension ;* Hengstenberg and Delitzsch *lowliness ;* Perowne and "Four Friends" *graciousness ;* Good *tenderness ;* Gesenius and Street *kindness* or *benignity ;* Kimchi *goodness ;* and other Jewish interpreters *providence, help,* and *goodwill.* All these readings may be traced from one or other of two roots, עָנָיו *Onov,* To be meek or gentle, and עָנָה *Innoh,* To chasten ; Horne using both meanings, "Thy *gentleness,* or Thy *afflictions.*" We must therefore admire the rendering in our Prayer-book, which unites both these significations. How much better, therefore, would it have been to be content with this rendering, which so well expresses what we want? Again, where our Old Translation gives " Lord," and " God," one author gives *Jehovah,* and another favours us with *Jahve,* another with *Yah,* and another with *Jhvh,* instead of Lord ; and with *Elohim,* and *Eloah,* instead of God !

Jebb's translation appeared in 1846 ; since then no further efforts have been made to restore the form of the original poetry, though many able and critical translations have appeared, in which the rendering is often more exact, and the true meaning better exhibited. This neglect of the study of Hebrew parallelism is certainly to be regretted : for if it be considered desirable to present to us the exact rendering of the words and idiom of the original, it might surely be considered desirable to present to us the balancing of such words. This balancing, or as Bishop Lowth called it, parallelism, is not without its use. Not merely does it denote that the original is poetry, but by the repetition of the same sentiment, like the prophet's "precept upon precept, precept upon precept, line upon line, line upon line," it tended to impress upon the ear and recollection of the people to whom it was written, as it does to all generations, the divine hymns which were written for their instruction and comfort by the inspired psalmist.

It has been, therefore, the particular effort in the present translation to restore the parallelism, not merely by restoring the division of the lines, but by restoring the use of the same word when repeated in the same distich ; to distinguish the stanzas or paragraphs which divide the poem ; and to point out the antiphon or chorus, which gives life to it when sung, and which made the psalm sung by the priest a psalm for the people also.

It has been alleged by some that the study of parallelism is useless, as it does not, they pretend, affect the meaning of the Bible : but when we consider that all modern translators adopt parallelism, it is unnecessary to refute such opinion. The fact is that parallelism is of the greatest use in enabling us to discover the true meaning of a word, which but for it might lead us astray. In the eightieth Psalm, for instance, we should understand by the word "branch," *the Branch,* and by "the man on Thy right hand," and "the son of man," *the Messiah, the Son of man.* And so accordingly the words have been taken by the Chaldee paraphrast, some of the Rabbies, R. Aben Ezra, and R. Obadiah, by the Seventy, and by some modern commentators, as Hengstenberg, Alexander, and the Bishop of Lincoln : but the parallelism shows us that this interpretation is erroneous. Let us then, seeing how easily we may go astray, endeavour to read the Psalms of David as they were written by him, and we shall then find not only that the sense becomes clearer, but that many beauties and niceties of expression exist, of which we before had no conception. As the Apostle resolves—" *I will sing with the spirit, and I will sing with the understanding also;"* so, in reading the Psalms of David, we are bound to do so with that attention which the Psalmist himself enjoins—

" Sing ye psalms with understanding."

THE BOOK OF PSALMS.

THE BOOK OF PSALMS.

PSALM I.

[INTRODUCTORY.]

BLESSED is the man
That walketh not in the counsel of the ungodly.
That standeth not in the way of sinners,
And that sitteth not in the seat of the scornful.
But whose delight is in the law of the Lord,
And in HIS law doth he exercise himself day and night.
And he shall be like a tree planted by the water-side,
That bringeth forth its fruit in due season :
His leaf also shall not wither ;
And whatsoever he doeth, it shall prosper.

As for the ungodly, it is not so with them :
But they are like the chaff which is scattered by the wind.
Therefore the ungodly shall not be able to stand in the judgment.
Neither sinners in the congregation of the righteous.

Antiphon. For the Lord knoweth the way of the righteous :
But the way of the ungodly shall perish.

PSALM II.

[By David. See Acts iv. 25.]

[*Placed in this position probably to show that the whole Book of Psalms was considered prophetical of the Messiah.*]

WHY do the heathen so furiously rage[1] together ?
And (why do) the people imagine a vain thing ?
The kings of the earth stand up,
And the rulers take counsel together,
Against THE LORD,
And against His Anointed !
" Let us break their bands asunder,
" And cast away their cords from us."

He that dwelleth in heaven shall laugh them to scorn ;
The Lord shall have them in derision.
Then shall He speak unto them in His wrath,
And vex them in His sore displeasure.
" Yet have I set my King
" Upon my holy hill of Sion.
" I will declare the decree :
" The Lord hath said unto me—
" Thou art MY SON :
" This day have I, even I, begotten Thee.
" Ask of me : and I will give Thee
" The heathen for Thine inheritance,
" And the uttermost parts of the earth for Thy possession.
" Thou shalt bruise them with a rod of iron ;
" Thou shalt break them in pieces, like a potter's vessel."

Be wise now therefore, O ye kings :
Be instructed, O ye judges of the earth.
Serve the Lord in fear,
And rejoice unto Him with reverence.
Kiss the Son, lest He be angry,
And so ye perish (from) the right way.
When His wrath is kindled, yea, but a little.
Blessed are all they that put their trust in HIM.

[1] *Heb.* "assemble."

PSALM III.

A Psalm of David:

When he fled from Absalom, his son.

[A MORNING HYMN.]

LORD, how are they increased that trouble me !
    Many are they that rise against me.
    Many there be that say of my soul—
"There is no help for him in his God."

Antiphon.

סלה

But THOU, O Lord, art my defender !
THOU art my glory, and the lifter up of my head.
I called upon the Lord with my voice,
And He heard me out of His holy hill.

סלה.

I laid me down, and I slept :
I rose up again : for THE LORD sustained me.
I will not be afraid of ten thousands of the people
That have set (themselves) against me round about.

Arise, O Lord :
Save me, O my God !
For Thou smitest all mine enemies (upon) the cheek bone.
Thou hast broken the teeth of the ungodly.

Antiphon.

Help[1] belongeth unto THE LORD :
And THY blessing is upon Thy people.

סלה

[1] See first antiphon.

PSALM IV.

To the chief Musician upon the stringed instruments.

A Psalm of David.

[AN EVENING HYMN.]

HEAR me when I call, O GOD, my righteousness!
Proem. Thou hast set me at liberty when I was in trouble :
Have mercy upon me, and hearken unto my prayer.

HOW long, O ye sons of men,
Will ye blaspheme my glory ![1]
Will ye love vanity !   Will ye seek after deceit !
סלה
But know that the Lord hath chosen the godly unto himself :
When I call upon the Lord, He will hear me.

Stand in awe, and sin not :
Commune with your own heart, and in your chamber.
    And be still.   סלה
Sacrifice the sacrifice of righteousness,
And put your trust in the Lord.

There be many that say—" Who will show us any good ?"
Lord, lift up the light of THY countenance upon us !
(Then) shalt Thou put gladness in my heart,
More than when their corn and their wine are multiplied.

Antiphon. I will lay me down in peace, and take my rest :
For it is THOU, Lord, only, that makest me dwell in safety.

[1] (The object of) "my glory." See note on Ps. xii. 2—4.

PSALM V.

To the chief Musician upon the wind instruments.

A Psalm of David.

[A MORNING HYMN.]

Procm. PONDER my words, O Lord!
Consider my meditation.
Hearken Thou to the voice of my calling, my King and my God!
For unto THEE will I make my prayer.

O LORD!
In the morning shalt Thou hear my voice;
In the morning will I prepare myself, and will look up.
For Thou art a God that hath no pleasure in wickedness;
    There shall no evil dwell with Thee.
    There shall no foolish persons stand in Thy sight;
For Thou hatest all them that work iniquity.
Thou wilt destroy them that speak falsehood;
The Lord will abhor both the blood-thirsty and deceitful man.

    But as for me:
I will come into Thine house, in the multitude of Thy mercy:
I will bow me down towards Thy holy temple, in Thy fear.
Lead me, O Lord, in Thy righteousness, because of mine enemies:
Make Thy way plain before my face.
For there is no faithfulness in his mouth;
Their inward parts are very wickedness:
Their throat is an open sepulchre;
They flatter with their tongue.
Declare their guilt, and destroy them, O God!
Let them perish through their own imaginations:
Cast them out in the multitude of their ungodliness;
For they have rebelled against THEE!

    But let all those that trust in Thee rejoice;
Let them give thanks for ever:
And do Thou watch over them,
And let them that love Thy name be joyful in Thee.

ntiphon. For Thou, Lord, wilt give Thy blessing unto the righteous:
And with Thy favour wilt Thou defend him, as with a shield.

PSALM VI.

To the chief Musician over the stringed instruments—Upon the eight-stringed lyre.

A Psalm of David.

O LORD!
Rebuke me not in Thine anger,
And chasten me not in Thy displeasure!
Have mercy upon me, O Lord;
    For I am weak:
Heal me, O Lord;
    For my bones are vexed.
My soul also is sore troubled:
But, Lord, how long (wilt Thou punish me)!
Turn Thee, O Lord, and deliver my soul;
Save me, for Thy mercy's sake:
For in death no man remembereth Thee;
And who can give Thee thanks in the pit!
    I am weary of my groaning:
Every night wash I my bed,
And water my couch with my tears:
Mine eye is consumed for very grief,
And worn away because of all mine enemies.

    Away from me, all ye that work iniquity!
⎧ The Lord hath heard the voice of my weeping;
⎨ The Lord hath heard my petition;
⎩ The Lord will receive my prayer.

Antiphon. All mine enemies shall be put to shame, and confounded:
They shall. be turned back, and put to shame suddenly.

PSALM VII.

A variable Song of David:

Which he sang unto the Lord, concerning the words of Cush the Benjamite.

O LORD, my GOD!
In THEE have I put my trust.
Save me from all them that persecute me, and deliver me:

Lest he devour my soul, like a lion ;
Tearing it in pieces, while there is none to deliver.

O Lord, my GOD !
If I have done any such thing,
If there be any wickedness in my hands,
If I have rewarded evil unto him that dealt friendly with me,
(If) even I have despoiled him that without cause is mine enemy—
Let mine enemy persecute my soul,[1] and take it ;
Let him tread my life down upon the earth ;
Let him lay mine honour in the dust.

סלה

Arise up, O Lord, in Thine anger :
Lift up Thyself, because of the rage of mine enemies ;
Awake up for me in the judgment that Thou hast commanded.
And so shall the congregation of the people come about Thee :
For their sakes, therefore, lift up Thyself again.
The Lord will judge the nations :
Judge me, O Lord,
According as righteousness and innocency are in me.
O put an end to the wickedness of the ungodly ;
But establish Thou the righteous :
For the righteous God
Trieth the very hearts and reins.
My defence cometh of GOD,
Who saveth them that are true of heart.
God judgeth the righteous,[2]
And God is provoked (with the wicked) every day.
If he will not turn, He will whet His sword ;
He hath bent His bow, and made it ready :
He hath prepared for him the instruments of death,
He hath made His arrows swift to overtake him.[3]

[1] Referring to previous paragraph—"Lest he devour my soul, like a lion."
[2] The three preceding verses justify this reading, rather than that of "God is a righteous judge," which the original might also signify ; but which would have no connexion here with the context. It is the same word used as in v. 8, "Judge me, O Lord," and not the word in the preceding line, "The Lord will judge the people," which signifies to *pass sentence* on them. "Rulers are not a terror to good works, but to the evil." See also Ps. ix. ; x. 20 ; xvii. 2 ; xxvi. 1 ; xxxv. 24 ; and xliii. 1.
[3] *Dolakeem*, "hot pursuers." See Ps. lxxvi. 3, *rishphai*, "quick motions," *met.* swift arrows.

Behold, he travaileth with iniquity :
He hath conceived mischief, and brought forth ungodliness.
    He made a pit, and digged it :
     And he is fallen himself into the ditch (which) he hath made.
His mischief shall return upon his own head,
And his violence shall come upon his own pate.

Antiphon. I will give thanks unto the Lord, according to His righteousness :
And I will sing psalms unto the name of the Lord Most High.

PSALM VIII.

To the chief Musician upon the Gathite harp.

A Psalm of David.

O LORD, OUR Lord !
Antiphon. How excellent is Thy name in all the world !
Thou hast set Thy glory above the heavens.

    Out of the mouth of babes and sucklings
    Hast Thou ordained strength,
Proem.   Because of Thine enemies ;
    To still the enemy and the revengeful.

WHEN I consider Thy heavens, even the works of Thy fingers,
The moon and the stars which Thou hast ordained,
What is man, that Thou art mindful of him ;
And the son of man, that Thou regardest him ?
Thou hast made him but little lower than Thyself ![1]
Thou hast crowned him with glory and worship !
Thou hast made him to have dominion of the works of Thy hands !
Thou hast put all things in subjection under his feet !
All sheep and oxen,
Yea, and the beasts of the field ;
The fowls of the air, and the fishes of the sea,
And whatsoever walketh through the paths of the sea.

    O Lord, OUR Lord !
Antiphon. How excellent is Thy name in all the world !

[1] *Heb.* "God."

PSALM IX. [AND X.]

To the chief Musician upon Muth-Labben.

A Psalm of David.

roem.

א I WILL give thanks unto Thee, O Lord, with my whole heart ;
א I will count up all Thy marvellous works.
א I will be glad and rejoice in Thee :
א I will sing psalms to THY name,
    O Thou Most Highest !

ב IN THE turning back of mine enemies,
   They fall and perish at Thy presence :
   For Thou hast maintained my right and my cause,
   Thou art set in the throne, judging righteousness.
ג   Thou hast rebuked the heathen,
     Thou hast destroyed the ungodly ;
*   Thou hast put out their name, for ever and ever :
ה   The destructions of the enemy are ended, for ever.
    Their cities Thou hast destroyed :
    Their memorial is perished with them.
ו But the Lord shall reign for ever :
   He hath prepared His throne for judgment.
ו For He will judge the world in righteousness,
   He will minister judgment to the nations in uprightness.
ו The Lord also will be a refuge for the oppressed,
   Even a refuge in time of trouble.
ו And they that know Thy name will put their trust in Thee,
   For Thou, Lord, hast never failed them that seek Thee.

ntiphon.

ז Sing psalms unto the Lord which dwelleth in Sion :
   Show forth among the nations all His doings.
   For when He maketh inquisition for blood, He remembereth
   He forgetteth not the complaint of the afflicted.   [them :

ח Have mercy upon me, O Lord !
   Consider the affliction which I suffer of them that hate me,
   O Thou that liftest me up from the gates of death,
   That I may show all Thy praises in the gates of the daughter
    I will rejoice in Thy salvation.   [of Sion.
ט The heathen are sunk down in the pit that they made :
   In the same net which they hid privily is their foot taken.

The Lord hath made Himself known : He hath executed judg-
The ungodly is trapped in the work of his own hands.   [ment :

הגיון סלה

י The wicked shall be turned into hell,
And all the people that forget God.
כ For the poor shall not always be forgotten :
The patient abiding of the afflicted shall (not) perish for ever.

　　　Arise, O Lord !
Let not man have the upper hand :
Antiphon.　　Let the heathen be judged in Thy sight.
Put them in fear, O Lord ;
That the heathen may know themselves to be but men.

סלה

[*Psalm X. commences here.*] [1]

ל Why standest Thou so far off, O Lord !
Why hidest Thou Thyself in the needful time of trouble !
The wicked in his pride doth persecute the afflicted :
They are taken by them in the devices which they have imagined.
For the wicked hath made boast of his own heart's desire :
He blesseth the covetous ! [2]
He despiseth THE LORD !
In the loftiness of his nostrils he seeketh not (GOD) !

---

[1] Psalms ix. and x. form one Psalm in the Septuagint and Vulgate, and in
some MSS. ; but most modern Translators make them independent.   It is
difficult to see how such an opinion can be formed, when we look at the
alphabetical arrangement, which is far more perfect than is generally stated ;
at the alliteration in the letters א and ו Ps. ix., and ת in Ps. x. ; at the agreement of the antiphon, "Arise, O Lord, Let not man have the upper hand,"
in Ps. ix., and "Arise, O Lord, Lift up Thine hand," in Ps. x. ; at the godly
"seeking after God," in Ps. ix., and the ungodly "seeking not after God," in
Ps. x. ; at the reference to the "wicked," twice repeated in Ps. ix., and six
times in Ps. x. ; the "afflicted" and "affliction" three times in Ps. ix., and
four times in Ps. x. ; the "oppressed" once in Ps. ix., and twice in Ps. x. ;
the "poor" in Ps. ix., and the "troubled in heart" repeated three times,
the "fatherless" twice, and the "innocent," and "miserable," once, in Ps. x.
[2] "He doth not abhor anything that is evil ;" (Ps. xxxvi. 5 :) "When
thou sawest a thief, thou hadst pleasure in him ;" (Ps. l. 18 :) "Who not
only do the same, but have pleasure in them that do them." (Rom. i. 32.)
Contrast Ps. xv. 4—"In whose eyes a vile person is contemned."

God is not in *any* of his thoughts :
His ways are grievous at *every* time.

ב Thy judgments are far above out of his sight :
All those whom he oppresseth he scoffeth at.[1]

* He hath said in his heart—" I shall not be moved :
" No harm shall ever happen unto me."

* His mouth is full of cursing, deceit, and fraud :
Under his tongue is ungodliness and iniquity.
He lieth in ambush in the streets,
In his secret places doth he murder the innocent,

ע His eyes are set against those who are troubled in heart :
He lieth in ambush in secret, as a lion in his lair,
He lieth in ambush to catch the afflicted,

* He catcheth the afflicted, and draweth him into his net.
He croucheth, he bends down,
That the troubled in heart may fall by the hand of his strong

* He hath said in his heart—" God hath forgotten : [ones.
"He hideth away his face : He will never see it."

ק Arise, O Lord !
Antiphon. Lift up Thine hand, O God :
Forget not those who are in misery.

Wherefore should the wicked despise God ?[2]
(While) he saith in his heart—" Thou wilt not require it."

ר Thou *hast* seen !
For Thou beholdest ungodliness and wrong,
To recompense it with Thy hand.
The troubled in heart committeth[3] (himself) unto Thee,
For Thou art the helper[3] of the fatherless.

ש Break Thou the power of the wicked and malicious,
Search after his wickedness till Thou find none.

The Lord is King for ever and ever !
And the heathen are perished out of the land.

---

[1] " I will help the oppressed from him that scoffeth at him ;" (Ps. xii. 5 ;)
" All they that see me laugh me to scorn ;" (Ps. xxii. 19 ;) " Which speak
scornful things against the righteous, being filled with pride and contempt ;"
(Ps. xxxi. 10 ;) " As with a sword in my bones mine enemies reproach me ;"
(Ps. xlii. 10 ;) "They speak wickedly (concerning their) oppression;"
(Ps. lxxiii. 8;) "Our enemies laugh us to scorn ;" (Ps. lxxx. 6 ;) " Our soul is
utterly filled with the scornful derision of the wealthy, and with the contempt
of the proud." (Ps. cxxiii. 4.) See also Is. lix. 13.
[2] See letter ל. [3] *Paronomasia.* *Ozar* and *Ozar.*

Catiphon. ת ⎰ Thou hast heard the desire of the afflicted, O Lord !
　　　　 ת ⎱ Thou preparest their heart,
　　　　 ת ⎰ Thine ear hearkeneth (thereto)—

Epiphonem. To judge the fatherless and oppressed,
That the man of the earth be no more exalted against them.

PSALM XI.

To the chief Musician.

A Psalm of David.

IN THE LORD put I my trust !
How say ye then to my soul—
" Flee (as) a bird (to) your hill :
" For lo, the ungodly bend their bow,
" And make ready their arrows upon the string,
" To shoot in ambush at those who are true of heart.
" For the foundations will be cast down :
" And what can the righteous do ?" [1]

THE LORD is in His holy temple !
THE LORD ! His seat is in heaven !
His eyes behold,
His eyelids try the children of men.
The Lord trieth the righteous ;　　　　　[soul abhorreth.
But the ungodly, and him that delighteth in wickedness, His
Upon the ungodly He shall rain snares,
Fire and brimstone, storm and tempest :
　　(This shall be) the portion of their cup.

Antiphon. For the righteous Lord loveth righteousness :
His countenance beholdeth the upright of heart.

[1] The Bishop of Lincoln well compares this to Ps. iv.—"There be many
that say—'Who will show us any good?' Lord, lift thou up the light of
Thy countenance upon us."

PSALM XII.

To the chief Musician upon the eight-stringed lyre.

A Psalm of David.

HELP me, O Lord !
For there is not one godly man left !
For the faithful are minished from among the children of men.
They speak of vanity[2] every man with his neighbour :
With a deceitful lip, and with a double heart,[1] do they speak.

The Lord shall root out all deceitful lips,
    And the tongue that speaketh proud[3] things.
      Which have said—" With our tongue will we prevail :
" Our lips are our own : who is Lord over us ? "

" Because of the oppression of the poor,
" Because of the deep sighing of the needy,
" I will arise," saith the Lord,
" I will help them from him that scoffeth at them."

[1] *Heb.* "with a heart and a heart."
[2,3] " Pride" and " vanity" in the Bible often have the meaning of infidelity and superstition, of atheism and idolatry. The proud of heart are described in Ps. x. and xiv. : the followers after vain gods in Deut. xxxii. 21 ; 1 Kings xvi. 13, 26 ; Jer. viii. 19 ; xiv. 22; and Jonah ii. 8. Often they are grouped together. Compare the following :—

    O ye sons of men,
How long will ye blaspheme (the object of) my glory ?
Will ye love vanity ? Will ye seek after deceit ? (Ps. iv. 2.)

Who hath not lifted up his soul unto vanity,
And hath not sworn to (idols of) deceit. (Ps. xxiv. 4.)

I have not sat with the followers of vanity,
And with the deceitful will I not hold fellowship. (Ps. xxvi. 4.)

Thou hatest all them that adhere to lying vanities. (Ps. xxxi. 6.)

And hath turned not unto the proud,
Nor to such as go after lying (gods). (Ps. xl. 4.)

D

The words of the Lord
    Are pure words ;
As silver refined in a furnace of fire,
    Purified seven times.
Thou wilt preserve them, O Lord ;
Thou wilt keep them from this generation for ever ;
(In which) the ungodly walk on every side,
When (they see) violent men exalted to power.

PSALM XIII.

To the chief Musician.

A Psalm of David.

HOW long wilt Thou forget me, O Lord !
    For ever !
How long wilt Thou hide Thy face from me !
How long shall I seek counsel in my soul,
    And be so vexed in my heart continually !
How long shall mine enemy triumph over me !

Look on me, and hear me, O Lord, my God !
Lighten mine eyes, lest I sleep the sleep of death ;
Lest mine enemy say—"I have prevailed against him ;
(Lest) they that distress me rejoice when I am troubled.

    But as for me :—
My trust is in Thy mercy,
Antiphon. My heart is joyful in Thy salvation :
I will sing unto the Lord ;
For He hath dealt lovingly with me.

PSALM XIV.

To the chief Musician.

A Psalm of David.

THE fool hath said in his heart—
" There is no God "!

Antiphon.	They are become corrupt, They are become abominable in their doings : There is none that doeth good !

The Lord looked down from heaven
Upon the children of men,
To see if there were (any that) would understand,
That would seek after God.

Antiphon.	They are all gone out of the way, They are all together become abominable : There is none that doeth good : There is not even one !

Have the workers of iniquity no knowledge,
Eating up my people, as they would eat bread !
They have not called upon the Lord !

There were they in great fear :
But God is in the generation of the righteous.
Ye have made a mock at the counsel[1] of the poor,
When THE LORD was his refuge !

Antiphon.	Oh that salvation were given unto Israel out of Sion ! When the Lord turneth the captivity of His people— Jacob shall rejoice, Israel shall be right glad.

---

[1] See 2 Kings xviii. 19, 20.—" What confidence is this wherein thou trustest ? Thou sayest, but they are but vain words, I have counsel and strength for the war. Now on whom dost thou trust ?"

PSALM XV.

A Psalm of David.

O LORD !
Proem. Who shall dwell in THY tabernacle?
Who shall rest upon THY holy hill?

HE who walketh uprightly,
   And worketh righteousness :
He who speaketh the truth from his heart,
   And hath not slandered with his tongue :
He who hath done no evil to his neighbour,
   And hath not taken up a reproach against him :
He in whose eyes a vile person is contemned,
   And who maketh much of them that fear the Lord
He who sweareth unto his neighbour,[1]
   And disappointeth him not :
He who giveth not his money upon usury,
   And who taketh no reward against the innocent.

Epiphonem. Whoso doeth these things
Shall not be moved for ever.

PSALM XVI.

"Michtam" of David.

Proem. PRESERVE me, O Lord,
For in THEE have I put my trust.

I HAVE said unto the Lord—
"THOU art my Lord !
"My desire[2] is to nothing[3] besides[3] THEE,
"And to the saints of the earth.

[1] *Heb.* "He who sweareth to his own disadvantage,
    "And changeth not."
[2] Compare Prov. xxii. 1.   [3,3] *Parænomasia.*

"They and the excellent (are my desire) :
" All my delight is in them."

They shall have great trouble [1]
That hasten after other (gods).[1]
I will not pour out their drink-offerings of blood :
I will not make mention of their names within my lips
⌈The LORD Himself is the portion of mine inheritance and of
│   Thou shalt maintain my lot.   [my cup :
│   The lines are fallen unto me in pleasant places :
⌊Yea, I have a goodly heritage.
I will thank the Lord for giving me warning :
My reins also chasten me in the night season
I have set the Lord always before me :
Because He is on my right hand, I shall not be moved.

Wherefore my heart is glad, and my soul[2] rejoiceth ;
My flesh also shall rest in hope.
For Thou wilt not leave my soul in hell :
Thou wilt not suffer Thy Holy One to see corruption.

Thou wilt show me the path of life :
ntiphon. In THY presence is the fulness of joy :
At THY right hand there are pleasures for evermore.

PSALM XVII.

A Prayer of David.

HEAR the right, O Lord !
    Consider my complaint :
ntiphon. Hearken unto my prayer
    Which goeth not out of feigned lips.

Let my judgment come forth from Thy presence,
Let Thine eyes look upon the thing that is right
Thou hast proved my heart,
Thou hast visited it in the night season :
Thou hast tried me, and shalt find nothing ;
For I am purposed that my mouth shall not transgress

[1,1] *Paronomasia :* the word *atsabbeem*, "idols," being understood.
        Heb. "glory," by *metonymy.*

As for this world :¹—By the words of Thy lips
I² have kept me from the ways of the destroyer.
O hold Thou up my goings in Thy paths,
That my footsteps slip not.

I² have called upon Thee :
Antiphon.　　For Thou wilt hear me, O God!
Incline Thine ear to me,
　　Hearken unto my words.

Show Thy mercy, Thou who savest them that trust (in Thee),
From such as resist Thy right hand.
Keep me as the apple of an eye ;
Hide me under the shadow of Thy wings ;
From the ungodly that trouble me,
From the enemies of my soul who compass me about.
They are enclosed in their own fat :
Their mouth speaketh proud things.
They have compassed us in our steps,
They have set their eyes bowing down to the earth,
Like a lion that is greedy of his prey,
And like a lion's whelp, lurking in secret places.

　　Arise, O Lord!
Disappoint his expectations : cast him down :
Deliver my soul from the ungodly (by) THY sword :³
From men who are but mortals, (by) THY hand,³ O Lord ;
From men who are but mortals of this world ;
Who have their portion in this life,
And whose bellies Thou fillest with Thy hid (treasure).
They have children at their desire ;
And they leave their substance to their babes.

　　As for me :
*Antiphon.*⁴I shall behold Thy presence in righteousness :
I shall be satisfied when I awake, with Thy likeness.

---

¹ *Heb.* "As to the works of man :—"
²․² The *I* in each case is emphatic in the original : in order to urge his request before God.
³․³ That "sword" and "hand" are not in apposition with the preceding substantives, as in authorized version, is evident from the whole context, but especially from the first distich in the foregoing paragraph—"From such as resist Thy right hand."
⁴ This antiphon corresponds with the antiphon of last Psalm.

PSALM XVIII.

To the chief Musician.—A Psalm of David, the servant of the Lord :

Who spake unto the Lord the words of this Song, in the day that the Lord delivered him from the hand of all his enemies, and from the hand of Saul. And he said :—

roem.   I WILL love[1] Thee, O Lord, my strength !

phon.   { The Lord (is) my Rock, my fortress, and my deliverer ;
My Rock (is) MY GOD :[2] in HIM will I trust !
(He is) my buckler, and the horn of my salvation ; my high tower !

roem.   I will call upon the Lord, who is worthy to be praised ;
So shall I be safe from mine enemies.

THE cords of death compassed me,
The floods of ungodliness[3] made me afraid :
The cords of hell came about me,
The snares of death overtook me.
In my trouble I called upon the Lord,
I cried unto my God.
So did He hear my voice out of His holy temple,
And my cry came before Him, even into His ears.

The earth trembled,[4] and was troubled ;[4]
The foundations of the mountains shook and were removed,
    Because He was wroth !
There went a smoke out of His nostrils,
And a consuming fire out of His mouth,
    So that coals were kindled at it.
He bowed the heavens, and came down,
And there was darkness under His feet :
He rode upon the cherubim, and did fly ;
He soared upon the wings of the wind.
He made darkness as a covering[5] round about His habitation :
Even dark waters, and thick clouds of the sky.

[1] *Rokham, to love tenderly.* Here only.
[2] *Heb.* "MY GOD is my rock." See v. 31, "Who is a rock except OUR GOD?" See also Ps. xxxi., where the Heb. is very emphatic :—

    "And be Thou my STRONG ROCK, and my castle of salvation :
    For my strong rock and my castle art THOU !"

[3] *Heb.* "Belial."   [4,4] *Paronomasia,* see Essay ii.
[5] *Heb.* "His secret place."

At the brightness of His presence
There issued from His thick clouds
   Hailstones and coals of fire.
The Lord thundered out of heaven,
And the Highest gave His thunder,
   Hailstones, and coals of fire.
He sent out His arrows, and scattered them :
He cast forth lightnings, and destroyed them.
The springs of waters were seen,
And the foundations of the world were discovered,
At THY chiding, O Lord,
At the blasting of the breath of Thy displeasure.

He sent from on high, He took me ;
He drew me out of many waters.
He delivered me from my strong enemy,
And from those who hated me, who were too mighty for me.
They pressed upon me in the day of my trouble :
But the Lord was my upholder.
He brought me forth also, into a place of liberty :
He delivered me, because He had a favour unto me.

Antiphon. The Lord will reward me after my righteous dealing :
After the cleanness of my hands will He recompense me.

Because I have kept the ways of the Lord,
And have not wickedly forsaken my God.
For all His statutes are before me ;
And His commandments will I not cast from me.
I was also uncorrupt before Him ;
I eschewed mine own wickedness.

Antiphon. Therefore will the Lord reward me after my righteous dealing ;
After the cleanness of my hands in His eyesight.

With the merciful, Thou wilt show Thyself merciful ;
With the upright, Thou wilt show Thyself upright :
With the pure, Thou wilt show thyself pure ;
And with the froward, Thou wilt show Thyself adverse.
For Thou wilt save the people that are in adversity ;
Thou wilt bring down the high looks of the proud.
For Thou wilt make my light to burn ;
The Lord my God will make my darkness to be light.
For by Thee I shall break through the host ;
And by the help of my God I shall scale the wall.

As for GOD : His way is perfect :
The word of the Lord is tried ;
He is the defender of all them that put their trust in Him.

ion. For who is God, but THE LORD ?
Or who is a Rock, except OUR GOD ?

It is GOD that girdeth me with strength,
And maketh my way perfect.
He maketh my feet like harts' feet,
And setteth me in high places.
He guideth my hands in the war ;
And mine arms shall break even a bow of brass.
Thou hast given unto me the shield of Thy salvation :
And Thy right hand shall hold me up,
And Thy loving correction shall make me great.
Thou wilt make wide my footsteps under me,
That my feet shall not slide.
I shall follow after mine enemies, and overtake them :
And I will not turn again, until I have destroyed them.
I will smite them that they shall not be able to stand ;
But they shall fall under my feet.
Thou hast girded me with strength unto the battle ;
Thou wilt subdue mine enemies under me.
The necks of mine enemies hast Thou given to (my feet) :[1]
And I shall destroy them that hate me.
They shall cry, but there will be none to help them :
Unto the Lord shall they cry ; but He will not help them.

[1] *Heb.* "given to me." The word "feet" occurs three lines previously. Compare Josh. x. 24, "Come near, put your feet upon the necks of these kings : and they came near and put their feet upon the necks of them."

Babylonian Cylinder in the Author's possession.

I shall grind them (as small) as the dust before the wind :
I shall cast them out, as the clay in the streets.
Thou wilt deliver me from the strivings of the people ;
Thou wilt make me the head of the heathen :
    A people whom I have not known, shall serve me.
As soon as they hear of me,[1] they shall obey me :
    The children of the stranger shall submit to me ;
    The children of the stranger shall fade away ;
And they shall be afraid in their borders.

    THE LORD LIVETH !

Antiphon. And blessed be my Rock,
    And praised be the God of my salvation !

It is GOD who hath avenged me,
    Who hath subdued the nations under me.
It is HE who hath delivered me from mine enemies,
    Who hath set me up above mine adversaries,
    Who hath rescued me from the man of violence.

Antiphon. Therefore will I give thanks unto THEE, O Lord, among the heathen :
    And unto THY Name will I sing psalms.

He giveth salvation unto His king,
And showeth mercy unto His anointed,
    Unto David, and to his seed, for evermore.

PSALM XIX.

To the chief Musician.—A Psalm of David.

THE heavens declare the glory of GOD,
And the firmament showeth HIS handiwork !
Day unto day uttereth speech,
And night unto night showeth knowledge !
There is neither speech[2] nor language
Where their voice is not heard :

---

[1] *Heb.* " At the hearing of the ear."
[2] To read here, as many modern commentators do—" *They have* neither speech
nor language," would be a contradiction to what has been already stated—

Their sound is gone out into all lands,
And their words unto the ends of the world.
In them hath He set a tabernacle for the sun,
Which is as a bridegroom, coming out of his chamber,
And rejoiceth as a giant to run his course.
It goeth forth from the uttermost part of the heaven,
And runneth about unto the end of it again ;
And there is nothing hid from the heat thereof.

The law of the Lord is perfect,
Converting the soul :
The testimony of the Lord is sure,
Giving wisdom unto the simple.
The statutes of the Lord are right,
Rejoicing the heart :
The commandment of the Lord is pure,
Giving light unto the eyes :
The fear of the Lord is clean,
Enduring for ever :
The judgments of the Lord are true,
And righteous altogether.
More to be desired are they than gold,
Yea, than much fine gold :
Sweeter also than honey,
And the droppings of the honey-comb.
Moreover by them is Thy servant taught,
And in keeping of them there is great reward.

Who can tell how oft he offendeth !
O cleanse Thou me from my secret faults.
Keep Thy servant also from presumptuous sins,
Let them not get dominion over me :
So shall I be undefiled,
And I shall be innocent from the great offence.

Antiphon.

Let the words of my mouth
And the meditations of my heart
Be acceptable in Thy sight,
O Lord, my strength, and my Redeemer !

"Day unto day uttereth speech :" (the same word in the Hebrew :) whereas the authorized version, referring to *nations* of different speech and language, agrees not only with the foregoing verse, but also with what immediately follows :—
"Their sound is gone out into all lands, and their words unto the ends of the world."

PSALM XX.

To the chief Musician.—A Psalm of David.

[A PRAYER FOR THE KING.]

THE Lord hear thee in the day of trouble,
The name of the God of Jacob defend thee :
Send thee help from the sanctuary,
And strengthen thee out of Sion :
Remember all thy offerings,
And accept thy burnt sacrifice.   סלה
Grant thee thy heart's desire,
And fulfil all thy mind.
We will rejoice in thy salvation,
We will triumph in the name of our God.
    The Lord perform all thy petitions.

Now know I that the Lord helpeth His anointed,
And will hear him from His holy heaven,
    Even with the saving strength of His right hand.
Some put their trust in chariots ; and some in horses :
    But we will remember the name of the Lord our God.
They are brought down, and fallen :
    But we are risen, and stand upright.

Antiphon.   Lord, save the king ;
And hear us in our prayer.

PSALM XXI.

To the chief Musician.—A Psalm of David.

[THE KING'S ANSWER.]

O LORD!
In THY strength shall the king be glad :
In THY salvation shall he exceedingly rejoice.
Thou hast given him his heart's desire,[1]
Thou hast not denied him the request of his lips.

סלה

[1] See verse 4 of preceding Psalm, line 7.

For Thou preventest him with the blessings of goodness ;
Thou settest a crown of pure gold upon his head.
He asked life of Thee ;
And Thou gavest him length of days, for ever and ever.
His glory is great in THY salvation :
Honour and majesty hast Thou laid upon him.
For Thou wilt give him everlasting felicity ;
Thou wilt make him glad with the joy of Thy countenance.
For the king putteth his trust in the Lord ;
And in the mercy of the Most High he shall not be moved.

All Thine enemies shall feel Thy hand :
Thy right hand shall find out them that hate Thee.
Thou shalt make them like a fiery furnace
In the time of Thy coming :[1]
The Lord shall swallow them up in His anger,
And the fire shall consume them.
Their fruit shalt Thou root out of the earth,
And their seed from among the children of men.
For they intended evil against Thee :
They imagined devices which they could not perform.
Therefore shalt Thou put them to flight ;[2]
The strings of Thy (bow) shalt Thou prepare against them.

Antiphon.   Be Thou exalted, O Lord, in Thine own strength !
(And) we will sing, and sing psalms to Thy power.

PSALM XXII.

To the chief Musician upon Ajileth[3]-Shahar.

A Psalm of David.

*E*LI, ELI !
Lama sabacthani !
MY GOD, MY GOD !
Why hast Thou forsaken me !
 . . . . so far from my help,
 . . . . . . the words of my complaint ![4]

---

[1] *Heb.* "presence. See Ps. ix. 3.   [2] *Heb.* "turn the shoulder."
[3] See Josh. x. 12 ; Judges xii. 12.   Probably a musical instrument of Ajalon.
[4] *Aposiopesis,* denoting intense feeling. The words $\left.\begin{array}{l}And\ art\\And\ from\end{array}\right\}$ being understood.

O my God !
I cry in the day-time, and Thou hearest not :
In the night season also, and that without ceasing.

But THOU art holy,
THOU who inhabitest the praises of Israel.
Our fathers trusted in THEE,
They trusted in THEE, and Thou didst deliver them.
They called upon THEE, and were holpen :
They put their trust in THEE, and were not confounded.

But as for me :—
I am a worm, and no man :
A reproach of men, and despised of the people.
All they that see me laugh me to scorn :
They shoot out the lip, they wag the head, (saying—)
" He trusted in God, that He would deliver him :
" Let Him deliver him, if He will have him."

But Thou art He that took me from the womb :
THOU wast my hope, when I hanged yet upon my mother's
Unto THEE was I cast, from the womb :   [breasts.
From the womb of my mother, THOU art my God.

Be not far from me :
Antiphon. For trouble is near ; there is none to help !

Many bulls have come about me :
Mighty (bulls) of Basan compass me about.
They gape upon me with their mouths,
As it were a ravening and a roaring lion.
I am poured out like water,
And all my bones are out of joint :
My heart is like wax ;
It is melted in the midst of my body.
My strength is dried up like a potsherd,
My tongue cleaveth to my jaws,   •
    And Thou hast brought me into the dust of death.
For dogs have surrounded me,
The congregation of the wicked have enclosed me.
They pierced my hands and my feet ;
I may tell all my bones.   •
As for them, they look (at me !)
They stare at me !

They part my garments among them,
And upon my vesture do they cast lots.

'iphon. But THOU, O God; be not far from me!
O my strength, haste Thee to help me!

Deliver my soul from the sword;
My life[1] from the power of the dog;
Save me from the mouth of the lion;
And hear me from the horns of the buffaloes.[2]

---

[1] *Heb.* "My only one."

[2] Various attempts have been made to determine what animal this was from which David had been delivered. Because we are told that in his occupation as a shepherd in his youth, he had to encounter wild animals, which he calls the "lion" and the "bear," commentators have sought to discover some formidable horned-animal which might have been living in Palestine at that time. The word in Hebrew is רֵים, or רְאֵם, *Raim* or *Reem*. In the passage before us "horns" are in the plural, but *raim* is also in the plural, "Raimeem"; but in Ps. xcii. 10 we have "horn" in the singular, and *raim* in the singular also. But in that passage there is an ellipsis, and we are not at all certain whether it should be supplied with the words "the horn" or "the horns." "Thou hast lifted my horn as (*that* or *those* of) the reim." We may, however, take it for granted that it was this particular passage which led the Seventy to translate the word by μονοκερώτων; from which we, following Jerome's Latin translation, have "*unicorn*." Now although it is not necessary to limit our choice to animals indigenous to Palestine, or even to take a realistic view of these passages, by supposing that David had ever been in danger from any such animal, yet we must have strong evidence adduced before we can assert that David believed in, or adopted, so fabulous an animal as a unicorn. If we accept the "one-horned" animal of the Septuagint, our choice will be between a unicorn and a rhinoceros. It has been remarked by a late writer that in Arabic and Persian monuments we have representations of an animal that looks like a unicorn. One of these monuments was bought by the author about thirty years ago at Aleppo. It is a metal vase of great antiquity, and bears the names of the twelve Imams who succeeded

Mahomet, under each of whom is an animal typifying the individual. One of these animals appears to be eating thistles or pomegranates. Though it looks

I will declare Thy name unto my brethren,
In the midst of the congregation will I praise Thee.

Antiphon. ⎰ Praise the Lord, all ye that fear Him :
     ⎱ Magnify Him, all ye seed of Jacob,
     ⎰ And fear Him, all ye seed of Israel :

---

like a unicorn, it bears the name of كى كيد *karkund*, rhinoceros; possibly because the Arabs have no special name for the unicorn. Curiously enough the word *reim* does occur in Arabic, رِم, but it is the name of the white doe.

The head and horn are certainly those of a unicorn, though the body, from its heaviness, might equally be taken for that of a rhinoceros. There is, however, no authority for this translation by the Seventy. Not only is the passage from which this hypothesis seems founded, equally capable, as we have seen, of referring to two horns instead of one horn; but in Deut. xxxiii. 17 we have "horns" in the plural, and *raim* in the singular, "the horns of a raim," and as this is the only positive example on the subject, we must conclude, notwithstanding the translation of the Seventy, that the animal was two-horned. In this last-mentioned passage, and in Is. xxxiv. 7, the *reim* is coupled with the bullock; in Ps. xxix. he is coupled with a calf; while in the book of Job, ch. xxxix., he is contrasted with an ox : thus showing an affinity with domestic cattle in all these passages : but the animal is wild, and possessed of great strength, (Num. xxiii. 22,) and is furnished with terrible "horns with which he pusheth to the ends of the earth." (Deut. xxxiii. 17.) He is an animal that cannot, like the ox, "serve" man, or "abide in the crib," or assist in "labour," or "bring home the seed," or "gather it into the barn." The *raim* of Job, then, is the wild buffalo, the bison, or the wild ox, (*urus*,) an animal which, from its resemblance to the ox, one might be tempted to think of employing as such, but which from its wildness would frustrate all efforts at so doing.

We shall find this deduction confirmed by the study of the *epanodos*. David, as a poet, made use of these animals and other illustrations, metaphorically. Behemoth, Belial, beasts of the field, and boars out of the wood, bulls of Bashan, calves, dogs, the hippopotamus or beast of the reeds, leviathan, the lion, the *raim* and the *tannrea*, sheep, swords and arrows, horn and heel, wings and feathers, vines, cedars, and olive branches—these and others are introduced figuratively to heighten the description. As an illustration of these metaphors, we will take a passage in the sixty-eighth Psalm—

He will rebuke the beasts of the reeds,
     With the herds of bulls,
         And the calves of the nations,
            Till they submit themselves with pieces of silver :
     He will scatter the nations that delight in war.
     Princes shall come out of Egypt,
Ethiopia shall stretch out her hands unto God.

Here we see that the "beasts of the reeds" designate Ethiopia; "bulls" represent the princes of Egypt; and "calves" the leaders of the nations. The *epanodos* has thus been of use in explaining some of these metaphors. Let us now apply it to the passage before us in the twenty-second Psalm—

He hath not despised nor abhorred
   The low estate of the poor :
He hath not hid his face from him ;
   But when he called upon Him, He heard him.

ntiphon. My praise is of THEE in the great congregation :
   My vows will I perform in the sight of them that fear Him.

The poor shall eat, and be satisfied ;
They who seek the Lord shall praise Him :
   Your heart shall live for ever.   [Lord :
All the ends of the world shall remember, and turn unto the
All the kindreds of the nations also shall worship before Him.
For the kingdom is THE LORD'S,
And HE is the Governor among the nations.
. Allthey that are in health[1] are fed (by Him) and worship (Him ;)
All they that go down to the dust shall bow before Him :
   And his own soul can no (man) keep alive.

Mighty (bulls) of Bashan compass me about :

. . . .
   As it were a ramping and a roaring lion.

. . . .
   For dogs have surrounded me.

. . . .
   They pierced my hands and my feet.

. . . .
   Deliver my soul from the sword,
   My life from the power of the dog :
Save me from the mouth of the lion,
And hear me from the horns of the *raim.*

By this it is quite clear that as "piercing" corresponds with "sword,"
"dogs" with "dog," and "lion" with "lion ;" so the *raim* corresponds
with "bulls of Bashan," or the wild buffalo of Job. The "dog" would refer
to the vilest of the people, the "lion" to those who lie in wait for blood, and
the wild buffalo to the headstrong and violent. Thus then, while we have
established that the animal here referred to is the wild buffalo, we are not
to suppose that David had ever been in danger from such an animal, or that
he prayed God to be delivered from it. The whole passage, like that in
Ps. lxviii., is figurative : and he prays God to deliver him from his enemies,
whose blasphemous rage he likens to the barking of a dog, their cruelty to
the tearing and rending of a lion, and their violence to the fury of a wild
buffalo.

[1] *Heb.* "All the fat upon earth." As both Jews and Pagans gave thanks
to God in eating, ("He that eateth, eateth to the Lord, and giveth God
thanks ;") so men, by the very act of eating, admit that they live only by
God.

E

(My) seed shall serve Him :
It shall be counted unto the Lord for a generation.
They shall come, and shall declare His righteousness,
Unto a people that shall be born,
    That HE hath done (it) ! [1]

PSALM XXIII.

A Psalm of David.

THE Lord is my Shepherd !
Therefore can I lack nothing !

He will feed me in a green pasture,
He will lead me forth beside the waters of comfort.
He will convert my soul.
He will bring me forth in the paths of righteousness,
    For His name's sake.
Yea, though I walk through the valley of the shadow of death,
I will fear no evil :
For THOU art with me !
THY rod and THY staff—they comfort me !
Thou preparest a table before me
Against them that trouble me :
Thou hast anointed my head with oil,
And my cup shall be full.

Truly, Thy loving-kindness and mercy shall follow me
    All the days of my life :
Antiphon. And I shall dwell in the house of the Lord
    For ever and ever ! [2]

---

[1] See John xix. 30, "It is finished : " or "(What) He hath wrought." See Num. xxiii. 23.
[2] *Heb.* "for length of days."

PSALM XXIV.

A Psalm of David.

Procm. THE earth is the Lord's, and all therein is :
The world, and they that dwell therein.
For he hath founded it upon the seas,
And prepared it upon the floods.

WHO shall ascend into the hill of the Lord ?
Or who shall rise up in His holy place ?

He that hath clean hands, and a pure heart ;
Who hath not lifted up his soul unto vanity,
And hath not sworn to (idols of) deceit.[1]
He shall receive the blessing from the Lord,
And righteousness from the God of his salvation.
This is the generation of them that seek Him ;
Even of them that seek Thy face, O Jacob.[2]

סלה

Lift up your heads, O ye gates,
And be ye lift up, ye everlasting doors :
        And the King of glory shall come in !

" Who is this King of glory ? "

It is THE LORD, strong and mighty !
It is THE LORD, mighty in battle !

Double antiphon.

Lift up your heads, O ye gates,
And be ye lift up, ye everlasting doors ;
        And the King of glory shall come in !

" Who is this King of glory ? "

It is THE LORD OF HOSTS !
He is the King of glory !

---

[1] See note to Ps. xii. 2—4.   [2] (O God of Jacob.)

E 2

PSALM XXV.

A Psalm of David.

א Unto thee, O Lord, will I lift up my soul, O my God!

Antiphon. ב In thee have I put my trust!
O let me not be confounded,
O let not mine enemies triumph over me.

ג For all they that hope in thee, shall not be ashamed:
They shall be ashamed who transgress without cause.

ד Show me Thy ways, O Lord:
Teach me Thy paths.

ה Lead me in Thy truth,

ו And teach me:
For thou art the God of my salvation;
In thee do I hope all the day long.

ז Remember Thy tender mercies, O Lord,
And Thy loving-kindnesses, which have been ever of old.

ח The sins and offences of my youth, remember not:
But according to Thy mercy remember Thou me;
For Thy goodness' sake, O Lord.

ט Gracious and righteous is the Lord:
Therefore will He teach sinners in the way.

י Them that are meek will He guide in judgment,
And such as are meek will He teach His way.

כ All the paths of the Lord are mercy and truth,
Unto such as keep His covenant, and His testimonies.

ל For Thy name's sake, O Lord,
Be merciful unto my sin: for it is great!

מ What man is he that feareth the Lord?
Him shall He teach in the way that He shall choose.

נ His soul shall dwell at ease,
And his seed shall inherit the land.

ס The secret of the Lord is with them that fear Him
And He will show them His covenant.

ע Mine eyes are ever looking unto the Lord:
For He shall pluck my feet out of the net.

פ Turn Thee unto me, and have mercy upon me:
For I am desolate, and in misery.

ע The sorrows of my heart are enlarged,
O bring Thou me out of my troubles.
* Look upon[1] my adversity and misery,
And forgive me all my sin.
ר Behold mine enemies, how many they are :
And they bear a tyrannous hate against me.

tiphon. ש O keep my soul, and deliver me :
Let me not be confounded, for I have put my trust in THEE.

ת Let integrity and uprightness preserve me :
For my hope hath been in THEE.

*itiphon
and
iphonem.*

Deliver Israel, O God,
Out of all his troubles.

PSALM XXVI.

A Psalm of David.

Antiphon.

Be thou my Judge, O Lord, *
For I have walked innocently :
My trust hath been also in the Lord ;
I will not swerve.[2]

Examine me, O Lord, and prove me :
Try out my reins and my heart.
For Thy loving-kindness is ever before mine eyes,
And I will walk in Thy truth.
I have not sat with the followers of vanity,
And with the deceitful will I not hold fellowship :
I have hated the congregation of the wicked,
And with the ungodly will I not sit.

---

[1] Good suggests that ראה "Look upon," or "Behold," has been substituted for קח *Take away,* or *Remove,* which would give the deficient letter ק.

[2] *Heb.* "I will not slide." This is the literal translation, and it agrees with the context.

[3] See note on Ps. xii. 2—4.

I will wash my hands in innocency,
And so will I go to Thine altar, O Lord
That I may show the voice of thanksgiving,
And that I may tell of all Thy wondrous works.
Lord, I have loved the habitation of Thy house,
And the place where Thine honour dwelleth.
O shut not up my soul with sinners,
Nor my life with the blood-thirsty :
In whose hands is wickedness,
And their right hand is full of gifts.

    As for me :
I will walk innocently :
Antiphon. O deliver me, and be merciful unto me.
My foot standeth right :
I will praise the Lord in the congregation.

PSALM XXVII.

A Psalm of David.

THE LORD is my light and my salvation !
    Whom then shall I fear ?
THE LORD is the strength of my life !
    Of whom then shall I be afraid ?
When the wicked came upon me,
    To eat up my flesh ;
Even mine enemies and my foes,
    They stumbled and fell.
Though a host encamp against me,
    Yet shall not my heart be afraid ;
Though war should rise against me,
    Yet will I put my trust in Him.

One (thing) have I asked of the Lord,
  That will I desire :—
Even that I may dwell in the house of the Lord
  All the days of my life :
To behold the fair beauty of the Lord,
  And to visit His temple.
For He will hide me in His tabernacle
  In the day of trouble :
He will hide me in the secret places of His pavilion ;
  He will set me on a rock.
And now will He lift up mine head
  Above mine enemies round about me.

Antiphon. I will sacrifice in His tabernacle sacrifices with shouting :
I will sing ; I will sing psalms unto the Lord.

Hearken unto my voice, O Lord, when I cry unto Thee :
Have mercy upon me, and hear me !
To Thee (saying)—" Seek ye my face,"
My heart answereth—Thy face, Lord, will I seek.
O hide not Thou Thy face from me,
O cast not Thou Thy servant away in displeasure.
Thou hast been my succour : leave me not,
Neither forsake me, O God of my salvation !
When my father and my mother forsake me,
The Lord taketh me up.
Teach me Thy way, O Lord,
And lead me in the right way,
  Because of mine enemies.
Deliver me not over into the will of mine adversaries,
For false witnesses are risen up against me, and such as breathe
Unless I had believed to see the goodness of the Lord   [violence.
In the land of the living—(I should utterly have fainted.)

Put thou thy trust in the Lord :
Antiphon. Be strong (in the Lord,) and He will strengthen thy heart.
Put thou thy trust in the Lord.

PSALM XXVIII.

A Psalm of David.

UNTO THEE, O Lord, will I cry, O my Rock!
    Be not silent unto me :
    Lest, (if) THOU be silent unto me,
I become like them that go down into the pit.
Hear the voice of my humble petitions
    When I cry unto Thee ;
    When I lift up my hands
Towards the mercy-seat of Thy holy temple.
O pluck me not away with the ungodly,
Nor with the workers of iniquity ;
Who speak friendly to their neighbours,
But imagine mischief in their hearts.
Give them according to their deeds ;
    According to the wickedness of their own inventions :
    According to the work of their hands give them ;
Pay them that they have deserved.
For (as) they regard not in their mind
    The works of the Lord,
    Or the operation of His hand ;
He will break them down, and not build them up.

Praised be the Lord !
For he hath heard the voice of my humble petitions.
The Lord is my strength, and my shield :

Antiphon. My heart hath trusted in Him, and I am helped :
Therefore my heart danceth for joy,
And in my song will I praise Him.

The Lord is my strength ;
And He is the saving strength of His anointed.
Save Thy people,
And give Thy blessing unto Thine inheritance
Feed them,[1] and carry them,
For ever !

[1] As a shepherd.

PSALM XXIX.

A Psalm of David.

Proem. GIVE unto THE LORD, O ye mighty,[1]
Give unto THE LORD glory and worship :
Give unto THE LORD the glory due unto His name ;
[2]Worship THE LORD in the beauty of holiness.

THE voice of THE LORD is upon the waters,
The God of glory commandeth the thunder,
THE LORD is upon many waters.

Antiphon. The voice of THE LORD is powerful,
The voice of THE LORD is full of majesty,
The voice of THE LORD breaketh the cedar trees.

THE LORD breaketh the cedars of Lebanon,
He maketh them also to skip like a calf,
Lebanon also, and Sirion,[3] like a young buffalo.

Antiphon. The voice of THE LORD cleaveth the flames of fire,
The voice of THE LORD shaketh[5] the wilderness;
THE LORD shaketh[5] the wilderness of Kadesh.

The voice of THE LORD maketh the hinds to shake,
He layeth bare the trees of the forest ;
In His temple doth everything speak of His glory.

Antiphon. THE LORD sitteth upon the water-flood,
THE LORD sitteth a King for ever !
THE LORD will give strength unto His people :
THE LORD will give His people the blessing of peace.

[It will be seen from the following arrangement that the foregoing Psalm forms an epanodos ; and it is remarkable that it is
precisely similar in form to that of the sixty-seventh Psalm.]

[1] *Heb.* "sons of God," *i.e.* the holy angels.
[2] In the original this line begins with the same letter.
[3] Mount Hermon, *i.e.* Anti-Lebanon. See Deut. iii. 8, 9.
[4] *Realm.*   [5, 5, 5] *Heb.* "to be in labour."

[Another Arrangement.]

GIVE unto THE LORD, O ye mighty,
Give unto THE LORD glory and worship:
Give unto THE LORD the glory due unto His name :
'Worship THE LORD in the beauty of holiness.
The voice of THE LORD is upon the waters,
The God of glory commandeth the thunder,
THE LORD is upon many waters.
The voice of THE LORD is powerful,
The voice of THE LORD is full of majesty,
The voice of THE LORD breaketh the cedar trees.
THE LORD breaketh the cedars of Lebanon,
He maketh them also to skip like a calf,
Lebanon also, and Sirion, like a young buffalo.
The voice of THE LORD cleaveth the flames of fire,
The voice of THE LORD shaketh the wilderness,
THE LORD shaketh the wilderness of Kadesh.
The voice of THE LORD maketh the hinds to shake,
He layeth bare the trees of the forest ;
In His temple doth every man speak of His glory.
THE LORD sitteth upon the water-flood,
THE LORD sitteth a King for ever !
THE LORD will give strength unto His people :
THE LORD will give His people the blessing of peace.

PSALM XXX.

A Psalm or Song, at the dedication of the house of David.

I WILL magnify THEE, O Lord !
Proem. For Thou hast set me up,
And hast not made my foes to triumph over me.

¹ See note in preceding page.

O LORD, MY GOD!
I cried unto Thee : and Thou hast healed me.
Thou, Lord, hast brought my soul out of hell,
Thou hast kept my life from them that go down to the pit.

Sing psalms unto the Lord, O ye saints of His,
And give thanks at the remembrance of his holiness.
antiphon. For His wrath endureth but the twinkling of an eye,
   And in His pleasure is life :
Heaviness may endure for a night,
   But joy cometh in the morning.

   As for me :—In my prosperity I said—
" I shall never be removed :
" Thou, Lord, of Thy goodness hast made my hill so strong."
   Thou didst turn Thy face from me ;
   And I was troubled.

   Unto THEE, O LORD, did I cry,
   And unto THE LORD did I make my supplication—
" What profit is there in my blood,
" When I go down to the pit?
" Shall the dust give thanks to Thee ?
" Shall it declare Thy truth ?
" Hear, O Lord, and have mercy upon me :
" Lord, be THOU my helper."

   Thou didst turn my heaviness into joy :
   Thou hast put off my sackcloth,
   And hast girded me with gladness.
antiphon. Therefore shall my soul sing psalms unto Thee,
   Without ceasing :
   O LORD, MY GOD!
   I will give thanks unto Thee, for ever !

PSALM XXXI.

To the chief Musician.—A Psalm of David.

IN THEE, O Lord, have I put my trust!
antiphon. Let me never be put to shame :
Deliver me in Thy righteousness.

Bow down Thine ear to me,
Make haste to deliver me :
And be Thou my STRONG ROCK,
And my castle of salvation :[1]
For THOU art my strong Rock, and my castle :
And because of Thy name, Thou wilt guide me and lead me.
Draw me out of the net which they have laid privily for me,
    For THOU art my strength.
Into Thy hands I commend my spirit,
    For THOU hast redeemed me.
O Lord, Thou God of truth,
Thou hatest all them that adhere to lying idols.[2]

Antiphon. But as for me :—I have trusted in THE LORD,
I will be glad, and rejoice in Thy mercy.

For Thou hast considered my trouble,
Thou hast known my soul in adversities.
Thou hast not given me over into the hand of the enemy ;
Thou hast set my feet in a large place.

Have mercy upon me, O Lord,
For I am in trouble :
And mine eye is consumed for very heaviness,
Yea, my soul and my body.
For my life is waxen old with heaviness,
And my years with mourning.
My strength faileth me because of mine iniquity ;
And my bones are consumed.
I became a reproach among all mine enemies,
But especially among my neighbours :
And they of mine acquaintance were afraid of me,
And they that did see me without fled from me.
I am clean forgotten, as a dead man out of mind ;
I am become like a broken vessel.
For I have heard the slander of the multitude ;
Fear was on every side :
While they conspired together against me,
And purposed to take away my life.

[1] *Heb.* "house of fortresses to save me."
[2] *Heb.* "lying vanities." See note to Ps. xii. 2—4.

But as for me :

Antiphon. My hope hath been in THEE, O Lord :
I have said—"THOU art my God."

My times are in THY hand : deliver me therefore
From the hands of mine enemies, and from my persecutors.
Show Thy servant the light of Thy countenance :
Save me for Thy mercy's sake.

Let me not be put to shame, O Lord,
    For I have called upon Thee :
Antiphon. Let the wicked be put to shame,
    And be put to silence in the grave.

Let the lying lips be put to silence,
Which speak scornful things against the righteous :
    (Being filled) with pride and contempt.

O how plentiful is Thy goodness,
    Which Thou hast kept for those that fear Thee,
    Which Thou hast prepared for those that put their trust in
Before the sons of men !   [Thee,
Thou shalt hide them in the hiding-place of Thy presence,
    From the combinings of men :
Thou shalt keep them secretly in Thy tabernacle,
    From the strife of tongues.

    Blessed be the Lord !
For He hath showed me marvellous great kindness
In a city of strength.
But as for me :—I said in my haste—
" I am cut off from the sight of Thine eyes."
Nevertheless Thou heardest the voice of my prayer,
When I cried unto Thee.

    O love the Lord, all ye His saints :
For the Lord preserveth them that are faithful,
Antiphon. And plenteously rewardeth the proud doer.
Be strong, and He shall strengthen your heart,
All ye who put your trust in the Lord.

PSALM XXXII.

A Psalm of David, giving instruction.

BLESSED is he whose unrighteousness is forgiven,
And whose sin is covered.
Proem.   Blessed is the man
Unto whom the Lord will not impute iniquity,
And in whose spirit there is no guile.

FOR while I held my tongue, my bones consumed away
    Through my complaining all the day long:
    For Thy hand was heavy upon me day and night;
And my moisture was turned into the drought of summer.

סֶלָה

I acknowledged my sin unto Thee,
And mine unrighteousness did I not hide.
I said—" I will confess my sins unto the Lord :"
And Thou forgavest the wickedness of my sin !

סלה

For this shall every godly man pray unto Thee
    In the time when (Thou) mayest be found :
    And in the time of the great water-floods
They shall not come nigh him.

Antiphon.   Thou art a place to hide me in,
    Thou shalt preserve me from trouble,
    Thou shalt compass me about with songs of deliverance.

סֶלָה

I will guide thee, and teach thee in the way thou shalt go ;
I will instruct thee with mine eye.
Be ye not like to horse and mule without understanding,
Whose mouths must be held with bit and bridle, to draw them
Great plagues shall be for the ungodly :   [unto thee.
But mercy shall embrace him who trusteth in the Lord.

Antiphon.   Be glad, and rejoice in the Lord, O ye righteous :
    Shout for joy all ye that are true of heart !

PSALM XXXIII.

SHOUT for joy unto the Lord, O ye righteous !
For praise is comely to the true of heart.[1]
phonal Give thanks unto the Lord with the harp,
oem. Sing psalms unto Him with the ten(-stringed) psaltery.
Sing unto Him a new song,
Strike the chords skilfully, with shouting.[2]

FOR the word of the Lord is true,
And all His works are faithful.
(He) loveth righteousness and judgment :
The earth is full of the goodness of the Lord.
By the word of the Lord were the heavens made,
And all the hosts of them by the breath of His mouth.
(He) gathereth the waters of the sea together, as a heap ;
(He) layeth up the deep, as in a treasure-house.
Let all the earth fear the Lord :
Stand in awe of him, all ye that dwell in the world.
For He spake—And it was done !
He commanded—And it stood fast !

The Lord bringeth the counsel of the heathen to nought ;
    He maketh the devices of the people to be of none effect.
The counsel of the Lord shall endure for ever :
    The devices of HIS heart from generation to generation.
Blessed is the nation whose God is THE LORD :
And the people whom He hath chosen to be His inheritance.
The Lord looketh down from heaven ;
    He beholdeth all the children of men :
From the habitation of His dwelling
    He considereth all them that dwell on the earth.
He fashioneth all the hearts of them ;
He understandeth all their works.

---

[1] The opening of this Psalm takes up the conclusion of the last.
[2] See Ps. xxvii. 6, " sacrifices with shouting."

There is no king that can be saved by the multitude of a host
    Neither is any mighty man delivered by much strength.
A horse is counted but a vain thing for safety :
    Neither shall it deliver by its great strength.
Behold, the eye of the Lord is upon them that fear Him
Upon them that put their trust in His mercy :
To deliver their soul from death,
And to feed them in the time of dearth.

Our soul waiteth upon the Lord :
For HE is our help and our shield.
Antiphon. For our heart shall rejoice in Him,
Because we have hoped in His holy name.
Let Thy merciful kindness, O Lord, be upon us :
Like as we do put our trust in THEE !

PSALM XXXIV.

A Psalm of David :

When he changed his behaviour before Abimelech ; who drove him away, and
he departed.

א I WILL give thanks unto the Lord at all times :
His praise shall ever be in my mouth.
Proem. ב My soul shall glory in the Lord :
The humble shall hear thereof, and be glad.
ג O praise the Lord with me,
And let us magnify His name together.

ד I SOUGHT the Lord, and He heard me :
Antipho'. And out of all my trouble He delivered me.

ה They had an eye unto Him, and were lightened :
ו And their faces were not ashamed.

Antiphon. ז This poor man cried, and the Lord heard Him :
And out of all his trouble He delivered him.

ח The angel of the Lord encampeth around them that fear Him,
And He delivereth them.
ט O taste and see how gracious the Lord is :
Blessed is the man that trusteth in Him.

﬩ O fear the Lord, ye that are His saints:
For they that fear Him lack nothing.

ﬤ The lions do lack and suffer hunger:
But they who seek the Lord shall not want any good thing.

ﬥ Come, ye children, and hearken unto me;
I will teach you the fear of the Lord.

ﬨ What man is he that lusteth to live,
And would fain see good days?

נ Keep thy tongue from evil,
And thy lips that they speak no guile;

ס Eschew evil, and do good;
Seek peace, and ensue it.

ע The eyes of the Lord are over the righteous,
And His ears are open unto their prayers:

פ But the face of the Lord is against them that do evil,
To root out the remembrance of them from the earth.

phon. צ They cried, and the Lord heard them;
And out of all their trouble He delivered them.

ק The Lord is nigh unto them that are of a contrite heart,
And He will save such as be of an humble spirit.

phon. ר Great are the troubles of the righteous;
But the Lord delivereth him out of all.

ש (He) keepeth all his bones,
So that not one of them is broken.

ת But misfortune shall slay the ungodly;
And they that hate the righteous shall be found guilty.

Antiphon and Epiphonem. The Lord delivereth the souls of His servants;
And all they that trust in Him shall not be found guilty

** The words "The Lord" occur sixteen times in this Psalm, and the pronoun referring to the Lord also sixteen times.

Err. The word "Him" in second antiphon should be altered to "him."

F

PSALM XXXV.

A Psalm of David.

STRIVE THOU, O Lord, with them that strive with me :
Fight THOU against them that fight against me.
Lay hand upon the shield and buckler,
And stand up to help me.
Stretch out the spear,
And stop the way against them that persecute me :
Say unto my soul—
" I AM THY SALVATION."

Antiphon.

Let them be put to shame and dishonour,
That seek after my soul :
Let them be turned back, and brought to confusion,
That devise my hurt.

Let them be as the chaff before the wind,
And the Angel of the Lord scattering (them) :
Let their way be dark and slippery,
And the Angel of the Lord pursuing them.
For without cause have they hid their net for me in a pit :
Without cause have they digged for my soul.
Let destruction come upon him unawares ;
Let his net which he hath hid, catch himself ;
And let him fall into his own destruction.

And my soul shall be joyful in the Lord,
It shall rejoice in His salvation.
All my bones shall say—
" O Lord, who is like unto Thee !
" Who deliverest the poor from him that is too strong for him :
" Yea, the poor and needy from him that spoileth him."

False witnesses did rise up :
They laid to my charge things that I know not.
They rewarded me evil for good,
Even to the bereaving of my soul.

As for me :—
When they were sick, I put on sackcloth,
I humbled my soul with fasting ;
  And my prayer returned to mine own bosom.
I behaved myself as towards my friend or my brother :
I went heavily, as one that mourneth for his mother.
But in mine adversity, they rejoiced, and gathered together !
The abjects gathered themselves against me :
And though I regarded not,[1]
They tore at me, and refrained not.
With unscrupulous parasites[2]
They gnashed upon me with their teeth.

O Lord, how long wilt Thou look upon this !
O deliver my soul from their destructions,
My life[3] from the power of the lions.

Second atiphon. I will give thanks unto Thee in the great congregation,
I will praise Thee among much people.

Let them not rejoice over me that are mine enemies unjustly :
Let them not wink with their eyes that hate me without a cause.

---

[1] Compare—

> I was as a deaf man, that heareth not,
>   And as one that is dumb, that doth not open his mouth
> I was as a man that heareth not,
>   And in whose mouth are no reproofs.   (Ps. xxxviii. 13, 14.)

> I will keep my mouth with a bridle,
> While the ungodly is in my sight.
> I held my tongue, and spake nothing :
> I kept silence, even from my right.   (Ps. xxxix. 1, 2.)

[2] *Heb.* "*mockers at feasts.*"—" **Trencher-friends**," *vulg.* " plate-lickers "
and " lick-spittles." There is a *paronomasia* in the original, לְעֵנֵי מָעוֹג.
Compare—

> Yea, even mine own familiar friend
>   Whom I trusted,
>   Who did also eat of my bread,
> Hath laid great wait for me.   (Ps. xli. 9.)

They are summer-friends, who bask in the sunshine of prosperity : but who
are the first to turn upon their benefactors in the hour of adversity.   There is
a good play upon words in the French language which distinguishes *l'ami de
cour* from *l'ami du cœur.*

[3] *Heb.* " My only one."

F 2

For their communing is not of peace :
But against the quiet in the land they devise deceitful things.
They open the mouth upon me : they say—
" Aha, aha ! our eyes have seen it ! "
This THOU hast seen, O Lord ! [1]   Be not silent :
Go not far from me, O Lord !
Awake, and stand up to judge my quarrel :
(Avenge Thou) my cause, my God, and my Lord.
Judge me, O Lord my God, according to Thy righteousness,
And let them not rejoice over me.
Let them not say in their hearts—" Aha ! so would we have it."[2]
Let them not say—" We have devoured him."

Let them be put to shame and confusion together,
First   That rejoice at my stroke : [3]
Antiphon. Let them be clothed with shame and dishonour,
That magnify themselves against me.

Let them be glad and rejoice
Second   That delight in my righteousness :
Antiphon. Let them say always—" O magnify the Lord ! "
That delight in the prosperity of His servant.

And as for my tongue :—
Epiphonem. It shall meditate on THY righteousness,
And of THY praise, all the day long.

[1] See Ps. x.   While he saith in his heart, " Thou wilt not require it."
Thou HAST seen !
[2] *Heb.* " Aha, our soul."
[3] This word, רעה, *Rooh*, "that which is *evil*, or *bad*," is evidently antithetical to "righteousness" in the second antiphon : and therefore would
signify chastisement resulting from supposed *sin* (compare above—" Aha,
aha ! our eyes have seen it !"). These two antiphons are remarkable for the
similarity of their structure, and the contrast of their prayer : the force of
which is heightened by employing the same words, "rejoice" and "magnify."

₊ While in this Psalm David's enemies rejoice at his trouble ; he himself
rejoices in God, and prays that the righteous may rejoice with him : and while
asserting his own innocence and "righteousness," he is mindful to ascribe it
to God, in meditating on HIS righteousness.

PSALM XXXVI.

To the chief Musician.

A Psalm of David, the servant of the Lord.

My heart showeth me the wickedness of the ungodly,
  That there is no fear of God before his eyes.
    For he flattereth himself (till he does not believe that) in His
His sin will be found to be hateful.   [eyes
The words of his mouth are unrighteous, and full of deceit :
He hath left off to behave himself wisely, and to do good.
He imagineth mischief upon his bed,
He hath set himself in no good way,
He doth not abhor anything that is evil.

Thy mercy, O Lord, (reacheth) unto the heavens,
And Thy faithfulness unto the clouds !
Thy righteousness (standeth) like the strong mountains ; [1]
Thy judgments (are) like the great deep !
Thou preservest man and beast, O Lord !
How excellent is Thy mercy, O God !   [wings.
  The children of men shall trust under the shadow of Thy
They shall be satisfied with the plenteousness of Thy house,
And Thou shalt make them drink of the river of Thy pleasures.
For with THEE is the well of life :
And in THY light shall we see light.

O continue Thy loving kindness unto them that know Thee ·
And Thy righteousness unto them that are true of heart.
O let not the foot of pride come against me,
And let not the hand of the ungodly cast me down.

antiphon. There are they fallen, all that work wickedness :
They are cast down, and shall not be able to stand.

[1] *Heb.* "mountains of God."

PSALM XXXVII.

A Psalm of David.

א
Antiphon.
FRET not thyself because of the ungodly ;
Be not thou envious because of evil doers.
For they shall soon be cut down, like the grass,
And they shall wither, like the green herb.

ב Put thou thy trust in the Lord, and continue faithful :
Dwell in the land, and verily thou shalt be fed.
Delight thou in the Lord,
And He shall give thee thy heart's desire.
ג Commit thy way[2] unto the Lord,
And trust in Him, and He will bring it to pass.
He will bring forth thy righteousness as the light,
And thy just dealing as the noon-day.
ד Hold thee quietly in the Lord,
And abide patiently upon Him.

Antiphon.
Fret not thyself against him whose way doth prosper,
Against the man that doeth after evil counsels.

ה Leave off from wrath, and let go displeasure :
Fret not thyself, else shalt thou be moved to do evil.
Wicked doers shall be rooted out :
But they that wait on the Lord,—they shall inherit the land

Antiphon.
ו Yet a little while, and the ungodly shall be clean gone :
Thou shalt look after his place, and he shall be away.
But the meek-spirited shall possess the earth,
And shall be refreshed in the multitude of peace.

ז The ungodly seeketh counsel against the just,
And gnasheth upon him with his teeth.
The Lord will laugh him to scorn,
For He hath seen that his day is coming.

---

[1] (Delitzsch.) *Heb.* "do good."
[2] *Heb.* "Roll thy way." See Ps. xxii. 8.

ר ⎧The ungodly have drawn out the sword,
⎪And have bent their bow;
⎨ To cast down the poor and needy,
⎪ To slay such as are of a right conversation:
⎪Their sword shall go through their own heart,
⎩And their bow shall be broken.

ש A small thing that the righteous hath
  Is better than great riches of the ungodly:
  For the arms of the ungodly shall be broken,
But the Lord alloweth the righteous.

ת The Lord knoweth the days of the godly,
And their inheritance shall endure for ever:
They shall not be confounded, in the time of evil,
And in the days of dearth, they shall have enough.

כ As for the ungodly, they shall perish:
  And as for the enemies of the Lord,—
Antiphon. They shall consume as the fat of lambs,
  They shall consume, even as the smoke.

ל The ungodly borroweth, and payeth not again:
  But the righteous is merciful and liberal.
  Such as are blessed of God shall possess the land:
  And they that are cursed of Him shall be rooted out.

מ The Lord ordereth a good man's going,
  And maketh his way acceptable to Himself.
  Though he fall, he shall not be cast away,
  For the Lord upholdeth him with His hand.

נ I have been young, and now am old:
  Yet saw I never the righteous forsaken, nor his seed begging
  (The righteous) is ever merciful, and lendeth;   [bread.
  And his seed is blessed.

ס Flee from evil, and do good,
  And dwell for evermore:
  For the Lord loveth the thing that is right;
  He forsaketh not His that be godly.

ע They are preserved for ever:[1]
  But the seed of the ungodly shall be rooted out.
Antiphon. The righteous shall inherit the land,
  And shall dwell therein for ever.

  [1] This line—"For ever they are preserved," would begin with the letter ע
were it not for the conjunction ל, "For," in front of it: and possibly this
may have been thought sufficiently near for the alphabetical arrangement:

צ The mouth of the righteous is exercised in wisdom,
And his tongue will be talking of judgment :
The law of his God is in his heart,
And his goings shall not slide.
ע The ungodly watcheth the righteous,
   And seeketh occasion to slay him :
The Lord will not leave him in his hand,
   Nor condemn him when he is judged.
ק Hope thou in the Lord,
And keep His way ;
And He shall promote thee to possess the land :
When the ungodly shall perish, thou shalt see it.
ר I myself have seen the ungodly in great power,
And flourishing like a green bay-tree :
But he passed away ; and lo, he was gone :
I sought him ; but his place could nowhere be found.

Antiphon.

שׁ Mark the perfect man, and behold the upright ;
For the end of that man is peace.
But transgressors shall perish together :
The end of the ungodly is, they shall be rooted out.

ת But the salvation of the righteous cometh of the Lord :
He is their strength in the time of trouble.
And the Lord will stand by them, and deliver them :
He will deliver them from the ungodly, and will save them ;

Epiphonem.   Because they put their trust in HIM.

---

and this idea is the more probable, as in this very Psalm the last verse, "The salvation of the righteous cometh of the Lord," beginning with ת, has the conjunction ו, "And" or "But," in front of it. Besides, several of the alphabetical Psalms exhibit still greater license. The Seventy, however, inserted a line—"The unrighteous shall be punished," so as to bring in this letter ; which interpolation we have followed in our Prayer-book translation. Should the Seventy have found authority for their translation, which is improbable, we should have to divide the lines thus :—

סFlee from evil,
And do good,
And dwell for evermore :
For the Lord loveth the thing that is right,
He forsaketh not His that be godly,
But they are preserved for ever.
ע The unrighteous shall be punished :
And the seed of the ungodly shall be rooted out.

But as each of the other letters of the alphabet, with one exception, has only a quatrain allotted to it, this interpolation is unjustified, and improbable.

PSALM XXXVIII.

A Psalm of David.

To bring to remembrance.

PUT me not to rebuke, O Lord, in Thine anger,
Neither chasten me in Thy displeasure :
For Thine arrows stick fast in me,
And Thy hand presseth me sore.
There is no soundness in my flesh, because of Thy displeasure ;
There is no rest in my bones, because of my sin :
For my wickednesses are gone over my head ;
As a heavy burden, they are too heavy for me (to bear.)
My wounds stink, and are corrupt,
Because of my foolishness.
I am troubled, I am bowed down greatly ;
I go mourning all the day long.
For my loins are filled with a sore disease,
And there is no soundness in my flesh.
I am feeble, and sore smitten ;
I have roared for the very disquietness of my heart.

tiphon. Lord, Thou knowest all my desire,
And my groaning is not hid from Thee.

My heart panteth, my strength hath failed me,
And the light of mine eyes is gone from me.
My lovers and my neighbours stood aloof from my trouble,
And my kinsmen stood afar off.
They laid snares for me that sought after my life,
And they that sought to do me evil—
Talked of wickedness,
And imagined deceit all the day long.
But as for me :—
I was as a deaf man, that heareth not ;
And as one that is dumb, that doth not open his mouth :
I was as a man that heareth not,
And in whose mouth are no reproofs.

iphon. But in THEE, O Lord, have I put my trust :
Thou wilt answer, O Lord my God.

For I said—(Hear me!) lest they rejoice over me ;
Lest, when my foot slippeth, they magnify themselves
But as for me—I am ready to halt ;   [against me.
And my heaviness is ever in my sight.
But I will confess my wickedness,
I will be sorry for my sin.
But mine enemies live, and are mighty :
And they that hate me wrongfully are many in number.
They also that reward evil for good are against me ;
Because I follow the thing that good is.

Antiphon. ת א Forsake me not, O Lord !
           ת א My God ! Be not far from me !
                Haste Thee to help me,
           ת א O Lord, my salvation !

PSALM XXXIX.

To the chief Musician—To Jeduthun.

A Psalm of David.

I SAID—
 " I will take heed unto my ways,
  " That I offend not with my tongue :
 " I will keep my mouth with a bridle,
  " While the ungodly is in my sight."
Proem. I held my tongue, and spake nothing ;
          I kept silence, even from (my) right :[1]
          But it was pain and grief to me,
          My heart burned within me.
          While I was thus musing, the fire kindled,
          And at the last I spake with my tongue :—

LORD, let me know mine end,
And the number of my days,
That I may know what it is,
And when I shall be called hence !

                    [1] *Heb.* "from good."

Behold, Thou hast made my days as it were a span long !
And mine age is even as nothing in Thy sight !

Verily, every man[1] living is altogether vanity ! סלה
Verily, man[2] walketh in a vain shadow !
phon. Verily, he disquieteth himself with vanity !
He heapeth up (riches) : and knoweth not who shall gather them !

And now, Lord, what is my hope ?
Truly my hope is even in THEE.
Deliver me from all mine offences,
Make me not a rebuke unto the foolish.
I held my tongue, and opened not my mouth :
For it was THY doing.
Take Thy plague away from me :
I am consumed by the means of Thy heavy hand.
Thou with rebukes dost chasten man for sin,   (by) the moth !
Thou makest his beauty to consume away, like the (garment eaten

phon. Verily, every man is vanity !
סלה

Hear my prayer, O Lord !
Give hear unto my cry :
Hold not Thy peace at my tears !
For I am a stranger with Thee,
And a sojourner, as all my fathers were !
O spare me a little, that I may recover my strength,
Before I go hence, and be no more seen !

PSALM XL.

To the chief Musician.—A Psalm of David.

I WAITED patiently for the Lord,
And He inclined unto me, and heard my calling.
He brought me also out of the horrible pit,
Out of the mire and clay,

---

[1] *Heb.* Every son of *Adam.*   [2] Even men of distinction.—"*Eesh.*"

And He hath set my feet upon the rock ;
He hath ordered my goings.
And He hath put a new song in my mouth,
Even a thanksgiving unto our God.
Many shall see[1] it and fear,[1]
And shall put their trust in the Lord, (and say—)
" Blessed is the man
" That hath set his hope in THE LORD ;
" And hath not turned unto the proud, [who regard not God,]
" Nor to such as go after lying (gods.)"[2]
Great are the things that Thou hast done, O Lord my God !
Even Thy wondrous works, and Thy thoughts which are to us-
    Who can recount them ?   [ward !
(If)[3] I should declare them, and speak of them,
They would be more[4] than I can number.[5]

Sacrifice and offering thou wouldest not,
    But mine ears hast Thou opened :
Burnt offerings and sacrifices for sin hast Thou not required ;
    Then said I—" Lo, I come,"
    In the roll of the Book it is written of me—
" I delight to do Thy will, O my God :
" Yea, Thy law is within my heart."
I have declared (Thy) righteousness in the great congregation
Lo, I will not refrain my lips, O Lord, Thou knowest.
I have not hid Thy righteousness within my heart ;
I have declared Thy faithfulness, and Thy salvation :
I have not concealed Thy loving mercy and truth
From the great congregation.

Antiphon. Withdraw not Thou Thy mercy from me, O Lord !
Let Thy loving kindness and Thy truth alway preserve me.

For evils are come upon me without number ![6]
    My sins have taken hold on me, and I am not able to look up[7]
They are more[7] in number than the hairs of my head !
    And my heart hath failed me !

---

1. [1] *Paronomasia,* יִרְאוּ and יִירָאוּ.   [2] See note on Ps. xii. 2—4.
[3] The conjunction is implied also in Ps. cxxxix. 18.
[5,6,7] In the first paragraph God's mercies are "*more*" than "*can be numbered:*" in the last his evils and his sins (and the collocation of the two together seem to imply that the one are caused by the other) are "*more*" than "*can be numbered.*"

iphon. O Lord, let it be Thy pleasure to deliver me.
Make haste to help me, O Lord!

Let them be ashamed and confounded together,
　That seek after my soul to destroy it:
Let them be driven backward, and put to confusion,
　That wish to do me evil.
Let them be desolate, and rewarded with shame,
　That say unto me—" Aha, Aha!"
Let them be joyful and glad in Thee, all they
　That seek after Thee.
Let them say alway—" The Lord be praised!"
　That love Thy salvation.

　As for me:—
I am poor and needy:
But the Lord careth for me.

iphon. Thou art my helper and Redeemer!
Tarry not, O MY GOD!

PSALM XLI.

To the chief Musician.—A Psalm of David.

Blessed be he that considereth the poor:
The Lord will deliver him in the time of trouble,
The Lord will preserve him, and keep him alive;
oem. 　And he shall be blessed upon earth,
　And he shall not be delivered unto the will of his enemies.
The Lord will support him when he lieth sick upon his bed:
Thou wilt make all his bed in his sickness.

　As for me, I said—
tiphon. O Lord, be merciful unto me:
Heal my soul; for I have sinned against Thee

　Mine enemies speak evil of me—
" When will he die, and his name perish?"
And if he come to see (me),
He speaketh deceitfully:
His heart gathereth iniquity within itself;
And he goeth out, and publisheth it.

All mine enemies whisper together against me,
Against me do they imagine evil—
" Some heavy crime presseth on him : [1]
" And now that he lieth, he will rise up no more."
Yea, even mine own familiar friend,
   Whom I trusted,
   Who did also eat of my bread,[2]
Hath lifted up his heel against me !

Antiphon. But be Thou merciful unto me, O Lord !
Raise Thou me up again, and I shall requite them.

By this I know that Thou acceptest me,
That mine enemy doth not triumph against me.
   As for me :—
Thou wilt uphold me in my uprightness :
Thou wilt set me before Thy face, for ever.

Blessed be the Lord God of Israel,
Antiphon. From everlasting to everlasting.
   Amen, and Amen.

[1] (French and Skinner.) *Heb.* " A matter of Belial presseth on him."
[2] Compare Matt. xxvi. 23 : " He that dippeth his hand with Me in the dish:"
and Ecclus. xx. 6—" They that eat my bread speak evil of me."

Turkish Dinner-table, Tray, and Dish.—From Damascus.
(In the Author's Collection.)

PSALM XLII [and XLIII].

To the chief Musician.—For the sons of Korah.

(Psalms) of instruction.

As the hart longeth after the water-brooks,
So longeth my soul after THEE, O God!
My soul is athirst for GOD, for the living God
When shall I come to appear before God?

My tears were my meat, day and night,
While they said unto me, all the day long—
"Where is thy God?"
This did I remember;[1]
I poured out my heart within me:
For I had gone with the multitude,
I had been with them in the house of God;
With the voice of joy and thanksgiving,
With such as keep holy day.[2]

iphon.

Why art thou so cast down, O my soul?
And why art thou so disquieted within me?
Trust thou in GOD: for I shall yet give Him thanks
For the help of His countenance.

O my God, my soul is cast down:
Therefore will I remember[3] THEE,

[1] [3] In the former case he remembers his troubles; in the latter, he remembers God.
[2] Such a procession seems represented to us in an Assyrian sculpture, now
in the British Museum.

Assyrian Musicians.—From Layard's "Discoveries in Nineveh and Babylon."

.Fromthe land of Jordan, and the Hermons ;
From the mountain of Mizar.
Deep calleth unto deep, at the noise of Thy water-spouts ;
All Thy waves and Thy storms are gone over me.
But in the day-time did the Lord command His loving kindness,
And in the night was my song of HIM,
    And my prayer unto the God of my life.

Antiphon.

I said unto God, my Rock—
    Why hast Thou forgotten me !
    Why go I so heavily,
While the enemy oppresseth me !

As with a sword in my bones, my enemies reproach me,
While they say unto me, all the day long—
    " Where is now thy God ? "

Antiphon.

Why art thou so cast down, O my soul !
And why art thou so disquieted within me !
Trust thou in GOD.   For I shall yet give Him thanks,
Who is the help of my countenance, and MY GOD !

[*Psalm XLIII. commences here.*]

JUDGE me, O God !
And plead my cause against an ungodly people,
O deliver me from the deceitful and wicked man.

Antiphon.[1]

For Thou art GOD my strength :
    Why hast Thou cast me from Thee !
    Why go I so heavily,
While the enemy oppresseth me !

O send out Thy light and Thy truth :
Let them lead me ;
Let them bring me to Thy holy hill,
And to Thy tabernacle :
That so I may go unto the altar of God,
Even unto the God of my joy and gladness :
And upon the harp will I give thanks unto Thee,
O GOD, MY God !

---

[1] See second antiphon of former Psalm.

Why art thou so cast down, O my soul!
And why art thou so disquieted within me
phon. Trust thou in GOD.   For I shall yet give
Who is the help of my countenance, and MY GOD!

***** The antiphons of Psalms xlii. and xliii. are examples of the variations
which will be constantly found in the antiphons.   Compare "My tears were
my meat," &c., and "As with a sword," &c.; "I will say unto God, my Rock,"
and "For Thou art God, my strength;" "Why hast Thou forgotten me?"
and "Why hast Thou cast me from Thee?" "Why go I so heavily?" and
"Why walk I so heavily?" "help of His countenance." and "help of my
countenance."

PSALM XLIV.

To the chief Musician.—For the sons of Korah.

(A Psalm) of instruction.

WE have heard with our ears, O God,
Our fathers have told us—
The works which Thou didst in their days,
Even in the days of old :—
(How) Thou didst drive out the heathen with Thy hand,
    And plantedst *them* in :
roem. (How) Thou didst destroy the nations,
    And madest *them* to stretch out ' (through the land).
For they gat not the land in possession by their own sword,
Neither was it their own arm that helped them ;
But THY right hand, and THINE arm,
And the light of THY countenance ; for THOU didst favour them.

THOU art my King, O God !
Send help unto Jacob.
Through THEE will we overthrow our enemies,   [against us.
Through THY name will we tread them under that rise up

1 See Ps. lxxx. 11 :—"She *stretched forth* her branches unto the sea.
                    And her boughs unto the river."
And Jer. xvii. 8 :—"For he shall be as a tree planted by the waters ;
                    And that *stretcheth out* her roots by the rivers."

For I will not trust in my bow,
It is not my sword that shall help me ;
But it is THOU that hast saved us from our enemies,
And that hast put them to confusion that hated us.
We make our boast of God all day long,
And will praise THY name for ever.

סֶלָה

But now Thou hast cast us off, and puttest us to confusion,
    And goest not forth with our armies !
Thou makest us to turn our backs upon our enemies,
    So that they which hate us spoil our goods :
Thou makest us to be eaten up like sheep,
    And Thou hast scattered us among the heathen :
Thou sellest Thy people for nought,
    And Thou takest no money for them :
Thou makest us to be rebuked of our neighbours,
    To be a scorn and derision of them that are round about us :
Thou makest us to be a by-word among the heathen,
    A shaking of the head among the nations.

My confusion is daily before me,
And the shame of my face hath covered me :
By reason of the slanderer and blasphemer,
By reason of the enemy and revengeful.

    All this has come upon us :—
Yet have we not forgotten Thee ;
Yet have we not been unfaithful to Thy covenant :
Our heart is not turned back ;
Our steps have not declined from Thy way :
Though Thou hast smitten us in the place of dragons,
And hast covered us with the shadow of death.
If we have forgotten the name of our God,
And holden up our hands to any strange God,
Would not God search it out ?
For He knoweth the very secrets of the heart !
For Thy sake are we killed all the day long :
We are accounted as sheep appointed to be slain.

Antiphon.   Awake, O Lord ! Why sleepest Thou !
              Arise, and cast not off for ever !

Why hidest Thou Thy face,
Why forgettest Thou our misery and trouble!
For our soul is bowed down to the dust,
Our belly cleaveth to the ground!

phon. Arise, and help us,
And deliver us for Thy mercy's sake!

** The second paragraph is a *replica* of the first.

PSALM XLV.

To the chief Musician.—Upon the six-stringed instruments.
For the sons of Korah.

(A Psalm) of instruction, and Song for "The Beloved," [1] *(i.e. Jedediah,*
or Solomon.) [2]

M Y heart is inditing of a good matter,
vorm. I speak of things touching the king.
My tongue is the pen of a ready writer.

[1] It is remarkable that David applied this name or epithet to himself, seven years before Jedediah was born (see Ps. lx. 5, and the occasion when that Psalm was written,) and that we find the name again used in Ps. cxxvii. 2, a Psalm having in its inscription, "For Solomon."

[2] That this Psalm was written primarily in regard to Solomon seems evident from a comparison of it with Ps. lxxii. In both these Psalms the title of "king" is mentioned; in both his kingdom is said to be that of righteousness; in both this kingdom is said to be established for ever and ever; in both the king's enemies are made to be subject unto him; in both presents are brought to him; and in both the royal psalmist concludes with an attribute of praise to God, praying that His name may endure for ever and ever. The Psalm appears to have been written at the same time as Ps. lxxii., when, after pouring out "a psalm of thanksgiving for God's powerful deliverance and manifold blessings" to him during all his life, (2 Sam. xxii.,) the aged monarch, feeling life drawing short, naturally looked forward to his son's succeeding him. This was not long before his death, and when Solomon was still under age. The father pictured to himself the prosperity of his son's reign, his distinguishing attributes, his marrying the daughter of the king of some neighbouring country:—entering into all the particulars thereof just in the same manner as the mother of Sisera did relative to the supposed par-

G 2

THOU art fairer than the children of men :
Full of grace are thy lips :
　　Therefore hath God blessed thee for ever !
Gird thy sword upon thy thigh,
O thou mighty one,
With thy glory, and thy majesty ;
And in thy majesty prosper thou.
Ride on, because of thy truth, and meekness, and righteousness ;
And thy right hand shall teach thee terrible things.
Thy arrows are sharp, and the people shall fall under thee ;
(They shall pierce) the hearts of those who are enemies to the king.

THY throne, O GOD, is for ever and ever ! [1]
A sceptre of righteousness is the sceptre of Thy kingdom.
Thou hast loved righteousness,
And Thou hast hated iniquity :
Therefore hath GOD anointed THEE ; even Thy God,
With the oil of gladness above Thy fellows.

All thy garments smell of myrrh, aloes, and cassia.
Out of the ivory palaces, whose instruments have gladdened thee.
King's daughters were among thine honourable women :
Upon thy right hand did stand the Queen, in gold of Ophir.
Hearken, O daughter, and consider ; incline thine ear ;
Forget also thine own people, and thy father's house :
So shall the king have pleasure in thy beauty,
For he is thy lord, and worship thou him.
And the daughter of Tyre shall be there with a gift :
The rich ones of the nations shall intreat thy favour.
　　The king's daughter is all glorious within :
Her clothing is of embroidery of gold ;
In raiment of needlework shall she be brought unto the king.
The virgins that follow her,
Even her companions, shall be brought unto thee :

ticulars of her son's victory. But while the *father* thus looked forward to
his son's prosperity, the *prophet* sees in the future the glorious establishment
of Messiah's kingdom, and abruptly changes his Psalm accordingly : but even
in those parts which he addresses to his son he unconsciously uses language
befitting rather the character of that Messiah who was promised to proceed
out of his loins.
　　[1] This paragraph is addressed to the Messiah. See Heb. i. 8, 9.

They shall be brought with joy and gladness,
They shall be brought into the palace of the king.
Instead of thy fathers, thou shalt have children,
Whom thou shalt make princes in all the earth.

I will remember THY name [1]
   From generation to generation :
iphon. Therefore shall the people give thanks unto THEE,
   For ever and ever.

PSALM XLVI.

To the chief Musician.—For the sons of Korah.

A Song upon the Alamoth [2] harp.

phon. GOD is our hope and strength :
A very present help in trouble !

   Therefore will we not fear—
Though the earth be moved,
Though the mountains be cast into the midst of the sea :
Though the waters thereof rage and swell,
Though the mountains shake at the tempest of the same.   סלה
The rivers of the flood thereof shall make glad the city of God,
The holy place of the tabernacle of the most High.
GOD is in the midst of her.
   Therefore shall she not be moved.
GOD shall help her,
   When the morn appeareth.
The heathen raged ;
   And the kingdoms were moved :—
He uttered His voice;
   And the earth dissolved.

[1] As the concluding antiphon of Psalm lxxii. is not addressed to Solomon, but to God ; so it would appear that this antiphon is addressed to God, the subject of it being identical.
[2] See 1 Chron. vi. 60.

Antiphon. The Lord of hosts is with us :
The God of Jacob is our refuge !

סלה

O come hither and behold the works of the Lord :
What destructions He hath brought upon the earth !
He maketh wars to cease in all the world,
He breaketh the bow, and knappeth the spear asunder,
He burneth the chariots in the fire.

" Be still then, and know that I AM GOD !
" I will be exalted among the heathen,
" I will be exalted in the earth."

Antiphon. The Lord of hosts is with us :
The God of Jacob is our refuge.

סלה

PSALM XLVII.

To the chief Musician.—For the sons of Korah.

A Psalm.

O CLAP your hands together all ye peoples !
Shout unto GOD with a song of rejoicing ![1]
Antiphon. For THE LORD is high, and to be feared :
He is the GREAT KING upon all the earth !

He will subdue the peoples under us,
And the nations under our feet.
He will choose out a heritage for us,
Even the excellency of Jacob whom he loved.

סלה

GOD is gone up with a shout,
THE LORD with the sound of the trumpet.
Antiphon. Sing psalms unto OUR GOD, sing psalms :
Sing psalms unto OUR KING, sing psalms.
For GOD is the KING of all the earth :
Sing ye psalms with understanding.

[1] *Heb.* " With the sound of a song of rejoicing."

GOD reigneth over the heathen :
GOD sitteth upon His holy seat.
The princes of the peoples are gathered in,
   (And become) the people of the God of Abraham :
For the powers of the earth are GOD'S !
   He is greatly exalted !

PSALM XLVIII.

A Song and Psalm.—For the sons of Korah.

Proem.

GREAT (is) THE LORD !
And highly to be praised !
In the city of our God,
(In) the mountain of His holiness.

Antiphon.

BEAUTIFUL for elevation,
The joy of the whole earth,
   (Is) the mountain of Sion !

Mount Sion.—From the south.
By David Roberts.

(On) the north side
(Is) the city of the GREAT KING ! [1]
God as a sure refuge
Is known in her palaces.
For lo, the kings were gathered ;
They passed by together.
They saw it—They marvelled :
They feared—They hasted away.
Trembling came there upon them,
And pangs, as upon one in travail.
Thou wilt break the ships of the sea
Through the east wind.

Antiphon.

Like as we have heard, so have we seen,
   In the city of the Lord of Hosts ;
   In the city of our God :
God will uphold the same for ever !

סלה

We wait for Thy loving-kindness, O God,
In the midst of Thy temple.
According to Thy name, O God,
So is Thy praise unto the world's end :
   Thy right hand is full of righteousness.

Antiphon.

Let the Mount Sion rejoice,
Let the daughters of Judah be glad,
   Because of Thy judgments !

Antiphon.

Walk about Sion ; go round about her ;
And tell the towers thereof. [2]
Mark well her bulwarks ; behold her palaces ;
That ye may tell them that come after.

Antiphon.

For this God is OUR GOD, for ever and ever :
He will be our guide, even unto death.

---

[1] For interpretation of this passage see Essay iii.
[2] Sion had sixty towers, and the lower city forty additional. (Josephus, *Bell.* 5, 4, § 3.)

PSALM XLIX.

To the chief Musician.—For the sons of Korah.

A Psalm.

Proem.

HEAR ye this, all ye peoples ;
Give ear, all ye inhabitants of the world :
Children of the rich, children of the poor,
High and low, one with another.[1]
My mouth shall speak of wisdom,
And my heart shall muse of understanding :
I will incline mine ear to parable,
I will show my dark speech upon the harp.

WHEREFORE should I fear in the days of evil,
When the wicked compass my heels round about?[2]
(Shall I be afraid of) those who trust in their goods,
And who boast in the multitude of their riches ?
No man can redeem his brother,
Or make atonement unto God for him—
For the redemption of their souls is precious ;
So that he must let that alone for ever—
Yea, though he live long,
And see not the grave.
But he will see it : (for even) wise men die ;
They perish together with the ignorant and foolish :
 And leave their riches for others.
Their inward thought is that their houses shall be for ever,
And their dwelling-places from generation to generation ;
 Calling the lands after their own names.

tiphon.

Man,[3] (who prides himself[4]) in his honour, will not abide :
He is like unto the cattle : there is no difference.

This is their foolishness :
And of those who after them shall speak in like manner.[5] סֶלָה
They are appointed to the grave, like sheep ;
Death gnaweth upon them :

---

[1] *Heb.* "Sons of *Adam*" (an ordinary man); "Sons of *Eesh*" (a man of distinction) : "Rich and poor together."
[2] *Heb.* "The wicked (or wickedness) of my heels encompasseth me." That this refers to the wicked is evident from the context.
[3] *Heb.* "*Adam.*" See note above.
[4] See concluding antiphon.   [5] *Heb.* "Are pleased with their mouth."

The righteous shall have dominion over them :
In a little time shall their form consume away :
  The grave shall be their habitation !
But God will redeem my soul from the hand of death,
When it shall receive me.

סלה

Be not thou afraid when a great man[1] is made rich,
  When the glory of his house is increased :
For he shall carry nothing away with him when he dieth,
  Neither shall his glory follow him.
Though while he lived he counted himself a happy man—
And (though) men praise thee when thou raisest thyself to
He shall go unto the generation of his fathers,   [distinction[2]—
And shall never see light.

Antiphon. Man,[3] (who prides himself) in his honour and hath no under-
Is like unto the cattle : there is no difference.   [standing,

---

PSALM L.

A Psalm.—For Asaph.

GOD, THE ALMIGHTY, JEHOVAH, hath spoken !
  And called the world,
    From the rising up of the sun,
    Unto the going down of the same.
  Out of Sion, the perfection of beauty,
GOD hath shined !
Our God will come,
Proem. And will not keep silence :
There will go before Him a consuming fire,
And a mighty tempest will be stirred up round about Him.
He will call the heavens from above,
And the earth, that He may judge His people.
" Gather My saints together unto me :
" Those that have made a covenant with Me by sacrifice."
And the heavens shall declare HIS righteousness,
For God is JUDGE Himself. סלה

[1] *Heb.* " Eesh." See note in preceding page.
[2] *Heb.* " When thou benefitest thyself."
[3] *Heb.* " Adam." See note in preceding page.

" HEAR, O my people, and I will speak :—
" O Israel, I will testify against thee :
" For I am GOD, even THY God.
" Not for thy sacrifices will I reprove thee,
" Nor for thy burnt offerings (which are) ever before Me :
" I will take no bullock out of thy house,
" Nor he-goat out of thy folds ;
" For all the beasts of the forests are Mine,
" And the flocks upon a thousand hills.
" I know all the fowls upon the mountains,
" And the wild beasts of the field are in My sight.
" If I were hungry, I would not tell thee :
" For the whole earth is Mine, and all that is therein.
" Shall I eat the flesh of bulls !
" Shall I drink the blood of goats !

" Sacrifice unto God thanksgiving,
" And pay thy vows unto the Most Highest :
onem· " And call upon Me in the time of trouble ;
" So will I hear thee, and thou shalt praise Me."

But unto the ungodly said God :—
" Why dost thou preach My laws,
" And take My covenant in thy mouth ?
" Seeing thou hatest to be reformed,
" And hast cast My words behind thee.
" When thou sawest a thief, thou consentedst unto him,
" And hast been partaker with the adulterer.
" With thy mouth thou hast spoken wickedness ;
" And with thy tongue thou hast set forth deceit.
" Thou satest, and spakest against thy brother ;
" Thou hast slandered thine own mother's son.
" These things hast thou done, and I held My tongue ;
" And thou thoughtest that I am even such an one as thyself :
" But I will reprove thee, and array (them) before thine eyes.
" O consider this, I exhort you, ye that forget God ;
" Lest I pluck you away, and there be none to deliver you."

honem· " Whoso sacrificeth thanksgiving, he honoureth Me :   [of God."
" And whoso walketh uprightly, to him will I show the salvation

PSALM LI.

To the chief Musician.

A Psalm of David:

When Nathan the prophet came unto him, after he had gone in to Bathsheba.

HAVE mercy upon me, O God!
　　According to Thy great goodness,
　　According to the multitude of Thy mercies
Do away my transgressions.

Antiphon.

Wash me throughly from mine iniquity,
　　And cleanse me from my sin:
For I acknowledge my transgressions,
　　And my sin is ever before me.

Against THEE, THEE only, have I sinned,
And done this evil in Thy sight;
That Thou mightest be justified when Thou speakest,
And be clear, when Thou dost judge.

Antiphon.

Behold, in iniquity was I brought forth,
And in sin did my mother conceive me.

Behold, Thou requirest truth in the inward parts,
Thou wilt make me to understand wisdom secretly
Thou wilt purge me with hyssop, and I shall be clean:
Thou wilt wash me, and I shall be whiter than snow.
Thou wilt make me hear of joy and gladness,
And the bones which Thou hast broken shall rejoice.

Antiphon.

Turn Thy face from my sins,
And blot out all mine iniquities.

Make me a clean heart, O God;
　　And renew a right spirit within me:
Cast me not away from Thy presence,
　　And take not Thy Holy Spirit from me.
Restore unto me the joy of Thy salvation,
　　And establish me with Thy free Spirit.
Then will I teach Thy ways unto the wicked,
And sinners shall be converted unto Thee.

tiphon. Save me from blood-guiltiness, O God, the God of my salvation.
And my tongue shall sing of Thy righteousness.

Thou wilt open my lips, O Lord :
And my mouth shall show forth Thy praise.
For Thou desirest no sacrifice, else would I give it Thee :
But Thou delightest not in burnt offerings.
The sacrifice of God is a troubled spirit :
A broken and contrite heart, O God, wilt Thou not despise.

O be favourable and gracious unto Sion :
Build Thou the walls of Jerusalem.
tiphon. Then shalt Thou be pleased
    With the sacrifices of righteousness ;
    With the burnt-offerings and whole burnt-offerings :
Then shall they offer young bullocks upon Thine altar.

PSALM LII.

To the chief Musician.

(A Psalm) of instruction, of David :

*When Doeg the Edomite came and told Saul, and said unto him—" David is
come to the house of Abimelech."*

W HY boastest thou thyself in evil, thou mighty man ?
The goodness of God endureth continually.
Thy tongue imagineth wickedness,
And with lies thou cuttest like a sharp razor.
Thou hast loved evil more than good,
   And lying rather than to speak righteousness :   סלה
Thou hast loved all words that may do hurt,
   O tongue of deceit.

Therefore will God destroy thee ;
He will take thee away for ever :
And will pluck thee out of thy dwelling,
And will root thee out of the land of the living.
סלה

The righteous shall see this, and fear,
And shall laugh him (to scorn) :—
" Lo, this is the man
" That took not GOD for his strength ;
" But trusted unto the multitude of his riches,
" And strengthened himself in his wickedness."
    As for me :—
I am like a green olive tree in the house of my God :
I will trust in the tender mercy of God, for ever and ever.

Antiphon.

I will always give thanks unto Thee
For that Thou hast done :
And I will hope in Thy name,
For Thy saints like it well.

PSALM LIII.

To the chief Musician upon the instruments of melody.

A Psalm of instruction, of David.

[A replica of Psalm XIV.]

THE fool hath said in his heart—
"There is no God."

Antiphon.

They are become corrupt,
They are become abominable in their wickedness :
    There is none that doeth good !

God looked down from heaven
Upon the children of men ;
To see if there were any that would understand.
That would seek after God.

Antiphon.

But they are all gone out of the way ;
They are all together become abominable :
There is none that doeth good,
There is not even one !

Have the workers of iniquity no knowledge?
That they eat up my people, as they would eat bread ;
   They have not called upon GOD !

There were they in great fear,
Even where no fear was :
For God hath scattered the bones of him that besieged thee ;
Thou hast put them to confusion ; for God hath despised them.

Oh that salvation were given unto Israel out of Sion !
When God turneth the captivity of His people,
iphon. Jacob shall rejoice ;
Israel shall be right glad.

PSALM LIV.

To the chief Musician upon the stringed instruments.

(A Psalm) of instruction, of David :

When the Ziphites came and said to Saul, " Doth not David hide himself with us ?"

SAVE me, O God, for Thy name's sake,
And avenge me in Thy strength.
Hear my prayer, O God :
Hearken unto the words of my mouth :
For strangers are risen up against me,
And oppressors seek after my soul.
   They set not GOD before their eyes !

סלה

Behold, GOD is my helper,
THE LORD is with them that uphold my soul.
He will reward evil unto mine enemies :
Destroy Thou them in Thy truth.
An offering of a free heart will I give Thee.
I will praise Thy name, O Lord ;
   For it is good.

For He hath delivered me out of all my trouble :
tiphon. And mine eye hath seen its desire upon mine enemies.

PSALM LV.

To the chief Musician upon the stringed instruments

(A Psalm) of instruction, of David.

HEAR my prayer, O God,
And hide not Thyself from my petition.
Take heed unto me, and hear me ;
How I mourn in my prayer, and am vexed ;
Because of the voice of the enemy,
Because of the oppression of the wicked :
For they cast iniquity upon me,
And in anger do they hate me.
My heart is disquieted within me,
And the fear of death is fallen upon me :
Fearfulness and trembling are come upon me,
And a horrible dread hath overwhelmed me.
　　And I said—
"Oh that I had wings like a dove ;
" For then would I flee away and be at rest :
" Lo, then would I get me away far off,
" I would remain in the wilderness : סלה
4 " I would make haste to escape,
" From the stormy wind and tempest."

10 Destroy them, O Lord, and divide their tongues :
For there is unrighteousness and strife in the city.
11 Day and night they go about the walls thereof ;
Antiphon.　　Mischief also and sorrow are in the midst of it :
Wickedness is in the midst of it ;
Deceit and guile go not out of their streets.

For it was not an enemy that reproached me,
For then I could have borne it :
Nor was it mine adversary that magnified himself against me,
For then I would have hid myself from him :

4 But it was even thou, my companion,
My guide, and mine own familiar friend !
We took sweet counsel of each other,
And walked together to the house of God.

Let death come hastily upon them,
tiphon. Let them go down quick unto the grave ;
For wickedness is in their dwellings,
And in the midst of them.

As for me :—
I will call upon GOD,
And THE LORD will save me.
At evening, and morning, and at noon-day will I pray :
I will cry aloud, and He will hear my voice.   [against me :
He hath delivered my soul in peace from the battle which was
For there were many round about me.
God will hear me, and reward them :
Even HE that abideth of old !

סלה

For they change not (for the better),
Neither do they fear God !
He laid his hand upon such as be at peace with him ;
He profaned his covenant.
His mouth was smoother than butter,
    Yet war was in his heart :
His words were softer than oil,
    Yet were they very swords.

O cast thy burden upon the Lord,
And HE will nourish thee :
    Neither will He suffer the righteous to be disturbed for ever.

Thou, O Lord, wilt bring (the wicked) into the pit of destruction :
The bloody and deceitful shall not live out half their days.
ntiphon. But as for me :—
My trust shall be in THEE.

H

PSALM LVI.

To the chief Musician upon the plaintive instrument.

" Michtam" of David:

When the Philistines took him in Gath.

E merciful unto me, O God!
For man goeth about to devour me;
　　He is daily fighting, and troubling me:
Mine enemies strive daily to devour me;
　　For there be many that fight proudly against me.
(Nevertheless,) when I am afraid,
I will put my trust in THEE.

I will praise God (because of) His word,
Antiphon. I have put my trust in God:
I will not fear what flesh can do unto me.

All the day long do they pervert my words:
All that they imagine is to do me evil.
They assemble, they hide, they mark my steps,
While they lay wait for my soul.
Destroy them, because of their iniquity:
Cast them down in Thine anger, O God!
Thou knowest my wanderings,
Thou takest account of my tears:
　　(All this is) noted in Thy book.
Whensoever I call upon Thee,
Then shall mine enemies be put to flight:
　　This I know: for GOD is with me!

I will praise God, because of His word,
　　　　　　I will praise the Lord, because of His word:
Antiphon. I have put my trust in God:
I will not fear what flesh can do unto me.

Unto Thee, O God, will I pay my vows,
Unto Thee will I give thanks.
For (as) Thou hast (ever) delivered my soul from death,
(So wilt Thou) not (now fail to deliver) my feet from falling,
That I may walk before God
In the light of the living.

PSALM LVII.

To the chief Musician on "al-taschith."

"Michtam" of David:

When he fled from Saul in the cave.

BE merciful unto me, O God!   Be merciful unto me!
For my soul trusteth in Thee!
And under the shadow of Thy wings will I trust,
Until this wicked enmity shall pass away.
I will call unto the Most High God,
Even unto GOD who will accomplish for me.   סלה
He will send from heaven, He will save me,
    When he reproaches that pants after me.
God will send forth His mercy, and His truth,
    (Though) my soul be among lions;
And (though) I lie among them that are set on fire,
Even the children of men ;
Whose teeth are spears and arrows,
And whose tongue is a sharp sword.

Antiphon.   Be Thou exalted, O God, above the heavens,
And Thy glory above all the earth !

They have laid a net for my feet,
    And have pressed down my soul :
They have digged a pit before me ;
    And they are fallen into the midst of it themselves.
            סלה

My heart is fixed, O God ! my heart is fixed :
I will sing : I will sing psalms.
Awake, my soul !
Awake, psaltery and harp !
I myself will awake right early.
I will give thanks unto Thee, O Lord, among the peoples :
I will sing psalms unto Thee among the nations.
For Thy mercy reacheth unto the heavens,
And Thy truth unto the clouds.

Antiphon.   Be Thou exalted, O God, above the heavens,
And Thy glory above all the earth !

PSALM LVIII.

To the chief Musician on " al-taschith."

" Michtam " of David :

Do ye speak in righteousness,
Do ye judge the thing that is right, O ye sons of men ?
Nay, your heart imagineth wickedness upon the earth,
And your hands deal in violence.
The ungodly are estranged from the womb,
They go astray as soon as they are born, speaking lies.
They are as venomous as the venom of a serpent,
They are like the deaf adder that stoppeth her ears ;
Which refuseth to hear the voice of the charmer,
Charm he never so wisely.

Break their teeth in their mouths, O God ;
Smite the jaw-bones of the young lions, ● Lord :
Let them melt away like the waters,
    Let them pass away :
And when one but strings the arrows,[1]
    Let them be cut in pieces.
As a snail which melteth,
    Let them consume away :
As the untimely birth of a woman,
    Let them not see the sun.
Or ever the thorns[2] make the pot to boil,
So, fed by Thy wrath,
    Let them be driven away as with a whirlwind.

The righteous shall rejoice, when he seeth the vengeance :
He shall wash his footsteps in the blood of the ungodly.
    And thus shall it be said :—

Antiphon. "Verily, there is a reward for the righteous :
"Verily, there is a God that judgeth the earth."

---

[1] See Ps. lxiv. 3. *Heb. " bends* the arrows," being a *syncope* of the full expression in Ps. xi. 2. " For lo, the ungodly *bend* the bow, and make ready *their arrows upon the string."* Compare Ps. lxiv. 8—
        "They shall flee away when anyone but looks at them."
[2] See Ex. xxii. 6 ; Ps. cxviii. 12 ; Eccl. vii. 6 ; Is. xxxiii. 12 ; Nahum, i. 10.

PSALM LIX.

To the chief Musician on "*al-taschith.*"

"*Michtam*" *of David:*

When Saul sent, and they watched the house to kill him.

DELIVER me from mine enemies, O my God!
  Defend me from them that rise up against me.
Deliver me from the wicked doers,
  And save me from the blood-thirsty men.
For lo, they lie waiting for my soul;
The mighty men are gathered against me;
Not for my transgression,
And not for any sin of mine, O Lord.
They run and prepare themselves, without my fault:
Arise Thou therefore to help me, and behold.
But Thou, O Lord God of hosts,
The God of Israel!
Awake to visit all the heathen;
And be not merciful to the workers of iniquity.   סלה

They assemble in the evening,
They make a noise like a dog, and go about the city.
Behold, they snarl with their mouths,
And swords are on their lips, (saying)—" Who hears ?"
But Thou, O Lord, wilt have them in derision :
Thou wilt laugh all the heathen to scorn.

  I will trust in THY strength ;
tiphon. For GOD is my refuge :
  The God who showeth mercy unto me[1] will preserve me.

God will let me see (my desire) upon mine enemies :
Slay them not, lest my people forget it,
But scatter them in Thy might,
And put them down, O Lord our defence.
Oh, the sin of their mouth!
Oh, the words of their lips!
But they shall be taken in their pride,
And for the cursing and lying which they utter.
Consume them in Thy wrath,
Consume them that they may perish :

  [1] *Heb.* "The God of my mercy."

And they shall know that it is GOD that ruleth in Jacob,
And unto the ends of the world.

סלה

But they will assemble again in the evening,
They will make a noise like a dog, and go about the city.
They will run here and there for meat,
They will murmur if not satisfied.

    As for me :—
I will sing of Thy power,
I will praise Thy mercy betimes in the morning :
For Thou hast been a defence to me,
And a refuge in the day of my trouble.

Antiphon. Unto THEE, O my strength, will I sing psalms :
For THOU, O God, art my refuge, and the God who showeth
                         [mercy unto me. [1]

PSALM LX.

To the chief Musician upon the six-stringed instrument.

(In remembrance of ?) the Testimony.[2]—" Michtam" of David: to teach.

When he strove with Syria of the two rivers, and with Syria of Zobah, when Joab returned, and smote of Edom in the Valley of Salt twelve thousand.

O GOD, Thou hast cast us off, Thou hast scattered us abroad :
Thou hast also been displeased ! O turn Thee unto us again.
Thou hast caused the land to tremble : Thou hast broken it :
Heal the breaches thereof: for it shaketh.
Thou hast showed Thy people heavy things :
Thou hast given us to drink of the wine of trembling.
(But) Thou hast given a standard [3] to such as fear Thee,
That they may stand up [3] because of the truth.   סלה
Therefore shall Thy beloved be delivered :
Save with Thy right hand, and hear me.

[1] In each case the Heb. is—" the God of my mercy."
[2] See Ps. xix. 7 ; lxxviii. 5 ; lxxxi. 5, and cxxii. 4, *Bib. Vers.* Hammond supposes the six-stringed instrument was played before the "Ark of the Testimony." See 1 Chron. xvi. 37—42.
[3,3] *Paronomasia,* see Essay ii. *Heb.* "To be displayed because of the truth."

God hath spoken in His holiness—
" I will rejoice : I will divide Schechem,
" I will mete out the valley of Succoth,
" Gilead is mine ; Manasseh is mine ;
" Ephraim also is the strength of my head ;
" Judah is my lawgiver ;
" Moab is my hand-basin ;[1]
" Over Edom will I cast out my shoe ;
" Over Philistia will I triumph."

Who will lead me into the strong city ?
Who will bring me into Edom ?
Wilt not Thou, O God, who has cast us off ?
Wilt not Thou, O God, go out with our hosts ?
O be THOU our help against the enemy :
For vain is the help of man !

Antiphon. Through GOD we shall do great acts :
For it is HE that will tread down our enemies.

[1] The office of hand-basin-holder is of great antiquity in the East. In one hand he holds the *tast*, or basin, with a napkin over the arm, and in the other the *ebrik*, or ewer. Elisha performed this office for Elijah. See 2 Kings iii. 11. The Shah of Persia was constantly attended by his *Ebrikdar* during his late travels in Europe.

Ebrik and Tast, in the author's collection.

PSALM LXI.

To the chief Musician upon the stringed instruments.

A Psalm of David.

Proem.

HEAR my crying, O God!
Give ear unto my prayer:
From the ends of the earth will I call upon Thee,
When my heart is in heaviness.

THOU hast set me upon a rock which is higher than I:
For Thou hast been my refuge,
And a strong tower for me against the enemy.
I shall dwell in Thy tabernacle for ever;
I shall trust under the covering of Thy wings.   סלה
For Thou, O God, hast heard my vows:
Thou hast given me an inheritance among those that fear Thy
Days upon days wilt Thou add unto the king: [name.
And his years shall endure from generation to generation.
He shall dwell before God, for ever:
Mercy and truth wilt Thou cause to guard him.

Antiphon.

Thus will I sing psalms to Thy name for ever,
And pay unto Thee my vows, day by day.

PSALM LXII.

To the chief Musician.—To Jeduthun.—A Psalm of David.

Antiphon.

ONLY upon GOD wait [1] thou, my soul:
For of HIM cometh thy salvation.
Only HE is my Rock, and my salvation:
He is my defence, so that I shall not greatly fall.

[1] *Heb.* "Be silent." We must not only trust in God in time of trouble,
but we must do so "without murmurings" and repinings. Phil. ii. 14.
See Ps. lxv. 1.

How long will ye conspire against a man: [1]
(How long) will ye all (seek to) destroy him?
(A man who is already) as a tottering wall,
As a broken fence! [2]
Only to thrust him down from his dignity do they devise,
Their delight is in lies :
They bless with their mouth,
But they curse inwardly.

סלה

phm.

Only upon GOD wait thou, my soul :
    For of HIM cometh thy salvation.
Only HE is my Rock, and my salvation :
    He is my defence, so that I shall not fall.

In GOD is my salvation and my glory:
The Rock of my might, and my refuge, is GOD !
O put your trust in Him alway, ye people :
Pour out your hearts before Him ;
    For God is our hope.

סלה

Only vanity are the children of common men ! [3]
A lie are the children of great men !
To be weighed in the balance,
They are all together lighter than vanity itself !
O trust not in wrong and robbery,
Give not yourselves unto vanity :
If riches increase,
Set not your heart upon them.

God spake once,
And twice I have also heard the same—
That power (belongeth) unto God ;
And that to Thee, O Lord, (belongeth) mercy :
For Thou rewardest to every man
According to his work.

---

[1] "*Eesh*," here signifying—an innocent, good man.
[2] See Ps. cix. 16. "But persecuted the man who was poor and afflicted,
        "And broken-hearted, (searching) to kill him."
[3] "*Adam*," man of the earth. } The Hebrew is in the singular in each case.
[4] "*Eesh*."

PSALM LXIII.

A Psalm of David:

When he was in the wilderness of Judah.

O GOD, Thou art MY God!
Early will I seek Thee.
My soul thirsteth for Thee,
My flesh also longeth after Thee ;
In a barren and dry land
Where no water is !
To see Thy power, and Thy glory,
So as I have seen Thee in the sanctuary.
For Thy loving-kindness is better than the life itself:
My lips shall praise Thee.
Thus will I magnify Thee as long as I live :
I will lift up my hands in Thy name.
Thou wilt satisfy my soul, as with marrow and fatness,
And my mouth shall praise Thee with joyful lips,
When I remember Thee upon my bed,
When I think of Thee in the night watches.
Because Thou hast been my helper,
Therefore under the shadow of Thy wings will I rejoice.
My soul hangeth upon Thee :
Thy right hand hath upholden me.

But as for them that seek the hurt of my soul,
They shall go under the earth :
They shall fall upon the edge of the sword,
They shall be a portion for jackals.

But the king shall rejoice in GOD :
Antiphon. All they also that swear by HIM shall be commended ;
But the mouth of them that speak lies shall be stopped.

PSALM LXIV.

To the chief Musician.—A Psalm of David.

HEAR my voice, O God, in my prayer ;
Preserve my life from fear of the enemy.
Hide me from the secret (designs) of the wicked,
And from the gathering together of the workers of iniquity :
Who have whet their tongues like a sword,
And have strung [1] their arrows, even bitter words,
That they may privily shoot at him that is perfect,
Suddenly do they shoot at him, and fear not.
They encourage themselves in deeds of evil ;
They commune among themselves how they may lay snares ;
They say—" Who will see it ?"
They search how they may do mischief ;
They have made search :
They search each one, both the inward parts,
And the depths of the heart.

But God will shoot at them with a swift arrow,
And suddenly shall they be wounded.
They shall fall, being convicted by their own tongues ;
They shall flee away when anyone but looks at them. [2]
And all men shall fear,
And they shall show forth God's deeds :
  For they will perceive that it is HIS work.

Antiphon.   The righteous shall rejoice in the Lord, and trust in HIM ;
And all they that are true of heart shall be glad.

---

[1] *Heb.* " inclined their arrows." See Ps. lviii. 8, and xi. 2.
[2] Compare Ps. lviii. 6—
                And when one but strings the arrows,
                Let them be rooted out.

₊ The second paragraph is God's answer to the wicked, whose words and actions are described in the first : punishing them with their own weapons and their own tongues.

PSALM LXV.

To the chief Musician.—A Psalm and Song of David.

SILENCE (and) praise (are offered) to Thee, O God, in Sion![1]
And unto Thee shall the vow be performed.
O Thou that hearest prayer,
Unto Thee shall all flesh come.
Iniquities prevail against me:
But our transgressions Thou wilt purge away.
Blessed is the man whom Thou choosest, and receivest unto
He shall dwell in Thy courts;   [Thee:
He shall be satisfied with the goodness of Thy house,
Even of Thy holy temple.
Thou wilt show us wonderful things in Thy righteousness,
O God of our salvation:
(Thou that art) the hope of all the ends of the earth,
And of them that remain in the broad sea.
Who in His strength setteth fast the mountains,
And is girded about with power:
Who stilleth the raging of the sea,
The raging of its waves, and the fury of the nations.
The uttermost lands shall fear Thee because of Thy judgments,
The lands of the far east and west[2] dost Thou make rejoice.

Thou visitest the earth, and blessest it exceedingly;
Thou enrichest it with the river of God, which is full of water;
(Which) Thou hast prepared (for) its corn;
For so Thou hast prepared it.

[1] "Silence" and "Praise." These two words are antithetical: and the antithesis seems marked by the absence of the copulative. As St. Paul reasons relative to the observance of appointed days, that whether men ate, or ate not, in either case they "gave God thanks;" (Rom. xiv. 6;) and as Mary's "silent" devotion was more than equally commended by our Lord, with Martha's more active service: so here the Psalmist declares that God is praised in Sion by the joyful shouting of some; those in prosperity; and by the submissive, confiding, unrepining faith of others: those in adversity or affliction. See Ps. lxii. 1. This is the rendering of Hammond, Gesenius, and Phillips. The Psalmist declares that that man is "blessed" who is "satisfied" with the consolations of religion; and that to such a man God will show "wonderful things in His righteousness;" He who is the "God of their salvation, and the hope of all the ends of the earth," and "who stilleth the raging of the sea, the raging of its waves, and the fury of the nations."
[2] *Heb.* "the outgoings of the morning and evening."

Thou waterest its furrows,
Thou breakest up its ridges :
Thou makest it soft with the drops of rain,
Thou blessest the increase of it.
Thou crownest the year with Thy goodness,
And Thy clouds drop fatness.
They shall drop upon the pastures of the wilderness,
And the hills shall rejoice on every side.
The meadows shall be clothed with flocks,
And the valleys shall stand thick with corn.
They shall shout for joy :
Yea, they shall sing.

PSALM LXVI.

To the chief Musician.—A Psalm or Song.

SHOUT unto God, all the earth !
Sing psalms unto the glory of His name :
Make His praise to be glorious.

roem
and   Say unto God—How wonderful are Thy works !
Antiphon.   Thine enemies shall submit themselves through the greatness
All the earth shall worship Thee.   [of Thy power ;
They shall sing psalms unto Thee,
They shall sing psalms to Thy name.

סלה׃

O COME hither, and behold the works of God :
How wonderful are His doings towards the children of men !
He turned the sea into dry land,
So that they went through the water on foot :
There did we rejoice in HIM.
He ruleth with His power for ever :
His eyes behold the nations :
Let not the rebellious exalt themselves.

סלה

Antiphon. O praise our God, ye nations,
And make the voice of His praise to be heard.

Who holdeth our soul in life,
And suffereth not our feet to slip.
For Thou, O God, hast proved us,
Thou also hast tried us, like as silver is tried.
Thou broughtest us into the snare,
Thou laidest trouble upon our loins.
Thou sufferedst men to ride over our heads,
We went through fire and water,
   And Thou broughtest us out into a wealthy place.

I will go into Thy house with burnt-offerings;
I will pay Thee my vows,
Which I promised with my lips,
And spake with my mouth, when I was in trouble.
I will offer unto Thee burnt-sacrifices of fatlings,
   With the incense of rams:
I will offer bullocks,
   With he-goats.

סלה

Oh, come hither, and hearken, all ye that fear God,
And I will tell you what He hath done for my soul.
I called unto Him with my mouth,
And gave Him praises with my tongue.
If I incline unto wickedness with my heart,
The Lord will not hear me:
But God hath heard me,
He hath considered the voice of my prayer.

Antiphon. Praised be God who hath not cast out my prayer,
Nor turned His mercy from me.

** In the third paragraph the Psalmist invites his hearers to consider God's goodness to his people: in the last he bids them listen to what God has done to himself.

PSALM LXVII.

To the chief Musician upon the stringed instruments.

A Psalm or Song.

Antiphon. Gᴏᴅ be merciful unto us, and bless us,
And cause His face to shine upon us.　לרֿ

That Thy way may be known upon earth,
Thy salvation among all nations.

Antiphon. Let the peoples praise Thee, O God :
Let all the peoples praise Thee !

O let the nations rejoice and be glad :
For Thou wilt judge the peoples righteously :
Thou wilt govern the nations upon earth.　סלה

Antiphon. Let the peoples praise Thee, O God :
Let all the peoples praise Thee !

Then shall the earth bring forth her increase,
And God, even our own God, will give us His blessing.

Antiphon. Gᴏᴅ will bless us,
And all the ends of the world shall fear Him.

(*Another Arrangement,*[1] see Ps. xxix.)

Antiphon. God be merciful unto us, and bless us,
And cause His face to shine upon us.
　　That Thy way may be known upon earth,
　　Thy salvation among all nations.
Antiphon. 　　Let the peoples praise Thee, O God :
　　Let all the peoples praise Thee !
　　　　O let the nations rejoice, and be glad :
　　　　　　For Thou wilt judge the peoples righteously,
　　　　The nations upon earth wilt Thou govern.
Antiphon. 　　Let the peoples praise Thee, O God,
　　Let all the peoples praise Thee !
　　Then shall the earth bring forth her increase,
　　And God, even our own God, will give us His blessing.
Antiphon. God will bless us :
And all the ends of the world shall fear Him.

Discovered by Jebb, *Lit. Trans.*

PSALM LXVIII.

To the chief Musician.

A Psalm or Song of David.

" LET God arise, and let His enemies be scattered ;
" Let them also that hate Him flee before Him." [1]
 As the driving away of smoke,
  So do Thou drive them away :
 As the melting of wax before the fire,
  So let the ungodly perish before the presence of God.
 But let the righteous be glad, let them rejoice before God,
 Let them also be merry and joyful.

 Sing unto God : sing psalms to His name.
Antiphon. Make way for Him that rideth in the wilderness in his name
 And rejoice before Him.   [JAH,[2]

 He is a Father of the fatherless, and a Judge of the widows ;
 Even GOD in His holy habitation.
 God maketh a home for the solitary,
 He bringeth the prisoners out of captivity :
  But maketh the rebellious dwell in a dry land.

 O God, when Thou wentest forth before the people,
 When Thou wentest through the wilderness, סלה

[1] The words used by Moses each time that the ark set forward. (Num. x. 35.)
[2] This is the modern interpretation, and is supported by Jerome, Chandler, Lowth, Horsley, Meyrick, and most German writers. Our Bible and Prayer-book translations are supported by the Jewish commentators, the Chaldee, Grotius, Mendelssohn, Fürst, Hammond, Jebb, and Good. Where there is such duality of signification we must look at the context, which there is no doubt refers to the children of Israel passing through the wilderness.

The earth shook, and the heavens dropped, at the presence of God;
Even Sinai,[1] at the presence of God, who is the God of Israel.
Thou, O God, sentest a gracious rain upon Thine inheritance,
And refreshedst it when it was weary.
Thy congregation shall dwell therein:
Thou, O God, hast of Thy goodness prepared for the poor.
The Lord gave the word:
Great was the company of those who published it.
Kings with their hosts[2] did flee, did flee;
And they of the household divided the spoil:[3]
Though they had lien[4] among the pots,[5]
(They were laden with spoil, as) the wings of a dove;
That is covered with silver,
And her feathers with bright gold.

[1] View of Mount Sinai.—*From a Photograph.*

[2] An ironical antithesis to "The Lord God of Hosts." (Böttcher.)
[3] See Num. xxxi. 27, and 1 Sam. xxx. 24—31.   [4] Remained at home.
[5] The word has also the meaning of "sheep-folds," or "cattle-pens;" but our authorized translation seems best to agree with the previous line. The author, on one occasion, when travelling in these countries, had engaged a new servant, and desired him to accompany him to the top of a mountain range to measure some antiquities. But the man refused, saying that he had never been accustomed to such work: that he had always remained at home "with the pots:" *i. e.* with the canteen and cooking utensils. These three verses have occasioned the greatest embarrassment to commentators, and have given rise to the wildest theories.

I

When the kings were scattered there by the Almighty,
(The spoils were plentiful as) the snow on Salmon.

The hill of God (is as) the hill of Bashan :
(Even) a high hill, (as) the hill of Bashan.
Why hop ye so, ye high hills?
(This is) the hill in which it pleaseth God to dwell ;
   Yea, the Lord will abide in it for ever.
The chariots of God are twenty thousand,
Even thousands of thousands ;
And the Lord is among them,
(As in) the holy place of Sinai.
Thou art gone up on high,
Thou hast led captivity captive,
Thou hast received gifts for men,
Even for the rebellious ;
   That the Lord God might dwell (among them).

Antiphon.   Praised be the Lord who daily loadeth us (with benefits ;)
Even the God of our salvation.

סלה

GOD is the God of our salvation :
THE LORD is the Lord by whom we escape death.
God will wound the head of His enemies :
The hairy scalp of such as walk in wickedness.
The Lord said—" I will bring (my people) from Bashan,
" I will bring (my people) through the depths of the sea :
" So that thy foot shall tread in the blood of thine enemies,
" And that the tongue of thy dogs (shall lick up) the same."
They have seen Thy goings, O God :
The goings of my GOD and KING in His holy place :—
The singers go before, the minstrels follow after ;
In the midst are the damsels playing on the timbrels :—

Antiphon.   " Bless ye God in the congregations ;
" Even THE LORD, ye that are of the fountain of Israel."

{ There is little Benjamin, their ruler,
  The princes of Judah, their council,
  The princes of Zebulon, and the princes of Naphtali.
Thy God hath sent forth strength for thee :
Strengthen the thing, O God, that Thou hast wrought in us.
For Thy temple's sake at Jerusalem,
Shall kings bring presents unto Thee.

He will rebuke the beasts of the reeds,[1]
  With the herds of bulls,
    And the calves of the nations,
      Till they submit themselves with pieces of silver.
    He will scatter the nations that delight in war:
  Princes shall come out of Egypt,
Ethiopia shall stretch out her hands unto God.

Antiphon.   Sing unto the Lord, all ye kingdoms of the earth,
Sing psalms unto the Lord. סֶלָה

To Him who sitteth in the heaven of heavens of old.
Lo, He doth send out His voice; yea, a voice of power.

    Ascribe ye power unto God!
Antiphon. His majesty (is displayed) over Israel,
And His power in the heavens.

O GOD, wonderful art Thou in Thy holy places:
Even the God of Israel!
He will give power and strength unto His people:
Blessed be God!

PSALM LXIX.

To the chief Musician upon the six-stringed instruments.

A Psalm of David.

SAVE me, O God!
For the waters are come in, even unto my soul.
Antiphon. I am sunk in the deep mire, where no ground is;
I am come into deep waters, so that the floods run over me.

I am weary of crying, my throat is dry,
My sight faileth me in waiting for my God.

---

[1] The hippopotamus or crocodile, as denoting Egypt and Ethiopia, mentioned immediately afterwards. "Bulls" are the mighty ones or princes, also mentioned afterwards; and "calves" would signify the minor leaders or heads of the people.

They are more than the hairs of my head,
   That hate me without a cause :
They are mighty that would cut me off,
   Being mine enemies unjustly :
(For) that which I took not away
I restored to them.

O God, Thou knowest my foolishness,
.And my sins are not hidden from Thee.
Let not those be ashamed on my account
   Who trust in Thee, O Lord (thou) Lord of hosts :
Let not those be confounded on my account
   Who wait on Thee, O God of Israel.
For I have suffered reproach for Thy sake,
Shame hath covered my face :
I am become a stranger unto my brethren,
And an alien unto my mother's children :
For the zeal of Thy house hath eaten me up,
And the reproaches of them that reproached Thee fell on me.
I wept (and chastened) myself with fasting,
   And that was turned to my reproach :
I put on sackcloth also.
   And they jested upon me.
They that sit in the gate speak against me,
And the drunkards make songs upon me.

   But as for me :—
I make my prayer unto Thee, O Lord,
In an acceptable time.
Hear me. O God, in the multitude of Thy mercy,
Even in the truth of Thy salvation.

Deliver me from the mire, that I sink not :
Deliver me from them that hate me, and from the deep waters.
Antiphon. Let not the water-flood drown me,
Let not the deep swallow me up,
And let not the pit shut her mouth upon me.

Hear me, O God, for Thy loving-kindness is comfortable ;
Turn Thee unto me, according to the multitude of Thy mercies :
And hide not Thy face from Thy servant, for I am in trouble ;
O haste Thee, and hear me.
Draw nigh unto my soul, and save it :
Deliver me, because of mine enemies.

Thou hast known my reproach, my shame, and my dishonour ;
Mine adversaries are all in Thy sight.
(Thy) reproach hath broken my heart,
I am full of heaviness :
I looked (for some) to have pity on me, but there was no man ;
And for comforters, but I found none.
They gave me gall to eat,
And when I was thirsty they gave me vinegar to drink.

Let their table be unto them as a trap ;
    And (let things) of peace (become) a snare :
Let their eyes be darkened, that they see not ;
    And make their loins continually to shake :
Let Thine indignation be poured out upon them ;
    And let Thy wrathful displeasure take hold of them :
Let their habitation be desolate ;
    And let their tents be without inhabitant :
For they persecute them, whom Thou hast smitten ;
And they add to the sorrows of those whom Thou hast wounded.
Let them fall from one wickedness to another,
    And let them not come into Thy righteousness :
Let them be blotted out of the book of life,
    And let them not be written among the righteous.

    But as for me :—
I am poor, and in heaviness,
But Thy salvation, O God, shall lift me up.
I will praise the name of God with a song,
I will magnify it with thanksgiving.
This also shall please the Lord,
Better than a bullock that hath horns and hoofs.
The humble shall consider this, and be glad ;
Seek ye after God, and your soul shall live :
For the Lord heareth the poor,
And despiseth not His afflicted ones,

Antiphon. Let heaven and earth praise Him ;
The sea, and all that moveth therein !

For God will save Sion, and build the cities of Judah,
That (men) may dwell there, and have it in possession.
The posterity also of His servants shall inherit it,
And they that love His name shall dwell therein.

PSALM LXX.

To the chief Musician.—A Psalm of David.   To bring to remembrance.

[A replica of part of Psalm XL.]

Antiphon. . . . . O God, to deliver me :
Haste Thee, O Lord, to my help !

Let them be ashamed
And confounded (together) [1]
   That seek after my soul :
Let them be driven backward
And put to confusion,
   That wish to do me evil.
Let them be desolate
And rewarded with shame,
   That say—"Aha, aha !"
Let them be joyful
And glad in Thee, all they
   That seek after Thee :
And let them say alway—
"Let God be praised,"
   That love Thy salvation.

   As for me :—
I am poor and needy :
Antiphon. Haste Thee unto me, O God !
Thou art my helper, and my deliverer !
Tarry not, O Lord !

PSALM LXXI.

IN THEE, O Lord, have I put my trust :
Let me never be put to confusion :
Antiphon. Deliver me in Thy righteousness, and free me ;
Incline Thine ear unto me, and save me.

[1] See Ps. xl.

Be Thou my abiding Rock,
   Whereunto I may always resort :
   Thou hast promised to help me,
For THOU art my Rock, and my castle.
Deliver me, O God, out of the hand of the ungodly,
Out of the hand of the unrighteous and cruel man :
For THOU, O Lord my Lord,[1] art the thing that I long for,
(THOU art) my hope, even from my youth :
Through THEE have I been holden up from the birth ;
Thou art HE that took me out of my mother's womb ;
   My praise shall be always of THEE.
I am become as it were a monster unto many,
But my sure trust is in THEE.
O let my mouth be filled with THY praise,
All the day long with THY honour.
Cast me not away in the time of age,
Forsake me not when my strength faileth.
For mine enemies speak against me,
And they that lay wait for my soul consult together, saying—
" God hath forsaken him :
" Pursue after him, and take him :
   " For there is none to deliver him."

O GOD, go not far from me :
O MY GOD, haste Thee to help me !
Let them be confounded and perish
   That are against my soul :
Let them be covered with shame and dishonour
   That wish to do me evil.

   As for me :—
I will patiently abide alway,
I will praise Thee more and more.

My mouth shall speak of Thy righteousness ;
All the day long of Thy salvation :
Antiphon.   For I know no end thereof.
I will go forth in the strength of the Lord Jehovah ;
I will make mention of Thy righteousness ; even Thine only.

O God, Thou hast taught me from my youth up ;
From my youth[2] have I declared Thy wondrous works.

---

   [1] *Heb.* " Lord Jehovah."   [2] *Heb.* " And until now."

Forsake me not then, O God,
In mine old age, when I am grey-headed,
Until I have showed Thy strength unto this generation,
And (Thy power) unto all them that are yet for to come.

Antiphon. Thy righteousness, O God, is very high ;
And great things are they that Thou hast done !

O God ! who is like unto Thee !
Who hast showed me such great troubles and adversities,
And yet Thou didst turn and refresh me,
Thou didst turn, and bring me up from the depths of the earth ;
Thou hast brought me to great honour,
Thou hast comforted me on every side.
Therefore will I praise Thee upon an instrument of music,
    Because of Thy faithfulness, O my God :
I will sing psalms unto Thee upon the harp,
    O thou Holy One of Israel.
My lips shall shout for joy unto Thee ;
My soul, which Thou hast redeemed, shall sing psalms.

All the day long also shall my tongue
Talk of Thy righteousness :
Antiphon. For they are confounded, for they are brought unto shame,
That seek to do me evil.

PSALM LXXII.

For Solomon.

GIVE Thy judgments, O God, unto the king,
And Thy righteousness unto the king's son.
Let him rule Thy people with righteousness,
    And Thy poor with judgment :
Let the mountains bring peace unto Thy people,
    And the hills righteousness :
Let him judge the poor of the people ;
Let him defend the children of the needy ;
Let him break in pieces the oppressor.
Let them fear THEE as long as the sun endureth,
As long as the moon shall last,
    From generation to generation :

Let him come down like rain upon the mown grass,
  Even as the showers which water the earth.
Let the righteous flourish in his days ;
  And abundance of peace so long as the moon endureth :
Let his dominion also be from the one sea to the other ;
  And from the river to the ends of the earth :
Let them that dwell in the wilderness kneel before him ;
Let his enemies lick the dust :
Let the kings of Tharsis and of the isles bring presents ;
Let the kings of Arabia and Saba bring gifts :
Let all kings fall down before him ;
Let all nations do him service.

For he will deliver the needy when he crieth,
  The poor also, and him that hath no helper :
He will be favourable to the poor and needy ;
  And he will preserve the souls of the needy :
He will deliver their souls from falsehood and wrong
  And dear shall their blood be in his sight.

May he live ! and let them give unto him
  Of the gold of Arabia :
Let them pray ever for him,
  Daily may they praise him.
Let there be abundance of corn upon the earth,
  Up to the top of the mountains :
Let its fruit shake like Lebanon,
Let it abound in the city, like grass upon the earth.
Let his name endure for ever !
Let his name be continued as long as the sun !
Let all men be blessed through him :
Let all the heathen call him blessed !

Antiphon. Blessed be the LORD GOD, even the God of Israel,
  Which only doeth wondrous things :
And blessed be the name of His majesty for ever,
And let all the earth be filled with His majesty.
                    Amen, and Amen.

The prayers of David the son of Jesse are ended.[1]

---

[1] That this line and the doxology form part of this particular Psalm, written shortly before David's death, see Ps. xlv. and Essay i. *Running titles*, " Solomon " and " Doxologies."

PSALM LXXIII.

A Psalm for Asaph.

TRULY God is loving unto Israel,
Even unto such as are of a clean heart:
    But as for me—
My feet were almost gone,
My treadings had well-nigh slipped.
For I was envious of the wicked,
When I saw the ungodly in such prosperity.
For they are in no peril of death,
But are lusty and strong.
They come in no misfortune like (other) folk,
Neither are they plagued like (other) men.
And this is the cause that they are so holden of pride,
And clothed with cruelty.
Their eyes swell with fatness,
Their hearts' desire floweth over.
They are corrupt, they speak wickedly (concerning their)
They speak loftily.   [oppression,[1]
Their mouth stretcheth up into heaven,
And their tongue runneth through the world.
Therefore fall the people unto them,
And waters of abundance shall be found by them.[2]
And they say—" How doth God know?
" Is there knowledge in the Most High?"
Lo, these are the ungodly;
These prosper in the world, and increase in riches.
Surely, in vain have I cleansed my heart,
And have washed my hands in innocency;
Have I been punished all the day,
And been chastened every morning!

If I should speak thus,
I should offend the generation of Thy children.
But when I endeavoured to understand this,
It was too hard for me:

---

[1] Compare Ps. x. 5, "all those whom he oppresseth he seedeth at."   See also Ps. lix. 12; and Is. lix. 13.
[2] Jebb, quoting Septuagint and three MSS.

Until I went into the sanctuary of God,
Then understood I the end of these men.
Surely, in slippery places dost Thou set them,
Thou dost cast them down to destruction.
How are they all brought into desolation, as in a moment!
They are brought to destruction, and consumed with terrors.
As a dream when one awaketh, so, O Lord,
On Thine arising shalt Thou despise their image.
Yet my heart was grieved,
And it went even through my reins :
So foolish was I, and ignorant,
Even as the beasts before Thee.

As for me :—I am always in Thy sight,
For Thou hast holden me by my right hand.
Thou wilt guide me with Thy counsel,
And after that Thou wilt receive me to glory.
Whom have I in heaven (but THEE)?
And there is none upon earth that I desire, beside THEE.
My flesh and my heart faileth :
But GOD is the strength of my heart, and my portion for ever.
For lo, they that forsake Thee shall perish :
Thou wilt destroy all them that go after other gods.[1]

Antiphon.
But as for me :—
It is good for me to draw me near to God,
To put my trust in the Lord my Lord,[2]
And to set forth all Thy doings.

PSALM LXXIV.

A Psalm of instruction.—To Asaph.

Antiphon.
WHY, O God, hast Thou cast us off for ever!
(Why) is Thy wrath so hot against the sheep of Thy pasture!

O think upon Thy congregation which Thou hast purchased,
Which Thou hast redeemed of old ;

[1] *Heb.* " commit fornication against Thee."   [2] *Heb.* " Lord Jehovah."

The rod of Thine inheritance,
The mount Sion wherein Thou hast dwelt !
Lift up Thy feet unto the perpetual desolations,   [sanctuary.
(And see) all that the enemy hath done wickedly in Thy
Thine adversaries roar in the midst of Thy congregation ;
They set up their ensigns as signs.[1]
They appear as though they were lifting up on high
    Their axes on the thick forests :
But lo ! all the carved work thereof
    Do they break down with axes and hammers.
They have devoted to the fire Thy holy place :
They have defiled to the ground the dwelling-place of Thy name !
They have said in their hearts—" Let us destroy them altogether."
They have burnt up all the houses of God in the land.
We see not our ensigns ; there is not one prophet more :
No, not one is there among us that can show us—how long ?

Antiphon. How long, O God, shall the adversary reproach ?
            Shall the enemy blaspheme Thy name for ever ?

Why withholdest Thou Thy hand, even Thy right hand ?
(Why withdrawest Thou it not) from Thy bosom to consume (them)?

But God is my King of old,
Working salvation in the midst of the earth.
Thou dividedst the sea through Thy power,
Thou breakedst the heads of the dragons in the waters :
Thou smotest the heads of Leviathan,
Thou gavest him to be food to the people in the wilderness :
Thou broughtest out fountains and waters (from the hard rock,)
Thou driedst up mighty rivers.
The day is Thine, and the night is Thine,
Thou hast prepared the light and the sun :
Thou hast set all the borders of the earth,
Thou hast made summer and winter.

Antiphon. Remember, O Lord, (how) the enemy hath reproached,
            And how the foolish people have blasphemed Thy name.

Give not over to (their) congregation the soul of Thy turtle-dove,
Forget not the congregation of the poor for ever.
Look upon the covenant :
For all the earth is full of darkness, and cruel habitations.

[1] *Paronomasia.*   See Essay ii.

O let not the oppressed go away ashamed :
Let the poor and needy give thanks unto Thy name.

Antiphon. Arise, O God, maintain Thine own cause :
Remember how the foolish man blasphemeth Thee daily.

Forget not the voice of thine enemies :
The tumult of them that hate Thee increaseth more and more.

PSALM LXXV.

To the chief Musician.

"Altaschith."—A Psalm or Song for Asaph.

Antiphon. WE give thanks unto THEE, O God, we give thanks :
For that Thy name is nigh Thy wondrous works declare.

When I appoint the set time,[1]
I, (even I,[2]) shall judge according unto right.
The earth and all its inhabitants are dissolved,
I, (even I,[2]) set up the pillars thereof.[3]

סֶלָה

I will say unto the fools—Deal not so foolishly ;
And unto the ungodly—Lift not up your horn :
Lift not up your horn on high ;
Speak not with a neck of arrogancy :
For lifting-up is not from the east or west,
Nor yet from the wilderness.[4]
For GOD is the judge : this man He putteth down,
And this man He lifteth up.

1 See the word so used in Ps. cii. 13.
2, 2 The *I* is emphatic in each case.
3 Compare—"For the pillars of the earth are the Lord's :
"And He hath set the world upon them." (1 Sam. ii. 8.)
See also Job. ix. 6.
4 The desert lay to the south.

For in the hand of the Lord there is a cup, and the wine is
It is full of mixture ; and He poureth out of the same.　[thick :
Surely, all the ungodly of the earth shall drink thereof,
And they shall wring out the dregs thereof.

　　As for me :——
I will talk of the God of Jacob,
I will sing psalms unto Him for ever !

All the horns of the ungodly also will I break :
But the horns of the righteous shall be lifted up.

PSALM LXXVI.

To the chief Musician upon the stringed instruments.

A Psalm or Song for Asaph.

GOD is known in Judah,
His name is great in Israel :
At Salem is His tabernacle,
And His dwelling-place in Sion.
There brake He the swift arrows[1] of the bow,
The shield, the sword, and the battle.

סלה

Thou art more glorious and excellent
Than the high mountains.
The proud are robbed ; they have slept their sleep :
And the hands of all the men of might have found nothing.
At THY rebuke, O God of Jacob,
Both the chariot and horse are fallen.[2]
THOU, even THOU, art to be feared :
And who may stand in Thy sight when Thou art angry !
Thou didst cause Thy judgments to be heard from heaven ;
The earth trembled, and was still ;

[1] "Quick motions."　See Ps. vii. 13, "swift pursuers."
[2] *Heb.* "fast asleep."

When God arose to judgment,
And to save all the meek upon earth.

סֶלָה

Surely, the wrath of man shall turn to Thy praise,
And the overflowings of wrath shall turn to Thy honour.[1]
Promise unto the Lord your God, and keep it ;
Bring presents, (all ye that approach Him,) in His fear.
He will refrain the spirit of princes ;
Ho will strike fear into the kings of the earth.

PSALM LXXVII.

To the chief Musician.—To Jeduthun.

A Psalm for Asaph.

WITH my voice I cried unto God :
With my voice unto God : and He gave ear to me.
In the day of my trouble I sought the Lord ;
My hand was stretched out in prayer all night :
　My soul refused comfort.

Antiphon. I remembered God (and His former mercies) ; and I was troubled :
I meditated (upon the past) ; and my spirit was overwhelmed.

סֶלָה

Thou withheldest sleep from mine eyes ;
I was so troubled that I could not speak :
I considered the days of old,
And the years that are past.

[1] *Heb.* "The remainder of wraths shalt Thou gird on (Thee.)" *i.e.* shalt
Thou use for Thine adorning. Compare Ps. xlvi. 3, 4 :—
　Though the waters thereof rage and swell,
　Though the mountains shake at the tempest of the same,
　The rivers of the flood thereof shall make glad the city of God ;
and Ps. lxxxiv. 6, Who going through the vale of misery, use it as a well,
　　　And the pools are filled with water.
It is thus, that by praising God for His chastisements and corrections, God's
"saints" are enabled to "rejoice in their beds," and to them —"the Valley
of Trouble" becomes a "Gate of Hope ;" (Hos. ii. 15 ;) the wilderness
becomes a standing water, and water-springs arise out of the dry ground.
　"Heaviness may endure for a night, but joy cometh in the morning."

Antiphon. I remembered my song in the night :
I meditated in my heart, and my spirit searched within me.

" Will the Lord cast off for ever ?
" And will He be no more entreated ?
" Is His mercy clean gone for ever ?
" Is His promise come utterly to an end for evermore ?
" Hath God forgotten to be gracious ?
" Hath He shut up His loving-kindness in displeasure ? "

סלה

But I said—This is my infirmity !   [High :
(I will call to mind)[1] the years of the right hand of the Most

Antiphon. I will remember the works of the Lord, and Thy wonders of old
I will think also of all Thy works :   [time.
I will meditate upon Thy doings.

Thy way, O God, is in the sanctuary :
Who is so great a God as our God !
Thou art the God that doeth wonders ;
Thou hast declared Thy power among the people.

Antiphon. Thou hast mightily delivered Thy people,
Even the sons of Jacob and Joseph. סלה
The waters saw Thee, O God !
The waters saw Thee, and were afraid :
The depths also were troubled.
The clouds poured out water,
The air thundered.
And Thine arrows were discharged.
The noise of Thy thunder (was heard) round about,
The lightnings shone upon the ground,
The earth was troubled, and shook withal.
Thy way is in the sea, and Thy paths in the great waters,
And Thy footsteps are not known.

Antiphon. Thou leddest Thy people, like sheep,
By the hands of Moses and Aaron.

---

[1] In the first and second paragraphs he "remembered" the past only to lament the present : now he remembers the past only to give confidence to the future. Compare Is. xlii.

* The *epanodos* at end of this Psalm can also be arranged as triplets. See Essay ii.

PSALM LXXVIII.

(A Psalm of) instruction.—For Asaph.

Proem.

GIVE ear to my law, O my people :
Incline your ear unto the words of my mouth.
I will open my mouth in a parable,
I will speak of God's dealings of the past; [1]
Which we have heard and seen,
And which our fathers have told us ;
That we should not hide them from our children,
Nor from the generations to come ;
But should show forth the praises of the Lord,
His might, and the wonderful works which He hath wrought.

HE gave a covenant unto Jacob,
And established a law unto Israel ;
Which He commanded our forefathers
To make known unto their children ;
That their posterity might know it,
And the children which were yet unborn ;
Who should grow up, and declare it unto their children—
That they should put their trust in God ;
And that they should not forget the works of God,
And that they should keep His commandments ;
And that they should not be as their forefathers,
A faithless and stubborn generation ;
A generation that set not their heart aright,
And whose spirit was not stedfast unto God.
The children of Ephraim,[2] though armed, and carrying bows,
Turned themselves back in the day of battle !
They kept not the covenant of God,
And they would not walk in His law ;
But they forgat what He had done,
And the marvellous works that He had showed for them.

[1] *Heb.* "I will declare hard sentences of old."
[2] *i.e.* Israel. The children of Israel, though adopted by God as a chosen people, as His people, and protected by Him, turned away after false gods. in the time of temptation !

K

Marvellous works did He in the sight of our forefathers.
In the land of Egypt, even in the field of Zoan.
He divided the sea, and let them go through,
He made the waters to stand as a wall ;
In the day-time also He led them with a cloud,
And all the night through with a light of fire ;
He clave the hard rocks in the wilderness,
And He gave them drink thereof, as out of the great depth ;
He brought forth streams out of the hard rock,
He made the water to run down like a river.

Yet for all this they sinned more against Him,
And provoked the Most Highest in the wilderness ;
And they tempted God in their heart,
     By requiring meat for their lust ;
And they spoke against God, saying —
  " Can God prepare a table in the wilderness ?
" He smote the rock indeed, that the waters gushed out,
" And the stream flowed withal :
" But can He give bread also,
" Or provide flesh for His people ? "

     The Lord heard this, and was wroth :
So the fire was kindled in Jacob,
And anger went out against Israel :
Because they believed not God,
And put not their trust in His help.
So He commanded the clouds from above,
And He opened the doors of heaven ;
And He rained down manna also upon them for to eat,
And He gave them food from heaven.
So man did eat angels' food ;
For He sent them meat enough :
He caused the east wind of heaven to blow,
And by His power He brought in the south wind ;
He poured flesh upon them as thick as dust,
And feathered fowl, like as the sand of the sea :
He let it fall among their tents,
Even round about their habitations.
     So they did eat, and were well filled ;
He gave them their own desire,
They were not disappointed of their desire.
But while the meat was yet in their mouths,
The heavy wrath of God came upon them,

And slew the wealthiest of them,
Yea, and smote down the chosen men that were in Israel.

But for all this they sinned yet more,
And believed not His wondrous works.
So He consumed their days in vanity,
And their years in trouble.
When He slew them, they sought Him,
And turned them early, and enquired after God :
And they remembered that GOD was their strength,
And that THE MOST HIGH GOD was their redeemer.
But they did but flatter Him with their mouth,
And dissembled with Him in their tongue :
For their heart was not right with Him,
Neither continued they stedfast in His covenant.

But HE was so merciful,
That He put away their misdeeds, and destroyed them not :
Yea, many a time turned He His wrath away,
And would not suffer His whole displeasure to arise :
For He remembered that they were but flesh,
And as it were a wind, that goeth, and cometh not again.
How often did they provoke Him in the wilderness,
And grieve Him in the desert !
They turned back, and tempted God,
And limited the Holy One of Israel !
They remembered not His hand,
Nor the day when He delivered them from their distress :
How He had wrought His miracles in Egypt,
And His wonders in the field of Zoan :
He turned their rivers into blood,
　　And their waters that they could not drink :
He sent swarms of flies to devour them,
　　And frogs to destroy them :
He gave their fruit unto the grasshopper,
　　And their labour unto the locust :
He destroyed their vines with hailstones,
　　And their mulberry trees with the frost :
He smote their cattle also with hailstones,
　　And their flocks with hot thunderbolts :
He cast upon them the furiousness of His wrath,
Anger, displeasure, and trouble ;
And sent evil angels (among them) :

K 2

He made a way to His indignation,
And spared not their soul from death,
But gave their life over to the pestilence :
And He smote all the first-born in Egypt,
The chief of their strength in the dwellings of Ham.

But as for His own people, He led them forth like sheep,
And He guided them in the desert like a flock :
He brought them out safely, that they should not fear,
But He overwhelmed their enemies in the sea :
And He brought them within the borders of His sanctuary,
Even to His mountain which He purchased with His right hand ·
   And He cast out the heathen before them,   [heritage,
And He caused their land to be divided among them for a
And He made the tribes of Israel to dwell in their tents.

But they tempted and provoked the Most High God,
And kept not His testimonies :
But turned back, and fell away like their forefathers,
Starting aside like a broken bow.
For they grieved Him with their hill altars,
And they provoked Him to jealousy with their images.

God heard this, and was wroth ;
And He took sore displeasure at Israel :
So that He forsook the tabernacle in Shiloh,
Even the tent which He had pitched among men ;
And He delivered His strength into captivity,
And His glory into the enemy's hands :
He gave His people also to the sword,
And He was wroth with His inheritance :
The fire consumed their young men,
And their maidens were not given in marriage :[1]
Their priests were slain with the sword,
And their widows made no lamentations.

Then the Lord awaked, as one out of sleep,
And as a giant refreshed with wine ;
He smote His enemies from behind,
And put them to a perpetual shame :
He refused the tabernacle of Joseph,
And chose not the tribe of Ephraim ;

---

[1] *Heb.* "were not praised."

But He chose the tribe of Judah,
And the hill of Sion which He loved :
And there He built His temple on high ;
He founded it, as the earth, for ever.
And He chose David His servant,
And He took him away from the sheep-folds,
As he was following the ewes He took him ;
That he might feed Jacob, His people,
And Israel, His inheritance.
And he fed them with a faithful and true heart,
And guided them prudently with all his power.

PSALM LXXIX.

A Psalm.—For Asaph.

O GOD !
The heathen are come into Thine inheritance !
They have defiled Thy holy temple !
They have laid Jerusalem in heaps !
The dead bodies of Thy servants have they given to be meat
   Unto the fowls of the air :
And the flesh of Thy saints
   Unto the beasts of the earth.
Their blood have they poured out¹ like water on every side of
And there was no man to bury them !   [Jerusalem ;

phon. We are become a reproach to our neighbours,
A very scorn and derision unto them that are round about us !

   How long, O Lord !
Wilt Thou be angry with us for ever !
Shall Thy jealousy burn like fire !
Pour out² Thine indignation upon the heathen
   That know Thee not ;
And upon the kingdoms
   That call not upon Thy name :
For they have devoured Jacob,
And laid waste his dwelling-place.

¹ ² Compare together with Note 1 of next page.

O remember not our old sins,
But have mercy upon us, and that soon ;
   For we are come to great misery.
Help us, O God of our salvation,
   For the glory of Thy name !
Purge us, and deliver us from our sins,
   For Thy name's sake !
Wherefore do the heathen say—
" Where is now their God ? "
Let Him be openly showed to the heathen in our sight,
By the avenging of Thy servants' blood which is poured out.
Let the sorrowful sighing of the prisoners come before Thee :
In the greatness of Thy power preserve Thou those that are
                                    [appointed to die.

Antiphon.
And render unto our neighbours sevenfold into their bosom,
For the reproach wherewith they have reproached Thee, O Lord.

Second Antiphon.
So we that are Thy people,
And the sheep of Thy pasture ;
Will give Thee thanks, for ever ;
And will show forth Thy praise, from generation to generation.

PSALM LXXX.

To the chief Musician upon the six-stringed instruments.

(In remembrance of?) the Testimony.[2]

A Psalm for Asaph.

HEAR, O thou Shepherd of Israel !
Thou that leadest Joseph like a sheep,
Thou that dwellest between the cherubim, shine forth !
Before Ephraim, Benjamin, and Manasseh,[3]
Stir up Thy strength, and come and save us !

Antiphon.
Turn us again, O God !
Show the light of Thy countenance, and we shall be saved.

[1] See Notes 1 and 2 of preceding page.
[2] See Ps. lx. *tit.*   [3] See Num. ii. 18, 20, 22.

How long, O Lord God of hosts !
Wilt Thou be angry with Thy people that prayeth ![1]
Thou hast made them eat of the bread of tears :
Thou hast made them drink of tears in great measure.
Thou hast made us a very strife to our neighbours,
And our enemies laugh us to scorn.

phon.

Turn us again, O God of hosts !
Show the light of Thy countenance, and we shall be saved.

Thou hast brought a vine out of Egypt ;
Thou hast cast out the heathen, and planted it :
Thou preparedst the land, and didst root it well ;
Thou didst cause it to fill the land :
The hills [2] were covered with the shadow of it,
And the boughs thereof were like the goodly cedar trees : [3]
She stretched forth her branches unto the sea,[4]
And her boughs unto the river.[5]

Three of the most ancient Cedars in Mount Lebanon.
From a Sketch by the Author, 1843.

" The righteous shall flourish like a palm tree,
   And shall spread abroad like a cedar in Lebanon."

[1] See Ps. lxxix. line 14.
[2,3,4,5] South, North, West, East.   (Delitzsch, referring to Deut. xi. 24

Why hast Thou then broken down her hedge,
So that all they that go by pluck off (her grapes
The wild boar out of the wood doth root it up,
And the wild beasts of the field devour it !

Turn, we pray Thee, O God of hosts !
Look down from heaven : behold and visit this vine
   And protect that which Thy right hand hath planted,
   And the branch[2] which Thou hast made strong for Thyself.
Antiphon.   It is burnt with fire, and cut down :
    (Thy people) perish at the rebuke of Thy countenance !
   Let Thy hand be upon the man of Thy right hand,[3]
   And upon the son of man[4] whom Thou hast made strong for
And so will we not go back[5] from Thee :   [Thyself.
Quicken us, and we will call upon Thy name.

Antiphon.   Turn us again, O Lord God of hosts !
   Show the light of Thy countenance, and we shall be saved.

---

[1] There is a *majuscule* here in the original—וּבֵנָּה אשר נטעה

[2] *Paronomasia.* The Psalmist has used three words before to signify a branch—*onoph, kotseer,* and *younaik* ; (vv. 10, 11 ;) but instead of again using one of these he chooses the word *bain,* which signifies both a *branch* and a *son,* and the word is intended to have this double signification in this passage :—*branch* as relating to the "vine," and *son* as relating to the children of Israel. The line therefore signifies, "And the children which Thou hast established for Thyself."

[3] See four lines above. The children of Israel whom God led out of Egypt.

[4] As the word "man" refers to the word "man" in the preceding line, so the "son of man" must signify the posterity of those whom God led out of Egypt—"the children which Thou hast established for Thyself :" which is exactly similar to what we have found four lines above.

[5] The word *soog,* "to slide back," or "go back," seems to have been chosen as a *paronomasia* with *shoov,* to "turn" or return, in order to complete the *epanodos,* and so give more importance to the concluding *antiphon,* which might otherwise have been taken for the concluding member of the *epanodos.*

PSALM LXXXI.

To the chief Musician upon the Gathite harp.

A Psalm.—For Asaph.

SING ye joyfully unto God our strength!
Shout aloud unto the God of Jacob!
Antiphon. Take the psalm, bring hither the tabret,
The pleasant harp, with the lute.
Blow ye the trumpet in the new moon,
At the time appointed, and upon our solemn feast-day.

For this was made a statute for Israel,
And a law of the God of Jacob:
This he ordained in Joseph for a testimony,
When he went out of the land of Egypt,
    And had heard a strange language.

" I eased his shoulder from the burden,
" And his hands were delivered from (making) the pots:
" Thou calledst upon Me in trouble,
" And I delivered thee;
" I heard thee in the secret place of thunder,
" I proved thee also at the waters of Meribah."

סלה

" Hear, O My people!
" And I will testify to thee, O Israel!
    " If thou wilt hearken unto Me—
" There shall no strange God be in thee,
" Neither shalt thou worship any other God.
" I, even I, am THE LORD THY GOD,
" Who brought thee out of the land of Egypt:
" Open thy mouth wide,
" And I will fill it."

" But My people would not hear My voice,
" And Israel would not obey Me.
" So I gave them up unto their own hearts' lusts,
" And let them follow their own imaginations."

" O that My people would have hearkened unto Me,
" For if Israel had walked in My ways,
" I should soon have put down their enemies,
" And turned My hand against their adversaries.
" The haters of the Lord should have been made to submit them-
" But *their* time should have endured for ever.   [selves :
" I would have fed them also with the finest wheat flour :
" And with honey out of the stony rock would I have satisfied thee."

PSALM LXXXII.

A Psalm.—For Asaph.

Proem. GOD standeth in the midst of His congregation :[1]
He is a JUDGE among those that execute judgment.[2]

" How long will ye judge unjustly,
" (How long) will ye accept the persons of the ungodly ?"

סלה

" Judge the poor and fatherless :
" Render justice to the afflicted and needy.
" Deliver the outcast and poor,
" Save them from the hand of the ungodly."

" They will not know ; nor will they understand ;
" They will walk in darkness :
       " All the foundations of the earth are out of course !"

       I have said :—
" Ye are gods,[3]
" And ye are all the children of the Most Highest :
" But ye shall die like men,[4]
" And fall like one of the princes."

Antiphon. Arise, O God, and judge THOU the earth :
For Thou shalt take all nations to Thine inheritance.

[1] *Heb.* " in the congregation of God."
[2] *Heb.* " in the midst of the gods."
[3] See Note 2.   [4] Like other men, like men of dust, *" Adam."*

PSALM LXXXIII.

A Song or Psalm.—For Asaph.

O GOD, be not silent :
Keep not still silence : refrain not thyself, O God !

Antiphon. For lo, thine enemies make a murmuring,
And they that hate Thee have lifted up their head :

They have devised craftily against Thy people,
And they have taken counsel against Thy secret ones.
 They have said—
" Come, and we will cast them off as a nation,
" So that the name of Israel may be no more in remembrance."
For they have consulted together with one consent,
And are confederate against Thee :
The tabernacles of the Edomites and the Ishmaelites,
The Moabites and the Hagarenes :
Gebal, and Ammon, and Amalek,
The Philistines, and they that dwell in Tyre :
Ashur also is joined to them ;
They have holpen the children of Lot.

סלה

But do Thou to them as unto the Midianites,
As unto Sisera, and as unto Jabin at the brook Kishon :
Who perished at Endor,
Who became as dung for the earth.
Make their princes as Oreb and Zeeb,
Yea, all their princes as Zebah and Zalmunna ;
Who said—" Let us take to ourselves
The houses of God in possession."
O my God, make them as a wheel,
And as the stubble before the wind ;
As the fire that consumeth a wood,
And as the flame that enkindleth the mountains :
Pursue them even so with Thy tempest,
And make them afraid with Thy storm :
Make their faces ashamed,
That they may seek after Thy name, O Lord :

Let them be confounded and troubled for ever,
And let them be put to shame and perish.

Antiphon. And they shall know that THOU, whose name alone is JEHOVAH,
Art the Most Highest over all the earth.

PSALM LXXXIV.

To the chief Musician upon the Gittite harp.

A Psalm.—For the sons of Korah.

HOW beloved are Thy tabernacles, O Lord of hosts!
My soul hath a desire and longing for the courts of the Lord!
My heart and my flesh cry out for the living God!
As the sparrow doth find her a house,
And the swallow a nest,[1] where they may lay their young,
(So longeth my soul after) Thine altars, O Lord of hosts,
My KING and my GOD!

Antiphon. Blessed are they that dwell in Thy house :
They will be alway praising Thee.

סלה

Blessed is the man whose strength is in THEE,
In whose heart are (Thy) ways :
Who, going through the vale of misery, use it as a well,
And the pools are filled with water.
They shall advance from strength to strength,
They shall appear before God in Sion.
     O LORD GOD OF HOSTS!
Hear my prayer :
Hearken, O God of Jacob! סלה
Behold, O God our defender!
And look upon the face of Thine anointed.
For one day in Thy courts
   Is better than a thousand :
I had rather lie (outside) the threshold of the house of my God,
   Than to dwell in the tents of ungodliness.

[1] There is a *majuscule* here in the original :—ודרור קן לה.

For the Lord God is a sun and shield ;
The Lord will give grace and glory :
Neither will He withhold good
From them that walk in uprightness.

Antiphon. O LORD OF HOSTS !
Blessed is the man that trusteth in THEE.

PSALM LXXXV.

To the chief Musician.

A Psalm.—For the sons of Korah.

THOU hast been gracious, O Lord, unto Thy land ;
Thou hast turned away the captivity of Jacob :
Thou hast forgiven the offence of Thy people ;
Thou hast covered all their sin :   סלה
Thou hast taken away all Thy displeasure ;
Thou hast turned Thyself from Thy wrathful indignation.

Turn us then, O God our Saviour,
And let Thine anger cease from us.
   Wilt Thou be angry with us, for ever !
Antiphon.   Wilt Thou stretch out Thy wrath, from generation to genera-
Wilt Thou not turn again, and quicken us,   [tion !
That Thy people may rejoice in Thee !

Show us Thy mercy, O Lord,
And grant us Thy salvation.

I will hearken to what the Lord God shall speak :
For He will speak peace unto His people, and to His saints,
   That they turn not again to folly.
For His salvation is nigh them that fear Him,
That glory may dwell in our land.
Mercy and truth are met (together) ;
   Righteousness and peace have kissed (each other):

Truth shall spring up out of the earth,[1]
   And righteousness hath looked down from heaven.
Yea, the Lord will give loving-kindness,
And our land shall give her increase.
Righteousness shall go before Him,
And He will direct our goings in His way.[2]

PSALM LXXXVI.

A Prayer of David.

BOW down Thine ear, O Lord, and hear me ;
   For I am poor, and in misery !
Preserve Thou my soul ;
   For I am holy :
Save Thou Thy servant, O my God !
   Who putteth his trust in Thee.
Be merciful unto me, O Lord :
   For unto Thee will I call, all the day long :
Comfort the soul of Thy servant ;
   For unto Thee, O Lord, do I lift up my soul.

Antiphon.   For Thou, Lord, art good, and ready to forgive,
And of great mercy unto all them that call upon Thee.

[1] This is one of the passages of the Bible selected by the Cabalists as exhibiting some occult meaning, or mystic significance. On arranging the letters in a square, they found that they presented the same words whether read perpendicularly or horizontally.

ת	ט	א
צ	רא	ט
תצ	ל	ת

(Phillips.—*Ps. in Heb.* i. 185.)
[2] This is not the exact translation ; but it appears to give the sense, and accords with the earth's response to heaven throughout the paragraph.

Give ear, Lord, unto my prayer,
And ponder the voice of my humble desires.
In the time of my trouble I will call upon Thee,
For Thou hearest me.

There is none among the gods like unto Thee, O Lord !
There are no (works) like Thy works !
  All nations whom Thou hast made
Shall come and worship before THEE, O Lord !
And shall glorify Thy name.
For Thou art great, and doest wondrous things,
Thou art God ; THOU only.
Teach me Thy way, O Lord ; and I will walk in Thy truth :
O knit my heart unto Thee, that I may fear Thy name.
I will thank Thee, O Lord my God, with all my heart,
And I will praise Thy name for evermore.

Antiphon. For great is Thy mercy toward me,
And Thou hast delivered my soul from the nethermost hell.

O GOD !
The proud are risen against me,
And the assemblies of violent men have sought after my soul,
  And have not set THEE before their eyes.
But Thou, O Lord, art a God full of compassion and mercy,
Long-suffering, plenteous in goodness and truth.
  O turn Thee then unto me, and have mercy upon me :
Give Thy strength unto Thy servant,
And help the son of Thine handmaid.
Show me some token for good,
That they who hate me may see it, and be ashamed :

Antiphon. For Thou, Lord, hast holpen me,
And comforted me.

PSALM LXXXVII.

A Psalm or Song.—For the sons of Korah.

HER foundation is upon the holy hills :
The Lord loveth the gates of Sion
More than all the dwellings of Jacob.

Glorious things are spoken of thee,
Thou city of God !

סלה

I will mention Rahab and Babylon as of them that know me:
Behold also Philistia, and Tyre, and Ethiopia : [1]
   Such a man was born there.

But of Sion it shall be reported—
" This man, and that man, were born in her :"
   And HE the Most High will stablish her.
The Lord will reckon them, when he writeth up the people—.
" This man was born in her."

סלה

   The singers also, and players on instruments (shall sing—)
Antiphon. " All my fountains [2] are in thee."

PSALM LXXXVIII.

A Psalm or Song.--For the sons of Korah.

*To the chief Musician upon the wind instruments.
For antiphonal response.*

A Psalm of instruction.———For Heman the Ezrahite.

Antiphon. O LORD God of my salvation !
In the day-time have I cried, and in the night, before Thee :

Let my prayer come before Thee,
Incline Thine ear unto my calling :
For my soul is full of trouble,
And my life draweth nigh unto the grave.
I am counted as one of them that go down into the pit,
I have been even as a man that hath no strength.

[1] See Is. xlv. 14 ; lx. 3 ; lxvi. 23 ; Zech. viii. 22.
[2] See *Introd.* p. 9, and Ps. lxviii., third antiphon.

Free (to go) among the dead,
Like the slain who lie in the grave;
Who are out of Thy remembrance,
And are cut off from Thy hand.
Thou hast laid me in the lowest pit,
In a place of darkness, and in the deep.
Thine indignation lieth hard upon me,
And thou hast vexed me with all Thy storms.   סלה
Thou hast put away mine acquaintance far from me,
Thou hast made me to be abhorred of them.
I am held fast (in prison); I cannot get forth:
Mine eye faileth by reason of my affliction.

ntiphon.   I have called daily, ● Lord, unto Thee:
I have stretched forth my hands unto Thee.

Shall the dead see Thy wonders!
Shall the dead rise up again, and praise Thee!   סלה
Shall Thy mercy be showed in the grave,
Thy faithfulness in destruction!
Shall Thy wondrous works be known in the dark,
And Thy righteousness in the land where all things are
[forgotten!

As for me:—
ntiphon.   Unto Thee have I cried, O Lord:
And early shall my prayer come before Thee.

Why, O Lord, castest Thou off my soul!
Why hidest Thou Thy face from me!
I am afflicted, and ready to die, from my youth up:
I have borne Thy terrors with a troubled mind.
Thy wrathful displeasure goeth over me:
Thy terrors have undone me.
They have surrounded me daily like water,
They have enclosed me on every side.
My lovers and friends hast Thou put away from me,
And hid mine acquaintance out of my sight.

⁎⁎⁎ This Psalm affords an instance of a double *replica*; each part beginning
with the antiphon.

PSALM LXXXIX.

A Psalm of instruction.—For Ethan the Ezrahite.

I WILL sing of the mercy of the Lord, for ever :
  With my mouth will I make known Thy truth, from generation
For I have said—Mercy shall be set up, for ever. [to generation.
Thy truth shalt Thou establish in the heavens.

Antiphon.

" I have made a covenant with My chosen,
" I have sworn unto David My servant—
" Thy seed will I establish, for ever,
" And will set up thy throne, from generation to generation."

סלה

O Lord, the heavens shall declare Thy wondrous works,
And Thy truth in the congregation of the saints :
For who in the heavens shall be compared unto the Lord !
And who among the gods shall be likened unto the Lord !
God is to be feared greatly in the congregation of the saints,
And to be had in reverence of all that are round about Him.
O Lord God of hosts ! who is like unto Thee !
Thy truth, most mighty LORD, is on every side.
Thou rulest the raging of the sea,
Thou stillest the waves thereof when they arise.
Thou hast subdued Egypt, and destroyed it :
Thou hast scattered Thine enemies abroad with Thy mighty arm.
The heavens are Thine : the earth also is Thine :
Thou hast founded the world, and all that therein is.
Thou hast made the north and the south :
Tabor and Hermon shall rejoice in Thy name.
Thou hast a mighty arm :
Strong is Thy hand, and high is Thy right hand.

Antiphon.

Righteousness and equity are the habitation of Thy seat :
Mercy and truth shall go before Thy face.

Blessed is the people, who know the shouting :[1]
They shall walk, O Lord, in the light of Thy countenance :

[1] See *Introduction.*

In Thy name shall they rejoice all the day,
And in Thy righteousness shall they be exalted.
For THOU art the glory of their strength,
And in Thy loving-kindness shall our horn be exalted.
For THE LORD is our defence:
The Holy One of Israel is our King!

Thou spakest sometime in vision to Thy servant, and saidst:—
" I have laid help upon one that is mighty,
" I have exalted one chosen out of the people:
" I have found David My servant;
" With My holy oil have I anointed him:
" My hand shall stablish him,
" Yea, Mine arm shall strengthen him:
" The enemy shall not be able to do him violence,
" The son of wickedness shall not hurt him:
" I will smite down his foes before his face,
" And I will plague them that hate him:
" My truth also, and My mercy shall be with him,
" And in My name shall his horn be exalted:
" I will set his hand on the sea,
" And his right hand on the rivers:[1]
" He shall say unto Me—'Thou art my Father,
" 'My God, and the Rock of my salvation:'
" And I will make him My first-born,
" Higher than the kings of the earth:
" My mercy will I keep for him for evermore,
" And My covenant shall stand fast with him:
" His seed also will I make to endure for ever,
" And his throne as the days of heaven.
" If[2] his children forsake My law,
" And walk not in My judgments,
" If they break My statutes,
" And keep not My commandments,
" I will visit their offences with the rod,
" And their skin with scourges:
" But My mercy[3] will I not take from him,
" Nor suffer My truth[3] to fail:
" My covenant will I not break,
" And that which has gone out of My lips will I not change;

[1] *West* and *East*. [2] There is no break here, as in P. B. version. It is no a denunciation of punishment, but a promise of forgiveness. See Ps. xcix. 8
[3,3] See Antiphons and above.

" Once have I sworn by My holiness—
" Shall I lie unto David !—
" ' His seed shall endure for ever,
" ' And his throne as the sun before Me :
" ' It shall stand fast for evermore as the moon,
" ' And as the constant witness in heaven.' "

סלה

But Thou hast cast off, and rejected,
Thou hast been wroth with Thine anointed :
Thou hast made void the covenant of Thy servant,
Thou hast cast his crown to the ground :
Thou hast broken down all his hedges,
Thou hast overthrown his strong-holds :
All they that go by spoil him ;
He is become a reproach to his neighbours :
Thou hast set up the right hand of his enemies,
Thou hast made glad all his adversaries :
Yea, Thou hast turned the edge of his sword,
And hast not given him victory in the battle :
Thou hast put out his glory,
Thou hast cast his throne to the ground :
Thou hast cut short the days of his youth,
Thou hast covered him with dishonour.

סלה

How long, O Lord !
Wilt Thou hide Thyself for ever !
Shall Thy wrath burn like fire !
O remember how short my time is :
Wherefore hast Thou made all men for nought !
What man is there that liveth, and shall not taste death !
And can he deliver his soul from the hand of the grave !

סלה

Antiphon. Lord, where are Thy old mercies,
Which Thou swarest to David in Thy truth !

Remember, O Lord, the reproach that Thy servants have,
And how I do bear in my bosom (the reproach of) many people :
Wherewith Thine enemies, O Lord, have reproached,
Wherewith they have reproached the footsteps of Thine
[anointed !

Antiphon. Blessed be the Lord for evermore.
Amen, and Amen.

PSALM XC.

A Prayer of Moses, the man of God

LORD, Thou hast been our dwelling-place
From generation to generation.
  Before the mountains were brought forth,
  Or ever the earth and the world were made,
Even from everlasting to everlasting,
Thou art GOD !

Thou turnest man to destruction :
Again Thou sayest—Return, ye children of men.

Antiphon. For a thousand years[1]
Are in Thy sight but as a day !
As yesterday when it is passed,
And as a watch in the night !

Thou scatterest them ;—they are as a dream[2] when the morning
They are as the grass which changeth :[4]   [cometh :
In the morning it is green, and groweth up ;[4]
In the evening it is cut down and dried up.
For we consume away in Thine anger,
And are afraid at Thy wrathful indignation.
Thou hast set our sins before Thee,
Our secret (sins) in the light of Thy countenance.

Antiphon. For when Thou art angry, all our days are gone,
We bring our years to an end, even as a tale that is told.

The days of our age are threescore years and ten ;
And though men be so strong that they come to fourscore years,
Yet is their strength then but labour and sorrow,
So soon passeth it away, and we are gone !

But who (alas) regardeth the power of Thine anger ?
For as (one neglects) Thy fear, so is Thy displeasure.

[1,2] " Years " and " dream."—There is a *paronomasia* between these two words.
[3] See Ps. lxxiii. 20—" As a dream when one waketh."
[4] *Paronomasia.*

Antiphon. So teach *us* to number our days,
That we may apply our hearts unto wisdom.

Turn Thee again, O Lord!   How long?
And be gracious unto Thy servants :
O satisfy us with Thy mercy, and that soon ;
So shall we be glad and rejoice all the days of our life.
Comfort us again now, after the time that Thou hast plagued us,
And for the years wherein we have suffered adversity :
Let Thy servants see Thy work, and their children Thy glory ;
And let the beauty of our Lord God be upon us :
Prosper Thou the work of our hands upon us ;
Prosper Thou even the work of our hands.

PSALM XCI.

Precen.   WHOSO dwelleth in the secret place of the Most High,
Shall abide under the shadow of the Almighty.

I WILL say unto the Lord—
(Thou art) my refuge, and my strong-hold,
My GOD!   In Him will I trust.
For He will deliver thee from the snare of the fowler,
And from the noisome pestilence :
He will defend thee under His wings,
And thou shalt be safe under His feathers ;
   His faithfulness shall be thy shield and buckler.
Thou shalt not be afraid for any terror by night,
Nor for the arrow that flieth by day :
For the pestilence that walketh in darkness,
Nor for the sickness that destroyeth in the noonday.
A thousand shall fall beside thee,
And ten thousand at thy right hand :
   But it shall not come nigh thee.
Only with thine eyes shalt thou behold,
And see the reward of the ungodly.

Because thou hast made THE LORD thy refuge,
Even the MOST HIGH thy habitation;
There shall no evil happen unto thee,
Neither shall any plague come nigh thy dwelling.
For He will give His angels charge over thee,
To keep thee in all thy ways.
They shall bear thee in their hands,
That thou hurt not thy foot against a stone.
Thou shalt tread on the lion and adder,
The young lion and the dragon shalt thou trample under thy feet.

" Because he hath set his love upon Me, therefore will I deliver
" I will set him up, because he hath known My name.   [him :
{ " He shall call upon Me : and even I will hear him :
" I will be with him in trouble :
{ " I will deliver him, and bring him to honour.
" With long life will I satisfy him,
" And I will show him My salvation."

_ This Psalm exhibits a double *replica*. At first the Psalmist speaks for himself in the name of the congregation ; in the next paragraph he speaks to them as a prophet ; and in the last the Almighty Himself confirms the utterance.

PSALM XCII.

A Psalm or Song for the Sabbath day.

IT is a good thing to give thanks unto the Lord,
And to sing psalms unto Thy name, O Most Highest !
To tell of Thy loving-kindness early in the morning,
And of Thy truth in the night-season ;
Upon (an instrument of) ten (strings), and upon the lute,
Upon the higgaion,[1] and upon the harp.
For Thou, Lord, hast made me glad through Thy works,
And I will rejoice in giving praise for the operation of Thy hands.

[1] See Ps. ix.

O LORD, how glorious are Thy works!
Thy thoughts are very deep!
An unwise man doth not well consider this:
And a fool doth not understand it.
When the ungodly are green as the grass,
And when all the workers of wickedness do flourish,
Then shall they be destroyed for ever:
But THOU, Lord, art the Most Highest for evermore!
For lo, Thine enemies, O Lord,
For lo, Thine enemies shall perish:
   And all the workers of iniquity shall be destroyed.
But Thou hast exalted my horn like (those of) the buffalo:
I am anointed with fresh oil.
Mine eye shall behold (the overthrow of) mine enemies:
And mine ear shall hear (the crying of) the wicked who rise up
                              [against me.
The righteous shall flourish like a palm-tree,
They shall spread abroad like a cedar in Lebanon.
Such as are planted in the house of the Lord,
Shall flourish in the courts of (the house of) our God.
They also shall bring forth more fruit in old age,
They shall be fat and well-liking.

Epiphonem. That they may show how true the Lord my Rock is:
And that there is no unrighteousness in Him.

Dromos of Palm-trees and Sphinxes, at Karnac.
From a Sketch by the Author.

PSALM XCIII.

THE Lord is KING! He is clothed with majesty :
The Lord is clothed with strength, wherewith He hath girded
The world is established, that it cannot be moved ;　　[Himself.
Thy throne was established of old :
　　THOU art from everlasting !

⎧ The floods have lifted, O Lord,
｜ The floods have lifted their voice,
⎩ The floods lift up their waves !
　More mighty than the voice of many waters,
　More mighty than the waves of the sea,
　　Is Jehovah in the highest !

honem.　Thy testimonies are very sure :
　　Holiness becometh Thine house, O Lord, for evermore !

PSALM XCIV.

O GOD, to whom vengeance belongeth,
O Lord God, to whom vengeance belongeth, show Thyself !
Arise, thou Judge of the world,
Reward the proud after their deserving.
How long, O Lord, shall the ungodly—
How long shall the ungodly triumph ?　[they speak scornfully ?
(How long) shall they pour forth (their malice ?　How long) shall
(How long) shall the workers of iniquity boast themselves ?
They smite down Thy people, O Lord,
And trouble Thine heritage.
They murder the widow and the stranger,
And put the fatherless to death.
And yet they say—" The Lord doth not see,
" The God of Jacob doth not regard it ! "

Understand, ye brutish among the people ;
And ye fools, when will ye be wise ?
He that planted the ear—shall He not hear !
He that formed the eye—shall He not see !
He that chastiseth the heathen—shall He not correct !
He that teacheth man knowledge—(It is) THE LORD !
Who knoweth the thoughts of man,
That they are vanity.

Blessed is the man whom Thou instructest, O Lord,
And teachest him in Thy law.
That Thou mayest give him patience in the time of adversity,
Until the pit be digged up for the ungodly.
For the Lord will not fail His people,
Neither will He forsake His inheritance :
For judgment shall be converted into righteousness,
And all they that are true of heart shall rejoice.[1]

Who will rise up for me against the wicked ?
Who will take my part against the evil doers ?
If the Lord had not helped me,
It had scarcely failed but my soul had dwelt in silence.
But when I said—" My foot hath slipped,"
Thy mercy, O Lord, held me up.
In the multitude of my thoughts within me,
Thy comforts have refreshed my soul.

Can the throne of wickedness have fellowship with Thee,
Which imagineth mischief as a law !
They gather them together against the soul of the righteous,
And they condemn the innocent blood.
But THE LORD is my defence :
And MY GOD is the Rock of my refuge.

Anti hon. He will turn upon them their own iniquity,
He will destroy them in their wickedness,
The Lord our God will destroy them.

[1] *Heb.* "shall (follow) after it."

PSALM XCV.

O COME, let us sing unto the Lord :
    Let us shout aloud unto the Rock of our salvation.
Antiphon.
Let us come before His presence with thanksgiving,
    Let us shout aloud unto Him with Psalms.

For the Lord is a GREAT GOD,
And a great King above all gods !
HE ! In whose hand are all the corners of the earth ;
    And the strength of the hills is His also.
HE ! For the sea is His, and He made it :
    And His hands prepared the dry land.

Antiphon.
O come, let us worship, and fall down :
Let us kneel before the Lord our Maker.

    For HE is our GOD :
And we are the people of His pasture,
And the sheep of His hand.

    To-day, if ye will hear His voice,
Harden not your hearts, as in the provocation,
As in the day of temptation in the wilderness ;
When your fathers tempted Me,
When they proved Me, and saw My works.
Forty years long
Was I grieved with this generation : and said—
" It is a people that do err in their hearts ;
" And they have not known My ways."
Of whom I sware in My wrath,
That they should not enter into My rest.

⁎⁎⁎ The third and fourth paragraphs form a *replica* of the first and second.

PSALM XCVI.

[By David.—See 1 Chron. XVI.]

Antiphon.
SING unto the Lord a new song,
Sing unto the Lord, all the whole earth :
Sing unto the Lord, and praise His name,
Show forth His salvation from day to day.

Declare His honour unto the heathen,
His wonders unto all people :
For the Lord is great, and cannot worthily be praised ;
He is more to be feared than all gods.
As for all the gods of the heathen, they are but idols :
But it is the Lord that made the heavens.
Glory and worship are before Him :
Power and honour are in His sanctuary.
Give unto the Lord, O ye kindreds of the people,
Give unto the Lord worship and power :
Give unto the Lord the honour due unto His name,
Bring offerings, and come into His courts.

Antiphon.
O worship the Lord in the beauty of holiness :
Let the whole earth stand in awe of Him.

Tell it out among the heathen—
"THE LORD IS KING !"
He hath established the earth that it cannot be moved :
He will judge the nations righteously.

Antiphon.
Let the heavens rejoice, and let the earth be glad ;
Let the sea make a noise, and all that is therein :
Let the field be joyful, and all that is in it :
Then shall all the trees of the wood rejoice before the Lord.

Epiphonem.
For HE COMETH !
For He cometh to judge the earth !
He will judge the world with righteousness,
And the nations with His truth.

PSALM XCVII.

THE Lord is King!
iphon. Let the earth rejoice :
    Let the multitude of the isles be glad thereof!

Clouds and darkness are round about Him,
Righteousness and judgment are the foundation of His throne.
There shall go a fire before Him,
And shall burn up His enemies on every side.
His lightnings gave shine unto the world.
The earth saw it, and was afraid :
The hills melted like wax at the presence of the Lord,
At the presence of the Lord of the whole earth :
The heavens have declared His righteousness,
And all the nations have seen His glory.
Confounded be all they that worship carved images,
That delight in idols :
    Worship HIM, all ye gods !

Sion heard of it, and rejoiced,
iphon. And the daughters of Judah were glad,
    Because of Thy judgments, O Lord !

For Thou, Lord, art higher than all that are in the earth ;
Thou art exalted far above all gods !

O ye that love the Lord,
See that ye hate the thing which is evil :
He will preserve the souls of His saints,
He will deliver them from the hand of the ungodly.
Light is sprung up for the righteous,
And joyful gladness for such as are true-hearted.

iphon. Rejoice in the Lord, ye righteous ;
    And give thanks at the remembrance of His holiness.

PSALM XCVIII.

A Psalm.

O SING unto the Lord a new song ;
For He hath done marvellous things :
Antiphon. With His own right hand, and with His holy arm,
Hath He gotten Himself the victory.[1]

The Lord hath declared His salvation :
  In the sight of the heathen
    He hath revealed His righteousness.
    He hath remembered His mercy and truth
  Towards the house of Israel :
All the ends of the world have seen the salvation of our God.

Shout aloud unto the Lord, all ye lands !
  Break forth, sing joyfully and sing psalms :
    Sing psalms unto the Lord upon the harp,
Antiphon.   With harp, and with the melody of psalm :
    With trumpets also, and with the melody of cornet,
Shout aloud unto the Lord the King !

Let the sea make a noise, and all that therein is,
The world, and they that dwell therein :
Second Let the floods clap their hands,
Antiphon. Let the hills be joyful together before the Lord :
  For He is come to judge the earth.

He will judge the world with righteousness,
And the nations with equity.

---

[1] *Heb.* " He hath saved for him (with) His right hand, and (with) the arm of His holiness."

PSALM XCIX.

[Ascribed to David by the Septuagint, Vulgate, Syriac, Arabic, and Ethiopic versions.]

THE LORD IS KING!
  Let the nations tremble :
He sitteth between the cherubim ;
  Let the earth be moved.
The Lord is great in Sion,
And high above all nations.

They shall give thanks unto Thy name,
'iphon. Which is great and wonderful :
    FOR IT IS HOLY !

The King's power loveth judgment :
Thou hast prepared equity :
Judgment and righteousness
Hast Thou wrought in Jacob.

O magnify the Lord our God,
'iphon. And fall down before His footstool :
    FOR HE IS HOLY !

Moses and Aaron among His priests,
And Samuel among such as call upon His name :
They called upon the Lord,
And He heard them.
He spake unto them out of the cloudy pillar :
For they kept His testimonies, and the law that He gave them.
Thou heardest them, O Lord our God ;
Thou forgavest them, O God :
    Though Thou punishedst their evil deeds.

O magnify the Lord our God,
'iphon. And worship Him upon His holy hill ;
    FOR THE LORD OUR GOD IS HOLY !

PSALM C.

A Psalm of praise.

SHOUT aloud unto the Lord, all ye lands !
Antiphon. Serve the Lord with gladness,
And come before His presence with a song.

Be ye sure that the Lord
HE IS GOD !
It is HE that hath made us, and not we ourselves :
We are His people, and the sheep of His pasture.

O come into His gates with thanksgiving,
And into His courts with praise :
Be thankful unto Him ;
Bless ye His name.

For the Lord is gracious :
Antiphon. His mercy is everlasting,
And His truth from generation to generation.

PSALM CI.

A Psalm of David.

I WILL sing of mercy and judgment :
Proem. Unto Thee, O Lord, will I sing psalms.

I WILL behave myself wisely in the way of uprightness .
O when wilt Thou come unto me !
I will walk with a perfect heart
In the midst of my house :
I will not set before mine eyes
Any thing of wickedness :
I will hate the sin of unfaithfulness ;
It shall not cleave unto me :

A froward heart shall depart from me ;
  I will not know a wicked person :
Whoso privily slandereth his neighbour,
  Him will I destroy :
Whoso hath also a high look and proud heart,
  I will not suffer him.

Mine eyes look upon the faithful of the land,
  That they may dwell with me :
Whoso walketh in the way of uprightness,
  He shall be my servant :
He that worketh deceit
  Shall not dwell within my house :
He that telleth lies
  Shall not tarry in my sight.
I shall soon destroy
  All the ungodly in the land :
That I may cut off from the city of the Lord
  All the workers of iniquity.

_{*} The last paragraph is a *replica* of the former: speaking of the ' way of
uprightness," in the beginning ; the hatred of wickedness, in the middle ; and
his resolution to destroy the wicked, in the end of each paragraph.

PSALM CII.

*A prayer of the afflicted, when he is overwhelmed, and poureth out his complaint
before the Lord.*

HEAR my prayer, O Lord,
  And let my crying come unto Thee.
    Hide not Thy face from me
Procm.   In the day of my trouble :
    Incline Thine ear unto me.
  In the day that I call
Answer me speedily.

FOR my days are consumed away like smoke,
And my bones are burnt up, as it were a firebrand.
My heart is smitten down, and withered like grass,
So that I forget to eat my bread.
For the voice of my groaning,
My bones cleave to my skin.

M

I am become like a pelican in the wilderness,
I am like an owl among desolate ruins.
I watch, and am even as a sparrow,
That sitteth alone upon the housetop.
Mine enemies revile me all the day long,
And they that are mad upon me are sworn together against me :
For I have eaten ashes as it were bread,
And have mingled my drink with weeping :
And that because of Thine indignation and wrath :
For Thou hast taken me up, and cast me down.
My days are gone like a shadow,
And I am withered like grass.

But Thou, O Lord, shalt endure for ever,
And Thy remembrance throughout all generations.
Thou wilt arise,
Thou wilt have mercy upon Sion :
For it is time that Thou have mercy upon her ;
For the time is come.
For Thy servants take pleasure in her stones,
And reverence her dust.

The " Wailing Place" at Jerusalem.

The heathen shall fear Thy name, O Lord,
And all the kings of the earth Thy majesty :
For the Lord will build up Sion,
And His glory shall appear.
He will turn Him unto the prayer of the poor destitute,
And despise not their desire.[1]

This shall be written for those who come after;
And the people which shall be born shall praise the Lord—
That He hath looked down from His sanctuary,
That the Lord from out of heaven did behold the earth ;
To hear the mourning of such as are in captivity,
To deliver the children appointed unto death ;
To declare the name of the Lord in Sion,
And His worship at Jerusalem ;
When the nations are gathered together,
And the kingdoms also to serve the Lord.

He brought down my strength in the way,
He shortened my days : and 1 said—
O my God, take me not away in the midst of mine age ;
As for Thy years, (they endure) throughout all generations.
Thou in the beginning hast laid the foundations of the earth,
And the heavens are the work of Thy hands.
They shall perish ; but Thou shalt endure :
  And they all shall wax old as doth a garment,   [changed :
  And as a vesture shalt Thou change them, and they shall be
But Thou art the same, and Thy years shall not fail.
The children of Thy servants shall continue,
And their seed shall stand fast in Thy sight.

[1] The verbs in these four lines are preterites in the original, describing God's deliverance with the eye of faith.

** The last paragraph is a *replica* of the first. That was written on the occasion of the event : this when looking back on his affliction, in after years.

PSALM CIII.

By David.

PRAISE the Lord, O my soul !
Antiphon. And all that is within me (praise) His holy name.
Praise the Lord, O my soul,
 And forget not all His benefits.

Who forgiveth all thy sin,
Who healeth all thine infirmities ;
Who saveth thy life from destruction,
Who crowneth thee with mercy and loving-kindness ;
Who satisfieth thy mouth with good things,
Who reneweth thy life as the eagle.

The Lord executeth righteousness and judgment
For all them that are oppressed with wrong :
He showed His ways unto Moses,
His works unto the children of Israel.

Antiphon. Merciful and compassionate is the Lord,
 Long-suffering, and of great mercy.

Not for ever will He be chiding,
And not for ever will He keep (anger).
Not according to our sins has He dealt with us,
And not according to our iniquities has He rewarded us.
For as the heaven is high above the earth,
 So great is His mercy toward them that fear Him :
As far as the east is from the west,
 So far hath He set our sins from us.

Antiphon. As a father is merciful unto his own children,
 So is the Lord merciful unto them that fear Him.

For He knoweth whereof we are made,
He remembereth that we are but dust.
The days of man are but as grass,
For he flourisheth as a flower of the field :
For as soon as the wind goeth over it it is gone,
And the place thereof shall know it no more.

Antiphon. But the mercy of the Lord is for ever and ever upon them that
And His righteousness upon children's children :   [fear Him,

Even upon such as keep His covenant,
And upon such as think upon His commandments to do them.
The Lord hath prepared His seat in heaven,
And His kingdom ruleth over all.

Praise the Lord, ye angels of His, mighty in strength,
    Ye that fulfil His word, and hearken to the voice of His word.
Praise the Lord, all ye His hosts,
Antiphon.   Ye servants of His that do His pleasure.
Praise the Lord, all ye works of His,
    In all places of His dominion :
Praise thou the Lord, O my soul !

PSALM CIV.

Praise the Lord, O my soul !
Antiphon. O Lord my God. Thou art become exceeding glorious,
Thou art clothed with majesty and honour.

Who decketh (Himself) with light as with a garment,
Who spreadeth out the heavens like a curtain ;
Who layeth the beams of His chambers in the waters ;
Who maketh the clouds His chariot ;
Who walketh upon the wings of the wind.
Who maketh His angels spirits,
His ministers a flaming fire.
Who laid the foundations of the earth,
That it should not be moved for ever.

Thou coveredst it with the deep as with a garment,
The waters stood above the mountains.
    At Thy rebuke they fled,
    At the voice of Thy thunder they hasted away.   [valleys,
They reached up to the mountains,—they went down into the
Even unto the place which Thou didst appoint for them.
    Thou hast set them their bounds which they shall not pass,
    Which they shall not turn, to cover the earth.

He sendeth the springs into the rivers
Which run amongst the hills :
All beasts of the field drink thereof,
The wild asses quench their thirst :
Beside them shall the fowls of the air have their habitation,
And sing among the branches.
He watereth the hills from above ;
The earth is filled with the fruit of Thy works.
He bringeth forth grass for the cattle,
And green herb for the service of man ;
That He may bring food out of the earth,
And wine that maketh glad the heart of man,
And oil to make him a cheerful countenance,
And bread which strengtheneth man's heart.

The trees of the Lord are full of sap,
The cedars of Lebanon which He hath planted ;
Wherein the birds make their nests,
And the fir-trees are a dwelling for the stork :
The high hills hath He given for the wild goats,
The stony rocks as a refuge for the coneys.

He appointed the moon for certain seasons,
And the sun knoweth its going down.
Thou makest darkness, that it may be night,
Wherein all the beasts of the forest do move :
The young lions roaring after their prey
Do seek their meat from God :
The sun ariseth, and they get them away together,
And lay them down in their dens :
While man goeth forth to his work
And to his labour, until the evening.

Antiphon.   O Lord, how manifold are Thy works !
In wisdom hast Thou made them all !

As the earth is full of Thy riches,
So is the great and wide sea also,
Wherein are things creeping innumerable,
Both small and great beasts,
There go the ships,
And that leviathan whom Thou hast made to sport therein.

These all wait upon Thee,
That Thou mayest give them meat in due season.
Thou givest it to them—they gather it ;
Thou openest Thy hand—they are filled with good.
Thou hidest Thy face—they are troubled ;
Thou takest away their breath—they die,
   And are turned again to their dust.
Thou sendest forth Thy spirit—they are created :
And Thou renewest the face of the earth.

Antiphon. The glory of the Lord shall endure for ever :
The Lord shall rejoice in His works.

He looketh upon the earth—and it trembleth :
He toucheth the mountains—and they smoke.

Antiphon. I will sing unto the Lord, as long as I live :
I will sing psalms unto my God, while I have my being.

My meditation of Him shall be sweet,
My joy shall be in the Lord.

Sinners shall be consumed out of the earth,
And the ungodly shall come to an end.

Antiphon. Praise thou the Lord, O my soul :
Praise ye the Lord !

PSALM CV.

[*By David.—See* 1 *Chron. XVI.*]

O GIVE thanks unto the Lord ! Call upon His name !
   Make known among the nations what things He hath done.
Antiphon. Sing unto Him : sing psalms unto Him :
   Talk ye of all His wondrous works.

Glory ye in His holy name ;
Rejoice in heart, ye that fear God.
Seek the Lord, and His strength,
Seek His face evermore.
Proem. Remember the marvellous works that He hath done,
His wonders, and the judgments of His mouth,
O ye seed of Abraham His servant,
Ye children of Jacob His chosen.

HE is the Lord our God,
His judgments are in all the world.
He hath remembered His covenant for ever,
The word which He commanded for a thousand generations :
(Even the covenant) which He made with Abraham,
And the oath that He swore unto Isaac ;
And appointed the same unto Jacob for a law,
And to Israel for a covenant for ever : saying—
" Unto thee will I give the land of Canaan,
" The lot of your inheritance,"
When there were yet but a few of them,
Yea, very few, and they strangers in the land.
What time as they went from one nation to another,
From one kingdom to another people,
He suffered no man to do them wrong,
But rebuked kings for their sake :—
" Touch not Mine anointed ones,
" And do My prophets no harm."

Moreover He called for a dearth upon the land,
And destroyed all the provision of bread :
But He had sent a man before them,
Even Joseph, who was sold to be a bond-servant ;
Whose feet they hurt in the stocks,
The iron entered into his soul ;
Until the time of (God's) appointment had come,
(While) the word of the Lord tried him.
The king sent and delivered him,
The prince of the people let him go free :
He made him lord also of his house,
And ruler of all his substance ;
That he might bind down his princes after his will,
And teach his senators wisdom.
And Israel went into Egypt,
And Jacob sojourned in the land of Ham.
And He increased His people exceedingly,
And He made them stronger than their enemies,
(Till) He turned their hearts to hate His people,
To deal untruly with His servants.

Then sent He Moses His servant,
And Aaron whom He had chosen,
And these showed His tokens among them,
And wonders in the land of Ham.

He sent darkness, and it was dark,
　　But they were not obedient unto His word :
He turned their waters into blood,
　　And slew their fish :
Their land brought forth frogs,
　　Yea, even in their king's chambers :
He spake the word, and there came swarms of flies,
　　And gnats[1] in all their quarters :
He gave them hailstones for rain,
　　And flames of fire in their land :
He smote their vines also, and fig-trees,
　　And destroyed the trees that were in their coasts :
He spake the word, and the locusts came,
　　And caterpillars innumerable,
And they ate up all the grass of their land,
　　And they ate up the fruit of their ground :
And He smote all the first-born in their land,
　　Even the chief of all their strength.
But He brought *them* forth also with silver and gold,
There was not one feeble person among their tribes.
Egypt was glad at their departing,
For they were afraid of them.

He spread out a cloud to be a covering,
　　And fire to give light in the night-season :
At their desire He brought quails,
　　And He filled them with the bread of heaven :
He opened the rock of stone, and the waters flowed out ;
　　So that rivers ran in the dry places.

For He remembered His holy promise,
And Abraham His servant :
And He brought forth His people with joy,
And His chosen with gladness :
And He gave them the lands of the heathen,
And they took the labours of the people in possession.

Epiphonem.　THAT THEY MIGHT KEEP HIS STATUTES,
　　　　　　AND OBSERVE HIS LAWS.

Antiphon.　Praise ye the Lord !

---

[1] Ex. viii. 16. *Eng. Vers.* "lice."

PSALM CVI.

[By David.—See 1 *Chron. XVI.]*

PRAISE ye the Lord!
Antiphon. O give thanks unto the Lord, for He is gracious,
For His mercy endureth for ever.

Who can express the noble acts of the Lord!
(Who) can show forth all his praise!
Blessed are they that keep judgment,
He that doeth righteousness at all times.
Proœm. Remember me, O Lord, in the favour Thou bearest to Thy people,
O visit me with Thy salvation.
⎧That I may see the felicity of Thy chosen,
⎨That I may rejoice in the gladness of Thy people,
⎩That I may give thanks with Thine inheritance.

WE have sinned with our fathers,
We have done amiss, and dealt wickedly :
Our fathers regarded not Thy wonders in Egypt,
They remembered not the multitude of Thy mercies ;
    But they rebelled at the sea, even at the Red Sea.
Nevertheless, He helped them for His name's sake,
That He might make His power to be known :
And He rebuked the Red Sea, and it was dried up ;
And He led them through the deep, as through the Wilderness :
And He saved them from the hand of the adversary ;
And He delivered them from the hand of the enemy :
But the waters overwhelmed their enemies ;
There was not one of them left.
Then they believed His words ;
They sang praise unto Him.
    But soon did they forget His works,
And would not abide His counsel :
But they lusted in their hearts in the wilderness,
And they tempted God in the desert ;
And He gave them their desire,
But sent leanness withal into their soul.

They angered Moses also in the camp,
And Aaron the saint of the Lord.
So the earth opened, and swallowed up Dathan,
And covered the congregation of Abiram;
And the fire was kindled in their company;
The flames burnt up the ungodly.

They made a calf in Horeb,
And worshipped a golden image.
Thus they changed their glory
Into the similitude of an ox that eateth hay!
And they forgat God their Saviour,
Who had done so great things in Egypt;
Wondrous works in the land of Ham,
And fearful things at the Red Sea.

So He said He would have destroyed them,
Had not Moses His servant
Stood before Him in the gap,
To turn away His wrath lest He should destroy them.

And they thought scorn of that pleasant land,
And they gave no credence unto His word;
And they murmured in their tents;
And they hearkened not unto the voice of the Lord.
Then lifted He up his hand against them,
To overthrow them in the wilderness:
To overthrow them among the nations,
And to scatter them in the lands.

And they joined themselves unto Baal-Peor,
And they ate the offerings of the dead:
And they provoked Him to anger with their own inventions;
And the plague broke out among them.
Then stood up Phinehas, and executed judgment;
And so the plague was stayed:
And that was counted unto him for righteousness,
Among all posterities for evermore.

They angered Him also at the waters of strife,
So that He punished Moses for their sakes:
For they provoked His spirit,
So that He spake unadvisedly with his lips.

They destroyed not the heathen,
As the Lord commanded them;
But were mingled among the heathen,
And they learned their ways.

And they worshipped their idols,
Which became a snare to them :
And they sacrificed their sons
And their daughters to devils;
And they shed innocent blood,
Even the blood of their sons and of their daughters ;
Whom they offered to the idols of Canaan,
And the land was defiled with blood.
Thus were they stained with their own works,
And served idols[1] of their own inventions.

Therefore was the wrath of the Lord kindled against His people,
Insomuch that He abhorred His own inheritance :
And He gave them over into the hand of the heathen,
And they that hated them were lords over them :
Their enemies oppressed them, and had them in subjection ;
Many a time did He deliver them ;
But they rebelled against Him with their own inventions,
And were brought down in their wickedness.
Nevertheless, when He saw their adversity,
He heard their complaint :
He thought upon His covenant, and pitied them,
    According to the multitude of His mercies :
He made them also to be pitied
    Of all them that carried them away captive.

Deliver us, O Lord our God,
And gather us from among the heathen ;
That we may give thanks unto Thy holy name,
And make our boast of Thy praise.

Blessed be the Lord God of Israel,
Antiphon. From everlasting to everlasting!
    And let all the people say
Amen ; Praise ye the Lord.

[1] *Heb.* " went a whoring with."

* This Psalm exhibits several instances of the introverted parallelism,
which would have confused the paragraphs had they been pointed out in the
text. Thus, " Red Sea " in ver. 7 corresponds with " Red Sea " in ver. 9 ;
"destroyed " in the beginning of ver. 23 corresponds with "destroy" in the
termination of the verse ; "land" in ver. 24 with "lands" in ver. 27 ;
"idols" and "sons and daughters" in ver. 36 with "sons and daughters" and
"idols" in ver. 37.

PSALM CVII.

ntiphon. O GIVE thanks unto the Lord, for (He is) gracious!
For His mercy endureth for ever!

Let the redeemed of the Lord say thus,
Whom he hath redeemed from the hand of the enemy,
Proem. And hath gathered them out of the lands;
From the east, and from the west,
From the north, and from the south.

THEY went astray in the wilderness, out of the way;
They found no city to dwell in:
Hungry and thirsty,
Their soul fainted in them.
ntiphon. But when they cried unto the Lord in their trouble,
He delivered them out of their distress.
And He led them by the right way,
That they might go to a city to dwell in.
ntiphon. Oh that men would therefore praise the Lord for His goodness,
And for the wonders that He doeth for the children of men!
For He satisfieth the empty soul,
And He filleth the hungry soul with gladness.

Such as sit in darkness, and in the shadow of death,
Being fast bound in misery and iron;
Because they rebelled against the words of the Lord,
And lightly regarded the counsel of the Most High:
Therefore did He humble their heart through heaviness;
They fell down, and there was none to help them.
ntiphon. But when they cried unto the Lord in their trouble,
He delivered them out of their distress.
For He brought them out of darkness, and out of the shadow of
And brake their bands in sunder.   [death,
ntiphon. Oh that men would therefore praise the Lord for His goodness,
And for the wonders that He doeth for the children of men!
For He hath broken the gates of brass,
And smitten the bars of iron in sunder.

Foolish men are plagued, because of their offence,
And because of their wickedness.
Their soul abhorred all manner of meat,
And they were even hard at death's door.

Antiphon. But when they cried unto the Lord in their trouble,
He delivered them out of their distress.
He sent His word, and healed them,
And they were saved from their destruction.

Antiphon. Oh that men would therefore praise the Lord for His goodness,
And for the wonders that He doeth for the children of men !
That they would sacrifice unto Him the sacrifices of thanksgiving,
And tell out His works with shouting.

They that go down to the sea in ships,
They that occupy their business in great waters—
These men see the works of the Lord,
And His wonders in the deep.
For at His word the stormy wind ariseth,
Which lifteth up the waves thereof:
They are carried up to the heaven, and down again to the deep;
Their soul melteth away, because of the trouble:
They reel to and fro, and stagger like a drunken man,
And are at their wits' end.

Antiphon. But when they cry unto the Lord in their trouble,
He delivereth them out of their distress.
For He maketh the storm to cease,
So that the waves thereof are still.
Then are they glad, because they are at rest,
And so He bringeth them unto the haven where they would be.

Antiphon. Oh that men would therefore praise the Lord for his goodness,
And for the wonders that He doeth for the children of men !
That they would exalt Him also in the congregation of the people ;
That they would praise Him in the seat of the elders.

He turneth the rivers into a wilderness,
And drieth up the water-springs :
A fruitful land maketh He barren,
For the wickedness of them that dwell therein :
Again, He maketh the wilderness a standing water,
And water-springs of a dry ground :
And there He setteth the hungry,
That they may build them a city to dwell in :

That they may sow their land, and plant vineyards,
To yield them fruits of increase.
He blesseth them, so that they multiply exceedingly,
And suffereth not their cattle to decrease.[1]

Again, if they are minished, and brought low,
Through oppression, through affliction, or sorrow—
He will pour contempt upon princes,
    Making them wander outcast into the wilderness :
While He will set on high the poor from affliction,
    Making them households, like a flock of sheep.

The righteous shall consider this, and rejoice ;
And the mouth of all wickedness shall be stopped.
phonem. Whoso is wise will ponder these things,
    Andthey shall understand the loving-kindness of the Lord.

    ⁎ There are nine letter *Nuns* reversed (נ) in this Psalm.

PSALM CVIII.

A Song or Psalm of David.

[A replica of Psalms LVII. and LX.]

O GOD, my heart is fixed !
I will sing, I will sing psalms.
(Awake,) my soul ;[2] awake, lute and harp !
I myself will awake right early.
I will give thanks unto Thee, O Lord, among the people,
    AndI will sing psalms unto Thee among the nations :
For Thy mercy reacheth unto the heavens,
And Thy truth unto the clouds.
Be Thou exalted, O God, above the heavens,
And Thy glory above all the earth.

---

[1] In this paragraph the Psalmist goes back to the subject of the first : speaking of " the wilderness," "a city to dwell in," and gifts of plenty.
[2] See Ps. vii. 5; xvi. 9; xxx. 12; and lvii. 8.

Then shall Thy beloved be delivered :[1]
Save with Thy right hand, and hear me.

    God hath spoken in His holiness—
" I will rejoice ; I will divide Shechem,[2]
" I will mete out the valley of Succoth.
" Gilead is Mine ; Manasseh is Mine ;
" Ephraim also is the strength of My head ;
" Judah is My lawgiver ;
" Moab is My hand-basin ;
" Over Edom will I cast out My shoe ;
" Over Philistia will I triumph."

    Who will lead me into the strong city ?
Who will bring me into Edom ?
Wilt not Thou, O God, who hast cast us off ?
Wilt not Thou, O God, go out with our hosts ?
O be THOU our help in trouble ;
For vain is the help of man.

Antiphon.
Through GOD we shall do great acts :
For it is HE that will tread down our enemies.

PSALM CIX.

To the chief Musician.—A Psalm of David.

BE not silent to me, O God of my praise !
For the mouth of the ungodly, the mouth of the deceitful, is opened
They have spoken against me with a lying tongue.   [against me.
They compassed me about also with words of hatred,
Proem. And they fought against me without a cause :
In return for my love, they are mine adversaries ;
But I betake myself unto prayer :
And they have rewarded me evil, in return for good,
And hatred, in return for love.

[1] This rendering is supported by the passage in Ps. lx. coming after a *Selah*, and therefore beginning a new sentence.
[2] The reader is requested to correct the spelling of this name in Ps. lx. p. 103.

SET Thou an ungodly man over him,
    And let an adversary stand at his right hand :
Let him be condemned when he is judged,
    And let his prayer be turned into sin :
Let his days be few,
    And let another take his office :
Let his children be fatherless,
    And his wife a widow :
Let his children be outcast, and beg,
    And let them beg in[1] desolate places :
Let the extortioner consume all that he hath,
    And let strangers spoil his labour :
Let there be no man to pity him,
    Nor to have compassion on his fatherless children
Let his posterity be destroyed,
    And in the next generation let his name be blotted out :
Let the wickedness of his fathers be remembered[2] by the Lord,
    And let not the sin of his mother be blotted out :
Let them be before the Lord continually,   [earth.
    And let Him root out the memorial of (the wicked) from off the
And that because he remembered[2] not to show mercy,
But persecuted the man who was poor, and afflicted,
And broken-hearted, (searching) to kill him.[2]
His delight was in cursing—Let it happen unto him :
He loved not blessing—Let it be far from him.
He clothed himself with cursing, as with a garment ;
Let it be in his bowels as water, and as oil in his bones :
Let it be unto him as the garment that he hath upon him,
And as the girdle that he is always girded withal.
Thus let it happen from the Lord unto mine enemies,
And to them who speak evil against my soul.

    But THOU, O Lord God ![4]
Deal Thou with me according to Thy name ;
For sweet is Thy mercy.
O deliver me ; for I am helpless and poor,
And my heart is wounded within me.

    [1] Or—[being driven away] from their
    [2],[2] Because he remembered not mercy, God remembered to him the wicked-
ness of his fathers.   [2] See Ps. lxii. 3.
    [4] *Heb.* "O Jehovah Lord."

I go hence like the shadow that departeth ;
I am driven away like the locust :
My knees are weak through fasting,
And my flesh is dried up for want of fatness.
I became also a reproach to them :
They that looked upon me wagged their heads.
Help me, O Lord my God !
Save me, according to Thy mercy !
And they shall know how that this is THY hand,
And that THOU, Lord, hast done it.
They may curse ; but Thou wilt bless :
They who rise up shall be ashamed ; but Thy servant shall rejoice.
Mine adversaries shall be clothed with shame ;
And they shall be covered with confusion, as with a cloak.

Antiphon.

I will give great thanks unto the Lord with my mouth,
I will praise Him among the multitude :
For He will stand at the right-hand of the poor,
To save him from those who condemn his soul.

PSALM CX.

A Psalm of David.

THE Lord said unto MY Lord—
" Sit Thou on My right-hand,
" Until I make Thine enemies Thy footstool."
The Lord will send the rod of Thy power out of Sion :
Be Thou ruler, even in the midst among Thine enemies.
Thy people shall be a free-will offering in the day of Thy power,
In the beauty of holiness :
The dew of Thy offspring [1]
Shall be as the womb of the dawn.

The Lord hath sworn, and He will not repent :—
" Thou art a priest for ever,
" After the order of Melchizedek."
The Lord upon Thy right-hand
Will wound even kings in the day of His wrath.

[1] *Heb.* " birth."

He will judge the heathen : He will fill (their land) with slain :
He will smite in sunder the heads over divers countries.
He will drink of the brook in the way :
Therefore will He lift up the head.

. The second paragraph is a *replica* of the first.

PSALM CXI.

Praise ye the Lord !

א I WILL give thanks unto the Lord with my whole heart,
ב Privately among the upright, and in the congregation.
ג The works of the Lord are great,
ד Sought out of all them that have pleasure therein.
ה His work is worthy to be praised, and had in honour,
ו And His righteousness endureth for ever.
ז He hath made His wonderful works to be remembered ;
ח The Lord is gracious, and full of compassion.
ט He hath given meat unto them that fear Him ;
י He will ever be mindful of His covenant.
כ He hath showed His people the power of His works,
ל That He may give them the heritage of the heathen.
מ The works of His hands are verity and judgment :
נ All His commandments are true.
ס (They) stand fast for ever and ever,
ע (And) are done in truth and equity.
פ He sent redemption unto His people,
צ He hath established His covenant for ever :
ק   Holy and reverend is His name.

ר The fear of the Lord is the beginning of wisdom ;
ש A good understanding have all they that do thereafter.

ת His praise endureth for ever.

PSALM CXII.

　　　　　　　　　Praise ye the Lord!

א Blessed be the man who feareth the Lord,
ב Who hath great delight in His commandments:
ג His seed shall be mighty upon earth,
ד The generation of the faithful shall be blessed
ה Riches and plenteousness shall be in his house,
ו And his righteousness remaineth for ever.
ז Unto the godly there ariseth up light in the darkness;
ח (He is) merciful, loving, and righteous.
ט Well is it with the man who is merciful and lendeth:
י He shall sustain his cause in the judgment.
כ For ever shall he not be removed:
ל For ever shall the righteous be had in remembrance.
מ He will not fear because of evil tidings,
נ For his heart standeth fast, believing in the Lord:
ס His heart is established, and will not fear,
ע Until he see (his desire upon) his enemies.
פ He hath dispersed abroad, and given to the poor;
צ His righteousness endureth for ever:
ק His horn shall be exalted with honour.

ר The ungodly shall see it, and it shall grieve him;
ש He shall gnash with his teeth, and consume away;
ת The desire of the ungodly shall perish.

Epiphonema.

PSALM CXIII.

Praise ye the Lord!
Praise, O ye servants of the Lord,
Praise ye the name of the Lord.
Antiphon. ⌠ Blessed be the name of the Lord
　　　　 ⎮ From this time forth for evermore;
　　　　 ⎮ From the rising up of the sun, unto the going down of the
　　　　 ⌡ Praised be the name of the Lord!　　　　　　[same—

The Lord is exalted above all heathen,
And His glory above the heavens.
Who is like unto the Lord our God,
   Who dwelleth so high ;
   Who humbleth Himself (nevertheless) to behold
The things that are in heaven and earth !
Who raiseth the poor from the dust,
And exalteth the needy from the dunghill ;
That He may set him with the princes,
Even with the princes of His people.
Who maketh the barren woman to keep house,
And to be a joyful mother of children.

Antiphon.   Praise ye the Lord !

PSALM CXIV.

WHEN Israel came out from Egypt,
And the house of Jacob from a strange people,
Judah was His sanctuary,
And Israel His dominion.
The sea saw (that), and fled ;
   Jordan was driven back :
      The mountains skipped like rams,
        And the little hills like young sheep !
What aileth thee, O thou sea, that thou fleddest,
   And thou Jordan, that thou wast driven back ?
      Ye mountains, that ye skipped like rams,
        And ye little hills, like young sheep ?
Tremble, thou earth, at the presence of the Lord,
At the presence of the God of Jacob !
Who turned the hard rock into a standing water,
And the flint stone into a springing well.

PSALM CXV.

N OT unto us, O Lord !
Not unto us, but unto Thy name give the praise :
For Thy loving mercy, and for Thy truth's sake.

Wherefore shall the heathen say—
" Where is now their God ?"
As for our God, He is in heaven :
He hath done whatsoever pleased Him.

Their idols are of silver and gold,
Even the work of the hands of *man !*
They have mouths—and yet they speak not ;
They have eyes—and yet they see not ;
They have ears—and yet they hear not ;
They have noses—and yet they smell not ;
They have hands—and yet they handle not ;
They have feet—and yet they walk not :
They cannot speak with their throat.
They that make them are like unto them ;
And so are all such as put their trust in them.

O Israel, trust thou in the Lord !
HE is their helper and defender.
O house of Aaron, put your trust in the Lord !
HE is their helper and defender.
Ye that fear the Lord, put your trust in the Lord !
HE is their helper and defender.

The Lord hath been mindful of us ; He will bless (us) :
He will bless the house of Israel,
He will bless the house of Aaron :
He will bless them that fear the Lord,
Both small and great.

The Lord shall add unto you,
Unto you, and to your children :
Ye are the blessed of the Lord,
Who made heaven and earth.
The heavens, even the heavens are the Lord's :
The earth hath He given to the children of men.

The dead praise not Thee, O Lord ;
Neither all they that go down into silence.

But we will praise the Lord,
Antiphon. From this time forth, for evermore.
     Praise ye the Lord.

<hr />

PSALM CXVI.

I LOVE THE LORD !
    Because He hath heard the voice of my supplication.
Proem. Because He hath inclined His ear to me,
Therefore will I call upon Him as long as I live.

THE sorrows of death compassed me round about,
The pains of hell got hold upon me ;
    I found trouble and heaviness.
Then called I upon the name of the Lord—
"O Lord, I beseech Thee, deliver my soul."

Gracious is the Lord, and righteous :
Yea, our God is merciful.
The Lord preserveth the simple :
I was in misery, and He helped me.
Turn again then unto thy rest, O my soul :
For the Lord hath dealt bountifully with thee.
For THOU hast delivered my soul from death,
Mine eyes from tears, and my feet from falling.
I shall walk before the Lord
In the land of the living.
I trust (in Thee): though I said (in my haste)—
    "As for me, I am sore troubled."
As for me. I said in my haste—
    "All men are vanity."

What return shall I make unto the Lord
For all the benefits that He hath done unto me !

Antipho- I will receive the cup of salvation,
And I will call upon the name of the Lord :
I will pay my vows unto the Lord
Now in the presence of all His people.

Right dear in the sight of the Lord
Is the death of His saints.
Truly, O Lord, I am Thy servant ;
I am Thy servant, and the son of Thine handmaid :
  Thou hast broken my bonds asunder.

Antiphon. I will sacrifice to Thee the sacrifice of thanksgiving,
And I will call upon the name of the Lord :
I will pay my vows unto the Lord,
Now in the presence of all His people ;
In the courts of the Lord's house,
Even in the midst of thee, O Jerusalem.
  Praise ye the Lord !

PSALM CXVII.

PRAISE the Lord, all ye heathen :
Praise Him, all ye nations !
Antiphon. For His merciful kindness is ever more and more towards us,
And the truth of the Lord endureth for ever.
  Praise ye the Lord !

PSALM CXVIII.

O GIVE thanks unto THE LORD, for He is gracious ;
  For His mercy endureth for ever.
*Precen
and
Antiphon.* Let Israel now confess—
    That His mercy endureth for ever.
Let the house of Aaron now confess—
    That His mercy endureth for ever.
Let them now that fear THE LORD confess—
    That His mercy endureth for ever !

IN my trouble I called upon THE LORD,
And THE LORD heard me, and (set me) at large.
THE LORD is on my side : I will not fear.
     What can *man* do unto me !
THE LORD is on my side with them that help me :
     Therefore shall I see (my desire) upon mine enemies.
It is better to trust in THE LORD,
     Than to put any confidence in man :
It is better to trust in THE LORD,
     Than to put any confidence in princes.
All nations compassed me about :
     But in the name of THE LORD will I destroy them.
They compassed me about—yea, they compassed me about :
     But in the name of THE LORD will I destroy them.
They compassed me about like bees—They are extinct as a fire of
     For in the name of THE LORD will I destroy them.   [thorns :
Thou hast thrust sore at me, that I might fall :
But THE LORD sustained me.
THE LORD is my strength, and my psalm,
And is become my salvation.
The voice of joy and salvation
Is in the dwelling of the righteous.
The right hand of THE LORD bringeth mighty things to pass ;
The right hand of THE LORD hath the pre-eminence ;
The right hand of THE LORD bringeth mighty things to pass.
I shall not die, but live,
And declare the works of THE LORD.
THE LORD hath chastened and corrected me,
But He hath not given me over unto death.
Open me the gates of righteousness,
     That I may go into them, and praise THE LORD.
This is the gate of THE LORD :
     The righteous shall enter into it.

I will thank Thee : for THOU hast heard me,
And art become my salvation.
The stone which the builders refused
Is become the head-stone in the corner.
This is THE LORD'S doing,
And it is marvellous in our eyes.
This is the day which THE LORD hath made ;
We will rejoice and be glad in it.

I beseech Thee, O LORD, Hosanna ;[1]
I beseech Thee, O LORD, send prosperity.
Blessed be he that cometh in the name of THE LORD :
We have blessed you out of the house of THE LORD.
God is THE LORD, and He hath showed us light :
Bind the sacrifice with cords unto the horns of the altar.
Thou art my GOD : and I will thank Thee !
Thou art MY God : and I will exalt Thee !

Antiphon. O give thanks unto THE LORD: for He is gracious :
For His mercy endureth for ever.

PSALM CXIX.

, *Four things are especially noticeable in this Psalm :—love of God's word ; singleness of that love ; hatred of evil ; prayer against those who are evil.*

א BLESSED are they who are undefiled in the way,
    Who walk in the law of the Lord :
א Blessed are they who keep His commandments,
    Who seek Him with their whole heart ;
א Who do no wickedness,
    Who walk in His ways.
א Thou hast charged—
    That we should diligently keep Thy commandments.
א Oh that my ways were made so direct,
    That I might keep Thy statutes !
א Then shall I not be confounded,
    While I have respect unto all Thy commandments.
א I will praise Thee with an unfeigned heart,
    When I shall have learned the judgments of Thy righteousness.
א I will keep Thy statutes :
א   O forsake me not utterly.

[1] *Heb.* "Save." See Matt. xxi. 9.

ב Wherewithal shall a young man cleanse his way?
    Even by ruling himself after Thy word.
ב With my whole heart have I sought Thee:
    O let me not go wrong out of Thy commandments.
ב Thy word have I hid within my heart,
    That I should not sin against Thee.
ב Blessed art Thou, O Lord!
    O teach me Thy statutes.
ב With my lips have I declared
    All the judgments of Thy mouth.
ב I have had as great delight in the way of Thy testimonies,
    As in all manner of riches.
ב I will meditate in Thy commandments,
    And have respect unto Thy ways.
ב I will delight in Thy statutes:
    I will not forget Thy word.

ג O be gracious unto Thy servant,
    That I may live and keep Thy word.
ג Open Thou mine eyes,
    That I may see the wondrous things of Thy law.
ג I am a stranger upon earth:
    O hide not Thy commandments from me.
ג My soul breaketh for the very fervent desire
    That it hath alway unto Thy judgments!
ג Thou hast rebuked the proud:
    Cursed are they that do err from Thy commandments.
ג Turn from me shame and reproach:
    For I have kept Thy testimonies.
ג Princes also did sit and speak against me:
    But Thy servant will meditate in Thy statutes.
ג For Thy testimonies
    Are my delight, and my counsellors.

ד My soul cleaveth to the dust!
    Quicken Thou me, according to Thy word.
ד I acknowledge my ways: and Thou heardest me:
    O teach me Thy statutes.
ד Make me to understand the way of Thy commandments,
    And so shall I talk of Thy wondrous ways.
ד My soul melteth away for very heaviness:
    Comfort Thou me according to Thy word.

צ Take from me the way of lying,
   And cause Thou me to make much of Thy law.
צ I have chosen the way of truth,
   And Thy judgments have I laid before me.
צ I have stuck unto Thy testimonies :
   O Lord, confound me not.
צ I will run the way of Thy commandments,
   When Thou hast set my heart at liberty.

ה Teach me, O Lord, the way of Thy statutes,
   And I shall keep it, unto the end.
ה Give me understanding, and I shall keep Thy law :
   Yea, I shall keep it with my whole heart.
ה Make me to go in the path of Thy commandments,
   For therein is my desire.
ה Incline my heart unto Thy testimonies,
   And not to covetousness.
ה Turn away mine eyes, lest they behold vanity ;
   And quicken Thou me in Thy way.
ה Stablish Thy word unto Thy servant,
   That I may fear Thee.
ה Take away the reproach that I am afraid of ;
   For Thy judgments are good.
ה Behold, my delight is in Thy commandments :
   O quicken me in Thy righteousness.

ו Let Thy loving mercy come also unto me, O Lord ;
   Even Thy salvation, according to Thy word.
ו So shall I answer him that reproacheth me ;
   For my trust is in Thy word.
ו O take not the word of Thy truth utterly out of my mouth ;
   For my hope is in Thy judgments.
ו So shall I alway keep Thy law,
   Yea, for ever and ever.
ו And I will walk at liberty,
   For I seek Thy commandments.
ו I will speak of Thy testimonies also, even before kings,
ו   And will not be ashamed.
ו And my delight shall be in Thy commandments,
   Which I have loved :
ו My hands also will I lift up unto Thy commandments, which I
ו   And my study shall be in Thy statutes.   [have loved ;

ז Remember Thy word unto Thy servant,
    Wherein Thou hast caused me to put my trust.
ז The same is my comfort in my trouble,
    For Thy word hath quickened me.
ז The proud have had me exceedingly in derision ;
    Yet have I not shrinked from Thy law.
ז For I remembered Thine everlasting judgments, O Lord,
    And received comfort.
ז Indignation hath seized me,
    Because of the wicked who forsake Thy law.
ז Thy statutes have been my psalms
    In the house of my pilgrimage.
ז I have thought upon Thy name, O Lord, in the night-season,
    And have kept Thy law.
ז This (comfort) I had,
    Because I kept Thy commandments.

ח THOU art my portion, O Lord !
    I have promised to keep Thy law.
ח I entreated Thy favour with my whole heart ;
ח   O be merciful unto me, according to Thy word.
ח I called mine own ways to remembrance,
    And turned my feet unto Thy testimonies.
ח I made haste, and delayed not,
    To keep Thy commandments.
ח The snares of the wicked are cast about me :
    But I have not forgotten Thy law.
ח At midnight I will rise to give thanks unto Thee,
    Because of Thy righteous judgments.
ח I am a companion of all them that fear Thee,
    Of them that keep Thy commandments.
ח The earth, O Lord, is full of Thy mercy :
ח   O teach me Thy statutes.

ט O Lord, Thou hast dealt graciously with Thy servant,
    According to Thy word.
ט O teach me true understanding and knowledge,
    For I have believed Thy commandments.
ט Before I was troubled I went wrong :
    But now have I kept Thy word.
ט Thou art good and gracious !
    O teach me Thy statutes.

ל The proud have imagined a lie against me ;
But I will keep Thy commandments with my whole heart.
ל Their heart is as fat as brawn :
But my delight hath been in Thy law.
ל It is good for me that I have been in trouble,
That I may learn Thy statutes.
ל The law of Thy mouth is dearer unto me
Than thousands of gold and silver.

י Thy hands have made me, and fashioned me ;
O give me understanding that I may learn Thy command-
י They that fear Thee will be glad when they see me,   [ments.
Because I have put my trust in Thy word.
י I know, O Lord, that Thy judgments are right,
And that Thou of very faithfulness hast caused me to be
י Let Thy merciful kindness be my comfort,   [troubled.
. According to Thy word unto Thy servant.
י Let Thy loving mercies come upon me, that I may live :
For Thy law is my delight.
י Let the proud be confounded, for they go wickedly about to
But I will meditate on Thy commandments.   [destroy me :
י Let such as fear Thee be turned to me;
And such as keep Thy commandments.
י Let my heart be sound in Thy statutes,
That I be not ashamed.

כ My soul faileth for Thy salvation :
I had hoped for (the accomplishment of) Thy word.
כ Mine eyes fail in looking for Thy promise, saying—
Oh when wilt Thou comfort me ?
כ For I am become like a (leathern) bottle in the smoke :
Yet do I not forget Thy statutes.
כ How many are the days of Thy servant ?
When wilt Thou be avenged of them that persecute me ?
כ The proud have digged pits for me,
Which are not after Thy law.
כ All Thy commandments are true :
They persecute me falsely : O be Thou my help !
כ They had almost made me fail upon earth :
But I forsook not Thy testimonies.
כ O quicken me after Thy loving-kindness :
And so shall I keep the testimonies of Thy truth.

ל O Lord, Thy word
  Endureth for ever in heaven!
ל Thy truth also remaineth from one generation to another:
  Thou hast laid the foundation of the earth, and it abideth.
ל They continue this day according to Thine ordinance;
  For all things serve Thee.
ל If my delight had not been in Thy law,
  I should have perished in my trouble.
ל I will never forget Thy commandments;
  For with them Thou hast quickened me.
ל I am Thine : O save me :
  For I have sought Thy commandments.
ל The ungodly laid wait for me, to destroy me :
  But I will consider Thy testimonies.
ל I see that all things come to an end :
  But Thy commandment is exceeding broad.

מ What love have I unto Thy word!
  All the day long is my study in it.
מ Thy precepts have made me wiser than mine enemies:
  For they are ever with me.
מ I have more understanding than my teachers :
  For Thy testimonies are my study.
מ I am wiser than the aged :
  For I keep Thy commandments.
מ I have refrained my feet from every evil way,
  That I may keep Thy word.
מ I have not departed from Thy judgments :
  For Thou teachest me.
מ Oh how sweet are Thy words unto my throat;
  Yea, sweeter than honey unto my mouth!
מ Through Thy commandments I get understanding :
  Therefore I hate all evil ways.

נ Thy word is a lantern unto my feet,
  And a light unto my paths :
נ I am sworn, and am stedfastly purposed
  To keep Thy righteous judgments.
נ I am troubled above measure :
  Quicken me, O Lord, according to Thy word.
נ Let the free-will offerings of my mouth please Thee, O Lord!
  And teach me Thy judgments.

צ My soul is alway in my hand :
  Yet do I not forget Thy law.
צ The ungodly have laid a snare for me :
  But yet I swerved not from Thy commandments.
צ Thy testimonies have I claimed as mine heritage for ever :
  For they are the very joy of my heart.
צ I have applied my heart to fulfil Thy statutes :
  Even alway, unto the end.

ק I hate them that are of a divided heart :
  But Thy law do I love.
ק Thou art my defence and shield :
  And my trust is in Thy word.
ק Away from me, ye wicked :
  I will keep the commandments of my God.
ק O stablish me according to Thy word, that I may live :
  And let me not be disappointed of my hope.
ק Hold Thou me up, and I shall be safe :
  Yea, my delight shall be ever in Thy statutes.
ק Thou hast trodden down all them that depart from Thy statutes :
  For they imagine but deceit.
ק Thou puttest away all the ungodly of the earth like dross :
  Therefore I love Thy testimonies.
ק My flesh trembleth for fear of Thee :
  And I am afraid of Thy judgments.

ע I deal with the thing that is lawful and right :
  O give me not over unto mine oppressors.
ע Undertake for Thy servant for good ;
  That the proud do me no wrong.
ע Mine eyes fail with looking for Thy salvation,
  And for the word of Thy righteousness.
ע O deal with Thy servant according unto Thy loving mercy,
  And teach me Thy statutes.
ע I am Thy servant :
  O grant me understanding, that I may know Thy testimonies.
ע It is time for Thee, Lord, to stretch out Thine hand ;
  For they have destroyed Thy law.
ע For I love Thy commandments
  Above gold and precious stone.
ע Therefore hold I straight all Thy commandments ;
  And all false ways I utterly abhor.

נ Thy testimonies are wonderful :
   Therefore doth my soul keep them.

נ The entrance of Thy word giveth light ;
   Making wise the simple.

נ I longed and panted after Thy word :
   For my delight was in Thy commandments.

נ O look Thou upon me, and be merciful unto me,
   As Thou usest to do unto those that love Thy name.

נ Order my steps in Thy word ;
   And let no wickedness have dominion over me.

נ O deliver me from the wrongful dealings of men :
   And so shall I keep Thy commandments.

נ Show the light of Thy countenance upon Thy servant,
   And teach me Thy statutes.

נ Mine eyes gush out with water ;
   Because men keep not Thy law.

צ Righteous art Thou, O Lord !
   And true are Thy judgments.

צ The testimonies that Thou hast commanded
   Are exceeding righteous and true.

צ My zeal hath even consumed me,
   Because mine enemies have forgotten Thy words.

צ Thy word is tried to the uttermost :
   And Thy servant loveth it.

צ I am small, and of no reputation :
   Yet do I not forget Thy commandments.

צ Thy righteousness is an everlasting righteousness,
   And Thy law is the truth.

צ Trouble and heaviness have taken hold upon me :
   Yet is my delight in Thy commandments.

צ The righteousness of Thy testimonies is everlasting :
   O grant me understanding, and I shall live.

ק I call with my whole heart :
   Hear me, O Lord ! I will keep Thy statutes.

ק Yea, even unto Thee do I call :
   Help me, and I shall keep Thy testimonies.

ק Early in the morning do I cry unto Thee :
   For in Thy word is my trust.

ק Mine eyes forestall the night watches,
   That I might meditate in Thy words.

 ק   Hear my voice, according to Thy loving-kindness :
      Quicken me, O Lord, according as Thou art wont.
 ק   They draw nigh that pursue wickedness,
      And that are far from Thy law.
 ק   But THOU art nigh at hand, O Lord !
      And all Thy commandments are true.
 ק   As concerning Thy testimonies I have known long since
      That Thou hast founded them for ever.

 ר   O consider mine adversity, and deliver me :
      For I do not forget Thy law.
 ר   Avenge Thou my cause, and deliver me :
      Quicken me, according to Thy word.
 ר   Salvation is far from the ungodly :
      For they regard not Thy statutes.
 ר   Great is Thy mercy, O Lord !
      Quicken me, according as Thou art wont.
 ר   Many there are that trouble me, and persecute me :
      Yet do I not swerve from Thy testimonies.
 ר   It grieveth me when I see the transgressors,
      Because they keep not Thy law.
 ר   Consider, O Lord, how I love Thy commandments ;
      O quicken me, according to Thy loving-kindness.
 ר   The whole of Thy word is true :   [more.
      And all the judgments of Thy righteousness endure for ever-

 ש   Princes have persecuted me without a cause :
      But my heart standeth in awe of Thy word.
 ש   I am as glad of Thy word,
      As one that findeth great spoil.
 ש   As for lies, I hate and abhor them :
      But Thy law do I love.
 ש   Seven times a day do I praise Thee,
      Because of Thy righteous judgments.
 ש   Great peace have they who love Thy law,
      And are not offended at it.
 ש   Lord, I have looked for Thy salvation,
      And done after Thy commandments.
 ש   My soul hath kept Thy testimonies,
      And loved them exceedingly.
 ש   I have kept Thy commandments and testimonies ;
      For all my ways are before Thee.

ﬨ Let my complaint come before Thee, O Lord !
　　Give me understanding, according to Thy word.
ﬨ Let my supplication come before Thee :
　　Deliver me according to Thy word.
ﬨ My lips shall speak of Thy praise,
　　When Thou hast taught me Thy statutes.
ﬨ Yea, my tongue shall speak of Thy word :
　　For all Thy commandments are righteous.
ﬨ Let Thine hand help me,
　　For I have chosen Thy commandments.
ﬨ I have longed for Thy salvation, O Lord ;
　　And in Thy law is my delight.
ﬨ O let my soul live, and it shall praise Thee ;
　　And Thy judgments shall help me.
ﬨ I have gone astray like a sheep that is lost :
　　O seek Thy servant, for I do not forget Thy commandments.

PSALM CXX.

A Song of the goings up.

WHEN I was in trouble, I called upon the Lord,
And He heard me.
Deliver my soul, ● Lord, from lying lips,
And from a deceitful tongue.
What shall be given unto thee,
Or what shall one add unto thee, thou deceitful tongue ?
Even sharp arrows of the Mighty ●ne,
With coals of juniper.
Alas, that I am constrained to dwell with Mesech,
That I have my habitation among the tents of Kedar !
My soul hath long dwelt among them
　　That are enemies to peace !
　　I am for peace :　　　　　　　　　　　　　　　[battle.
But when I speak unto them thereof, they make them ready to

PSALM CXXI.

A Song of the goings up.

I WILL lift up mine eyes unto the hills,
　From whence cometh my help.
　My help cometh even from THE LORD,
Who hath made heaven and earth !
He will not suffer thy foot to be moved,
　He that keepeth thee will not slumber :
　Behold, He will neither slumber nor sleep,
That keepeth Israel.
THE LORD is thy keeper !
THE LORD is thy defence upon thy right hand.
So that the sun shall not burn thee by day,
Neither the moon by night.
The Lord will keep thee from all evil :
(Yea, it is even) HE (that) will keep thy soul.
The Lord will keep thee in thy going out, and thy coming in,
From this time forth, for evermore.

PSALM CXXII.

A Song of the goings up.—By David.

I WAS glad when they said unto me—
" Let us go into the house of the Lord :
" Our feet shall stand in thy gates, O Jerusalem."
　Jerusalem is built as a city
　Which is compacted well together.
For thither the tribes *go up,*
Even the tribes of the Lord ;
(As) a testimony to Israel,
To give thanks unto the name of the Lord.
For there is the seat of judgment,
Even the seat of the house of David.

O pray for the peace of Jerusalem![1]
   They shall prosper that love thee.
Peace be within thy walls,
   And prosperity within thy palaces!
Because of my brethren and companions,
   I will say—"Peace be within thee!"
Because of the house of the Lord our God,
   I will pray for thy good.

[1] *Heb.* "O pray for the peace of *Abode of Peace.*"
This passage is often chosen by the seal engravers of Jerusalem as a motto, both for Jews and Christians.

Another favourite motto is that taken from Ps. cxxviii. 5, "The Lord bless thee out of Zion," or "The Lord from out of Zion give thee His blessing." This passage ought to have been included in the list of Antiphons in p. 15, as it occurs here, and in Ps. cxxxiv. 3. The seal, or device, has an olive branch in the middle, the emblem of *peace*, (Gen. viii. 11,) and the type of God's people. (Jer. xi. 16.)

But the subject generally selected by Christian engravers is the Cross of Jerusalem, with the name of the city above, surrounded by an olive garland. Not only was an olive tree the emblem of the city, when God's peace rested upon it; but olive trees formerly abounded in its neighbourhood, and are still grown there. We may presume that the Mount of Olives was formerly covered with these trees.

With this key to the significance of the olive, we can better understand the psalmist, when in Ps. cxxviii. he likens the children of a good man, living in the perpetual verdure of peace and love one with another, to the flourishing stems of an aged olive trunk, shooting upwards side by side, with their branches locked together in indissoluble unity.

PSALM CXXIII.

A Song of the goings up.

UNTO Thee, O Lord, lift I up mine eyes,
O Thou that dwellest in the heavens !
 Behold, even as the eyes of servants
  Look unto the hand of their masters,
 And as the eyes of a maiden
  Unto the hand of her mistress,
Even so our eyes wait upon the Lord our God,
Until He have mercy upon us.
Have mercy upon us, O Lord, have mercy upon us :
 For we are utterly filled with contempt.
 Our soul is utterly filled   [of the proud.
With the scornful derision of the wealthy, and with the contempt

PSALM CXXIV.

A Song of the goings up.—By David.

IF THE LORD had not been on our side,
 Now may Israel say :
If THE LORD had not been on our side,
 When men rose up against us—
Then they had swallowed us up alive,
 When they were so wrathfully displeased at us :
Then the waters had drowned us,
 The stream had gone over our soul.
 Then there had gone over our soul
Even the deep waters of the proud !

But praised be THE LORD,
Who hath not given us over for a prey unto their teeth.
Our soul is delivered, even as a bird out of the snare of the
The snare is broken, and we are delivered.   [fowler :

ohon. Our help standeth in the name of THE LORD,
Who hath made heaven and earth.

PSLAM CXXV.

A Song of the goings up.

THEY that trust in the Lord shall be as the Mount Sion,
Which shall not be removed, but standeth fast for ever.
The hills stand round about Jerusalem :
Even so doth the Lord stand round about His people,
  From this time forth for evermore.
For the rod of the ungodly cometh not into the lot of the righteous ;
Lest the righteous put their hands unto wickedness.
Do well, O Lord, unto those that are good,
Unto those that are upright of heart.

As for such as turn back unto their own wickedness,
iphon. The Lord will lead them forth with the evil-doers ;
  But peace shall be upon Israel.

Jerusalem, from the Mount of Olives.
From a sketch by the Author.

PSALM CXXVI.

A Song of the goings up.

WHEN the Lord turned the captivity of Sion,
Then were we like unto them that dream:
Then was our mouth filled with laughter,
And our tongue with joy.
Then said they among the heathen—
"The Lord hath done great things for them!"
The Lord HATH done great things for us!
Whereof we rejoice.

Turn our captivity, O Lord,
As the rivers in the south.
They that sow in tears,
Shall reap in joy.
He that walketh in the path of weeping,
Bearing forth good seed,
Shall come back in the path of rejoicing,
Bearing his sheaves with him.

PSALM CXXVII.

A Song of the goings up.—For Solomon.

EXCEPT the Lord build the house,
Its builders have but toiled in vain!
Except the Lord keep the city,
Its keepers have but watched in vain!
It is in vain that ye rise up early,
And that ye late take rest,
And that ye eat the bread of labour:
For (God) giveth to His beloved[1] sleep.

Lo, children are an heritage of the Lord,
And the fruit of the womb is (His) reward.
Like as arrows in the hand of a mighty man,
Even so are the young children.

[1] "Jedediah," the early name of Solomon. See Ps. xlv., *title* and note.

Happy is the man that hath his quiver full of them :
He shall not be ashamed ; but shall withstand his enemies in
[the gate.

PSALM CXXVIII.

A Song of the goings up.

Blessed are all they that fear the Lord,
That walk in His ways !
For thou shalt eat the labours of thy hands ;
Blessed art thou, and happy shalt thou be.
Thy wife shall be as the fruitful vine,
  Upon the walls of thine house :
Thy children like the olive stems,
  Round about thy table.

Old Olive-trunks—with interlacing stems.
Garden of Gethsemane. See p. 197.

Lo, thus shall the man be blessed
That feareth the Lord.
    The Lord from out of Sion shall give thee His blessing ;—
And Thou shalt see Jerusalem in prosperity
    All thy life long :
And thou shalt see thy children's children,
    And peace upon Israel.

PSALM CXXIX.

A Song of the goings up.

MANY a time have they afflicted me from my youth up,
    May Israel now say :
Many a time have they afflicted me from my youth up :
    But they have not (prevailed) against me.
The ploughers ploughed upon my back,
They made long furrows.
But the Lord is righteous,
And hath hewn the snares of the ungodly in pieces.

Let them be confounded, and turned backward,
    As many as have evil will at Sion :
Let them be as the grass growing upon the house-tops,
    Which withereth afore it be plucked up :
Whereof the mower filleth not his hand,
Neither he that bindeth up the sheaves, his bosom.
So that they say not, who pass by—" The Lord bless you !
" We bless you in the name of the Lord."

PSALM CXXX.

A Song of the goings up.

OUT of the deep have I called unto Thee, O Lord :
Lord, hear my voice !
O let Thine ears consider well
The voice of my complaint.

If Thou shouldst be extreme to mark iniquity, O Lord,
Lord, who may abide it !
But there is mercy with Thee :
Therefore shalt Thou be feared.

I wait for the Lord : my soul doth wait for Him :
In His word is my trust.
My soul waiteth for the Lord,
More than they who watch long for the morning.[1]

O Israel, trust in the Lord !
For with THE LORD there is mercy,
Antiphon. And in HIM is plenteous redemption.
And He will redeem Israel
From all his sins.

PSALM CXXXI.

A Song of the goings up.—By David.

LORD, I am not high-minded,
I have no proud look :
I do not exercise myself in great matters,
In things which are too high for me :
But I refrain my soul, and keep it low,
Even as a child which is weaned from his mother ;
My soul is even as a weaned child.

Antiphon. O Israel, trust in the Lord !
From this time forth, for evermore.

---

[1] *Heb.* "more than they who watch for the morning, watching for the morning."

PSALM CXXXII.

A Song of the goings up.

LORD, remember David,
And all his troubles.
How he sware unto the Lord,
And vowed a vow unto the mighty God of Jacob—
" I will not come within the habitation of my house,
" I will not go up to the couch of my bed :
" I will not give sleep to mine eyes,
" Nor slumber unto mine eyelids—
" Until I find out a place for (the temple of) the Lord,
" A habitation for the mighty God of Jacob."
Lo, we heard of the same at Ephrata ;
We found it in the fields of the wood.[1]
We will go into His tabernacle ;
We will bow down before His footstool.

Antiphon.

Arise, O Lord, into Thy resting-place,
Thou, and the ark of Thy strength ![2]
Let Thy priests be clothed with righteousness,
And let Thy saints shout with joyfulness.

For Thy servant David's sake
Turn not away the face of Thine anointed.
The Lord hath sworn[3] unto David, in His truth :
He will not turn from it :—
" Of the fruit of thy body will I set upon thy throne.
" If thy children will keep My covenant,
" And My testimonies that I shall learn them,
" Their children also shall sit upon thy throne for evermore."

For the Lord hath chosen Sion for Himself,
He hath longed for it as His habitation.
" This shall be My rest for ever :
" Here will I dwell, for I have longed for it.

---

[1] The fields outside of *Kirjath-jearim*, the " city of woods."
[2] Taken from the words used by Moses each time that the ark rested, (Num. x. 36,) and applied afterwards by Solomon. (2 Chron. vi. 41.)
[3] In the first paragraph David swears to the Lord. Here the Lord swears to David.

" I will bless her victuals with increase ;
" I will satisfy her poor with bread.
" I will clothe her priests with salvation,
" And her saints shall shout for joy, and rejoice with shouting
" There will I make the horn of David to flourish ;
" I have ordained a lamp for Mine anointed.
" As for his enemies, I will clothe them with shame ;
" But upon himself shall his crown flourish."

, The fourth paragraph is a *replica* of the second and third. It first
refers to God's house, then to his priests, and lastly to David and his posterity.

PSALM CXXXIII.

A Song of the goings up.—By David.

BEHOLD, how good and joyful a thing it is
For brethren to dwell together in unity.
It is like the precious ointment upon the head,
   Which fell down upon the beard, upon the beard of Aaron ;
   Which fell down to the skirts of his clothing.
It is like the dew of Hermon,
   Which falls down upon the hill of Sion.

Mount Lebanon, covered with clouds or dew,
As seen from Hermon, or Anti-Lebanon.
From a sketch by the Author.

For there the Lord promised His blessing,
Even life for evermore.

PSALM CXXXIV.

A Song of the goings up.

BEHOLD now, bless ye the Lord,
All ye servants of the Lord,
Antiphon. Ye that by night stand in the house of the Lord ;
Lift up your hands in the sanctuary,
And bless ye the Lord !

The Lord that made heaven and earth,
Give thee blessing out of Sion !

PSALM CXXXV.

Praise ye the Lord.

PRAISE ye the name of the Lord,
Praise it, O ye servants of the Lord !
Antiphon. Ye that stand in the house of the Lord,
In the courts of the house of our God.
Praise ye the Lord : for the Lord is gracious !
Sing psalms unto His name, for it is lovely.

For the Lord hath chosen Jacob unto Himself,
And Israel for His own possession.
For I know that the Lord is great,
And that our Lord is above all gods.
  Whatsoever the Lord pleased, that did He,
In heaven, and on earth,
In the sea, and in all deep places.
He bringeth forth the clouds from the ends of the earth,
He sendeth forth lightnings with the rain,
  Bringing the winds out of His treasure.

He smote the first-born of Egypt,
  Both of man and beast:
He sent tokens and wonders into the midst of thee, O Egypt,
  Upon Pharaoh, and all his servants:
He smote divers nations,
  And slew mighty kings:
{ Sihon, king of the Amorites,
  And Og, the king of Basan,
{ And all the kingdoms of Canaan:
And He gave their land to be a heritage,
Even a heritage unto Israel His people.

Antiphon. Thy name, O Lord, endureth for ever:
Thy remembrance, O Lord, from generation to generation!

For the Lord will avenge His people,
And be gracious unto His servants.

The idols of the heathen are but silver and gold,
The work of the hands of man!
    They have mouths—and yet they speak not;
      They have eyes—and yet they see not;
      They have ears—and yet they hear not;
    Neither is there any breath in their mouths.
They that make them are like unto them;
And so are all they that put their trust in them.

O house of Israel, bless ye the Lord!
O house of Aaron, bless ye the Lord!
O house of Levi, bless ye the Lord!
Antiphon. Ye that fear the Lord, bless ye the Lord!
Blessed be the Lord out of Sion,
Which dwelleth at Jerusalem!
    Praise ye the Lord!

PSALM CXXXVI.

[An antiphonal Psalm.]

O GIVE thanks unto the Lord : for He is gracious :
    And His mercy endureth for ever !

*Full
Antiphon.* O give thanks unto the God of all gods :
    For His mercy endureth for ever !
O give thanks unto the Lord of all lords :
    For His mercy endureth for ever !

To Him who only doeth great wonders :
    For His mercy endureth for ever !
To Him who by wisdom made the heavens :
    For His mercy endureth for ever !
To Him who stretched out the earth above the waters :
    For His mercy endureth for ever !
To Him who made great lights :
    For His mercy endureth for ever !
The sun, for the ruling of the day :
    For His mercy endureth for ever !
The moon and the stars, for the ruling of the night :
    For His mercy endureth for ever !
To Him who smote Egypt in their first-born :
    For His mercy endureth for ever !
And brought out Israel from the midst of them :
    For His mercy endureth for ever !
With a mighty hand, and with a stretched-out arm :
    For His mercy endureth for ever !
To Him who divided the Red sea into two parts :
    For His mercy endureth for ever !
And made Israel to go through the midst of it :
    For His mercy endureth for ever !
But who overthrew Pharaoh and his host in the Red sea :
    For His mercy endureth for ever !
To Him who led His people through the wilderness :
    For His mercy endureth for ever !

To Him who smote great kings :
    For His mercy endureth for ever !

Yea, and slew mighty kings :
　For His mercy endureth for ever !
Sihon, king of the Amorites :
　For His mercy endureth for ever !
And Og, the king of Basan :
　For His mercy endureth for ever !
And who gave their land to be a heritage :
　For His mercy endureth for ever !
Even a heritage unto Israel His servant :
　For His mercy endureth for ever !

Who remembered us in our low estate :
　For His mercy endureth for ever !
And hath delivered us from our enemies :
　For His mercy endureth for ever !
Who giveth food to all flesh :
　For His mercy endureth for ever !

Full　O give thanks unto the God of heaven :
Antiphon.　For His mercy endureth for ever !

PSALM CXXXVII.

BY the waters of Babylon we sat down ;
And we wept when we remembered (thee, O) Sion !
Upon the willows in the midst of it
We hanged up our harps !
For they that led us away captive asked of us then a song,
And they that wasted us, melody :—
　" Sing us one of the songs of Sion ! "

How shall we sing the Lord's song
In a strange land !
　If I forget thee, O Jerusalem,
May my right hand forget (how to play) ;[1]
May my tongue cleave to the roof of my mouth :

---

[1] *Aposiopesi.*

If I remember thee not,
If I think not of Jerusalem,
  Above my chief joy.

Remember, O Lord, the children of Edom,
In the day of Jerusalem:
Who said—" Raze it, raze it,
" Even to its foundations."
    O daughter of Babylon, who art to be destroyed,—
Blessed shall he be that rewardeth thee,
  As thou hast rewarded us :
Blessed shall he be that seizeth and dasheth
  Thy children against the stones.

PSALM CXXXVIII.

By David.

I WILL give thanks unto Thee, (O Lord),[1] with my whole heart :
Even before the gods will I sing psalms unto Thee.
I will worship toward Thy holy temple,
Antiphon. And I will give thanks unto Thy name,
Because of Thy mercy, and because of Thy truth :
Because[2] Thou hast magnified Thy name above all, (according to)
                                         [Thy promise.[3]

When I called upon Thee, Thou heardest me,
And enduedst my soul with much strength.
All the kings of the earth shall give thanks unto Thee, O Lord,
When they shall hear the words of Thy mouth.
Yea, they shall sing in the ways of the Lord,
That great is the glory of the Lord.
For though the Lord be high, yet hath He respect unto the lowly :
As for the proud, He beholdeth them afar off.

[1] *Aposiopesis.*
[2] Although this word is not the same in the Hebrew as in the parallel hemistich, the word "above," which follows, is the same word.
[3] This is the reading of Bishop Horsley. See the remarks of Hammond, Phillips, and Perowne, on this difficult verse.

Though I walk in the midst of trouble, yet wilt Thou refresh me:
Thy hand wilt Thou stretch forth upon the fury of mine enemies,
And Thy right hand will save me.
The Lord will accomplish for me:
O Lord, Thy mercy (endureth) for ever:
Forsake not then the work of Thine own hands.

PSALM CXXXIX.

To the chief Musician.—A Psalm of David.

O LORD!
on. ⎰Thou hast searched me out, and known me!
⎱Thou knowest my down-sitting, and mine up-rising,
 Thou understandest my thoughts long before.

Thou art about my path, and about my bed,
And Thou spiest out all my ways!
For lo, there is not a word in my tongue,
But Thou, O Lord, knowest it altogether!
Thou hast fashioned me behind and before,
And laid Thine hand upon me.

Such knowledge (is) too wonderful for me;
It is excellent: I cannot attain unto it!
Whither can I go then from Thy spirit?
Or whither can I flee from Thy presence?
If I climb up into heaven—Thou art there:
If I go down to hell—Thou (art there also).
If I take the wings of the morning,
If I dwell in the uttermost parts of the sea,
Even there shall Thy hand lead me,
And Thy right hand shall hold me!
If I say—surely the darkness shall cover me,
Then shall my night be turned to day:
⎰Yea, the darkness is no darkness to Thee,
⎱But the night is as clear as the day,
 The darkness as the light.
 For Thou hast possessed my reins,
 Thou hast covered me in my mother's womb.
 I will praise Thee: for I am fearfully and wonderfully made!
 Wonderful are Thy works: and that my soul knoweth well!

P 2

My bones were not hid from Thee,
When I was made secretly,
When I was fashioned beneath in the earth.
Thine eyes did see my embryo state,
And in Thy book were all (my members) written,
(As in) the days they were fashioned,
When as yet there was none of them.[1]

How dear are Thy counsels unto me, O God !
How great is the sum of them !
If I tell them, they are more in number than the sand !
When I wake up, Thou art still present in my thoughts !

Thou wilt surely slay the wicked, O God :
Depart from me, ye bloodthirsty men.
For they speak unrighteously against THEE ;
Thine enemies take (THY NAME) in vain.
Do not I hate them, O Lord, that hate Thee ?
And am I not grieved with them that rise up against Thee ?
Yea, I hate them right sore :
I count them as MINE enemies.

Antiphon.

Search me, O Lord, and examine[2] my heart ;
Prove me, and examine[2] my thoughts :
And see if there be any way of wickedness in me,
And lead me in the way everlasting.

PSALM CXL.

To the chief Musician.—A Psalm of David.

Antiphon.

DELIVER me, O Lord, from the evil man ;
Preserve me from the wicked man ;

Who imagine mischief in their heart :
They stir up strife all the day long.

[1] The passage might be understood as having a *prolepsis :*—" And in Thy book were all (my actions) written, (even the actions of) the days (when) they were fashioned, when as yet there was none of them :" but the context shows that it relates to the material structure of man.

[2,2] The same word, ידע, "know," or "examine," as in verse 1.

They have sharpened their tongues like a serpent :
Adders' poison is under their lips.

סלה

Antiphon. Keep me, O Lord, from the hands of the ungodly ;
Preserve me from the wicked man ;

Who have purposed to overthrow my goings ;
The proud have laid a snare for me, and cords :
They have spread a net by the way-side,
They have set traps for me.

סלה

  I said unto the Lord :—
Thou art my God !
Hear the voice of my prayer, O Lord.
O Lord my God ![1] thou strength of my salvation,
Thou hast covered my head in the day of battle.

Antiphon.   { Let not the ungodly have his desire, O Lord ;
Let not his devices prosper ;
Let them not be exalted.

סלה

  As for those that compass me about ;—
{ Let the mischief of their own lips cover them ;
Let hot burning coals fall upon them ;
Let them fall into pits, that they rise not up again.
A man full of words shall not prosper upon the earth :   [thrown.
A man full of violence shall be hunted by evil till he be over-

Sure I am that the Lord will maintain
The cause of the poor, and the right of the helpless.
Antiphon. The righteous shall give thanks unto Thy name,
And the just shall continue in Thy sight.

    [1] *Heb.* "Jehovah, Lord."

PSALM CXLI.

A Psalm of David.

LORD, I cry unto Thee!   Haste Thee unto me:
And consider my voice when I cry unto Thee.
Let my prayer be set forth in thy sight as the incense,
And the lifting up of my hands as an evening sacrifice.

Set a watch, O Lord, before my mouth;
Keep the door of my lips.
Let not my heart be inclined to any evil thing,
Let me not be occupied with ungodly works,
With the men that work wickedness;
And let me not partake of their pleasures.
If the righteous were to strike me, (I would regard it as) a mercy;
And if he were to rebuke me, (I would regard it as) oil upon the head:
(So even the wickedness of the ungodly) shall not break my head;
But their wickedness shall provoke only to prayer.[1]
(When) their princes were cast down by the side of the rock,
They listened to my words, for they were sweet:[2]
(Though) our bones (then) lay scattered at the mouth of the pit,
Like as when one breaketh and heweth (wood) upon the earth.

But unto THEE, O Lord God![3] do I direct mine eyes:
In THEE is my trust: O cast not out my soul.
Keep me from the snare which they have laid for me,
And from the traps of the wicked doers.

Antiphon. Let the ungodly fall into their own nets together,
And let me ever escape them.

---

[1] See Ps. cix. 4:—"In return for my love, they are mine adversaries:
   But I betake myself unto prayer."
[2] See 1 Sam. xxiv., xxvi.   [3] *Heb.* "Jehovah, Lord."

PSALM CXLII.

'A Psalm of instruction. — By David.   A prayer when he was in the cave.

WITH my voice unto the Lord did I cry;
With my voice unto the Lord did I make my supplication :
I poured out my complaint before Him ;
I showed Him of my trouble.
When my spirit was in heaviness,
    Thou knewest my path :
    In the way wherein I walked
Have they privily laid a snare for me.
I looked on my right hand,
    But there was no man that would know me :
I had no place to flee unto;
    And there was no man that cared for my soul.

    I cried unto THEE, O Lord !   I said—
THOU art my refuge,
And my portion in the land of the living.
Consider my complaint,
For I am brought very low.
Deliver me from my persecutors,
For they are too strong for me.
Bring my soul out of prison,
That I may give thanks unto Thy name.

    The righteous [1] shall compass me about :
antiphon. For Thou wilt deal bountifully with me !

[1] Instead of the *wicked*, as above, and in the former Psalm.

*** This Psalm exhibits the *replica*.

PSALM CXLIII.

A Psalm of David.

Antiphon.
HEAR my prayer, O Lord !
Give ear to my supplications :
Hearken unto me for Thy truth and righteousness' sake.
And enter not into judgment with Thy servant :
For in Thy sight shall no man living be justified.

For the enemy hath persecuted my soul,
He hath smitten my life down to the ground :
He hath laid me in the lowest darkness,
As the men which have been long dead.
Therefore is my spirit vexed within me,
And my heart within me is desolate.
I remember the time past,
I muse upon all Thy works,
I meditate on the works of Thy hands :
I stretch forth my hands unto Thee,
My soul gaspeth for Thee as a thirsty land.

סלה

Antiphon.
Hear me, O Lord, and that soon,
    For my spirit waxeth faint :
Hide not Thy face from me,
    Lest I be like unto them that go down into the pit.

O let me hear Thy loving-kindness betimes in the morning,
    For in THEE is my trust :
Show Thou me the way that I should walk in :
    For I lift up my soul unto THEE.
Deliver me, O Lord, from mine enemies,
    For I flee unto THEE to hide me.
Teach me to do Thy will,
    For THOU art my God.
Let Thy loving spirit lead me forth
Into a land of quietness.
Quicken me, O Lord, for Thy name's sake,
And for Thy righteousness' sake bring my soul out of trouble.
And of Thy goodness cut off mine enemies,
And destroy all them that vex my soul ;
    For I am Thy servant.

PSALM CXLIV.

By David.

BLESSED be the Lord, my strength !
Who teacheth my hands to war,
And my fingers to fight.
Proem. My hope and my fortress,
My castle and deliverer,
My defender in whom I trust,
Who subdueth my people that is under me.

LORD, what is man,[1] that Thou regardest him ?
Or the son of man,[2] that Thou thinkest of him ?
Man is like a thing of nought :
His time passeth away like a shadow !
Bow Thy heavens, O Lord, and come down :
Touch the mountains, and they shall smoke.
Cast forth Thy lightnings, and scatter them :
Shoot out Thine arrows, and destroy them.

Send down Thy hand from above :
Save and deliver me
From the great waterfloods,
ntiphon. From the hands of strange children ;[3]
Whose mouth talketh of vanity,
And whose right hand is a right hand of falsehood.

I will sing a new song unto Thee, O God !
I will sing psalms unto Thee upon a ten-(stringed) lute :
Who giveth victory unto kings,
Who hath delivered David Thy servant from the peril of the sword.

Save and deliver me
From the hands of strange children ;
ntiphon. Whose mouth talketh of vanity,
And whose right hand is a right hand of falsehood.

---

[1] Man of dust, "*Adam.*"   [2] Man of distinction, "*Eesh.*"
[3] *Heb.* "Sons of the stranger."

That our sons may be as plants
   Which grow up (vigorously) in their youth
That our daughters may be as corner-stones,
   Which are fitted for the temple.
That our garners may be full,
   Affording all manner of store:
That our sheep may bring forth thousands,
   And ten thousands in our fields.[1]
That our oxen may be heavy laden,
That there be no breaking down:
And that there be no going forth,
And no complaining in our streets.

Antiphon.

Blessed are the people who are in such a case:
Blessed are the people who have THE LORD for their God!

PSALM CXLV.

Praise of David.

Proem.

א I WILL magnify Thee, O God my King!
   I will bless Thy name for ever and ever!
ב Every day will I give thanks unto Thee;
   I will praise Thy name for ever and ever!

ג GREAT is the Lord, and highly to be praised.
   There is no end of His greatness!
ד One generation shall praise Thy works unto another,
   And shall declare Thy power!
ה As for me, I will be talking of Thy worship,
   Thy glory, Thy praise, and wondrous works!
ו So that man shall speak of the might of Thy marvellous acts,
   And I will also tell of Thy greatness!
ז The memorial of Thine abundant kindness shall be showed,
   And men shall sing of Thy righteousness.

ח Gracious and merciful is the Lord;
   Long-suffering, and of great goodness!
Antiphon. ט Loving is the Lord to every man:
   And His mercy is over all His works!

[1] *Heb.* "Open places." See Job, v. 10; Prov. viii. 26.

א All Thy works praise Thee, O Lord !
    And Thy saints give thanks unto Thee.
כ They show the glory of Thy kingdom,
    And talk of Thy power !
ל That Thy power, Thy glory, and the mightiness of Thy kingdom
    Might be known unto men.
מ Thy kingdom is an everlasting kingdom ;
    And Thy dominion endureth from generation to generation !

Antiphon. נ [Faithful is the Lord in His words,
    And holy in all His works ! [1]]

ס The Lord upholdeth all such as fall,
    And lifteth up all those that are bowed down.
ע The eyes of all wait upon THEE, O Lord :
    And Thou givest them their meat in due season !
פ Thou openest Thy hand,
    And fillest all things living with plenteousness !

Antiphon. צ Righteous is the Lord in all His ways !
    And holy in all His works !

ק The Lord is nigh unto all them that call upon Him :
    Yea, to all such as call upon Him faithfully.
ר He will fulfil the desire of them that fear Him :
    He also will hear their cry, and will help them.
    The Lord preserveth all them that love Him ;
    But scattereth abroad all the ungodly.

Antiphon. ת My mouth shall speak the praise of the Lord !
    And let all flesh give thanks unto His holy name,
        For ever, and ever !

[1] This verse, which appears in the Septuagint, is found also in the Syrian, Arabic, and Vulgate versions, and in one Hebrew MS. of the fourteenth century. It is vindicated by the learned Dr. Hammond. Though a fair presumption that the Seventy may have interpolated it in order to bring in the deficient letter *Nun*, it is equally fair to presume that the letter was not originally omitted, and that it might have been preserved in one copy which the Seventy consulted. Another presumption in its favour is that it forms an antiphon, which it is not likely that the Seventy would have thought of, had they restored the letter.

PSALM CXLVI.

PRAISE ye the Lord !
Praise the Lord, O my soul !
I will praise my God while I live :
I will sing psalms to my God while I have my being.

O put not your trust in princes, or in any child of man ;
For there is no help in them :
For when the breath of man goeth forth, he shall turn again to his
And in that day all his thoughts perish !   [earth,

Blessed is he that hath the God of Jacob for his help,
And whose hope is in the Lord his God ;
Who made heaven and earth,
The sea, and all that therein is,
    Who keepeth His promise for ever.
Who helpeth them to right that suffer wrong,
Who feedeth the hungry.
The Lord looseth men out of prison,
The Lord giveth sight to the blind :
The Lord helpeth them that are fallen,
The Lord careth for the strangers :
He raiseth the fatherless and widow ;
(While) the way of the ungodly He turneth upside down.

The Lord shall reign for ever !
Thy God, O Sion, from generation to generation !
    Praise ye the Lord !

PSALM CXLVII.

P̲RAISE ye the Lord!

utiphon. For it is a good thing to sing psalms unto our God;
For it is a joyful and pleasant thing to sing praises.

The Lord doth build up Jerusalem,
He doth gather together the outcasts of Israel.
He healeth those that are broken in heart,
He bindeth up all their sorrows.
He telleth the number of the stars,
He calleth them all by their names.
Great is our Lord, and great is His power:
Yea, and His wisdom is infinite!
The Lord setteth up the meek:
He casteth the ungodly down to the ground.

ntiphon. O raise the antiphon unto the Lord, with thanksgiving:
Sing psalms upon the harp unto our God!

Who covereth the heaven with clouds,
Who prepareth rain for the earth:
Who maketh grass to grow upon the mountains for the cattle,
Their food for the young ravens that call upon him.
He hath no pleasure in the strength of a horse,
He hath no delight in any man's legs:
But the Lord's delight is in them that fear Him,
In them that put their trust in His mercy.

ntiphon. Praise the Lord, O Jerusalem:
Praise thy God, O Sion!

For He hath made fast the bars of thy gates,
He hath blessed thy children within thee.
Who maketh peace in thy borders,
    He filleth thee with the flower of wheat.
Who sendeth forth His commandment upon earth;
    His word runneth very swiftly.
Who giveth snow like wool;
    He scattereth the hoar-frost like ashes.

Who casteth forth His ice like morsels :
Who is able to abide His frost ?
He sendeth out His word, and melteth them :
He bloweth with His wind, and the waters flow.
Who showed His word unto Jacob,
His statutes and ordinances unto Israel.

Epiphonem.   He hath not dealt so with any nation :
        Neither have (the heathen) knowledge of His laws.

Antiphon.   Praise ye the Lord !

PSALM CXLVIII.

Antiphor.   Praise ye the Lord !

PRAISE the Lord, in the heavens,
Praise Him, in the height !
Praise Him, all ye angels of His,
Praise Him, all His hosts !
Praise Him, sun and moon,
Praise Him, all ye stars of light !
Praise Him, ye heaven of heavens,
And ye waters that are above the heavens !
    Let them praise the name of the Lord ;
    For He commanded, and they were created !
    He hath made them fast for ever and ever :
    He hath given them a law which shall not be broken !

Praise the Lord, upon earth,
Ye dragons, and all deeps !
Fire and hail, snow and vapours,
Wind and storm, fulfilling His word !
Mountains and all hills,
Fruitful trees and all cedars,
Beasts and all cattle,
Creeping things, and fowls of the air ;
Kings of the earth, and all peoples,
Princes, and all judges of the world :
Young men and maidens,
Old men and children—
    Praise the name of the Lord !

For His name only is excellent,
His praise above heaven and earth !
He will exalt the horn of His people,
All His saints shall praise Him :
Even the children of Israel,
A people dear unto Him !

Antiphon.   Praise ye the Lord !

PSALM CXLIX.

Antiphon.   Praise ye the Lord !

O SING unto the Lord a new song,
(Sing to) His praise in the congregation of the saints !

Let Israel rejoice in Him that made him,
Let the children of Sion be joyful in their King !
Let them praise His name in the dance,
Let them sing psalms unto Him with tabret and harp :
For the Lord hath pleasure in His people,
He will give help to the meek-hearted.
Let the saints be joyful with glory,
Let them rejoice in their beds :
Let the praises of God be in their mouths,
And a two-edged sword in their hands,
To be avenged of the heathen,
And to rebuke the people :
To bind their kings with chains,
And their nobles with links of iron :
To execute on them the judgment written—
" This honour have all His saints."

Antiphon.   Praise ye the Lord !

PSALM CL.

[An Antiphon.]

Praise ye the Lord !

PRAISE God in His holiness,
Praise Him in the firmament of His power !
Praise Him in His noble acts,
Praise Him according to His excellent greatness !
Praise Him with the sound of the trumpet,
Praise Him upon the lute and harp :
Praise Him with the cymbals and dances,
Praise Him on the stringed-instruments and pipes :
Praise Him upon the well-tuned cymbals,
Praise Him upon the loud cymbals.

Epiphonem. Let everything that hath breath
Praise the Lord !

Antiphon. Praise ye the Lord.

ESSAY I.

THE PSALMS OF DAVID RESTORED TO DAVID.

I.

THE PSALMS OF DAVID RESTORED TO DAVID.

OF the hundred and fifty psalms in the Book of Psalms exactly one hundred have titles, and of these latter seventy-three are assigned to David, and twenty-seven have other names attached. As, therefore, about one half of the psalms are not attributed to David, and some of them bear other names, commentators have, in all ages of the Church, been permitted to assume that any of the fifty psalms which are without titles may be by unknown authors, and that they may have been written at various times. As more and more learning and investigation have been made to bear upon the subject, attention has been directed to peculiarities of style in certain psalms, to supposed references to historical events, to similarity to other psalms and to other portions of Scripture ; and the result has been that many of the psalms which bear the name of David are "proved" by this "internal evidence" to be not by him ; till at last few or no psalms remain which by the consent of all writers we can confidently assign to him whose name they bear. Carried away by the great learning of these writers, we have accepted their conclusions, and taken their arguments as granted : so that now if any writer in the present day ventures to express a contrary opinion, he is immediately refuted by a reference to the *dicta* of these learned men. But this deference to the assertions of these great writers has been too easily conceded : and it is the object of the present essay to show that some of the principal arguments relied on by them are not conclusive, while others may be adduced of a contrary character : by which means we shall come back to the old opinion, that, though some of the psalms were probably written by other authors, the great bulk of the psalms were written by David, and the book as a whole may be justly attributed to the royal psalmist.

The Psalms are called the "Psalms of David," because the greater part of them were supposed to be written by him, and one half of them, as we have seen, bear his name. Some of them, however, bear the names of his three directors of the choir, Asaph, Heman, and Ethan; some appear to be written by the sons of Korah; one bears the name of Moses; two that of Solomon; while others have no name attached to them. But although these names appear to the Psalms, it is by no means certain that they represent the authors: for the same particle ל *le*, which is attached to them may be translated *of*, *by*, *to*, or *for*; and thus we find the word very properly rendered in the margin of our Bibles, with this double interpretation, whenever it precedes any other name than that of David. One example will explain this ambiguity. In the heading of the eighty-eighth psalm we have—"A psalm ל *for* the sons of Korah, ל *to* the chief musician upon Mahalath, ל *for* antiphonal response, a song of instruction, ל *to* or *of* Heman the Ezrahite." It is therefore evident that the particle ל in front of a name, as "a psalm ל Asaph," does not necessarily prove that the psalm was written *by* Asaph, for it might have been written *to* or *for* Asaph, as one of the three directors of the choir. This is further evident from 1 Chron. xvi. 7, where we read that "David delivered this psalm into the hands of Asaph and his brethren."[1] On the other hand, it would appear from 2 Chron. xxix. 30, where we are told that Hezekiah sang praises unto the Lord "in the words of David and of Asaph the seer," that Asaph did compose some psalms; unless, indeed, as is probable, that in Hezekiah's time these psalms were attributed to Asaph simply from the ambiguity of the particle ל *le*. This Asaph, from being called a seer, has been erroneously supposed to have been a different Asaph to David's chief singer, and to have lived in the time of Hezekiah: while others, from the mournful character of his psalms, have placed him in the time of the Babylonian captivity. Now if Asaph is supposed to have lived at the time of the "Babylonian captivity," the reference to an Asaph living in the time of Hezekiah

---

[1] Hammond indeed objects from this very circumstance, that as Ps. xcvi. cv. and cvi. are not inscribed "To Asaph," therefore the inscription in other psalms of לאסף cannot be taken to mean *To* Asaph, but *Of* Asaph. But this objection is easily answered: for if these particular psalms do not bear the inscription of "To Asaph," neither do they bear the inscription "Of" or "By David," although we are informed of both these facts: for as the absence of David's name cannot disprove their being his, when we know from other authority that they were written by him; so the absence of Asaph's name cannot disprove their being addressed to him, when we learn from the above passage that they were so addressed.

is of no use to us. There was, indeed, an earlier Babylonian captivity, but this did not take place in the reign of Hezekiah, but in that of his successor, Manasseh : besides which, we read only of the king being taken prisoner. (2 Chron. xxxiii. 11.) It is true that Israel was taken captive in the reign of Hoshea, (2 Kings xvii. xviii.,) who was contemporary with Hezekiah : but then it must be remembered that these kingdoms of Judah and Israel were at continual enmity ; and that only fifteen years before, 120,000 men of Judah were slain by the men of Israel, and 200,000 carried away captive : (2 Chron. xxviii:) besides which, even the captivity of Israel was five years after the occasion when Hezekiah ordered " the psalms of David and of Asaph the seer " to be sung. As regards Hezekiah, there was an Asaph whose name is connected with his reign : but he is not called a seer, and we find but one mention of his name ; it is when we are told that " Joah the son of Asaph was Recorder ; " (2 Kings xviii. 18, 37 ;) whose office probably his father Asaph had held before him : moreover, as his son was contemporary with Hezekiah, it is possible that he himself might then have been dead. As the name of Asaph, therefore, is no authority for supposing that the psalm-writer of that name lived in the time of Hezekiah ;—although we know from Is. xxxviii. 20, that Hezekiah wrote psalms or songs, or ordered them to be written, for the service of the temple worship ;—so we shall find that the title of seer given to Asaph in 2 Chron. xxix. 30, is no authority for supposing him to be a different person from David's chief singer. The three directors of the choir appointed by David were Asaph, Heman, and Jeduthun. Heman is called a seer in 1 Chron. xxv. 5 ; and Jeduthun is called a seer in 2 Chron. xxxv. 15. What wonder then that Asaph also should be a seer ? Possibly they were of the school of the prophets,[1] out of which God was pleased to call up one from among the rest, to give forth his prophecies, on particular occasions.[2]

If we have had to overcome difficulties in determining the individuality of Asaph, we have equal apparent difficulty respecting that of Heman and Ethan, whose names are attached to Ps.

[1] 1 Sam. x. 5 ; xix. 20—24 ; 2 Kings ii. 3—15.

[2] 1 Kings xx. 35 ; 2 Kings ix. 1—10. Some confirmation of this attribution to David or David's time, of the psalms which bear the name of Asaph, arises from the peculiar structure of the *epanodos*, which naturally leads us to suppose that all psalms in which we find this peculiarity were written by the same author. Now, Ps. xxix. and xxx. were written by David, and it is probable therefore that Ps. lxvii. and lxxvii., where we also find this peculiarity, were likewise written by David, though one of these has no title, and the other bears the name of Asaph.

lxxxviii. and lxxxix., and who are called Ezrahites. Now it so
happens that in 1 Kings iv. 31, we read that Solomon "was wiser
than all men, than Ethan the Ezrahite, and Heman, and Chalcol,
and Darda, the sons of Mahol ; "[1] while in 1 Chron. ii. 6, we find
that "the sons of Zerah (Judah's son) were Zimri, and Ethan, and
Heman, and Calcol, and Dara;" who are called Ezrahites para-
gogically from Zerah their father. This has led the compiler of the
Book of Psalms to place these two psalms, lxxxviii. and lxxxix.,
next to Ps. xc., which is a psalm of Moses, and prior to his,
as being of greater antiquity : and so Athanasius and Eusebius
held them to be, notwithstanding the frequent mention of David's
name in Ps. lxxxix., which is, of course, a proof to the contrary. The coincidence of these names is certainly very remarkable : but the internal character of the two psalms forbids us to
attribute them to an earlier period than that of David. If it be
objected, why then are Heman and Ethan called Ezrahites, when
we know from 1 Chron. vi. that they were Levites, and not descended from Judah ; Asaph being descended from Gershon, the
eldest son of Levi ; Heman being the descendant of Kohath, the
second son ; and Ethan being descended from Merari, the youngest
son of Levi?—we might ask, Why is only Ethan called an Ezrahite
in 1 Kings iv. 31, and not Heman, and Chalcol, and Darda also ?
This difficulty has led to various ways of accounting for the same ,
and Heman and Ethan have been supposed to be called Ezrahites,
not from family descent, but from some other cause. Good supposes the word to mean *encircled with a chaplet*, as a *Laureate ;*
Hengstenberg supposes Heman and Ethan to have been living
among the descendants of Zerah, Judah's son, and so bearing their
name ; and adduces instances of like effect ;[2] while Weiss also believes
them to be *sojourners*, as all the Levites were, and assigns this as the
reason, deriving the name from Ezrah, to *sojourn*. The Bishop of
Bath and Wells (Lord Arthur C. Hervey) suggests that " Heman
the Kohathite, or his father, (and of course we may suppose the
same of Ethan the Merariite,) married an heiress of the house of
Zerah, as the sons of Hakkaz (?) did of the house of Barzillai, (see
Ez. ii. 61 ; Neh. vii. 63,) and was so reckoned in the genealogy
of Zerah, and was called after their name."[3]   "Or it might

---

[1] Mahol is supposed to be Zerah's wife.
[2] "There are not wanting examples of Levites being spoken of as belonging
to the family of which, in their capacity of citizens, they formed part. Thus,
Samuel the Levite, 1 Sam. i. 1, is called an Ephraimite ; and in Judges xvii. 7
there follows immediately after the words 'of the family of Judah,' the remark,
' who was a Levite, and he sojourned there.' " (On Ps. lxxxviii.)
[3] Smith's *Dict. of the Bible*, art. "Heman."

also be possible that Heman and Ethan were properly of the tribe of Judah, but on account of their gift of song were incorporated with the Levitical family of singers."[1]   Be this as it may, there is no doubt that the Heman and Ethan whose names are attached to these two psalms were the same Heman and Ethan who were directors of the choir in the time of David.   But here we meet with a fresh difficulty : for while in 1 Chron. vi. 44, and xv. 17, 19, the three chiefs or directors are called Heman, Asaph, and Ethan ; in other passages, as in 1 Chron. xii. 41, 42 ; xxv. 1 ; 2 Chron. v. 12 ; xxix. 13, 14 ; and xxxv. 15, they are called Asaph, Heman, and Jeduthun ; and in 1 Chron. xxv. 6, Asaph, Jeduthun, and Heman.   Ethan and Jeduthun are therefore identical ; and nothing is commoner in the Old Testament than for the same person to have two names; as Abram, Jacob, Solomon, and Daniel had.[2]   Ethan, then, whose name signified *strong*, appears to have had the name of Jed-Ethan, or Jeduthun, given him, signifying, *who giveth praise*, because it was his duty to " prophesy with a harp, to give thanks, and to *praise* the Lord." (1 Chron. xxv. 3.) A further difficulty arises with regard to the name of Jeduthun, —that although Ps. xxxix. is headed ל To Jeduthun, Ps. lxii. and lxxvii. are headed על *Upon* Jeduthun, as though it were the name of some musical instrument.   Some suppose the letter על to have been inserted by copyists in mistake, others that some ellipsis takes place here : but all are agreed that the true meaning is that given by our translators—*To* Jeduthun.   Heman and Ethan, or Jeduthun, being seers, it is *possible* that they may have written these two psalms, as Asaph may have written others ; yet it seems probable from the subject of the psalms that David was the author ; and that, as he addressed some of his psalms ל *To* the chief musician ; ל *To* Jeduthun ; ל *For* the sons of Korah ; so in these instances it may have been ל *To* Heman ; ל *To* Ethan.

In the same manner we may conclude that Ps. lxxii. and cxxvii. were addressed ל *To* Solomon, and not *By* Solomon.   So, in like manner, it does not appear at all certain that the psalms which bear the name of Asaph were composed by him.   It is true that the compiler of the Book of Chronicles says that Hezekiah praised God in the words of David and of Asaph the seer.   But we must remember that Hezekiah lived three hundred years after the time of David ; and it is probable that the psalms bearing Asaph's name were attributed to him in his reign, only for the same reason that they have

[1] *Impl. Bible Dict.*, art. " Heman."
[2] See also numerous examples in the margin of our Bible, in the genealogies given in the First Book of Chronicles.

been attributed to him subsequently—because they have the particle
ל before Asaph's name, which, as we have seen, may be either *by*
or *to*. And only one hundred years after the time of Hezekiah
we find that all the book of the law was lost, and all knowledge of
God's Word forgotten. (2 Chron. xxiv.) Moreover we know that
David "delivered his psalms into the hands of Asaph and his
brethren," and that he "praised by their ministry." (2 Chron.
vii. 6.) We have psalms To Jeduthun, To the chief musician,
For the sons of Korah: which of the psalms are we to put down
as "To Asaph," as "delivered into his hands" for the service of
song? Doubtless those which bear his name. It will thus be seen
that it is quite possible, and indeed probable, that David may have
been the author of psalms which have other names attached to
them, and that they were merely delivered to them to be set to
music, for the arrangement of the solos, and for the chorus.

We have said that the preposition *le* makes it probable that
Ps. lxxii. and cxxvii. were addressed *To* Solomon, and not
written *by* Solomon. Let us now examine these psalms, together
with Ps. xlv., "a song of the beloved," which also relates to Solomon. On reading these psalms carefully, with the observations we
have made on the latter psalm, it will be evident that they were all
written shortly before the death of David; when, his life drawing
to a close, he summed up all God's gracious deliverances and manifold blessings to him; he thought of his son who was to succeed
him, according to God's promise; and, according to that same
promise, of the Messiah who was to spring from his loins. He
poured out a prayer and prophecy on behalf of his son, in two of
these psalms, (lxxii. and xlv.,) in the latter of which especially his
thoughts were often directed to the Messiah; and he ends each
psalm with praise to God; thus acknowledging God as the only
giver of all good.

> Blessed be the Lord God, the God of Israel,
> Which only doeth wondrous things:
> And blessed be the name of His majesty for ever,
> And let all the earth be filled with His majesty.
> > Amen, and Amen.
> I will remember THY name
> > From generation to generation:
> Therefore shall the people give thanks unto Thee
> For ever and ever.

And as Dædalus furnished wings for Icarus, and then cautioned
him how to use them, which caution was disregarded by his son:
so we find David giving the kingdom to Solomon, and cautioning

him in like manner : which caution was in like manner disregarded, so far as fidelity to God was concerned.   In Ps. cxxvii. he says—

> Except the Lord build the house,
>   Their labour is but lost that build it :
> Except the Lord keep the city,
>   The watchman waketh but in vain.

And then, blessing his son in the words of Ps. lxxii., he adds :

> The prayers of David the son of Jesse are ended.[1]

With this agrees what we read in the Second Book of Samuel—

> Now these be the last words of David :—
> David the son of Jesse said,
> And the man who was raised up on high ;
> The anointed of the God of Jacob,
> And the sweet psalmist of Israel said :
> The Spirit of the Lord spake by me,
> And His word was in my tongue ;
> The God of Israel said,
> The Rock of Israel spake to me—

Nothing can exceed the solemnity with which these words are brought out.   We expect what he has to say to follow after every one of the nine preceding lines ; but line follows after line, and still it is delayed ; and at last we find that, instead of its proceeding from David himself, it proceeds from the Spirit of the Lord speaking in him : it proceeds from God himself.   And what are these words ?   They are an injunction to him who is anointed king, to rule in justice and righteousness ; followed by an assurance of blessing and prosperity from God, if he does so :—

> He that ruleth over men must be just,
> Ruling in the fear of God.
> And he shall be as the light of the morning, when the sun ariseth,
> Even a morning without clouds :
> As the tender grass springing out of the earth,
> By clear shining after rain.   (2 Sam. xxiii. 1—4.)

And now if we turn back to the seventy-second psalm, we see how identical are the thoughts expressed.   The psalmist begins by praying God to fill the heart of the king, and the king's son, with righteousness and judgment ; and then describes the blessings which will follow.   In each case David calls himself " David the son of Jesse : " above he likens his son to the " tender grass springing out

[1] Calvin also makes this verse apply to the psalm itself, not to the book.

of the earth, by clear shining after rain ; " and in the psalm he
describes him as "coming down like rain upon the moist grass,
even as the showers which water the earth : " in the history he
concludes by saying—"Now these be the last words of David the
son of Jesse," and he concludes the psalm by saying—"The prayers
of David the son of Jesse are ended."

If this reasoning be admitted, if these psalms were written of or
concerning Solomon, and not by Solomon, then we must see that
the *lamed* is of no authority for supposing that where it is joined
to the names of Asaph, Ethan, Heman, or the sons of Korah in
certain psalms, it denotes that these psalms were written *by* them,
instead of being directed *to* them.

Let us now see whether there is any authority for supposing
that the psalms which bear the name of "the sons of Korah"
were written *by* them, instead of *for* them. The twelve psalms,
(xlii.[1]—xlix., lxxxiv.—lxxxviii.,) in the inscriptions of which the
sons of Korah are referred to, will be found on examination to
accord perfectly with the various phases of David's life, and with
the various emotions of his heart :—now oppressed ; now pouring
out his thanksgivings to God ; now describing his personal individual longing for God's sanctuary from which he is separated ; now
full of joyful exultation on behalf of Sion ; now cast down and
afflicted ; now trustful in God's help, and defiant and full of disdain
of all God's enemies ; now looking forward (as we have seen in Ps.
xlv.) with pride and pleasure to the thought of his son's succeeding
him, and prophesying of the Messiah who should come after him.
Some writers indeed have supposed all these psalms to be written
by the Maccabees, but the general opinion has been that Ps. xliv.
belongs to the time of the Babylonian captivity, and Ps. lxxxv. to
the time of the return from that captivity.

Although David's choir of two hundred and eighty-eight singers
was divided into twenty-four lots of twelve singers each, represent-
ing the four sons of Asaph, the six of Jeduthun, and the fourteen
of Heman the descendant of Korah, we find that Asaph's choir,
which was in such a minority, outlived its rivals. Notwithstanding
the idolatries introduced by Solomon and his descendants, the
triple choir of Asaph, Jeduthun, and Heman, was still in being in
the reign of Jehoshaphat, B.C. 896,[2] and even so late as the reign of
Hezekiah, B.C. 726.[3] But one hundred years after this, in the

---

[1] Of the first psalms in this group, xlii., xliii., Dr. Kay says—"The
situation is that of David in 2 Sam. xv. 25."

[2] 2 Chron. xx. 19.   [3] 2 Chron. xxix. 12—14.

reign of Josiah, B.C. 623, the choirs of Jeduthun and of the sons of Korah had disappeared,[1] leaving only the choir of the sons of Asaph. This was only thirty-five years before the captivity, which happened in his son's time; on returning from which, in the time of Zerubbabel, B.C. 536, we find only the choir of the sons of Asaph,[2] which was still alone in the time of Nehemiah, B.C. 445,[3] unless indeed the choir of Jeduthun had then revived, which is not probable.[4] Thus we see that the choir of the sons of Korah had disappeared for about two hundred years, and consequently that these psalms could not have been written by the sons of Korah[5] during or after the return from the captivity. We must go back, therefore, to the time of David: a conclusion which is confirmed by the title of the eighty-eighth psalm, which is addressed "ל *For* the sons of Korah. ל *To* the chief musician . . . . Maschil ל *Of* Heman the Ezrahite." A further objection has been noticed by Delitzsch, who observes[6]:—"It is certainly remarkable that instead of an author, it is always the family that is named." But the fact just noted that one of those psalms bearing the name of the sons of Korah is said to be by Heman the Ezrahite, shows that the inscription must be read "*To* or *for* the sons of Korah." Otherwise we might indeed wonder, if all these psalms had been *by* the sons of Korah, that we have none by the *sons of* Asaph, when we know that his descendants retained their office for many generations; especially when it is believed by these writers that one of his most eminent descendants was inspired by God to write psalms in the reign of Hezekiah. If it be still pressed upon us that some of these psalms, especially the forty-fourth[7] and

---

[1] 2 Chron. xxxv. 15.   [2] Ezra ii. 41, iii. 10; Neh. vii. 44.

[3] Neh. xii. 35, 36.   [4] Comp. Neh. xi. 17 and 22.

[5] As for the psalms bearing the names of "the sons of Corah, Eman, Ethan, and Jeduthun, it cannot be concluded that those psalms were composed by them; it being more probable that they were to be sung by them—as of the sons of Corah seems clear—or that it is upon some other account that their names are there mentioned." Hammond, *Annot. on Titles of Ps.* Delitzsch also shows how Ps. lxxxv. and lxxxvii., both of which bear the name of the sons of Korah, "have points of contact" with Ps. lxxxvi., which is by David; and how Ps. xlix., also bearing the same title, (sons of Korah,) "in its didactic character harmonizes with the psalms of the time of David."

[6] *Bibl. Com.* ii. 52.

[7] "A series of expositors from Calvin to Hitzig have referred this psalm to the times of the Maccabees." See this disproved by Hengstenberg. Others, looking at the objections to this theory, attribute it to the time of Jehoiakim or his son Jehoiachin, while others, as De Burgh, seeing these dates fit in no better, put it down as prophetical of the times of the early

eighty-fifth,[1] refer to and mention a " captivity ;" we would answer first, as we shall presently see, that there was a captivity in the time of David ; and secondly, that the word שְׁבוּת *shevooth* does not necessarily mean captivity in a foreign land ;[2] and thirdly, that such mention may be prophetical.

---

church. Hengstenberg, Keil, Weiss, Delitzsch, Kay, and Bishop Wordsworth concur in believing it to be David's. Hengstenberg directs attention to the striking resemblance between passages in this psalm and others in Ps. lx. ; which are indeed so identical, that we may well conclude them both to have been written when David "strove with Aram-Maharaim and with Aram-Zobah, when Joab returned, and smote of Edom in the Valley of Salt twelve thousand."

Ps. xliv. 9—11.	Ps. lx. 1.
But *Thou hast cast us off*, and puttest us to confusion,	O God, *Thou hast cast us off*, Thou hast *scattered us abroad*.
And goest not forth with our armies.	
Thou makest us to turn our backs upon our enemies,	
So that they which hate us spoil our goods.	
Thou makest us to be eaten up like sheep,	
And hast *scattered us among the heathen*.	
verses 5—7.	verses 11, 12.
Through Thee will we push down our enemies :	O be Thou our help in trouble ; For vain is the help of man.
Through Thy name will we *tread them under that rise up against us*.	*Through God* we shall do great acts : *For it is He* that will *tread down our enemies*.
For I will not trust in my bow ; It is not my sword that will help me : *But it is Thou* that savest us from *our enemies*,	
And puttest them to confusion that hate us.	

[1] Bishop Wordsworth, accepting the arguments of Hengstenberg in the following note as to the meaning of "captivity," ascribes this psalm to David's time :—"In Ps. lxxxiv. the psalmist had expressed an intense desire for restoration to God's favour and presence, and he had prayed to God for his banished king—'Look on the face of Thine anointed !' In the present psalm we see that his prayer is granted."

[2] Hengstenberg, in Ps. xiv. 7, adduces several passages to show that "captivity" in the Bible is often put for affliction. "And the Lord turned the captivity of Job." Job xlii. 10. "I turn myself to the captivity of Jacob's tents." Jer. xxx. 18. "I will return to their captivity, the captivity of Sodom and her daughters." Ez. xvi. 53. And he shows that the words "cords," "bands," "prisoners," "darkness" are used in like manner to denote affliction of soul.

We have now to consider the authorship of those psalms which bear no name. Some of these we know to have been by David, from the subject matter contained in them ; others contain extracts from other psalms by David ; others are attributed to him by the word of God, as Ps. xcvi., cv., and cvi., which are given in 1 Chron. xvi. ; while eleven other psalms are attributed to David in the Septuagint, and several Oriental MSS. Psalm xcvi. is attributed to David by St. Paul. (Heb. iv. 7.) That Ps. x. is by David is evident from its being a continuation of Ps. ix., as shown by the alphabetical arrangement. That many of these anonymous psalms were probably written by David, we have internal evidence to show. It is in those cases where we find a striking similarity of form and treatment between such psalms and others which bear the name of David, and where such similarity has led to their being placed together. Thus, as Ps. xxxii. ends with the antiphon—

> *Be glad and rejoice in the Lord, O ye righteous :*
> *Shout for joy all ye that are true of heart !*

we may conclude that the anonymous psalm which follows is also by David, as it begins with the antiphon—

> *Shout for joy unto the Lord, O ye righteous !*
> *For praise is comely to the true of heart :*

thus forming an anadiplosis or epiploce. Again, as in Ps. ciii., by David, we have—

> The days of man are but as grass ;
> For he flourisheth as a flower of the field,

we may conclude that the preceding anonymous psalm is also by him, as we there find—

> My heart is smitten down, and withered like grass,
> So that I forget to eat my bread.
>
> My days are gone like a shadow
> And I am withered like grass.

This similarity of thought and treatment in adjoining psalms has been pointed out by many commentators. In Delitzsch, an impartial evidence, as he does not deduce the same conclusion, we shall find several instances of this ; thus leading us to acknowledge some dozen psalms which appear anonymous to have been written by

David ; and this of course leads us to consider it as probable that
others were so likewise.[1]

[1] Thus, of Ps. li. by David, he says—"The same depreciation of the external
sacrifice that is expressed in (the anonymous psalm) Ps. l. finds utterance in
Ps. li., which supplements the former, according as it extends the spiritualizing
of the sacrifice to the offering for sin." In Ps. lxv.—lxviii. we have a group
of "psalm-songs." The first and last of this group are by David. Delitzsch
says—"This series, as is universally the case, is arranged according to the
community of prominent watchwords. In Ps. lxv. 2 we read—'To Thee is
the vow paid,' and in Ps. lxvi. 13—'I will pay Thee my vows.' In Ps. lxvi.
20—'Blessed be Elohim,' and in Ps. lxvii. 8—'Elohim shall bless us.' Like
Ps. lxv., Ps. lxvii. also celebrates the blessing upon the cultivation of the
ground. As Ps. lxv. contemplated the corn and fruits as still standing in the
fields, so this psalm contemplates, as it seems, the harvest as already gathered
in, in the light of the redemptive history." "Is it not an admirably delicate
tact with which the collector makes the psalm-song Ps. lxviii. follow upon
the psalm-song Ps. lxvii.? Ps. lxvii. began with the echo of the benediction
which Moses puts into the mouth of Aaron and his sons; Ps. lxviii. with
a repetition of those memorable words in which, at the breaking up of the
camp, he called upon Jahve to advance before Israel. (Num. x. 35.)"
Ps. xcviii., which is anonymous, is almost identical with Ps. xcvi., which we
have shown to be by David. Ps. cii., which is anonymous, is between two
psalms bearing David's name. We have already shown the connexion
between it and the latter psalm, and Delitzsch thus compares it with the
former—"Ps. ci. utters the sigh—'When wilt Thou come unto me?' and
Ps. cii. has—'Let my prayer come unto Thee.' Ps. ciii., by David, is
followed by another anonymous psalm. Ps. ciii. begins 'Bless, O my soul,
Jahve.' With these same words begins the anonymous psalm, Ps. civ. also,
in which God's rule in the kingdom of nature, as there in the kingdom of
grace, is the theme of praise; and as there the angels are associated with it."
Ps. cvii. is anonymous, and it is followed by one by David. Of this latter
psalm Delitzsch says—"The אוֹדְךָ in v. 4, and the whole contents of this
psalm, is the echo to the הוֹדוּ of the preceding psalm." Of the group
Ps. cxxi.—cxxv., the first and last and middle one are anonymous. Of
Ps. cxxii. Delitzsch says—"If by 'the mountains' in Ps. cxxi. the mountains
of the Holy Land are to be understood, it is clear for what reason the collector placed this song of degrees, which begins with the expression of joy
at the pilgrimage to the house of Jahve, and therefore to the holy mountain,
immediately after the preceding song. By its peace-breathing contents also
it touches close upon Ps. cxx.," another anonymous psalm. "Ps. cxxiii.
is joined to the preceding psalm by the community of the divine name
'Jahve our God.' " Of Ps. cxxiv. he says—"The statement 'the stream
had gone over our soul' of this fifth song of degrees, coincides with the
statement 'our soul is full enough' of the fourth : the two psalms also meet
in the synonymous new formations שְׁאֹנָג and זֵידוֹנִים, which also look very
much as though they were formed in allusion to contemporary history." Of
Ps. cxxv. he says—"The favourite word 'Israel' furnished the outward
occasion for annexing this psalm to the preceding. The situation is like
that in Ps. cxxiii. and cxxiv." Of Ps. cxxxiv. he says—"The psalm begins,
like its predecessor, with the word 'Behold.' There it directs attention to an
attractive phenomenon, here to a duty which springs from the office."

There is one psalm, however, cxxxvii., which appears more than any other to bear the stamp of a later date, by the direct allusion to the Babylonian captivity. But even this, though highly probable, and however certain we may all feel in respect of it, is not conclusive; for when we consider how prophetical David's psalms are of our Saviour, is it a great matter that the Babylonian captivity was also revealed to him? If Abraham saw Christ nearly two thousand years before His advent, is it extraordinary that David should do so one thousand years nearer to such event? If David saw by revelation the doings of Christ one thousand years before it took place, is it extraordinary that he should foresee the destruction of Jerusalem which occurred in less than half that period? If Isaiah (xxxix.) and Jeremiah (xxv.) prophesied of the Babylonian captivity, and its duration for seventy years, and the return from that captivity, without being considered by critics, from such "internal evidence," as having lived after the event, may we not equally suppose that David "being a prophet," and "seeing this before," (Acts ii. 30, 31,) may have prayed to God prophetically for assistance, may have praised him prophetically for his subsequent deliverance? It is satisfactory to find at least one writer in the present day doing justice to the power of prophecy. The reader will see in the note[1] what De Burgh writes on this subject.

In Ps. xiv. and liii., both written by David, we find him saying—

Who will give salvation unto Israel, out of Sion?
When the Lord turneth the captivity of His people,
Then shall Jacob rejoice,
And Israel shall be glad.

Some German critics, it is true, followed by some English writers, speak of "internal evidence" as proving that many of the psalms which bear the name of David were written long after his time. But leaving aside for the moment David's prophetical claim, we are

[1] "As an instance of how little of the directly prophetical character is allowed to the Psalms, and how low a view is taken of their inspiration, it is taken for granted that this psalm (cii.) could not have been written by David, because Jerusalem is spoken of as desolate in v. 14; and accordingly it, with the many others in which there are like allusions, is referred, for no other reason, to other authors, and to the time of the Babylonish captivity . . . . And even the mention of the 'Sanctuary' and the 'House of the Lord' in other psalms has been by some considered conclusive of the same fact, because the Temple was not erected in David's time!" (De Burgh, Commentary on the Book of Psalms, 1860, i. 9.) Although it was only a tabernacle before the time of Solomon, we find it spoken of as the "house of the Lord" in Josh. vi. 24, and 2 Sam. xii. 20.

not sure that all these descriptions of the desolation of Jerusalem
and its captivity refer to the Babylonian captivity ; for what can
be more positive on this ground, with the exception of the mention
of Babylon, just referred to, than the following ?—

> Deliver us, O Lord our God,
> And gather us from among the heathen ;
> That we may give thanks unto Thy holy name,
> And make our boast of Thy praise. (Ps. cvi. 47.)

Who would not attribute this prayer to the period of the Babylonian captivity ?   And yet we find that it was written by David,
when he brought up the ark of the covenant to Mount Zion.
(1 Chron. xv.)   So again, when we read—

> He delivered His strength into captivity,
> And His glory into the enemy's hands:
> He gave His people also to the sword,
> And He was wroth with His inheritance :
> The fire consumed their young men,
> And their maidens were not given in marriage :
> Their priests were slain with the sword,
> And their widows made no lamentations ; (Ps. lxxviii. 62—65 ;)

who would not attribute this terrible picture of captivity for those
who escaped fire and sword, to the same sad occasion ?   And yet
we find that it relates to the time of Saul : for God's selection of
David is mentioned afterwards.   So again, when we read—

> O be favourable and gracious unto Sion,
> Build Thou the walls of Jerusalem ; (Ps. li. 13 ;)

might we not from this "internal evidence" suppose that Jerusalem
had been laid waste by the Babylonians, and that the captive prophet prayed for a return to the Holy Land, and for the rebuilding of
its waste places ?   But may we not equally suppose [1] that David
put up this prayer when he had taken the city of the Jebusites, and
making it the city of his God, called upon God to assist him while
he "built round about, from Millo and inward?" (2 Sam. v. 9 ;)
which building of the walls occupied David all his life-time ; for
they were not completed till after his death : for "Solomon built

---

[1] "The prayer *Build Thou the walls of Jerusalem*, is not inadmissible in
the mouth of David : since בנה signifies not merely to build up what has
been thrown down, but also to go on and finish building what is in the act
of being built ; as in Ps. lxxxix. 4." Delitzsch, *Bib. Com.* ii. 142.

Millo, and repaired the breaches of the city of David his father."
(1 Kings xi. 27.)

Carried away by the weight of their supposed "internal evidence,"
these critics find it necessary to dismiss the Superscriptions as being
worthy of no credit, for these superscriptions attribute psalms to
David which they in their wisdom pronounce emphatically to be
not by him. Thus in the verses which we have quoted from two
psalms, each of which bears the name of David,—

> Who will give salvation unto Israel out of Sion?
> When the Lord turneth the captivity of His people—

these critics allege that this can refer only to the Babylonian captivity : but may we not equally suppose it to have been written by
David, when we remember that the land of Israel was in subjection
to the Philistines during all the reign of Saul? In the second
year of his reign we find him raising, evidently with difficulty,
three thousand men to free his country from its enemies ; but no
sooner did the Philistine trumpet blow, than the Israelitish army
vanished into air, and the people " hid themselves in caves, and in
thickets, and in rocks, and in high places, and in pits ;" so that
only six hundred men remained with him, and these six hundred,
with the exception of Saul and Jonathan, were entirely unarmed.
And though subsequently he threw off the yoke, yet there was
" sore war against the Philistines all the days of Saul," and at last,
after nearly forty years' reign, he and three of his sons were slain
in battle, and the whole nation "forsook their cities and fled, and
the Philistines came and dwelt in them." And when, after such
calamity, David on ascending the throne established himself on
every side, so that, instead of being subject to the Philistines, he
annexed their country, together with those of the Ammonites, the
Edomites, the Moabites, the Hagarenes, the Amalekites, and the
Syrians, we may well conceive his adding—

> Then shall Jacob rejoice,
> And Israel shall be glad.

Again, in the sixty-ninth psalm we read—

> For God will save Sion, and build the cities of Judah,
> That men may dwell there, and have it in possession.
> The posterity also of His servants shall inherit it,
> And they that love His name shall dwell therein.

Now, not only does this psalm bear the name of David, not only
does St. Peter affirm it to be written by him, (Acts i. 16—20, referring to v. 25 of this psalm,) but it contains as many, and as

R

distinct and detailed prophecies of Christ, as the twenty-second
psalm, which also bears the name of David. It is impossible to
conceive of any other than David thus prophesying of Christ: and
indeed we ought to be very careful how we do anything to question
the authorship of these prophecies. Sceptics first question the authen-
ticity of some of the books of the New Testament, from alleged
" internal evidence," and then deny the doctrines which they contain. We do not, of course, call these *sceptics* who have written on
the Psalms of David, for they are all learned, laborious, careful, and
pious Christian men, whose works one cannot read without instruction, profit, and admiration : but we do think that system dangerous
by which, through the plea of "internal evidence," some of these
writers dismiss the Superscriptions as being worthy of no credit ;
ignore the assertions of Apostles as to the authorship of the Psalms ;
divide some psalms into two parts, pretending that David might
indeed have written a portion of such psalms, but that somebody
else wrote the other portion ; and affirm that in those psalms which
they acknowledge to have been written by him, where any passage
occurs which seems prophetical of the Captivity, such passage was
added afterwards : and there is no doubt that such method of
handling Holy Scripture is highly suggestive to those who *are*
sceptics ; and we feel no doubt that much of the rationalism
which exists in Germany has arisen from the over-straining of this
so-called "internal evidence."

We have seen that Asaph, whose name appears in the superscription of many of the psalms, must be the Asaph whom David made
one of the chief directors of his choir: and we have shown the
high probability that all these psalms were written by David, and
" delivered into the hands of Asaph and his brethren." We must
therefore suppose that the detailed descriptions which we have in
two of these psalms, lxxiv. and lxxix., were written *prophetically*,[1]
the more especially as some of the particulars are said to accord
more with the destruction of Jerusalem by the Romans, than with
any other event.[2] We have already shown by an examination of
Ps. xliv., which is addressed, " For the sons of Korah," the probability which exists of attributing that psalm to the author of
Ps. lx., which we know to be by David: let us now compare
this same psalm, lx., with one of those just mentioned addressed to

---

[1] The Chaldee says of the seventy-ninth psalm that it was "on the destruction of the house of the sanctuary," and that the psalmist "spake by the
spirit of prophecy." Hammond, *Annot.* on Ps. lxxiii.

[2] Phillips, *Ps. in Heb.* ii. 162.

Asaph, and we shall see ground for supposing that these also were written by the same person :—

Ps. lx. 1.	Ps. lxxiv. 1.
O God, *Thou hast cast us off*,	Why, O God, *hast Thou cast us off*
Thou hast scattered us abroad.	for ever !
	Why is Thy wrath so hot against the
	sheep of Thy pasture !

v. 4.	v. 4.
Thou hast *given a banner* to such as	Thine adversaries roar in the midst
fear Thee ;	of Thy congregations :
To be displayed because of the truth.	They *lift up their banners* for tokens.

v. 5.	v. 11.
Therefore shall Thy beloved be de-	Why withdrawest Thou Thy hand,
livered ;	even *Thy right hand* !
Save with *Thy right hand*, and hear	Why withdrawest Thou it not from
me.	Thy bosom to consume them ? [1]

So again, if we compare this psalm, lxxiv. with Ps. xliv., we shall see a striking similarity between them :—

Ps. xliv. 9, 23—26.	Ps. lxxiv. 1, 22, 23.
But *Thou hast cast us off*, and puttest	Why, O God, *hast Thou cast us off* for
us to confusion.	ever !
And goest not forth with our armies.	Why is Thy wrath so hot against the
	sheep of Thy pasture !
Arise, O Lord, why sleepest Thou !	*Arise, O God*: maintain Thine own
	cause :
Awake, and *cast us not off* for ever.	Remember how the foolish man blas-
Wherefore hidest Thou Thy face, and	phemeth Thee daily.
forgettest our misery and trouble !	*Forget* not the voice of Thine enemies:
Arise, and help us,	The tumult of them that hate Thee
And deliver us for Thy mercy's sake!	increaseth more and more.

Thus we see that these three psalms, which bear such a striking resemblance to each other, and which we have compared together in every way, Ps. xliv. with Ps. lx.; Ps. lx. with Ps. lxxiv; and Ps. xliv. with Ps lxxiv. ; and which bear the names of David, Asaph, and the Sons of Korah ;—must have been written, or rather, were in all probability written by one and the same person, and that this psalmist could have been no other than David.

Another of the psalms bearing the name of Asaph, lxxxiii., mentions "Assur," as though it were written after the time of

---

[1] In like manner we might compare the prayer for help in v. 2 of the former to that of v. 3 of the latter ; and the ascription of power in vv. 6—8 of the former to what we find in vv. 13—15 of the latter.

Sennacherib: but if we examine the psalm we shall find that all
the nations there mentioned were the nations which David himself
subdued, as the Edomites, the Ishmaelites, the Ammonites, the
Moabites, the Amalekites, and the Philistines: and though we find
all these nations mentioned in subsequent history, we do not find
all these at any time combining together against the children of
Israel. Assur may have given secret help to some of these petty
nations in the time of David, which indeed the words "have
holpen" seem to suppose; but Assyria was too great a country to
be mentioned in this secondary manner afterwards.

The eighty-fifth psalm commences—

> Lord, Thou art become favourable to Thy land,
> Thou hast turned again the captivity of Jacob.

But this psalm is addressed to the Sons of Korah, and therefore
evidently in David's time; for, independently of what we have
already advanced, it would be preposterous to suppose that twelve
psalms were written by the sons of Korah collectively: and the
restoration from captivity would refer to that which took place immediately after the death of Saul.

We have now, we believe, but three psalms remaining which
speak of the desolation of Sion, and the captivity of her people—
cii., cxxvi., and cxxxvii. The former of these, Ps. cii., has a peculiar
superscription; and as all the other historical superscriptions refer
to David, it is probable that this one does so also: and we have
already seen what De Burgh says of this psalm against those who
deny David to be the author:[1] Hengstenberg also speaks of the
"Davidic character which it bears" throughout: the other two
have no name or superscription, and as they abound in minute
particulars, the latter one especially mentioning Babylon by name,
we are justified in attributing these psalms, if we think fit, to the
Babylonian captivity: but even here we must not be too positive:
for if we make no allowance for metaphor, or poetical license, or
Oriental hyperbole, many of these particulars will be found no
exaggeration of the miserable state of the country at the death of
Saul, which we have already depicted. Take for instance the
hundred and twenty-sixth psalm:—

> When the Lord turned the captivity of Sion,
> Then were we like unto them that dream:
> Then was our mouth filled with laughter,
> And our tongue with joy.

[1] See note, p. 239.

> Then said they among the heathen—
> " The Lord hath done great things for them."
> The Lord *hath* done great things for us !
> Whereof we rejoice.

Moreover, do we not see a striking resemblance between this passage and that which we have already quoted from Ps. xiv. and liii., written by David :—

> Who will give salvation unto Israel out of Sion ?
> When the Lord turneth the captivity of His people,
> Then shall Jacob rejoice,
> And Israel shall be glad.

But let us carefully guard against expecting to find exact accordance in historical events with the particulars mentioned in the Psalms, many of which we know to be prophetical. Who shall explain the meaning of the *gall and vinegar*, the *piercing of hands and feet*, the *parting of garments*, and *casting lots upon the vesture*, the dead body not being *left in the grave*, and being *incapable of corruption*, the *ascension on high*, and *receiving gifts for men*, and *leading captivity captive*, the being a *priest for ever after the order of Melchisedek ?*[1] If then we find so many minute particulars prophesied of Christ, which are incapable of application to any historical circumstance relating to David or his successors, may we not, ought we not, to believe that equally minute particulars would be prophesied of the destruction of Jerusalem, and the captivity of its people ?

To say nothing of Olshausen and Hupfeld, who do not attribute a single psalm to David ;[2] or of Ewald and others who give him but fourteen out of the seventy-three which bear his name ; or of Hitzig who assigns all those after Ps. lxxii. to the Maccabees,[3] let us examine the chronological arrangement of one of these German

---

[1] See the author's chain of David's prophecy of Christ, in *David's Vision.* 1872.

[2] " If there are any, as St. Augustine saith there are, *De Civit. Dei,* xvii. 14, which would allow David to be the author of none of those psalms which were inscribed *ipsi David* in the dative case, they of all others are most worthy refuting, there being no other form of mentioning David in any of the psalms, but that of לְדָוִד, which is by the Latin indifferently rendere sometimes *Psalmus David,* sometimes *ipsi David;* who yet, if we will believe our Saviour, Luke xx. 42, was the author of some of them."—Hammond, *Annot.* Tit. of the Ps.

[3] Maccabean psalms are contested by Gesenius, Hengstenberg, Havernick, Keil, Ewald and others.

writers of the new school, ("Higher Criticism school,") Ewald, which
has been given to the English reader by some able writers under the
signature of "Four Friends."[1] In this arrangement the superscriptions are ignored, and consequently Moses is ignored as the author
of Ps. xc.; and the Apostles St. Peter and St. Paul are ignored, who
attribute Ps. xvi., lxviii. and lxix. to David; and our Lord Himself is ignored in those wonderful prophecies of Him contained in
Ps.ii., xxii. and lxix.;[2] though compensation is supposed to be
made by chapters relating to the Jews' expectation of a Messiah.
It is no wonder then that out of the seventy-three psalms ascribed
to David in the superscriptions, and twenty-four addressed to his
precentors, only fourteen psalms and three verses from two other
psalms are given to him in this chronological arrangement. If our
readers will take the trouble to compare the chronological arrangements of any two such writers, say of Weiss, Ewald, Hitzig,
Townsend,[3] Good or Hibbard, they will see how utterly discordant
and unreliable all such arrangements are, and how they necessarily
tend to unsettle God's Holy Word.

Proof by "internal evidence" of later authorship has also been
adduced by reference to the alleged frequent occurrence of Chaldaisms : but this has been disputed by various writers.[4] Besides

[1] *The Psalms chronologically arranged.* By Four Friends, 1867. — Although
we object to this which we think rationalistic tendency of the arrangement, we
cannot but admire the care and religious spirit with which this work is written,
the interesting historical introduction to each psalm, and especially the
ingenuity with which the alphabetical psalms are exhibited. For other
attempts at acrostic rendering, see Delitzsch, *Commentar über den Psalter;*
Ewald, *Die Dichter des alten Bundes;* Dr. W. Binnie, *The Psalms;* Dalman
Hapstone, *The ancient Psalms in appropriate metres.*

[2] If one set of writers deny all reference to our Lord in the Book of
Psalms, and if others were to do the same in the Book of Isaiah, we should
not have much left of ancient prophecy to prove the divinity of our Lord,
notwithstanding that He said "Search the Scriptures, for . . . . they are
they which testify of Me;" and "all things must be fulfilled which were written
in the law of Moses, and in the Prophets, and in the Psalms, concerning Me."

[3] Townsend attributes Ps. cii. to Daniel, quoting as an authority Dan. ix.
27, though what it has to do with the psalm we cannot make out. Neither
can we see what the personal affliction and misery described in vv. 3—11 of
the psalm, or the "shortening of days" in vv. 11 and 23, have to do with the
constant prosperity and regal state of Daniel, who must have been between
eighty and ninety years of age when he died. Hengstenberg believes the
fourth and fifth books to be in chronological order. *Com.* iii. p. xl.

[4] "These Chaldaisms consist merely in the substitution of one letter for
another very like it in shape, and easily to be mistaken by a transcriber,
particularly by one who had been used to the Chaldee idiom." "The occurrence of an apparent Chaldaism in this psalm (cxxii.) has induced some
critics to assign it to a later period. Little dependence, however, is to be

which, we must never forget the tendency which always exists among later copyists in transcribing, to make the spelling conformable to the custom of the day.

Another proof by "internal evidence" of late authorship is adduced from supposed ruggedness of style in early productions, as in those of David, and from a soft flowing one in later. But these critics forget to mention that this diversity of style occurs in works by the same author, especially in poetry, where in one case he wishes to describe something sad or terrible, and in another something joyous. If a ruggedness of style characterizes many of David's psalms, what shall we say to the soft, melodious, tender character of Ps. xxiii., which by "an almost universal feeling" has been attributed to the sweet psalmist of Israel? or why indeed should he be called the "*sweet* psalmist of Israel," if his compositions are always of a rugged character? So, when we consider the vicissitudes of David's life, we may well suppose that some of his psalms would

placed upon apparent marks of this kind. These indications are very slight in the Psalms, and may easily be accounted for by the alteration in the transcript of the older Scriptures, probably without design, by the later Jews. In the instance before us, however, it appears very evident that the supposed Chaldaism is an ancient though rarely used Hebrew idiom. It occurs not only in the Book of Judges . . . . but in Job . . . . in Eccles. . . . . in Cant. . . . . It is not a mere poetical license, but an ancient and established idiom, as the above passages ought to prove: unquestionably one of the age of Solomon." "Dr. Kennicott, in speaking of this psalm, observes that the internal marks of several of the following psalms, particularly Ps. cxxiii. and cxxxvii., will make it probable that this abbreviation is the work of a later age, and at least as recent as the Captivity: but the same abbreviations occur in the Books of Judges and of Job." (Jebb, *Lit. Transl.* 1846, i. 276; ii. 300, 307.)

"The fact, however, that these Chaldaisms, as they are called, occur in psalms undoubtedly composed by David, and in the earlier books of Scripture, shows how rash is the criticism which on this ground only would deny to many psalms his authorship, and assign them to a later date." "The use of the prefix here, (Ps. cxxii. 3, 4,) has been urged as a decisive proof that the Hebrew of this psalm is of a later age than David's; notwithstanding the fact that it occurs frequently as early as the Book of Judges . . . . " —Ps. cxl. 3. "In qualification of the assertion that this . . . . is an exclusively Chaldee word, it is to be observed that it occurs in Leviticus, chs. . . . ." —v. 5. "There is not *a word*," &c. "This occurs before in Ps. xix. 5, in 2 Sam. xxiii. 2, and in Prov. xxiii. 9: whence not a mere Chaldaism." —Ver. 20. "Only once besides in this sense, 1 Sam. xxxviii. 16, which, however, again disproves the assertion that it is an exclusively Chaldee word." (De Burgh, *Com.* ii. 903, 953-955.) See also his comment on Ps. cxvi. 7. Perowne thinks it possible that "the tendency to Aramaisms is to be regarded as evidence of a variation merely of dialect, perhaps the dialect of northern Palestine." *Bk. of Ps.*, Ps. cxxxix.

See Dr. Margoliouth's opinion in note, p. 277.

be written in a joyful, some in a trustful, some in a mournful, and some in a dejected style.[1] Besides, if a rough, unpolished style is a proof of antiquity, how is it that we find this characteristic in the writings of Ezekiel, who prophesied in the time of the Captivity?

Another proof by "internal evidence" of later authorship is alleged from the supposed resemblance of phrases in certain psalms to the style of Isaiah, Jeremiah, or later prophets; but may we not equally, or rather, far more justly suppose that such coincidences of style or phrase prove that these later prophets borrowed from David,[2] just as we see that David in his time copied occasionally from Moses, and other earlier poets. Take, for instance, the following :—

Moses' Song.	*David's Psalm.*
The Lord is my strength and my song,	The Lord is my strength and my song,
And He is become my salvation.	And is become my salvation.
Thy right hand, O Lord, is become glorious in power:	The right hand of the Lord doeth valiantly.
Thy right hand, O Lord, hath dashed in pieces the enemy.	The right hand of the Lord is exalted,
Exod. xv. 2, 6.	The right hand of the Lord doeth valiantly. Ps. cxviii. 14—16.

Deborah's Song.	*David's Psalm.*
Lord, when Thou wentest out of Seir,	O God, when Thou wentest forth before the people,
When Thou wentest out of the field of Edom,	When Thou wentest through the wilderness,
The earth trembled, and the heavens dropped,	The earth shook, the heavens also dropped, at the presence of God:
The clouds also dropped water.	Even Sinai itself was moved at the presence of God, the God of Israel.
The mountains melted from before the Lord,	Ps. lxviii. 7, 8.
That Sinai from before the Lord God of Israel. Judges v. 4, 5.	

---

[1] "In the didactic psalms of David we meet with a style differing from that of his other psalms; and where the doings of the ungodly are severely rebuked we find a harsher and more concise mode of expression, and a duller, heavier tone." (Delitzsch, *Bib. Com.* Ps. xlix.) "The same David who writes elsewhere so beautifully, tenderly, and clearly, is able among his manifold transitions to rise to an elevation at which his words as it were roll along like rumbling thunder through the gloomy darkness of the clouds, and more especially where they supplicate, or predict, the judgment of God." (*Ib.* on Ps. lviii.)

[2] See this advocated by Delitzsch, relative to Ps. xxxi. ; and in Ps. lxxvii. relative to the supposed priority of Habakkuk. See also Perowne on Ps. lxxix.

Hannah's Song.

He raiseth up the poor out of the
　dust,
He lifteth up the beggar from the
　dunghill,
To set them among princes,
And to make them inherit the throne
　of glory :
For the pillars of the earth are the
　Lord's,
And He hath set the world upon
　them.　　　　1 Sam. ii. 8.

David's Psalm.

Who raiseth the poor from the dust,
And lifteth the needy from the
　dunghill,
That He may set him with the
　princes,
Even with the princes of His people.
　　　　　　　Ps. cxiii. 7, 8.
The earth and all the inhabitants
　thereof are dissolved :
I bear up the pillars of it.
　　　　　　　Ps. lxxv 3.

Wandering in the Desert.

When the ark set forward, Moses
　said—
Rise up, Lord, and let Thine enemies
　be scattered :
Let them also that hate Thee flee
　before Thee.　　　Num. x. 35.

David's Psalm.

Let God arise, and let His enemies be
　scattered :
Let them also that hate Him flee
　before Him !　　　Ps. lxviii. 1.

As well might we suppose from this "internal evidence" that Moses and Deborah and Hannah lived after the time of David!

We have seen that it is the fashion of modern critics, since the appearance of Vogel's *Inscript. Psal.*, to dismiss the Superscriptions as being worthy of no credit. Let us examine their validity. One objection is made to their genuineness from the fact that those in the Septuagint and in some Oriental versions do not agree with those in the Hebrew; but equal objection might be made that the headings in our Bibles, giving the contents of the psalm or chapter, are not authorized. No doubt, later translators and editors of God's Word, as the "Seventy," put new headings, as they thought they were justified, and sometimes apparently from mere caprice. While the Seventy ascribe psalms to Haggai and Zechariah, the Chaldee attributes the eighty-eighth to Abraham! and in Ps. xcvi., which has no title in the Hebrew, although the occasion of writing it is given us by the author of the Book of Chronicles,—the Seventy, and all the Oriental translators, affixed as title—" When the house was built after the Captivity—a Song of David." There is no doubt this psalm was used then, in consequence of its having been composed by David, and used by him on the occasion of bringing up the ark to Mount Sion; just as on the death of Judas Maccabeus his brothers buried him, lamenting over him, "How is the mighty man fallen!" thus adapting David's lamentation over Saul and Jonathan, "How are the mighty fallen !" But this fact shows that the titles in the Greek and Oriental versions being written later, are not to be put in opposition to those of the Hebrew.

Another objection is made to them because they do not always appear to correspond with the subject-matter of the Psalms : and accordingly they have been set aside as worthless, and adjudged to be the comment merely of the compiler. But surely this is not sound reasoning. Were these headings written by subsequent annotators, they would have made them fit with the subject of the psalms : and the desire to find out the occasions when the several psalms were written would have led them, as it has led many modern commentators, to fix the occasions, and to put headings to every psalm : instead of which we find only thirteen such incidents specified. Moreover, let us look at three such occasions. The third psalm is said to have been written when David " fled from Absalom his son," and on the same occasion was written the seventh psalm, " when he sang unto the Lord concerning the words of Cush the Benjamite." But if *we* were to write fresh headings to the Psalms, we should probably select for this occasion the *thirty-fifth*, where he calls upon God to plead his cause, and to fight against those that fought against him, and to punish his adversaries ; where he complains of the false charges of Shimei, and contrasts his own patience under injury ;—or the *forty-second* and *forty-third*, where his enemies taunt him with " Where is now thy God ?"—or the *sixty-ninth*, where he also complains of the reproaches of the wicked, notwithstanding his own innocence ;—or the *seventy-first*, where he calls upon God to deliver him from the cruel and wicked man, and where he speaks twice of his own great age ;—or the *eighty-ninth*, where he speaks of his own abasement, and of the reproaches of his enemies.

Again, if we were required to select a psalm suitable for the " dedication of the house of David," the subject of Ps. xxx., we should probably select the *sixteenth*, where he says, " The lines are fallen unto me in pleasant places : yea, I have a goodly heritage ;" —or the *sixty-first*, where he again speaks of having the heritage of those who fear God's name ;—or the *hundred and first*, where he lays down rules for the management of his house, and for the selection of his servants ;—or the *hundred and twelfth*, where he shows the blessedness of those who fear the Lord, and how God giveth to His saints—power, honour, riches, blessing, light in darkness, calmness in times of trouble, and everlasting remembrance after death ;—or the *hundred and twenty-first*, where he shows how God is his keeper and preserver from all trouble ;—or the *hundred and twenty-seventh*, where he shows that, " Except the Lord build

the house, their labour is but lost that build it," and how all efforts
and all industry are vain without God's help ;—or the *hundred and
twenty-eighth*, where he describes the domestic blessedness of the
godly ;—or the *hundred and forty-fifth*, where he praises God for all
His goodness, and for His constant providence.

Again the fifty-first psalm is said to have been written "when
Nathan the prophet came unto him, after he had gone in to Bathsheba." How natural would it have been for the compiler, had he
written the titles, to give the same title to all the other so-called
"Penitential Psalms."

Now if, in the cases we have mentioned, these three titles had
been given to all these psalms, we should have held, were we to
adopt the reasoning of these critics, that all such titles were
genuine : whereas, from this not being the case, we ought to
conclude that the titles, where they do occur, not being placed
perhaps where we should place them, are for that very reason
more likely to be genuine : for although we are told the occasion
when any such psalm was written, we are not told what were the
feelings and thoughts of the psalmist under such occasion. Critics
might expect to find the actual mention of the names of Doeg, of
Shimei, of Achish, or of Joab, in the psalms which refer to these
several persons, and detailed circumstances connected with them ;
but the divine psalmist, in the midst of his personal suffering,
thinks chiefly of God, and of God's people, and strives to make his
psalm useful to God's church to the latest posterity. He general-
izes his subject therefore, and instead of dwelling on his own
personal events, he allows his heart to soar upwards to God, and
to give expression to thoughts far removed from things of this
life.

Instead therefore of adopting the conclusion of those who hastily
consider that the apparent want of connection between the titles of
several of the psalms and the subject-matter of such psalms is a
proof that such titles were written afterwards, and on insufficient
grounds ; we ought rather, as we say, to conclude that the titles are
for that very reason genuine. But to this negative evidence we
can add some positive evidence ; for one such title we can prove to
have been given by David. It is that of the eighteenth psalm ; for
we find this title given at length in 2 Sam. xxii., a book which is
supposed to have been written by the prophets Gad and Nathan.
We may also assume this to be the case from the Superscription of
Ps. xxxiv., which Hupfeld maintains has been blindly taken from
1 Sam. xxi. 14. But this, as Delitzsch observes, cannot be the
case : " for the psalm does not contain any express reference to that

incident in Philistia." The compiler, had he added the superscription, would never have thought of this incident, for there is nothing
in the psalm to suggest it : and if he had, he would have inserted
the name Achish, as given in Samuel; instead of which he gives the
name Abimelech, the title of the Philistine kings.   It is objected,
indeed, that in another case where the psalm is given in duplicate,
(1 Chron. xvi.,) the supposed title of Ps. cvi., " Praise ye the
Lord," does not appear.[1]   In the first place, however, we think it
evident that what we find in the Book of Chronicles was not composed from the three psalms in the Book of Psalms ; for we are told
that " Then on that day David delivered *first* this psalm to thank
the Lord :" but rather that this psalm was subsequently elaborated
by David into the three psalms ; and secondly, that it is not at
all certain that the words " Praise ye the Lord " form a title,
although Phillips asserts it to be the case in all the Hallelujah
psalms.[2]   In Ps. cxi., cxii., cxxxv., cxlviii., cxlix., and cl. the
words may form a title, though perhaps they are only an antiphon :
but in some other instances it is quite clear that they form part of
the psalm itself.   Thus in Ps. cxvi. we have—

> Praise ye the Lord :
> Praise ye the Lord, O my soul !

and in the following psalm—

> Praise ye the Lord :
> כִּ *For* it is a good thing to sing psalms unto our God :
> כִּ *For* it is a joyful and pleasant thing to sing praises.

But even if we were to give up both these points, and suppose that
the chronicle was written after the psalms, and that the words " Praise
ye the Lord" constituted a title, even then the insertion of such a
title was unnecessary ; for the historical narrative itself states that
David gave this psalm " to thank and to praise the Lord," and the
psalm as there given being composed, as Phillips and others
suppose, of portions of three psalms, " so making together a poem
adapted to the particular occasion," [3] and Ps. cvi. being the last
portion, it would have broken the continuity of the composition, if
the titles (if any) of the two psalms which came last had been
introduced.

We may therefore conclude from the proof of the title of Ps.
xviii., that all the titles are genuine,[4] and this conclusion is rendered

---

[1] Phillips, *The Psalms in Heb.* Introd. p. xli.
[2] *Ibid.* ii. 379.   [3] *Ibid.* ii. 365.
[4] See the validity of the superscriptions advocated in Tholuck, *Trans. and
Com.*, p. 13.

positive by the titles which we find in the other books of Scripture.[1]
Thus we see that it was the *rule* to affix a superscription to the
sacred writings; and finding them therefore so frequently attached
to the Psalms of David, we are not at liberty to discard them.
Why indeed should not ancient poets have put their names at
the top of their compositions, when we cannot take up a modern
serial without seeing the authors' names attached to their pieces
of "poetry" at the bottom? Some slight weight also must be
attached to the fact of the superscription forming part of the
psalm itself in the Hebrew Bibles as is shown by the division

[1] As "The words of Nehemiah," "The Proverbs of Solomon," "These are
also Proverbs of Solomon," "The words of Agur the son of Jakeh, even the
prophecy," "The words of King Samuel, the prophecy which his mother
taught him," "The words of the Preacher, the son of David, King of Jerusalem," "The Song of songs, which is Solomon's," "The vision of Isaiah, the
son of Amos," "The writing of Hezekiah, King of Judah, when he had been
sick, and was recovered of his sickness," "The burden of Babylon, which
Isaiah did see," "The year that Ahaz died was this burden," "The burden of
Moab," "The burden of Damascus," "The burden of Egypt," "The burden
of the desert of the sea," "The burden of Dumah," "The burden upon
Arabia," "The burden of the valley of vision," "The burden of Tyre," "In
that day shall this song be sung in the land of Judah," "The burden of the
beasts of the earth," "The words of Jeremiah," "The word that came from
Jeremiah to the Lord," (Jer. vii., xi., xviii., xxi., xxvi., xxvii., xxx., xxxii.,
xxxv., xl.,) "The word that came to Jeremiah concerning—" (Jer. xiv.,
xxv., xliv.,) "now these are the words of the letter that Jeremiah the prophet
sent—" (Jer. xxix.,) "The word that Jeremiah the prophet spake unto
Baruch," (Jer. xlv.,) "The word of the Lord which came to Jeremiah the
prophet against the Gentiles," (Jer. xlvi.,)—"against the Philistines," (Jer.
xlvii.,) "The word that the Lord spake against Babylon," (Jer. l.,) "The
word of the Lord that came unto Hosea," "The beginning of the word of the
Lord by Hosea," "The word of the Lord that came to Joel," "The words of
Amos," "The vision of Obadiah," "The word of the Lord that came to
Micah," "The burden of Nineveh : the book of the vision of Nahum,"
"The burden which Habakkuk the prophet did see," "A prayer of Habakkuk
the prophet upon Shigionoth," "The word of the Lord which came unto
Zephaniah," "The burden of the word of the Lord in the land of Hadrach,"
"The burden of the word of the Lord for Israel," by Zechariah, "The burden
of the word of the Lord to Israel," by Malachi, "The Revelation of Jesus
Christ which God gave unto him?" &c. To these may be added other instances,
as Num. xxi. 17 ; xxiv. 3, 4 ; xxxi. 23, 30 ; Deut. i. 1 ; xxxi. 19, 22, 30 ;
xxxii. 44 ; the headings of many chapters in Ezekiel ; and especially, as connected with our present subject, those passages in the historical books where
David's psalms are referred to ; such as 2 Sam. i. 17 ; xxii. 1 ; xxiii. 1 ;
1 Chron. xvi. 7 :—"and David lamented with this lamentation over Saul and
over Jonathan his son ;" "Then on that day David delivered first this psalm
to thank the Lord ;" "and David spake unto the Lord the words of this song
in the day that the Lord had delivered him out of the hand of all his
enemies, and out of the hand of Saul ;" "These be the last words of David."

of the verses; which division is attributed to the Masorites in the sixth century.[1]

But it may be said—If we allow the titles or superscriptions to stand, it is clear that as these superscriptions tell us which were written by David, those which have no superscription were not written by him. But this does not at all follow, as we have already seen: for Ps. xcvi. cv. and cvi. bear no superscriptions, and yet we know from the Book of Chronicles that they were written by David: and so there is every reason to suppose that others also which have no superscription were written by him.

How unsatisfactory then is the opinion of those who hold that the superscriptions were written by the compiler of the Book of Psalms! What possible reason could he have for assigning Ps. xc. to Moses, and Ps. lxxxviii. to Heman? Why should he assign several psalms to Jeduthun, and only one to him under his former name of Ethan? Why, in those which bear the name of Asaph, should there be no distinction between an earlier and a later Asaph, if, as these critics suppose, there was an interval of three hundred or five hundred years between them? Why should particular psalms be assigned to the sons of Korah, when this portion of David's choir no longer existed?[2] Why should he direct some psalms to be sung to the accompaniment of the sistrum, or of cymbals; and others to that of wind instruments; and others to that of stringed instruments; and of these latter why should some be of six strings, others of eight strings, and others of ten strings? Why should he suppose some to be adapted for instruments the very names of which were unintelligible only some two hundred and fifty years after the Captivity, when the Seventy commenced their labours? Or, more astonishing still, if, as some suppose, the canon of the Book of Psalms was not completed till the time of the Maccabees, when they allege the greater number of the psalms were written, how the Maccabean compiler could have written these Hebrew titles, when the Seventy had written such very different Greek titles one hundred years before! In conclusion we would allege that the titles themselves furnish both negative and positive evidence of their genuineness; negative, inasmuch as, if the compiler had prefixed them, he would have given the title of "the Psalm by David" to Ps. xcvi., cv., and cvi., which he would know from the Book of Chronicles were written by him, and he would have given titles to many of the anonymous psalms, where the subject of the psalm seems to justify it; and

[1] Hupfeld and Riehm attribute it to an earlier origin.
[2] Indeed, Ewald says, "Why this song has been attributed to the Korahites, that to Asaph or Ethan, I know not."

positive, not only from what we have adduced relative to the title
of Ps. xviii., but from the fact which we shall presently notice, that,
finding the names of Heman and Ethan the Ezrahites attached to
Ps. lxxxviii. and lxxxix. he *mistook* them for the grandsons of
Judah !

We have now to consider the arguments against the reputed
authorship of the Psalms which arise from the supposed division of
the Psalms into " Five Books." These books, as is well known, are
supposed to terminate at Ps. xli., lxxii., lxxxix., cvi., and cl. ; the
four former psalms concluding with a similar doxology : and this
subdivision into five books has been considered a most convincing
proof that the Psalms were written at different times, and by different men, and collected together into books at different times.
David's psalms are thought by many to be confined to the first and
second books, from the words with which the second book concludes
—" The prayers of David the son of Jesse are ended." The later
books are thought to contain psalms written in the time of Hezekiah, of Ezra, and of the Maccabees.[1] Supposing this theory correct,
it would follow that all psalms occurring in the later books, which
bear the name of David in the superscription, would be looked at
with suspicion, either as having been placed inadvertently in those
later books, or as having false superscriptions. Let us then examine this supposed division into five books. The earliest notice
we have of it is in the Syrian translation, and in Jerome, and
some other of the early fathers.[2] The division into five books is
supposed to be in imitation of the Five Books of Moses.[3] Some
imagine the collections to have been made at five different times;
others that Ezra or Nehemiah, others that someone in the
time of the Maccabees, after collecting the Psalms together, divided
them into five books. It is evident that this opinion has been
founded chiefly on the doxologies at the end of the first four supposed
books. It is to these doxologies therefore that we must first direct
our attention.

We have already seen that the doxology at the end of Ps. lxxii.
forms part of that psalm, and that it cannot be separated from it.[4]
This we have deduced from 2 Sam. xxii., 1—4, which refers to the

[1] The Talmud attributes some of the psalms to Adam, Melchizedek, and
Abraham. The eighty-eighth is attributed to Abraham by the Chaldee.

[2] Hammond, *Paraphrase*, 1850, *Annot.* vol. ii : Jebb. *Lit. Trans.* ii. 224.

[3] The Midrash on Ps. i. 1. Mendelssohn, Pref. 3, supposes this division to
have been made by David. Hilary, however, says this belief in a division
into five books was held but partially among the Jews.

[4] See p. 232.

close of David's life . but if we now examine 1 Chron. xxix. 19, 20, which refers to the same event, we find a still more striking confirmation of this opinion.   Ps. lxxxii. begins—

> Give the king Thy judgment, O God,
> And Thy righteousness unto the king's son.

So here David says—"Give unto Solomon my son a perfect heart, to keep Thy commandments, Thy testimonies, and Thy statutes." After which we read—"And David said to all the congregation, Now bless the Lord your God. And all the congregation blessed the Lord God of their fathers, and bowed down their heads, and worshipped the Lord :" thus confirming in a most remarkable manner the connection between the doxology at the end of Ps. xxii. and the psalm itself. But we have here to observe that if these doxologies had been added by the compiler when he divided the Book of Psalms into five books, the doxologies would be found at the *end* of each of such psalms. Here, however, we have a line *after* the doxology,—"The prayers of David the son of Jesse are ended," and we have seen that this line is intimately connected with the psalm. The doxology, therefore, in this instance could not have been added afterwards. Its applicability to the subject-matter of the psalm has been pointed out, and we now find confirmation of such opinion by the fact of this line following the doxology. Another proof of this doxology forming a portion of the psalm itself occurs in the double epiploce or anadiplosis which is here observable. The word "name" which appears twice in the preceding verse, reappears in the doxology ; and the word "blessed " which appears twice in the preceding verse, once in the form of *Borakh*, to bless, and once in the other form of *Oshar*, to be happy, is repeated twice in the doxology. This is so common a feature in the Psalms of David, that we cannot refuse to pay attention to it. A further confirmation of this appears by comparing this doxology or antiphon with the concluding antiphon of another psalm on behalf of Solomon, (xlv.,) in which mention is also made of the eternal remembrance of God's name. And a further confirmation, if more be needed, occurs in the fact that if, as is alleged, Ps. lxxii., were written *by* Solomon, instead of *to* or *for* Solomon, and that "Books " I. and II. were collected in his reign, the words "The prayers of David the son of Jesse are ended " would have been placed after Ps. lxxi. instead of after Ps. lxxii. which is affirmed to be by Solomon.[1] This reduces the five books to four books.

[1] In order to support the theory of the doxologies having been written subsequently—a theory only too commonly accepted in the present day—

The doxology at the end of Ps. cvi. is proved to be part and parcel of that psalm, by reference to 1 Chron. xvi., where we find the occasion of this psalm being used, with part of the psalm itself given, including its doxology; and here also, as in Ps. lxxii., we have the doxology followed by another verse or line— "Praise ye the Lord," corresponding with the first verse, an arrangement which we find in so many of the "Hallelujah psalms," and which therefore cannot be set aside. This proves, as in the former case, that the doxology was not added afterwards. Perowne, however, who follows in the opinion of Delitzsch, supposes the chronicle to be written after the psalm, and considers this extra line part of the doxology, because we read in the chronicle that "the people said, Amen, and *praised the Lord*."[1] That it is not part of the original doxology appears both from comparing it with the doxologies at end of Ps. xli., lxxii., and lxxxix.; and from the account in the Book of Chronicles being evidently historical, and written from records taken at the time: "and all the people said, Amen, and praised the Lord." Had the chronicler copied from the Book of Psalms, he would have given us the whole psalm as he found it, or at least such portion as he chose to copy; but if the author of the psalm composed and elaborated that psalm[2] from what was used on that solemn occasion, he could not copy the words "and all the people praised the Lord," for this would be adding prose to poetry; but he threw the recital into the form of an antiphon, "Praise ye the Lord." To suppose, as these critics do, that the chronicler described an act, "and they praised the

Delitzsch, finding that the doxology of Ps. lxxii. does not occur at the end of the psalm, where it naturally ought to be, if added, does not hesitate to say— "*The collector certainly has removed this subscription* (The prayers of David the son of Jesse are ended) *from its original place* close after Ps. lxxii. 17, by the interpolation of the *beracha*, vv. 18, 19, but left it at the same time untouched." (*Bib. Com.* 1874, i. 16.) What is this but to found a theory first, and then to alter Scripture in order to accord with it!

[1] "The last verse is merely a doxology added at a time subsequent to the composition of the psalm, to mark the close of the book . . . . The chronicler who quotes this verse changes the words 'Let all the people say, Amen,' into the historic tense—'And all the people said, Amen, and praised Jehovah.'" (Perowne, ii. 259.) "The chronicler, in the free manner which characterizes Thucydides or Livy in reporting a speech, there reproduces David's festal hymn . . . . and he does it in such a way that after he has once fallen into the track of Ps. cvi., he also puts into the mouth of David the *beracha* which follows that psalm." (Delitzsch, *Bib. Com.* i. 15.)

[2] Delitzsch rightly states this natural procedure, in speaking of Ps. cxliv. 1, 2, which, according to the Seventy and the Midrash, were the words addressed to God by David when about to fight Goliath—when he says, "*The psalm has grown out of* this utterance of David."

S

Lord," from the words of a psalm which had been written previously to the event, would be writing history of present actions
ex post facto; which, to use language which Perowne in one place
employs towards Hengstenberg, (ii. 55,) but contrary to his usual
style, would be maintaining a theory "at the risk of any absurdity."[1]

These critics suppose that the first book, containing psalms by
David, was edited by Solomon; that the second and third were
collected in the time of Hezekiah, who placed those of David
and his contemporaries in the second book, and those of Asaph
and others in the third; and that the fourth and fifth collections
were made in the times of Ezra and Nehemiah, to which were added
other psalms afterwards, "inserted here and there" among the five
books.[2] Delitzsch says—" Even in the time of the writer of the
Chronicles, the Psalter was a whole divided into five parts, which
were indicated by these landmarks (the doxologies.) We infer this
from 1 Chron. xvi. 36. From this we see that the Psalter was
already divided into (five) books at that period."[3] Perowne says—
" The fact that he has incorporated this verse as well as the preceding in his psalm, is a proof that already in his time the Psalter
was divided, as at present, (?) into books, the doxology being regarded as an integral portion of the psalm."[4] But this *petitio·
principii* is altogether unjustified. Both these writers believe
that some of the psalms are Maccabean. Delitzsch indeed says,
" they can at any rate only be few :" (i. 14:) but that "no age

[1] Delitzsch in one place is even more invective in his language. The
reasons of those opposed to him he there calls "miserable attempts," and
"artifices." (See Ps. lxxviii. and lxxix., vol. ii. p. 24, 33.) This, however, is
a solitary instance; and in his *Preface* is a passage which does honour to
himself and also to his bitter critic Hupfeld. It is an extract from a letter
from the latter: " I have only just seen your complaint of my judgment at
the close of my work on the Psalms. The complaint is so gentle in its tone,
it partakes so little of the bitterness of my verdict, and at the same time
strikes chords that are not yet deadened within me, and which have not yet
forgotten how to bring back the echo of happier times of common research,
and to revive the feeling of gratitude for faithful companionship, that it has
touched my heart and conscience." Would that such writing and such
feeling were more common among writers, especially writers on theology! It
is no doubt right to "be zealously affected always in a good cause," but it is
also our duty, where we see others taking what we believe to be a wrong
course, to "restore such in the spirit of meekness, considering ourselves, lest
we also be tempted." When critics write thus, even when they differ from
us, we may say—

    If the righteous strike me, [I will regard it as] a kindness :
    And if he rebuke me, it shall be as oil upon the head.

[2] Delitzsch, i. 15—19; Perowne, 1870. i. 73—79.
[3] *Bib. Com.* i. 16; iii. 151.   [4] *Book of Psalms*, 1871, ii. 259.

could be regarded as better warranted in incorporating some of its
songs in the Psalter than the Maccabean, the sixty-third week
predicted by Daniel, the week of suffering bearing in itself the
character of the time of the end:" (ii. 327:) but Perowne says
—"Notwithstanding the positive and contemptuous manner in
which Dr. Pusey has recently expressed himself on this subject,
(*Lectures on Daniel*, 56, 292, &c.,)[1] there is not a shadow of proof
that the canon was closed before the Maccabean era." (ii. 73.)[2]
Other writers, however, as we have seen, attribute the greater
portion of the Psalter to the Maccabees; but whether such psalms
were few or many, we cannot suppose that the division into five
books took place before the canon was completed.[3] This division
therefore must have been, according to this supposition, subsequent
to the time of the Maccabees, say B.C. 150; whereas the Book of
Chronicles is supposed to have been written by Ezra, 300 years
earlier. But even if we throw over this Maccabean theory,[4] and
suppose that the latest psalms were written on the return from
exile, and thus make the age of the latest psalms, the supposed
division into five books, and the writing of the Book of Chronicles, to synchronize, even then it is manifestly beginning at the
wrong end to suppose that the record of historical events which
took place in the year 1000 B.C. was written subsequently to the
supposed division into five books more than 500 years afterwards:
for although the *history* may have been written more than 500
years after the event, it is quite evident that records and materials must have existed for such history to be written:[5] and
we may therefore conclude with certainty from 1 Chron. xvi. 36,

[1] Hengstenberg also argues strongly against the Maccabean theory, saying—
"While the Maccabees were good soldiers and zealous for the law of their
fathers, they were not men full of the Holy Spirit: not one example of this
sort meets us throughout the whole period. But that the co-operation of the
Spirit of God was considered as a necessary mark of a song, we have already
seen. How deeply they were themselves conscious of the absence of this
Spirit appears from 1 Mac. iv. 46; ix. 27; xiv. 41." (*Com. on the Psalms*,
Appendix, p. xviii.) He further argues that as the author of the Book of
Maccabees gives us all the speeches of the heroes, we might expect to find the
psalms or songs written by them, if any such existed. Even Ewald attributes
no psalms to the Maccabean period. See also note 3 in p. 245.

[2] See also i. 18, 346, and ii. 72—75.

[3] We might indeed have thought so if we found *all* the psalms attributed
to David in the first book; all those of his choir in another, and later ones
afterwards in strict chronological order. But this is not the case.

[4] A theory not adopted by Ewald, and "Four Friends:" who moreover
acknowledge a subdivision into only four books.

[5] Delitzsch acknowledges the former existence of such records. In com-
menting on Ps. cxliv. 1, 2, he says—"In one of the old histories, just as

that the doxology at the end of Ps. cvi. formed part of the original composition,[1] instead of being written afterwards. Moreover, the compound word, "Hallelujah," or "Praise ye the Lord," constitutes the usual termination of what are called the "Hallelujah psalms." of which this is one; and we therefore require it for part of the psalm. And the doxology itself, "Blessed be the Lord," must be considered as an appropriate termination to a psalm which begins —"O give thanks unto the Lord, for He is good, and His mercy endureth for ever." A further proof that Ps. cvi. cannot have formed the conclusion of a book, appears from the fact which is attested by those who hold to the "Five Books," that Ps. cvi. and cvii. are too intimately connected with each other to be divided.[2] The "five books" now are reduced to three.

Another of the supposed books ends with Ps. lxxxix. Now it is evident that the compiler of the Book of Psalms, finding the names of Heman and Ethan the Ezrahites attached to Ps. lxxxviii. and lxxxix. (or, if you wish it, he himself attaching the names to them,) believed them to be the same as the grandsons of Judah, of those names, and consequently of greater antiquity than

several of these lie at the foundation of our Books of Samuel as sources of information that are still recognizable, it was intended," &c.

1 Hitzig regards the songs in the Chronicles as the original, and the respective parallels in the Psalms as "layers" or "shoots."

2 "We must not be surprised if Ps. cvi. and cvii. are closely connected, in spite of the fact that the boundary of the two books lies between them. The psalms civ.—cvii. really to a certain extent form a tretralogy . . . . nevertheless the connection of Ps. civ. with cv.—cvii. is by far not so close as that of these three psalms among themselves. These three anonymous psalms form a trilogy in the strictest sense : they are a tripartite whole from the hand of one author. The observation is an old one." And he then gives an extract from the "Harpffe Davids mit Teutschen Saiten bespannet," a translation of the Psalms which appeared in Augsburg in 1659. And after long detailed proofs of correspondence Delitzsch concludes—"Everything therefore favours the assertion that Ps. cv., cvi. and cvii. are a 'trefoil'—two Hodu psalms and a Hallelujah psalm in the middle." Delitzsch, Bib. Com. on Ps. cvii.

"Ps. cvii. stands in close relationship to Ps. cvi. The similarity of the beginning at once points back to this psalm. Thanks are here given in v. 3 for what was there desired in v. 47. The praise of the Lord which was promised in Ps. cvi. 47 in the case of redemption being vouchsafed, is here presented to Him after redemption vouchsafed." Hengstenberg, Com. on same psalm.

"There is no reason, as Ewald has observed, why Ps. cvi. should be separated from Ps. cvii." Perowne, Book of Psalms, in same place.

"Ps. cvi. is so closely connected with Ps. cvii. that neither can be understood apart from the other." Four Friends, The Psalms chronologically arranged, p 405.

Moses,[1] the author of Ps. xc., and therefore *placed these three psalms together*, giving the priority to Heman and Ethan, as being the elder. Is it likely, then, after putting these three psalms together in immediate sequence, that the compiler would at the same time, or indeed anyone after him, separate them by putting two of them in one book, and the third in another! This is preposterous: and indeed we may look upon this as a clear proof not only that Ezra,[2] or whoever might be the compiler of the Book of Psalms, did not divide the collection into "five books," but that *he did not write the titles*. Instead of writing them, he *mistook* them, and finding the name of Ezrahite attached to each of these two names, and finding these names mentioned in the Book of Chronicles as the sons of Zerah, he naturally concluded them to be the same persons, and therefore placed their supposed productions immediately before that assigned to Moses. But independently of this argument, which we think is unanswerable, let us look at the object of the doxology, and the reason for its insertion. We find that the first eighteen verses constitute a thanksgiving and song of praise for God's mercies, and the next nineteen verses a calling to remembrance God's promises: it was natural therefore after laying his trouble before God, which the psalmist does in the following fourteen verses, that he should terminate in praise to God, *believing* that the same God who had done so much for him before, would continue to do so for ever Another proof that there can be no separation between these psalms exists in the extraordinary similarity of arrangement in the *replicas* of Ps. lxxxviii. and xci. Thus we get rid of another supposed division: and the alleged "five books" are now reduced to two.

The customary form of doxology being absent in Ps. cl., there remains but one instance of it to which to attach any extrinsic significance: and as the whole force of the argument lies in the fact of the same doxology appearing no fewer than four times, and as we have shown that in three of these instances the doxology has no extrinsic value, we cannot but conclude that where we find it in

[1] This view, as we have seen, p. 230, was held by Athanasius and Eusebius, and recently by Lightfoot and the author of "The Psalms in chronological order," who places these two psalms at the beginning of the book. It is true Ps. lxxxix. disproves this antiquity: but it is evident that the antiquity was believed in by the compiler of the Book of Psalms.

[2] It seems more probable, however, from 2 Mac. ii. 13, that Nehemiah was the collector and compiler of the Book of Psalms; for we read—that Nehemiah "founding a library, gathered together the acts of the kings, and the prophets, and of David."

Ps. xli., it is to be considered as part and parcel of the psalm itself. As Phillips truly says—"What is found at the end of Ps. xli., lxxxix., &c., is as appropriate for ending the particular psalm of which it is a part, as it is for ending a book." [1]

Thus we see that the fictitious authority attributed to this imaginary division into "five books," from the five books of Moses, vanishes into thin air. The truth is, we find almost all of David's psalms terminating with praise to God; as in Ps. civ., "Bless thou the Lord, O my soul. Praise ye the Lord;" and the thanksgiving to God at the end of Ps. xlv.: and accordingly, one writer divides the Psalter into seven books, [2] the two extra books terminating at Ps. cxvii. and cxxxv., in consequence of their terminations of praise; and so natural is this praise, that the Church has added its own doxology to every one of the psalms: why then should we think it anything peculiar, and foreign to the nature of other psalms, that four of these psalms should terminate with the same ascription of praise to God?

This breaking down of the supposed division into five books is further confirmed by some writers, as Ewald and others, dividing the Book into *four* parts, by Dr. Forbes dividing it into *seven* parts, and by Augustine being first disposed to divide it into *ten* parts of fifteen psalms each, and afterwards into *three* parts of fifty psalms each. It may be interesting to read his arguments, as a specimen of the absurd mystical interpretation of some of the Fathers, and of Augustine in particular; by means of which they were enabled to prove anything they pleased. [3]

---

[1] *The Psalms in Hebrew*, 1846. Introd. p. xvi.

[2] Dr. J. Forbes, *Symmet. Structure of Scripture*, pp. 134, 135.

[3] "Although the arrangement of the Psalms, which seems to me to contain the secret of a mighty mystery, hath not yet been revealed unto me, yet, by the fact that they in all amount to one hundred and fifty, they suggest somewhat even to us who have not as yet pierced with the eye of our mind the light of their entire arrangement, whereon we may, without being over bold, so far as God giveth, be able to speak. Firstly, the number *fifteen*, whereof it is a multiple, ... signifieth the agreement of the Two Testaments. For in the former is observed the Sabbath, which signifies rest; in the latter the Lord's day, which signifieth resurrection. The Sabbath is the seventh day: but the Lord's day coming after the seventh must needs be the eighth . . . . Further, seven and eight make fifteen. Of the same number are the psalms which are called 'of the steps,' because that was the number of the steps of the Temple. Furthermore, also the number *fifty* in itself also containeth a great mystery. For it consisteth of a week of weeks, which with the addition of one as an eighth complete the number *fifty*. For seven multiplied by seven make forty-nine, whereto one is added to make *fifty*. And this number *fifty* is of so great a meaning, that it was on the *fiftieth* day exactly from the Lord's resurrection the Holy Spirit descended upon the disciples. And this seven-

An argument, however, in corroboration of this pretended division into five books is adduced by Delitzsch and various authors, from the separation of the *Jehovah* and *Elohim* psalms. Hengstenberg, after pointing out this circumstance, sums up by saying—"The arrangement, then, is as follows:—The *first* book contains the Davidic-Jehovah psalms; the *second* the Elohim-psalms of the singers of David, of the sons of Korah, Ps. xlii.—xlix., of Asaph, l., of David himself, li.—lxxi., and of Solomon, lxxii; the *third* the Jehovah-psalms of Asaph, lxxiii.—lxxxiii., of the sons of Korah, Ps. lxxxiv.—lxxxix."[1] This certainly looks at first sight like a very strong, if not conclusive argument in favour of the division into five books; and it is necessary therefore to examine into the supposed fact. It is pretended that "the first

fold operation is thus mentioned by Isaiah, xi. 2—'And the spirit of the Lord shall rest upon him, the spirit of wisdom and understanding, the spirit of counsel and of might, the spirit of knowledge and of the fear of the Lord.' The number one hundred and fifty containeth this fifty *three* times, as though it were multiplied by the Trinity. Wherefore for this reason, too, we make out that this number of the Psalms is not unsuitable. For in the number of the fishes, too, which were caught in the nets, which were let down after the Resurrection, by the adding of three to one hundred and fifty, we seem to have a kind of suggestion given us, into how many parts that number ought to be divided, viz., that it should contain three *fifties*." [Though of this origin and meaning he does not appear quite sure, for he finds "by setting down all the numbers from 1 to 17 in a column, and adding them together," he arrives at the same amount, 153, which he thinks "more deep and pleasing."]

"Now in that some have believed that the Psalms are divided into five books, they have been led by the fact that so often at the end of the psalms are the words 'So be it, so be it.' But when I endeavoured to make out the principle of this division, I was not able: for neither are the five parts equal to one another, either in quantity of contents or yet even in number of psalms, so as for each to contain thirty. And if each book end with 'So be it, so be it,' we may reasonably ask why the fifth and last book hath not the same conclusion? We, however, following the authority of the canonical Scripture, where it is said, 'For it is written in the Book of Psalms,' know that there is but one Book of Psalms." [He then shows that the Book may yet be divided into parts or portions, and then concludes by saying]—"Whichever then of these is understood . . . . this Book of the Psalms in its parts of *fifty* psalms each, if it be questioned by these very divisions of fifties, gives an answer important, and very worthy of consideration. For it seems to me not without significance that the *fiftieth* is of penitence, the *hundredth* of mercy and judgment, the *hundred and fiftieth* of the praise of God in his saints. For thus do we advance to an everlasting life of happiness; first, by condemning our own sins, then by living upright; that having condemned our ill life, and lived a good life, we may attain to everlasting life. For it is written—'Moreover whom He did predestinate, them He also *called*; and whom He called, them He also *justified*; and whom He justified, them He also *glorified*.' But the *three* which remain are wrought in us, calling, justifying, glorifying."—(*On the Psalms*, Ps. cl.)   [1] *Com.* iii. p. xliv.

book contains the Davidic-Jehovah psalms." How is it, then, that the Jehovah-psalms, lxxxvi. in the third book, ci.—ciii. in the fourth book, and sixteen such psalms in the fifth book, all by David, are not included in the first book? Again, if "the second book contains the Elohim-psalms of the singers of David, and of David himself," how is it that David's Elohim-psalm cviii. in the fifth book, and the eleven Elohim-psalms of Asaph [1] in the third book, were not also included in the second book? The Elohim-psalms, instead of being confined to book ii., Ps. xlii.—lxxii., as the five-book theory would require, extend more than half-way into the third book, consisting of Ps. xlii.—lxxxiv., as stated by Delitzsch—"There are in all forty-four Elohim-psalms, xlii.—lxxxiv. They form the middle portion of the Psalter, and have on their right forty-one, and on their left sixty-five Jahve-psalms." [2] Thus Delitzsch, though advocating the division into five books, practically divides the Psalter into three parts, and this no doubt, as we shall see further presently, forms a key for the classification by Nehemiah or Ezra. The argument, therefore, of five books based on the distinction of the Elohistic and Jehovah psalms, breaks down. But it has been argued that a striking confirmation of the validity of the doxologies as marking the division into five books, exists in the fact that the doxology at the end of the second book differs from the others in the circumstance that "it is more full-toned than that of the first book, and God is intentionally here called ' *The Lord* ELOHIM, *the God of Israel*,' because the second book contains none but Elohim-psalms ; and not, as there, ' *The Lord, the God of Israel*.' " [3] But Delitzsch has already shown that the third book also is chiefly composed of Elohim-psalms, and therefore, had there been this significance in the introduction of the name *Elohim*, it would have been inserted also in the doxology at the end of the third book ; and, indeed, Hengstenberg does not fail to point out that the absence of this name at the end of the third book should, according to Delitzsch's argument, be considered as a proof that the third book consists exclusively of Jehovah-psalms [4] : which we see it does not.

But though the arrangement of Elohistic and Jehovah-psalms does not support the pretended division into five books, it may

---

[1] Hengstenberg, carried away by the force of theory, endeavours, though in vain, to make out that these eleven psalms of Asaph are Jehovah-psalms, and not Elohistic : for the name of God occurs in them exactly twice as many times as that of Jehovah. See *Com*. iii. p. xlv.

[2] *Bib. Com*. i. 19, 22.

[3] Delitzsch, ii. 306.

[4] *Com*. 1851. iii. p. xliv.

yet be supposed to throw some light on the reputed age and
authorship of the Psalms; as it would seem, say these writers, to
indicate that in the early psalmody David made use of the name
Jehovah; that Asaph and some of the sons of Korah at a later age
made use of the name *God*, (Elohim,) while others of the descendants of Korah, and other unknown psalmists at a still later age, went
back again to the name *Jehovah*. Neither, however, can this be
admitted: for while the great bulk of David's psalms are Jehovistic,
there are eighteen of his which are Elohistic; of those of the sons
of Korah there are eight Elohistic and four Jehovistic; and of those
of Asaph eleven are Elohistic and one Jehovistic. The truth is that
this distinction of Jehovistic and Elohistic psalms is imaginary; for

1.	In Book	i. the name Jehovah occurs 277 times, and God 63 times.					
2.	,,	ii.	,,	,,	40	,,	216 ,,
	,,	iii. up to Ps. lxxxiv. ,,			18	,,	68 ,,
3.	,,	,, from Ps. lxxxv.	,,		39	,,	12 ,,
	,,	iv.	,,	,,	112	,,	25 ,,
	,,	v.	,,	,,	273	,,	39 ,,

Thus we see that in the whole Book of Psalms the name *Jah*
or *Jehovah* occurs about seven hundred and sixty times, and the
name *El*, *Elohe*, or *Elohim* about four hundred and twenty times;
and that the Psalmist appears to use one or the other as the occasion
required, sometimes addressing God as the universal GOD, the God
of Sabaoth, the God of hosts, the God of all the earth; sometimes
and more particularly the God of Israel, JEHOVAH, "which was, and
is, and is to come:" sometimes the absolute title of *God* is made
personal by addressing Him as *my* God, or *our* God; sometimes, and
very often, the two titles are joined together, to show in one case
that the God of the world is the Lord Jehovah, the God of Israel;
in the other that the God of Israel is GOD, THE GOD. The same
may be observed in other books of the Old Testament. Thus in
the Book of Proverbs the name Jehovah is said to occur 59 times
and Elohim 6 times; in the Book of Ezra, Jehovah 37 times and
Elohim 97 times; and in Nehemiah, Jehovah 17 times and Elohim
74 times.[1] While therefore a distinction was evidently made by the
collector of the Book of Psalms, it is not at all clear but that the
words *God* and *Jehovah* were used indifferently by the Psalmist;
sometimes indeed the two appellations are interchanged without
apparently any reason except to avoid tautology. Thus in Psalm x.
we have in one place, "The wicked despiseth *the Lord!*" and shortly
afterwards we have in the same psalm, "Wherefore should the
wicked despise *God?*" Again, in the same psalm we have, "Arise,

[1] Bishop Browne, *The Pentateuch, and Elohim Psalms*, second edition, p. 50.

O Lord! Lift up Thine hand, O God!" Similar examples occur all through the Book of Psalms :—

Arise, O Lord !
Save me, O my God ! (Ps. iii.)

As for God, His way is perfect :
The word of the Lord is tried. (Ps. xviii.)

Unto Thee, O Lord, will I lift up my soul :
My God, I have put my trust in Thee. (Ps. xxv.)

God is gone up with a shout,
The Lord with the sound of the trumpet. (Ps. xlvii.)

The mighty God, even the Lord, hath spoken. (Ps. l.)

Behold, God is my helper :
The Lord is with them that uphold my soul. (Ps. liv.)

I will call upon God,
And the Lord will save me. (Ps. lv.)

I will praise God, because of His word,
I will praise the Lord, because of His word. (Ps. lvi.)

Break their teeth in their mouths, O God :
Smite the jaw-bones of the young lions, O Lord. (Ps. lviii.)

Power belongeth unto God :
And to Thee, O Lord, belongeth mercy. (Ps. lxii.)

. . . . The Lord will not hear me :
But God hath heard me. (Ps. lxvi.)

Bless ye God in the congregations,
Even the Lord, ye that are of the fountain of Israel.
Sing unto God, O ye kingdoms of the earth,
Sing psalms unto the Lord. (Ps. lxviii.)

I make my prayer unto Thee, O Lord, in an acceptable time :
Hear me, O God, in the multitude of Thy mercy. (Ps. lxix.)

Haste Thee, O God, to deliver me :
Haste Thee, O Lord, to my help.
Haste Thee unto me, O God !
Tarry not, O Lord ! (Ps. lxx.)

. . . . with my voice unto God, and He gave ear unto me :
In the day of my trouble I sought the Lord. (Ps. lxxvii.)

Thou art God alone :
Teach me Thy way, O Lord. (Ps. lxxxvi.)

Who among the gods shall be likened unto the Lord ?
God is to be feared greatly in the congregation of the saints. (Ps. lxxxix.)

O give thanks to the God of gods :
O give thanks to the Lord of lords. (Ps. cxxxvi.)

Praise ye the Lord !
Praise God in His sanctuary. (Ps. cl.) [1]

---

[1] Many other instances might be quoted, as Ps. xviii. 6 ; xxxi. 14 ; xxxviii. 21 ; xlvi. 11 ; xlviii. 1, 8 ; lxviii. 4 ; lxxxiv. 2 ; xci. 2 ; xciv. 22 ; civ. 33 ;

It is impossible that in these instances any distinction can be here intended, beyond that which we have just indicated. Here, however, it is necessary to explain how it is that according to the above table we assert the name *God* to appear sixty-four times in the fourth and fifth books, whereas Delitzsch makes it to appear but once in the fifth book, viz. in Ps. cxliv., and not once in the fourth book;[1] and this statement is quoted by Perowne;[2] while Hengstenberg, more correctly, allows seven mentionings of the name in the fifth book;[3] he being followed by Bishop Wordsworth:[4] none of these writers, however, reckoning the occurrence of the name in Ps. c. of the fourth book, and in the title of Ps. xc. in the same book. This divergence arises from Delitzsch distinguishing the full name of Elohim from the abbreviations of such name. It is necessary for us therefore to make a further examination of the Psalter, in order to ascertain whether anything can be gathered from the recurrence of this name. Accordingly we find that the name *Elohim*, as distinguished from its abbreviations *El* and *Elohe*, occurs as follows :—

1.	In Book	i. the full name of Elohim occurs	13	times.
2. {	,,	ii.	167	,,
{	,,	iii. to Ps. lxxxiv.	40	,,
3. {	,,	,, from Ps. lxxxv.	3	,,
{	,,	iv.	2	,,
{	,,	v.	7	,,
	In the whole Psalter	. . . .	232[5]	,,

From this we see not only that the compiler divided the Book of Psalms into three divisions, i.— xli. : xlii.—lxxxiv.; and lxxxv.— cl.; but also that the first of these divisions contained the Jehovistic-Elohim psalms, the second the Elohistic-Jehovah psalms, and the third the Jehovah psalms: and this view is still further strengthened if we suppose that Ps. cviii., which contains the full name of Elohim six times, fell into the fifth book inadvertently, as it ought to have followed Ps. lx. in the second book, which was written on the occasion when "Joab smote of Edom in the Valley of Salt twelve thousand." If then we take out this psalm from the fifth book, there will remain but three occasions in which the

cxvi. 5; cxviii. 28; cxxxv. 2; cxlvi. 2; cxlvii. 1, 7, 12; and cl. 1. These all occur in the same verse; but the list might be very greatly enlarged if adjoining verses were quoted.

[1] *Bib. Com.* i. 22.   [2] *Book of Psalms*, i. 74.
[3] *Com.* iii. p. xl.   [4] *Book of Psalms* 1870, p. x.
[5] *El* occurs about 70 times, and *Elohe* 120 times.

full name of Elohim is mentioned in the latter part of the third book, one in the fourth, besides that in the title of Ps. xc., and one in the fifth, making but six in almost half of the Book of Psalms, a clear proof of intention in the grouping of the psalms together; and that this intention was not to attempt a chronological arrangement, or division of authors, but simply to classify the psalms according to some given principle, whether of subject or treatment: and we must perceive, from what we have shown above, that the carrying out of this principle is too perfect to allow us for one moment to suppose that the "five books" were collected together and compiled, as many suppose, at five different eras of Jewish history.

Thus we see that, as the psalms were written on different occasions and on separate rolls, the collector of them who compiled the Book of Psalms bestowed the greatest care in the sorting and arranging his materials, and that from the awe and solemnity with which God sometimes revealed His name in Scripture, one of the first things would be the counting of the names of God, and placing together those psalms in which the same name of God appeared most frequently. Other methods of classification would be the placing those together which begin in the same manner, or in which any peculiar expression occurs, or which refer to the same graces, as that of patience under injuries, or to the same occasions; and accordingly commentators have pointed out numerous instances of what they believe to be "double psalms," or "pairs of psalms." Hengstenberg adduces five different motives for grouping such psalms together.[1] Not to mention minor particulars which led to this grouping, we have large divisions of the "Songs of degrees," and the "Hallelujah psalms," the "Hodu psalms," and "Psalmsongs;" while most of those bearing the name of Asaph are grouped together, as are also most of those with the name of the sons of Korah. Thus it happens that Ps. lxxii., which ought to be at the end of the psalms of David, is placed in the middle of the collection, the compiler evidently thinking less of chronological arrangement than of casting the collection into a perfect whole, beginning with introductory psalms, with morning and evening hymns, and terminating with ascriptions of praise to God, placing in the middle, and sorting according to the best of his judgment, all the other psalms, whether lyric or didactic, whether of prayer or praise, whether historical or personal, whether of meditation or of instruction, whether of complaint or rejoicing.

[1] *Com.* iii. p. xlvi.—xlix. See also Jebb, *Lit. Transl.* ii. Diss. iii.; Perowne, *Book of Psalms,* i. 79; but particularly Delitzsch, i. 22; and in his commentary to each psalm.

But though we have disposed of the figment of the division into five books; even if we were to admit its reality, we should be no better able to discover any evidence therefrom as to the reputed authorship of the Psalms: for if the reader will only take the trouble (which the author has done for his own instruction) of exhibiting in parallel columns the chronological arrangements of those who have thus written on the Psalms, he will see at once how conflicting are the views of such writers, and how hopeless is the task of endeavouring to establish an exact chronological arrangement of them. Let us take one example from the chronological arrangement of "Four Friends:"—

"In these psalms (xlii.—xliii., lxxxiv.), the language is that of the captivity. The terrible blow had come at last: the king and the nobles were carried away to Babylon. Jeremiah and Ezekiel abound with expressions which indicate the poignancy of the national anguish at this overwhelming calamity. The last of David's line, the lion cub of the house of Judah" [They then quote from Stanley's *Lectures on the Jewish Church*, 2nd series, p. 541, as follows:] "was cast away like a broken and despised vessel; (Jer. xxii. 24, 28;) the voice of the young lion (Ezek. xix. 3-6) should no more be heard on the mountains of Israel; the topmost and tenderest shoot of the royal cedar tree (Ezek. xvii. 4) had been plucked off by the eagle of the East, and planted far away in the merchant city of Euphrates. From the top of Lebanon, from the heights of Bashan, from the ridges of Abarim, the widowed country shrieked aloud, as she saw the train of her captive king and nobles disappearing in the distant East. From the heights of Hermon, from the top of Mizar, it is no improbable conjecture that the departing king poured forth his exquisitely plaintive song, in which, from the deep disquietude of his heart, he longs after the presence of God in the Temple, and pleads his cause against the impious nation, the treacherous and unjust man, who in spite of plighted faith (Ps. xliii. 1, 2; Joseph. *Ant.* x. 9) had torn him away from his beloved home."

This is beautiful writing: but is it true? Let us hear what holy Scripture says of this same man, this holy man, this injured man, this loving man!

It is sad when we find the children of good men turning out evil: a result frequently arising from the want of restraint on the part of their parents. With the example of Aaron and his two sons, but especially of Eli and his children, before his eyes, one wonders to see the sons of Samuel turning out evil. Here we have another sad example, and one entailing the greatest misfortune to the land,

arising from the manner in which the sons of good King Josiah
were brought up.   Let us give his pedigree :—

	Zebudah	=	Josiah b. 649 k. 641 d. 610	=	Hamutal	

Eliakim	=	Nehushta	Shallum [1]		Mattaniah	=
Jehoiakim			Johanan		Zedekiah	
b. 635			Jehoahaz		b. 620	
k. 610,			b. 623		k. 599,	
d. 599 on his			k. 610		taken cap-	
way to Babylon			reigned 3 months		tive to	
			taken captive		Babylon	
			to Egypt.		588.	

Coniah		Zedekiah		Sons all
Jeconiah				slain.
Jehoiachin				
b. 607				
k. 599				
reigned 3 months				
taken captive				
to Babylon.				

Shealtiel	=	Several other
Salathiel		sons.

Zorababel
Zerubbabel
   returned to
Jerusalem.

By this we see how immediately connected with Josiah were the
last four kings of Judah.   With the exception of a grandson, who

---

[1] The compiler of the genealogies in the Book of Chronicles makes Shallum
the fourth son of Josiah ; Zedekiah the brother of Coniah, instead of being his
uncle ; and Zerubbabel the grandson of Coniah by Pedaiah, instead of by
Shealtiel.   In one respect, however, he appears to be right in making Coniah
eight years old when he ascended the throne, instead of eighteen, as stated by
the chronicler of the Book of Kings.   It is curious, moreover, to find that
though Eliakim was born two years before Shallum, he did not succeed his
father.   This is explained by the fact mentioned by the chronicler that "the
people of the land took Jehoahaz the son of Josiah, and made him king in his
father's stead in Jerusalem."

reigned but three months, they were all the sons of Josiah. They all bore names compounded from the awful name of GOD himself, and signifying HIS grace, HIS possession, HIS arising, HIS strength. HIS steadfastness, HIS justice ; names, alas, which betokened their father's piety, rather than their own deserving. Being the children of such a parent, God had promised them, if they would follow the example of their parent,—" If ye do this thing indeed, then shall there enter in by the gates of this house kings sitting upon the throne of David, riding in chariots and on horses; he, and his servants, and his people. But if ye will not hear these words, then shall this house become a desolation." How did they accept God's offer? Of the eldest, Jehoahaz, we read that he and his people forsook the covenant of the Lord their God, and worshipped other gods, and served them, (Jer. xxii. 9,) and that—

He did that which was evil in the sight of the Lord,
According to all that his fathers had done. 2 Kings xxiii. 32.

Of his elder brother, Jehoiakim, we read that he was guilty of all manner of unrighteousness to God, and of injustice to man ; that he robbed the poor, and oppressed his neighbour ; that he rejoiced in deeds of violence and in shedding of innocent blood ; that he defied God's threatenings, and scoffed at His pleadings ; that he burnt the word of God in defiance of the Most High, and that when God's judgments were about to fall upon the land, he built himself a palace, and lined it with cedar, and painted it with vermilion, so that—

" The stone cried out from the wall,
And the beam out of the timber did answer it ;"

so that the mournful dirge is repeated of him—

And he did that which was evil in the sight of the Lord,
According to all that his fathers had done.
2 Kings xxiii. 37 ; 2 Chron. xxxvi. 5.

So great indeed was his wickedness that, like wicked Jezebel, his dead body was denied burial, and was cast into the highway. " Therefore, thus saith the Lord concerning Jehoiakim, the son of Josiah, king of Judah—

They shall not lament for him, saying –
" Ah ! my brother !" or " Ah ! sister !"
They shall not lament for him saying—
" Ah ! Lord !" or " Ah ! his glory !"
He shall be buried with the burial of an ass,
Drawn and cast forth beyond the gates of Jerusalem.
Jer. xxii. 13—19 ; xxxvi. 24, 30, 31.

Jeconiah, or Jehoiachin, the next king, is likened to a "despised broken idol," a "vessel wherein is no pleasure;" (Jer. xxii. 28;) and of him again we hear the mournful dirge—

And he did that which was evil in the sight of the Lord,
According to all that his father had done.   2 Kings xxiv. 9.

Of Zedekiah, the last king, who was as weak as he was wicked, who broke faith with the poor of his people in refusing to enfranchise them in the seventh year, we are told that he "hardened his heart from turning unto the Lord God of Israel;" (2 Chron. xxxvi. 13;) so that, notwithstanding that God pleaded with him also, even as it were up to the last moment, (Jer. xxi. 12—14,) and would have heard him, if he had confessed his sins, even as he heard wicked Ahab, (1 Kings xxi. 27—29,) and wicked Manasseh, (2 Chron. xxxiii. 12, 13,) and remitted their punishment ; but all in vain : we hear the dirge,[1] repeated for the last time—

And he did that which was evil in the sight of the Lord,
According to all that Jehoiakim had done.

And here we may remark that in the last two cases it is no longer said "according to all that his *fathers* had done," referring especially to Manasseh, but according to all that "his *father*," or "Jehoiakim," had done : thus showing that their wickedness, as wickedness always does, had gone on increasing, "until, at length, the wrath of the Lord arose against His people, till there was no remedy." (2 Chron. xxxvi. 14—16 ; Jer. xxii. 9.)

These are the last kings of Judah : they were all captive kings. Which of them is the pious king whom these writers delight to honour? Let them take their choice.[2] And now let anyone read what the talented writer referred to justly styles that "exquisitely plaintive song" (xlii.) which King Jehoiakim is supposed to have written ; beginning—

As the hart longeth after the water-brooks,
So longeth my soul after THEE, O God !
My soul is athirst for GOD, for the living God !
When shall I come to appear before God ?

---

[1] Compare the dirge in the seventy-eighth psalm—

" But for all this they sinned yet more,
And believed not His wondrous works."

[2] Ewald ascribes the forty-second psalm to Jehoiakim, and the eighty-fourth to Jehoiachin ! The reader will understand from v. 9 of this latter psalm, " Look upon the face of thine anointed," that it was necessary to find a king as the author of this psalm.

Or that other equally beautiful one (lxxxiv.) which they ascribe to his son Jehoiachin—

> How lovely are Thy tabernacles, O Lord of hosts!
> My soul hath a desire and longing for the courts of the Lord,
> My heart and my flesh cry out for the living God!

And he need not be a Solomon to declare who is the author of them. While the forty-second and forty-third psalms are ascribed by these writers to the infamous Jehoiakim, and the forty-fourth to the "despised broken idol" Jehoiachin, the forty-fifth is supposed by one critic [1] to have been written in honour of the marriage of Ahab (of whom it is written that "there was none like unto Ahab, which did sell himself to work wickedness in the sight of the Lord") with "wicked Jezebel!" and by another [2]—on the occasion of the marriage of Jehoram, king of Judah (who murdered all his brothers and many of the princes of Israel, (Judah,) 2 Chron. xxi. 4) with Athaliah, the wicked daughter of wicked Ahab and wicked Jezebel, who murdered all her grandchildren! (2 Kings xi. 1.) So much for the application of "internal evidence!"

We have spoken rather depreciatingly of "internal evidence," as thus adduced in reference to the authorship of the Psalms. Let it not be supposed that we disregard internal evidence : it would be foolish in anyone to do so on any subject : and we ourselves have made considerable use of internal evidence in the foregoing essay : but what we object to is that such evidence, as it is called, which is often no *evidence* at all, but mere conjecture, is pushed beyond its limits. In almost every such case the proper language would be—from this or that circumstance *we may suppose*, or *we may conclude*, or *it is probable*, or *an argument may be drawn*. An instance of this perversion of "internal evidence" occurs in relation to Numb. vi. 24—26, which from its resemblance to Ps. lxxvii. 1, is supposed by Colenso to have been "probably written by a disciple of Samuel, contemporary with David, who first introduced the name of Jehovah!" And from such evidence, and from the number of times that the names of God—Elohim and Jehovah—occur in the Pentateuch, he comes to the conclusion that the first four books and the Book of Joshua were written by Samuel and his disciples, and that the Book of Deuteronomy was written probably by Jeremiah! It has been said that "with numbers we can prove anything," and certainly with "internal evidence" used in this manner we can prove whatever we please. Another instance is afforded us by Delitzsch, who, fancying he sees a strong resem-

---

[1] Hitzig.   [2] Delitzsch.

T

blance between Ps. lxxxviii., which bears the name of Heman,
and the Book of Job, "both as regards linguistic usage and
single thoughts, and also the suffering condition of the poet, and
the whole manner in which this finds expression," concludes that
the Book of Job was written by Heman, who with Ethan he supposes "belonged to the wise men of the first rank at the court of
Solomon!"[1] Sometimes indeed this "internal evidence" is con-
futed by some passage in the psalm itself: but in such cases we are
led to suppose that there has been "an addition by a later hand,"
that it is a "liturgical addition," that "a portion of another psalm
has slipped in," that there is "a mutilation by loss," "a transposi-
tion of the text," an insertion of "a fragment belonging to some other
psalm, and here altogether out of place." With these liberties taken
with the text, and the superscriptions cast aside, we can indeed prove
anything we please.[2] Again, it is strange when critics have sought
so eagerly for "internal evidence," that they should have limited
their inquiries to material facts, to matters of history, to ruggedness
of style, or to a soft and flowing one; and should have taken no care
to examine the *external evidence* of prophecy or revelation, or the
internal evidence of piety. The result of this neglect has been that
writers have got more and more lost in the mazes of uncertainty,
till at last the psalms of the "sweet psalmist of Israel," the "man
after God's own heart," are attributed to perhaps the most wicked
king of the house of Judah, who was buried with the burial of an
ass; or to his son, who was likened to a despised broken idol; or
to the miserable and wicked last king, whose eyes were put out
for his rebellion against the King of Babylon, and for his apostasy
towards God! We cannot, indeed, take up any modern exposition
of the Psalms without seeing how every writer has felt the difficulty of determining who are the writers of the several psalms:
for no two writers agree.[3] In treating of Ps. cxli. Perowne writes:

[1] *Bib. Com.* iii. 23, 24.

[2] Delitzsch points out an amusing instance of one of these criticisms.
"Böttcher transposes the verses in the alphabetical Ps. cxi., and *corrects* the
initial word of another, Ps. cxii.; in the warmth of his critical zeal he runs
against the boundary posts of the letters marking the order, without observing
it." *Bib. Com.* ii. 197. And of another critic, Hitzig, he says, "only his
clairvoyant-like historical discernment is able" to fill up the *nun*-strophe of
the alphabetical Ps. cxlv. with v. 6 of Ps. cxli. *Ib.* iii. 388.

[3] Thus with regard to Ps. xlii.—xliii, Delitzsch writes—"What a variegated
pattern card of hypotheses modern criticism opens out in connection with this
psalm! Vaihinger regards it as a song composed by one of the Levites, who
was banished by Athaliah. Ewald thinks that King Jeconiah, who was
carried away to Babylon, may have composed this psalm, and in fact when
(and this he infers from the psalm itself) on the journey to Babylon, he may

" It is curious that whilst De Wette, describing the psalm as ' a very original, and therefore difficult psalm,' holds it to be one of the oldest in the collection, Maurer, almost on the same grounds, sets it down as belonging to a comparatively late period."

The sixty-eighth psalm, however, forms the most extraordinary instance. Reuss wrote a book—*Der acht-und-sechzigste Psalm, ein Denkmal exegetischer Noth und Kunst zu Ehren unser ganzen Zunft, Jena*, 1851—in which he collects and exhibits the opinions of no fewer than 400 rival interpreters, and which Hupfeld describes as " written with much humour, full of points and antitheses in the grouping, and very amusing to read." Perowne says :—" There is the greatest difference of opinion both as to the occasion for which, and the period at which the psalm was written : some, as Gesenius, Ewald, Hupfeld, Olshausen, Reuss, regarding it as one of the later, or even of the very latest of Hebrew poems ; and others, as Böttcher, De Wette, Hitzig, classing it with the very earliest. One set of critics sees in it every evidence of antiquity and originality : another sees in it every mark of a late age, and a great absence of originality."—*Book of Psalms*, I. 498, 499. What weight indeed can be attached to criticism thus uncontrolled, when we find writers like Hitzig, Von Lengerke, and Olshausen ascribing the greater part of the Psalter to the Maccabees : viz., all the psalms in what are called the third, fourth, and fifth books, and many of those in the first and second ! We have seen what are the consequences of this disagreement : how that not merely the psalms which bear no superscription are supposed to be written at a later time, but that many of the psalms which bear the name of David are declared to be written by someone else ; till at length, as with Hitzig, not one psalm remains for the author of the Book of Psalms, the declarations of our Lord and of His apostles notwithstanding ! Let us then, seeing how possible it is that all the psalms, with perhaps some few exceptions, were written by David, ascribe them, if only

have been detained just a night in the vicinity of Hermon. Reuss (Nouvelle Revue de Théologie, 1858) prefers to suppose it is one of those who were carried off with Jeconiah (among whom there were also priests, as Ezekiel). Hitzig, however, is no less decisive in his view that the author is a priest who was carried off in the direction of Syria at the time of the wars of the Seleucidæ and Ptolemies, probably Onias III., high priest from 199 B.C., [whom he regards as] the collector of the Second Book of Psalms, and whom the Egyptians under the general Skopas carried away to the citadel of Paneas. Olshausen even here, as usual, makes Antiochus Epiphanes his watchword." To these may be added Paulus, who, with De Wette, ascribes it to the time of Jeroboam. It has been well said by Maurer—" Quærendo elegantissimi carminis scriptore frustra se fatigant interpretes."

for convenience, if only for usefulness of devotion, to him whose
name they bear when considered collectively. We may infer from
the fact of Ps. xcvi., cv., and cvi., bearing no titles, notwithstanding the statement in the Book of Chronicles of David's being the
author, and from what we have already said, that Nehemiah, or
the compiler of the Book of Psalms, by not putting a title to these
particular psalms, believed that David was the author of all of
them ; from the fact of there being no division into books in the
Septuagint and the Chaldee, we may conclude that the authors of
these translations looked upon the whole as one book ; from Luke
xx. 42, and Acts i. 20, we may assume that our Lord and St. Peter
knew of no such division ; while from 2 Mac. ii. 13, and Heb. iv.
7, we may infer that from the time of the Maccabees to the Christian era the whole collection went by the name of David ;[1] "saying
in David," as St. Paul writes. It is not extraordinary, therefore,
that we find Origen, Ambrose, Chrysostom, Theodoret, Augustine,
and Cassiodorus ascribing the whole collection to David, or that the
framers of our Liturgy have done so, who call the book collectively
"The Psalms of David," or that Chrysostom and the early Church
should call the Psalter "David," or that the Æthiopic Psalter
should conclude with "David is ended ; " or that the Syriac trans-

lations should call it ⁘ ܩܠܐ ܕܓܒܪ̈ܐ ܘܨܠ̈ܘܬܐ ܕܕܘܝܕ ܡܠܟܐ ⁘
"The Psalms of David the King and Prophet."

In conclusion, then, we would say, that though, were we writing
a history of David, we should be extremely desirous to ascertain
the occasion when each psalm was written, so as to place them all
in chronological arrangement ; and thereby investigate the character
of David ; showing how it was influenced and matured by the
chequered circumstances of his life, and how these circumstances
wrought in him a higher and more chastened expression of holiness :
yet, considering that the Psalms, like all the Scriptures, are written
for our instruction and comfort in Divine things, and not to teach
us history ; just as we find that Holy Scripture does not teach us
astronomy, or geology, or genealogy, or national annals, when unconnected with the history of God's Church, even when these subjects are referred to ; let us endeavour to receive them as the WORD
OF GOD, written for ourselves, and not perplex ourselves about so
comparatively unimportant a thing as chronological arrangement. It
has pleased God that the Book of Psalms has come down to us

---

[1] Rabbi Meir in the Talmud, *Pesachim* 117a, and two modern commentators,
Klauss, 1832, and Randegger, 1841, attribute the whole collection to David.
(Delitzsch, i. 51.)

in its present state, the penitential psalms and the psalms of rejoicing being mixed together, so that we may more frequently mourn for our sins, more frequently rejoice in God's mercy. Let us, then, rather think of the application of the psalms to ourselves, than be *over*-curious to find out the particular occasions when they were written; lest our minds should be so engrossed with applying every circumstance in the psalms to these historical particulars, that we fail in deriving any benefit to our own souls. But while we avoid being over-curious, we are justified in forming and encouraged to have a *positive* idea of the authorship of the psalms, in order that we may have a more confident conception of their divine inspiration. Our Lord, in quoting them, said:—"David himself says in the Book of Psalms;" and St. Paul also says:—"Wherefore *he* (David) says also in another psalm." It is therefore from a fear lest the belief in the Divine inspiration of Scripture be weakened by such over-curious research, that we protest against the system of chronological arrangement of these critics, on reading which one is led to doubt that any of the psalms were written by David: for if they reject most of those which bear his name, how are we sure that they may not be mistaken in the attribution to him of those which remain?[1]

[1] We may judge of what the Jews thought on this subject, by the fable which we read in the Midrash on Ps. iii. where we are told that when Joshua Ben Levi was endeavouring to put the Psalms in order, a voice from heaven cried out to him—"Arouse not the slumberer!" *i.e.* Disturb not David! (Delitzsch, i. 17.)

Note to Page 247, *too late for insertion*:—" As far as the structure of the Hebrew language is concerned, we are unable to trace, with any minuteness, its various transitions. The poems of David, of Isaiah, of Jeremiah, or Habakkuk, are not in this way so broadly distinguished from earlier compositions, as we find to be the case in the dates of merely human songs. It is sheer ignorance of this circumstance which made some rash Biblical critics hazard certain theories respecting the dates and authorship of some portions of the Bible. The German philogists, and their British disciples, reason on unsafe premises. It is this ignorance which betrayed some of the former, and misled some of the latter, to propound the preposterous idea that the Books of Moses, Isaiah, Daniel, were penned by various writers who flourished at different periods in the annals of the Jewish Church, than those believed in."—*The Poetry of the Hebrew Pentateuch.* By Dr. Moses Margoliouth, 1871.

ESSAY II.

ON THE EXTERNAL FORM OF HEBREW POETRY AS EXHIBITED IN THE BOOK OF PSALMS.

II.

ON THE EXTERNAL FORM OF HEBREW POETRY AS EXHIBITED IN THE BOOK OF PSALMS.

THE Hebrew Poetry differs from that of other nations in its possessing neither rhyme nor metre. This assertion must startle an ordinary reader, who would be unable to understand how that could be poetry which is wanting in these two qualifications, at least the latter; no less than a classic student, who would deny that to be poetry which is incapable of being scanned. After the dispersion of the Jews consequent upon the destruction of Jerusalem, less attention was gradually given to Hebrew literature, and those who studied the Sacred Books were mostly ignorant that any portion of the text was written in a poetic form, the Rolls being written in continuous lines, instead of having the lines separated as in modern poetry. Of the Sacred MSS. which have come down to us, two-thirds are written in continuous lines, like prose; and sometimes indeed with all the letters joined together;[1] though some of these, which have the Masoretic points, have the lines indicated by accents.[2] These Masoretic copies, as well as those which are written stichometrically, appear to be more recent than the others. Were it otherwise, were they more ancient, we should then be in no doubt as to the dividing or pointing of the lines in our translations: all that we should have to do would be to follow the Masoretic divisions. But as such divisions are no part of the original Hebrew, we cannot be sure that they always correspond

[1] Le Clerc says, "In codicibus antiquissimis Hebraicis Judæi fatentur, voces nullis interstitiis sejunctas, nec ullis interpunctionibus separatas esse; aut saltem, quam plurimas ita conjunctas, quasi essent una vox." Kennicot, *Dissert. Generalis*, § 124.

[2] Dr. Schiller-Szinessy observes that in the "Prideaux Pentateuch" belonging to the Society of Biblical Archæology, "between verse and verse there is generally a somewhat wider space left than between word and word."

with the original poetry. Any attempt, therefore, to print the
translation in a poetic form must be attended with great uncertainty, and regarded as a mere tentative effort, and only looked
upon as authoritative when most simple and most evident, and
most resembling those instances which we have in the Alphabetical
Psalms, where the initial letters leave no doubt as to the beginning
and end of each line. Though the Hebrew rolls were written in
the form of continuous prose, it is evident that the Jews knew
that some portions were poetical, for Josephus so speaks of them
in his "Jewish Antiquities." Like Josephus, Philo-Judæus,
Origen, Eusebius, Isidore, and other fathers of the Church, thought
the poetry was written in classic metre, as the hexameter and
pentameter. Jerome, however, seems to have noted the existence
of parallelism in the Book of Psalms; for his translation, which
was executed in the fourth century, is written stichometrically, or
in lines.

Delitzsch observes that—"There is no Hebrew MS. which could
have formed the basis of the arrangement of the Psalms in stichs:
those which we possess only break the Masoretic verse—if the
space of the line admits of it—for ease of writing into two halves,
without even regarding the general injunction. . . . that the breaks
are to be regulated by the beginnings of the verses and the two
great pausal accents. Nowhere in the MSS. which divide and
break up the words most capriciously, is there to be seen any trace
of the recognition of those old םיקוספ being preserved. These were
not merely lines determined by the space, as were chiefly also the
στίχοι or ἔπη, according to the number of which the compass of
Greek words was recorded, but lines determined by the sense, κῶλα
(Suidas: κῶλον ὁ ἀπηρτισμένην ὅ τοιαν ἔχων στίχοι) as Jerome wrote
his Latin translation of the Old Testament after the model of the
Greek and Roman orators, (e.g. the MSS. of Demosthenes,) per
cola et commata, i.e. in lines breaking off according to the sense."
(Bib. Com. 1, 27, 28.) The result is that none of the Hebrew
MSS. possess any absolute authority for the division of the lines:
they differ from each other in the pointing, and this pointing is
often not merely capricious, but evidently false, and opposed alike
to parallelism and construction. All that we can conclude from
these MSS., whether written stichometrically or divided by the
Masoretic accents, is that the early copyists perceived that what
they were copying was poetry, and that they tried, though often in
vain, to arrange it as such. It follows, therefore, that, however
the original was written, as the earliest copies are written continuously, and the later ones only occasionally written stichometri-

cally, but never agreeing in the division of the lines, it is hopeless
to expect that we shall ever discover with absolute certainty,
having neither metre nor rhyme to assist us, what was the original
division of the verse; and that we can only arrive at an approxi-
mate realization of the original disposition and arrangement, by the
study and comparison of successive efforts to restore such arrangement. Every fresh attempt, therefore, to exhibit the arrangement
of the Hebrew poetry should be based, not upon the writer's
caprice or imagination, but upon a careful examination of all previous efforts, to see whether in some instances the writer's arrangement, instead of being an improvement on former essays, may not
be a falling back from what has been already done.

The revival of the study of Hebrew literature took place immediately after the discovery of printing in the fifteenth century,
when several editions of the Hebrew Scriptures were published by
learned Jews, in which the poetical parts of Scripture were distinguished from the prosaic portions. In the sixteenth century, Rabbi
Azarias noted the existence of parallelism in the Hebrew poetry;
and a few years after him, in 1560, Professor Morell, of Paris, published the first and second psalms in the form of verse. In the
seventeenth century, Gomarus in 1637, Meibomius in 1674, and
others, thought to improve upon the writers of the preceding century, by discovering that Hebrew poetry resembled that of the
Greeks and Romans in the arrangement of its metre—a conceit
which was still further improved upon towards the end of the
century and the beginning of the next, by Le Clerc, Garofalo, and
Fourmont. who pretended to discover the existence of rhyme also.
Bishop Hare, towards the middle of the eighteenth century, in-
veighed against these fancies, though he still thought that Hebrew
poetry contained some of the Greek measures. But it was not till
1763 that parallelism was reasserted to be the sole base of the
Hebrew poetry. In this year, Dr., afterwards Bishop, Lowth
brought out his *Prælectiones*, "Lectures on the Sacred Poetry of
the Hebrews," in which he divides this parallelism into three
kinds: 1,—Synonymous: when the several lines express the same
sense, as in Ps. i. v. 1:—

> Blessed is the man that walketh not in the counsel of the ungodly;
> That standeth not in the way of sinners;
> And that sitteth not in the seat of the scornful.

2,—Antithetic: when the lines are contrasted with, or opposed to
each other, as in v. 7:—

> For the Lord knoweth the way of the righteous;
> But the way of the ungodly shall perish.

3.—Synthetic : when there is a diversity of figure, but a similarity of construction and signification, as in v. 4 :—

> His leaf also shall not wither ;
> And look, whatsoever he doeth, it shall prosper.

These three varieties of Bishop Lowth may for our present purpose be united under one class which we will call *direct* or regular. The opposite to this is the *inverted*, as in v. 2 :—

> But whose delight is in the law of the Lord,
> And in His law doth he exercise himself day and night ;

which would be converted into a direct parallelism by reading—

> And who exercises himself day and night in His law.

But though this principle of parallelism forms the general characteristic, it will be frequently found to fail, as in v. 3, where no parallelism whatever can be detected :—

> And he shall be like a tree planted by the water-side, that will bring
>   forth his fruit in due season.

It is evident that this verse, standing in the middle of other verses in the psalm, all of which are divisible into two lines which are parallel with each other in one of the above-mentioned ways, must also be divided into two lines, though its parts run only in continuation of each other, as in ordinary prose : —

> And he shall be like a tree planted by the water-side,
> That will bring forth his fruit in due season.

It follows that the verse, though not appearing to conform to the law of parallelism, must be judged to be poetical, because it is in the midst of other verses which we know to be such ; provided that the verse from its structure is capable of division into two lines, and that these lines correspond with the lines of the other verses. Indeed, it is generally admitted in poetry that the occasional introduction of a less artificial form of composition gives greater force and value to those parts which are more studied, as well as greater variety. Sometimes, however, the verse appears incapable of subdivision into two lines, and exhibits an apparent want of correspondence and apposition with those adjoining it, in all of which we find parallelism to be evident, while in this particular verse we see only harshness and incongruity ; but on more carefully examining any such verse, we shall invariably find that its superfluous part disposes of itself in one or other of the following ways : either, it is capable of subdivision into two lines, however short; or we may indent it, so as to form the commencement or the conclusion of a paragraph; or we shall find that what appears as the superfluous part of one verse ties in with the superabundant part of the following verse, so that what is divided into two verses in our Bibles, ought to have been divided into three verses.

We will first consider some instances in which the line is capable of division into two short lines; and we will begin by adducing an instance where we have undoubted authority for such short lines. It is in Ps. xxv., where the lines are marked by the letters of the alphabet :—

> ה Lead me in Thy truth,
> ו And teach me.

And in another alphabetical psalm it appears equally evident; for in the thirty-fourth psalm we find each letter of the alphabet occupying a distich; and therefore each of the following letters should do so also :—

> ה They had an eye unto Him,
>   And were lightened;
> ו And their faces
>   Were not ashamed.

These short lines are, however, generally used when it is desired to give peculiar solemnity to some word, as, for example, to the name of God :—

> And upon the harp will I give thanks unto Thee,
> O GOD, MY GOD ! (Ps. xliii. 4.)
>
> —Thine altars, O Lord of hosts,
> My KING and my GOD ! (Ps. lxxxiv. 3.)
>
> Be ye sure that the Lord
> HE IS GOD ! (Ps. c. 3.)

The name of God in such instances becomes invested with peculiar awe and reverence; and there is no doubt that, however disproportioned a short line may appear to the eye, as connected with a long line; to the ear, the slow and reverend manner with which the name of God in such instances would be pronounced, would be considered as a sufficient equivalent.

When the line is incapable of thus forming a distich, it may be found to commence a paragraph :—

> Arise, O Lord !
> Let not man have the upper hand :
> Let the heathen be judged in Thy sight. (Ps. ix. 19.)

Arise, O Lord!
Lift up Thine hand;
Forget not the poor.   (Ps. x. 13.)

The Lord liveth!
And blessed be my Rock,
And praised be the God of my salvation.   (Ps. xviii. 47.)

But unto the ungodly said God—
" Why dost thou preach My laws,
" And takest My covenant in thy mouth ? "   (Ps. l. 16.)

But the king shall rejoice in God :
All they also that swear by Him shall be commended :
But the mouth of them that speak lies shall be stopped.
(Ps. lxiii. 12.)

But as for me,
I make my prayer unto Thee, O Lord,
In an acceptable time.   (Ps. lxix. 13.)

And many other instances.

But the greatest number of examples of this kind occur in the
beginning of psalms, where the line forms a kind of title, or proem,
among which may be mentioned the following :—

Blessed is the man
That walketh not in the counsel of the ungodly,
That standeth not in the way of sinners,
And that sitteth not in the seat of the scornful.   (Ps. i.)

In the Lord put I my trust !
How say ye then to my soul—
" Flee as a bird to your hill ? "   (Ps. xi.)

Help me, O Lord !
For there is not one godly man left !
For the faithful are minished from among the children of men.
(Ps. xii.)

I will magnify Thee, O Lord !
For Thou hast set me up,
And hast not made my foes to triumph over me.   (Ps. xxx.)

In Thee, O Lord, have I put my trust !
Let me never be put to confusion :
Deliver me in Thy righteousness.   (Ps. xxxi.)

Blessed is he that considereth the poor.
The Lord will deliver him in the time of trouble :
The Lord will preserve him and keep him alive.   (Ps. xli.)

Judge me, O God !
And plead my cause against an ungodly people :
O deliver me from the deceitful and wicked man.   (Ps. xlii.)

Be merciful unto me, O God !
For man goeth about to devour me :
  He is daily fighting and troubling me.
Mine enemies strive daily to devour me ;
  For there are many that fight proudly against me. (Ps. lvi.)

Hear, O Thou Shepherd of Israel !
Thou that leadest Joseph like a sheep,
Thou that dwellest between the cherubim, shine forth !
                                  (Ps. lxxx.)

How beloved are Thy tabernacles, O Lord of hosts !
My soul hath a desire and a longing for the courts of the Lord !
My heart and my flesh cry out for the living God ! (Ps. lxxxiv.)

The Lord is King !
Let the earth rejoice,
Let the multitude of the isles be glad thereof ! (Ps. xcvii.)

The Lord said unto my Lord—
" Sit Thou on My right hand,
" Until I make Thine enemies Thy footstool." (Ps. cx.)

I was glad when they said unto me—
" Let us go into the house of the Lord,
" Our feet shall stand in thy gates, O Jerusalem." (Ps. cxxii.)

Blessed be the Lord my strength !
Who teacheth my hands to war,
And my fingers to fight. (Ps. cxliv.)

Praise ye the Lord !
For it is a good thing to sing praises unto our God,
For it is a joyful and pleasant thing to sing praises. (Ps. cxlvii.)

Sometimes the supernumerary verse forms a striking termination :—

I will be glad and rejoice in Thee ;
Yea, my songs will I make of Thy name,
  O Thou Most Highest ! (Ps. ix. 2.)

He will convert my soul,
He will bring me forth into the paths of righteousness,
  For His name's sake. (Ps. xxiii. 3.)

Thou sufferedst men to ride over our heads ;
We went through fire and water ;
  And Thou broughtest us out into a wealthy place. (Ps. lxvi. 11.)

More mighty than the voices of many waters,
More mighty than the waves of the sea,
  Is Jehovah in the highest ! (Ps. xciii. 5.)

> Confounded be all they that worship carved images,
> That delight in vain gods ;
>   Worship Him all ye gods !
> Sion heard of it, and rejoiced,
> And the daughters of Judah were glad,
>   Because of Thy judgments, O Lord !   (Ps. xcvii. 7, 8.)

And so in many other instances.

The last way in which the supernumerary line is disposed of is by connecting it with the supernumerary line of another verse. This is done in two ways : by connecting it with the first line of the following verse, thus forming an anadiplosis :—

> Lift up your heads, O ye gates ;
> And be ye lift up, ye everlasting doors ;
>   And the King of Glory shall come in !
> " Who is this King of Glory ?"
> It is the Lord, strong and mighty !
> It is the Lord, mighty in battle !   (Ps. xxiv. 7, 8 ; and also 9, 10.)

or, which is more common, by connecting it with the corresponding line of the following verse :—

> The earth trembled, and was troubled ;
> The foundations of the mountains shook and were removed ;
>   Because He was wroth !
> There went a smoke out of His nostrils,
> And a consuming fire out of His mouth,
>   So that coals were kindled at it.
>
> At the brightness of His presence
> There issued from his thick clouds
>   Hailstones and coals of fire.
> The Lord thundered out of heaven,
> And the Highest gave His thunder,
>   Hailstones and coals of fire.   (Ps. xviii. 7, 8 ; 12, 13.)

But the most beautiful example of this description occurs in Ps. lxx., which will be exhibited presently.

Of course it is not necessary to speak of triplets, the occasional use of which gives great beauty to the composition.

> The voice of the Lord is upon the waters,
> The God of glory commandeth the thunder,
> The Lord is upon many waters.
>
> The voice of the Lord is powerful,
> The voice of the Lord is full of majesty,
> The voice of the Lord breaketh the cedar trees.
>
> The voice of the Lord divideth the flames of fire,
> The voice of the Lord shaketh the wilderness,
> The Lord shaketh the wilderness of Kadesh.   (Ps. xxix. 3—8.)

That walketh not in the counsel of the ungodly,
That standeth not in the way of sinners,
And that sitteth not in the seat of the scornful.   (Ps. i. 1.)

Let destruction come upon him unawares,
Let his net which he hath hid catch himself,
And let him fall into his own destruction.   (Ps. xxxv. 8.)

He imagineth mischief upon his bed,
He hath set himself in no good way,
He doth not abhor anything that is evil.   (Ps. xxxvi. 4.)

Let not the water-flood drown me,
And let not the deep swallow me up,
And let not the pit shut her mouth upon me.   (Ps. lxix. 16.)

The waters saw Thee, O God!
The waters saw Thee, and were afraid:
The depths also were troubled.

The clouds poured out water,
The air thundered,
And Thine arrows were discharged.

The voice of Thy thunder was heard round about,
The lightnings shone upon the ground,
The earth was moved and shook withal.

Thy way is in the sea,
Thy paths in the great waters,
And Thy footsteps are not known.   (Ps. lxxvii. 16—19.)

The floods have lifted, O Lord,
The floods have lifted their voice,
The floods lift up their waves!   (Ps. xciii. 4.)

The right hand of the Lord bringeth mighty things to pass,
The right hand of the Lord hath the preeminence,
The right hand of the Lord bringeth mighty things to pass.
                                    (Ps. cxviii. 16.)

Sihon, King of the Amorites,
And Og, the King of Basan,
And all the kingdoms of Canaan.   (Ps. cxxxv. 11.)

I remember the time past,
I muse upon all Thy works,
I exercise myself in the works of Thy hands.   (Ps. cxliii. 5.)

In one case we find a double triplet :—

How long wilt Thou forget me, O Lord!
   For ever?
How long wilt Thou hide Thy face from me!
How long shall I seek counsel in my soul,
   And be so vexed in my heart!
How long shall mine enemy triumph over me!   (Ps. xiii. 1, 2.)

U

From all this it will be evident that a third line, as it appears in modern translations following the Masoretic division of the verses in our Bibles, is inadmissible, unless it can be disposed of in one of these methods; either in forming a triplet, or as the commencement or termination of a distich. Want of attention in this respect has caused the parallelism to be frequently obscured. Thus, in Ps. lxvi., owing to three lines being placed together in the beginning, we have in v. 3 :—

> Say unto God—How terrible Thou art in Thy works;
> Through the greatness of Thy power shall Thine enemies submit them-
>   selves unto Thee,

which gives no connection : but if we make use of the third line we restore the parallelism and restore the sense :—

> Make His praise to be glorious!
> Say unto God—How wonderful are Thy works!
> Thine enemies shall submit through the greatness of Thy power :
> All the earth shall worship Thee.

Starting from this principle, that a single or odd line is inadmissible, it becomes necessary, if we wish to exhibit the parallelism of the original, to disregard the division of the Psalms into verses, whether as respects the division exhibited in the Hebrew, or that of our Bible version, or that of our Prayer-book version. In our Paragraph Bible it will be found that there are sixteen verses which contain but one line each ; 310 which contain three lines each ; and three which contain five lines each : thus making 359 odd lines. Thirty-six of these are portions of triplets ; so that there still remain 323 odd lines which *ought to have been accounted for*, and which the reader will find disposed of in the accompanying exposition. The reader can compare Ps. lix. as here given with the psalm as exhibited in the Paragraph Bible, which contains nine verses of three lines each.

Hitherto we have considered Hebrew parallelism as affecting the two hemistichs of any single verse ; but we must now enlarge our notion of this parallelism, and consider it as capable of extending to adjoining verses, or even to distant verses, as in the *epanodos*.

Sometimes the parallelism is alternate, and sometimes introverted. The alternate parallelism is almost as frequent as the regular or direct. It forms a quatrain, of which sometimes only two lines correspond, but sometimes the other two also. In most instances this correspondence is visible in our translation.

Have mercy upon me, O Lord,
  For I am weak :
Heal me, O Lord,
  For my bones are vexed. (Ps. vi. 2.)

The Lord looketh down from heaven ;
  He beholdeth all the children of men :
From the habitation of His dwelling
  He considereth all them that dwell on the earth. (Ps. xxxiii. 13.)

Except the Lord build the house,
  The builders have but toiled in vain !
Except the Lord keep the city,
  The watchman waketh but in vain ! (Ps. cxxvii. 1, 2.)

Thy wife shall be as the fruitful vine
  Upon the walls of thy house ;
Thy children like the olive branches
  Round about thy table. (Ps. cxxviii. 3, 4.)

But in other instances it has not been sufficiently noticed by our translators, though evident enough in the original :—

When the wicked came upon me
  To eat up my flesh :
Even mine enemies and my foes,
  They stumbled and fell. (Ps. xxvii. 2.)

He that walketh in the path of weeping,
  Bearing forth good seed ;
Shall come back in the path of rejoicing,
  Bearing his sheaves with him. (Ps. cxxvi. 7.)

Sometimes the two lines are not equal, but one line is shorter than the other. It is called "a half-brick upon a brick, and a brick upon a half brick." אריח על־גבי לבנה ולבנה על־גבי אריח.
The nineteenth psalm affords a specimen :—

The law of the Lord is perfect,
  Converting the soul :
The testimony of the Lord is sure,
  Giving wisdom unto the simple.
The statutes of the Lord are right,
  Rejoicing the heart :
The commandment of the Lord is pure,
  Giving light unto the eyes.
The fear of the Lord is clean,
  Enduring for ever :
The judgments of the Lord are true,
  And righteous altogether.

The alternate parallelism is not confined to occasional verses, but frequently, as in the above instance, is exhibited in a long series,

u 2

and with considerable beauty. A portion of a psalm is composed
in *direct* parallelism, and then changes to *alternate* parallelism, and
then perhaps changes back again to direct parallelism. Ps. xix.,
xxvii., xl., xliv., lviii., lxxviii., cv., cix., and cxviii. are thus
written; while Ps. xv., ci., and cxxxvi. are written entirely in
alternate parallelism.

But the alternate parallelism is not confined to quatrains: the
following example exhibits a hexastich :—

> He lieth in ambush in the streets :
>   In his secret places doth he murder the innocent :
>   His eyes are set against those who are troubled in heart.
> He lieth in ambush in secret places, as a lion in his lair :
>   He lieth in ambush to catch the afflicted :
>   He catcheth the afflicted, and draweth him into his net.
>   (Ps. x. 8, 9.)

And the following a double quatrain, or octostich :—

> The sea saw that, and fled :
>   Jordan was driven back,
>   The mountains skipped like rams,
>   And the little hills like young sheep.
> What ailed thee, O sea, that thou fleddest,
>   And thou, Jordan, that thou wast driven back?
>   Ye mountains that ye skipped like rams,
>   And ye little hills like young sheep?   (Ps. cxiv. 3—6.)

We now come to the introverted parallelism. This frequently
appears as a quatrain; of which sometimes only two lines correspond; sometimes the other two also :—

> The Lord himself is the portion of mine inheritance and of my cup :
>   Thou shalt maintain my lot.
>   The lot is fallen unto me in a fair ground,
> Yea, I have a goodly heritage.   (Ps. xvi. 6, 7.)

> Thou shalt make them like a fiery oven
>   In the time of Thy wrath :
>   The Lord shall destroy them in His anger,
> And the fire shall consume them.   (Ps. xxi. 9.)

> Give them according to their deeds,
>   According to the wickedness of their own inventions :
>   According to the work of their hands give them :
> Pay them that they have deserved.   (Ps. xxviii. 4, 5.)

> Then the waters had drowned us,
>   The stream had gone over our soul :
>   Then there had gone over our soul
> Even the deep waters of the proud.   (Ps. cxxiv. 3, 4.)

Very frequently it is difficult to tell whether the parallelism is to
be treated as inverted or introverted ; that is to say, whether it is
intended as a distich or as a tetrastich or quatrain : the rule appears
to be, that when too long for a distich it is to be made a quatrain ;
as in the foregoing instances : and when too short for a quatrain,
unless very emphatic, it is to form a distich : but in reading these a
slight cæsura should be made use of, in the places where the division
would be were the distich converted into a quatrain :—

There have surrounded me | many bulls :
Mighty bulls of Basan | compass me about.   (Ps. xxii. 12.)

I will give thanks unto the Lord | at all times :
Continually | shall His praise be in my mouth.

The Lord is nigh | unto them that are of a contrite heart :
And such as be of an humble spirit | He will save.
                                               (Ps. xxxiv. 1, 18.)

Misfortune shall slay | the ungodly :
And they that hate the righteous | shall be desolate.
The Lord delivereth | the souls of His servants :
And all they that trust in Him | shall not be destitute.
                                     (Ps. xxxiv. 1, 18, 21, 22.)

Whoso dwelleth | under the defence of the Most High,
Under the shadow of the Almighty | he shall abide.   (Ps. xci. 1.)

For the Lord will not fail | His people ;
And his inheritance | He will not forsake.   (Ps. xciv. 14.)

But though the introverted parallelism is sometimes too short to
form a quatrain, as in the foregoing examples of inverted parallelism,
in some cases it is much longer, and then forms an *Epanodos*, as in
the following hexastichs :—

Behold he travaileth with iniquity :
He hath conceived mischief, and brought forth ungodliness.
  He made a pit, and digged it :
  And he hath fallen himself into the pit which he hath made.
His mischief shall return upon his own head,
. And his violence shall come upon his own pate.   (Ps. vii. 14—16.)

Thou hast rebuked the heathen,
Thou hast destroyed the ungodly :
  Thou hast put out their name for ever and ever.
  The destructions of the enemy are ended for ever.
Their cities are destroyed,
Their memorial is perished with them.   (Ps. ix. 6, 7.)

The ungodly have drawn out the sword,
And have bent their bow,
 To cast down the poor and needy,
 To slay such as are of a right conversation.
Their sword shall go through their own heart,
And their bow shall be broken.   (Ps. xxxvii. 14, 15.)

Turn us then, O God our Saviour!
And let Thine anger cease from us.
 Wilt Thou be angry with us for ever!
 Wilt Thou stretch out Thy wrath from generation to generation!
Wilt Thou not turn again and quicken us,
That Thy people may rejoice in Thee!   (Ps. lxxxv. 4—6.)

Lord, Thou hast been our dwelling-place,
 From generation to generation.
  Before the mountains were brought forth,
  Or ever the earth and the world were made,
 Even from everlasting to everlasting,
Thou art God!   (Ps. xc. 1, 2.)

The Lord hath declared His salvation.
 In the sight of the heathen
  He hath revealed His righteousness.
  He hath remembered His mercy and truth
 Towards the house of Israel :
All the ends of the world have seen the salvation of our God.

Shout aloud unto the Lord, all ye lands!
 Break forth, sing joyfully, sing psalms.
  Sing psalms unto the Lord upon the harp,
  With harp, and with melody of psalm :
  With trumpets also, and with melody of cornet.
Shout aloud unto the Lord the King!   (Ps. xcviii. 2—6.)

Unto Thee lift I up mine eyes,
O Thou that dwellest in the heavens!
 Behold, even as the eyes of servants
  Look unto the hand of their masters,
 And the eyes of a maiden
  Unto the hand of her mistress,
Even so our eyes wait upon the Lord our God,
Until He have mercy upon us.   (Ps. cxxiii. 1, 2.)

The idols of the heathen are but silver and gold,
The work of the hands of man!
 They have mouths, and yet they speak not ;
 They have eyes, and yet they see not ;
 They have ears, and yet they hear not ;
  Neither is there any breath in their mouths.
They that make them are like unto them ;
And so are all such as put their trust in them. (Ps. cxxxv. 15—18.)

But in many cases the epanodos is octostich, decastich, or even longer :—

> Thou hast mightily delivered Thy people,
> Even the sons of Jacob and Joseph.
> The waters saw Thee, O God !
> The waters saw Thee, and were afraid ;
> The depths also were troubled.
> The clouds poured out water,
> The air thundered,
> And Thine arrows were discharged.
> The noise of Thy thunder was heard round about,
> The lightnings shone upon the ground,
> The earth was troubled, and shook withal.
> Thy way is in the sea, and Thy paths in the great waters,
> And Thy footsteps are not known ! [1]
> Thou leddest Thy people, like sheep,
> By the hands of Moses and Aaron.   (Ps. lxxvii. 15 – 20.)

Lastly, on referring to Ps. xxix. and lxvii. in the text, the reader will see that in some instances the whole psalm is composed as an *epanodos :* the former of these examples being also composed in triplets. That this attention given to the *epanodos* is of use, is evident from Ps. lxxx. where it enables us to understand the meaning of the terms " branch," " man of Thy right hand," and "son of man," which have led some commentators astray.   It is by means of the *epanodos* also that we are able in some cases to explain metaphors, and to determine the correct meaning of some disputed word.   See note on the word *Raim,* translated "unicorn," in Ps. xxii.

In treating of parallelism, we must not omit to notice a kind of double parallelism evident in many of the psalms : the same line being connected with two other lines ; so that it is sometimes difficult to tell with which it should be joined.   This ambiguity imparts a more pleasing character, and greater richness to the composition, though it necessarily creates a great difficulty and uncertainty as to the kind of parallelism intended. The following examples will suffice as an illustration.   The first is from the seventy-second Psalm :—

> Give Thy *judgments,* O Lord, unto the *king,*
> And Thy *righteousness* unto the *king's son :*
> Let him rule *Thy people with righteousness,*
> And *Thy poor with judgment.*

Or it may be read thus :—

> Give Thy *judgments,* O Lord, unto the king,
> And Thy *righteousness* unto the king's son
> Let him rule Thy people with *righteousness,*
> And Thy poor with *judgment.*

---

[1] This example is the more remarkable, that it is at the same time composed in triplets. See p. 289.

Or if we take in the next verse, it may read thus :—

> Give Thy judgments, O Lord, unto the *king*,
> And Thy *righteousness* unto the *king's* son :
>   Let him rule Thy people with righteousness,
>   And Thy poor with judgment.
> Let the *mountains* bring peace unto Thy people,
> And the *hills righteousness*.

The next is from the hundred and twenty-first psalm :—

> I will lift up mine eyes unto the hills
> From whence cometh my help :
> My help cometh even from the Lord
> Who made heaven and earth ;

Or—

> I will lift up mine eyes unto the hills
>   From whence cometh my *help* ;
>   My *help* cometh even from the Lord
> Who made heaven and earth.

Again, in the same psalm :—

> He will not suffer thy foot to be moved,
> He that *keepeth* thee will not slumber.
>   Behold, He will not *slumber*,
>   And will not *sleep*, that keepeth Israel.
> The Lord is thy *keeper* :
> The Lord is thy defence upon thy right hand.

Or—

> He will not suffer thy foot to be moved,
>   He that keepeth thee will not *slumber*.
>   Behold, He will neither *slumber*, nor sleep,
> That keepeth Israel.
> *The Lord* is thy keeper.
> *The Lord* is thy defence upon thy right hand.

Or—

> He will not suffer thy foot to be moved,
> He that keepeth thee will not slumber.
> Behold, He will neither slumber, nor sleep,
>   That *keepeth* Israel.
>   The Lord is thy *keeper* ;
> The Lord is thy defence upon thy right hand.

Or—

> He will not suffer thy foot to be moved,
>   He *that keepeth* thee will not slumber.
> Behold, He will not slumber,
>   And *will not sleep that keepeth* Israel.

Again, in the hundred and ninth psalm, where, from the words " In return for my love," we may either put as parallel the first and third lines, the first and fourth lines, or the third and fourth—

> In return for my love they are my adversaries :
> But I betake myself unto prayer.
> And they have rewarded me evil, in return for good,
> And hatred, in return for love.

If the reader will now further compare the two renderings of Ps. xxix., the rendering of verses 16—21 of Ps. xl., as given in the rendering of that psalm in its proper place, and as these same words appear in Ps. lxx., where they constitute an entire psalm ; if he will compare the two arrangements of Ps. lxvii.; as also Ps. lxxvii., as given in pages 289 and 295 ; he will perceive how the same psalm may be exhibited in totally different ways, and yet how each manner may exhibit a peculiar elegance.

From these examples we may see how very difficult it is to determine in all cases what are the corresponding lines ; and from this very difficulty perhaps we may perceive why the Hebrew poetry was written continuously like prose, the division of the lines being left to the skill and appreciation of the reader.

The importance of the study of parallelism cannot be too strongly insisted on : for many instances will occur where the true meaning of obscure passages may be discovered by this means.

> Thou hast rebuked the heathen,
> Thou hast destroyed the ungodly,
>   Thou hast put out their name for ever and ever.
>   The destructions of the wicked are ended for ever.
> Their cities are destroyed ;
> Their memorial is perished with them.   (Ps. ix. 5, 6.)

> Have mercy upon me, O Lord !
> Consider the affliction which I suffer of them that hate me ;
> O Thou that liftest me up from the gates of death,
> That I may show all Thy praises in the gates of the daughter of Sion.
>   (Ps. ix. 13, 14.)
> Into Thy hands I commend my spirit :
> For Thou hast redeemed me.
> O Lord, Thou God of truth,
> Thou hatest all them that adhere to lying idols.   (Ps. xxxi. 5, 6.

> But in my adversity they rejoiced and gathered together ;
> The abjects gathered against me :
> And though I regarded not,
> They tore at me, and refrained not.   (Ps. xxxv. 15.)

Lord, let me know my end,
And the number of my days;
That I may know what it is,
And when I shall be called hence.   (Ps. xxxix. 4.)

Or ever the sticks make the pot to boil,
So, fed by Thy wrath, let them consume away.   (Ps. lviii. 9.)

For a thousand years
Are in Thy sight but as a day!
As yesterday when it is past,
And as a watch in the night!
Thou scatterest them—they are as a dream when the morning cometh;
They are as the grass which changeth.   (Ps. xc. 4, 5.)

He will pour contempt upon princes,
    Making them wander outcast into the wilderness;
While He will set on high the poor from affliction,
    Making them households like a flock of sheep.   (Ps. cvii. 40, 41.)

While in the twenty-fifth psalm, one of the alphabetical psalms,
a deficient letter of the alphabet, ו, which is wanting in former
translations, is restored:—

ה Lead me forth in Thy truth,
ו And teach me:
    For Thou art the God of my salvation:
    In Thee do I hope all the day long.

This example is the more important as it shows that the lines are
sometimes exceedingly short: and it might have been this length of
line, sometimes short and sometimes long, which induced Josephus,
in writing to Greeks and Romans, to describe the Hebrew poetry as
consisting of, that is to say, assimilating in form to, trimeters and
tetrameters, as well as hexameters and pentameters.

Before quitting the subject of parallelism, it may not be irrelevant
to notice a seeming coincidence between the Hebrew and Chinese
poetry, pointed out by Dr. Morrison; though the force of the connection is lessened by the examples which he gives being confined
to proverbs:—

The white stone, unfractured, ranks as most precious:
The blue lily, unblemished, emits the finest fragrance.

The heart which is harassed, finds no place of rest:
The mind, in the midst of bitterness, thinks only of grief.

With the cravings of the heart, the health is flourishing:
With many anxious thoughts, the constitution decays.

Many other examples of Chinese parallelism are given in Sir John Francis Davis's "Poetry of the Chinese;" from which we take the following :—

> Unsullied poverty is always happy :
> Impure wealth brings many sorrows.

> Prosecuting virtue, is like ascending a steep :
> Pursuing vice, like rushing down a precipice.

> Consider not any vice as trivial,
>   And so practise it ;
> Regard not any virtue as unimportant,
>   And so neglect it.

So far with regard to parallelism. But in addition to this feature we find other peculiarities ; the first of which is that many of the psalms are supposed to exhibit a dramatic character, being divided into strophes of different length, sometimes supposed to be spoken by different persons, as God, the Messiah, the Psalmist, the church, and the wicked. Many translators have attempted to exhibit these instances of *Prosopopæia ;* but no two such writers agree, and this disagreement adds to the repugnance with which we see any addition made to the Word of God. The divisions are generally sufficiently marked for the reader to know by whom the parts are supposed to be spoken ; more especially as some such words as — " But unto the wicked said God," or, "Lo, these are the ungodly ;" or, "Then said I," are inserted, to teach us the meaning. That some of the psalms were divided into stanzas or strophes, is evident from Ps. cxix ; and Psalms xiv., xvi., (capable of being divided into seven stanzas,) xxix., liii., lxvii., lxxxvii., xcviii., and cxl., may be cited as instances : but these instances must be regarded only as exceptions to the general rule.

The next characteristic, and one which demands more attention, is the introduction of an *Antiphon*, or refrain ; or what we would call a chorus, having borrowed the term from the ancient chorus. These antiphons are recognizable in most of the psalms, and were doubtless sung by the whole choir, as noticed at large in the *Introduction*. David appointed Asaph, Heman, and Jeduthun, as directors of his choir; under them as assistants were the four sons of Asaph, the fourteen sons of Heman, and the six sons of Jeduthun : and each of these twenty-four had a band of twelve relatives under him, thus making a total of two hundred and ninety-one performers or singers : (1 Chron. xxv :) to whom were joined four thousand Levites, (1 Chron. xxiii. 5,) to "praise the Lord ;" while thirty-four thousand other Levites had other functions attached to them. It

cannot be an idle conjecture, then, that with such an apparatus
the Psalms of David were sung with all the accessorial accompani-
ments which the division into full choruses and semi-choruses would
produce; especially when we remember that prophesying and singing were so identical. The antiphons in some psalms may be
readily recognized, as in the forty-second and forty-third, which
form one psalm; and in the hundred and seventh; because in
these instances the same words appear repeatedly: but in other
psalms where the words are different, they have to be searched for.
Most of the psalms have an antiphon at the conclusion: very frequently they commence with one: while in many others the antiphon recurs frequently throughout the psalm, as in Ps. xxxi., xxxiv.,
xxxvii., xlii.—xliii., xlix., li., lxxxviii., xcix., ciii., civ., cxl., cxlv.,
and cxlvii., thus giving great unity and force to the entire composition. In several of the psalms there is a double antiphon, as
in Ps. xviii., xxii., xxxv., lxxvii., lxxix., and cvii. Sometimes the
antiphon forms an alternate stanza, as in Ps. xxix., lxvii., xcviii.,
and cxxxvi. The antiphons are sometimes identical, and sometimes extremely varied, resembling each other rather in sense than
in words.[1]

Connected with the antiphon is the frequent occurrence of a
Replica, or repetition of part of the psalm, an instance of which is
shown in Ps. lxxxviii., which is headed *Leannoth*, an "antiphonal
song," and which consists of three parts, each corresponding with
the others, and which must have resembled our glees. Other
instances occur in Ps. xxiv., xxx. xliv., lxiv., lxvi., lxxxviii., xci.,
xcv., ci., cii., cxxxii., cxlii. Instances of a reversed replica occur in
Ps. xxii., where we have "bulls," "lion," "dog," and "piercing,"
followed by "sword," "dog," "lion," and "unicorns;" and in
Ps. lxxxviii., where we have "acquaintance," "affliction," "calling
upon the Lord, and stretching out the hands" [in prayer], and
"dead;" followed by "dead," "crying unto the Lord," and
"prayer," "afflicted," and "acquaintance."

The *Anaphora*, or running phrase at the beginning of a paragraph,
is often met with, as in Ps. lix., 6 and 14, "They assemble in the
evening, they make a noise like a dog, and go about the city;" in
Ps. lxii. 1, 5, 9— "Only upon God wait thou my soul," "Only upon
God wait thou my soul," "Only vanity are the children of men;" in

[1] This variation is noticed by Hengstenberg, (Ps. xlii. 5,) and by Delitzsch—
"...... in accordance with the custom in the Psalms of not allowing the refrains
to occur in exactly the same form." (On Ps. lvi. 12.) "The refrain varies
according to recognized custom." (On Ps. cvii. 21.) Delitzsch makes the
antiphon a peculiarity of the *Michtam* psalms (xvi., lvi.—lx). See his *Bib.
Com.* on Ps. xvi. *Introd.*, lvi. *Introd.*, and lviii. *Introd.*

Ps. cxlii. 1, 5,—" With my voice unto the Lord did I cry," " I cried unto Thee, O Lord ; I said—" in Ps. cxlviii. 1, 7, " Praise the Lord in the heavens," " Praise the Lord upon earth."

An *Epistrophe*, or running phrase, at the end of a paragraph, occurs in Ps. xlii. and xliii. " Why art thou cast down, O my soul ?" &c., and in Ps. cvii. " But when they cried unto the Lord in their trouble," &c., and " Oh that men would therefore praise the Lord," &c., and in Ps. cxxxvi. " For His mercy endureth for ever."

We frequently detect the *Proem* in the beginning of a psalm, as in Psalms xxxix., xlv., xlix., l., lxxviii., lxxx., xcii., ci., cix., and many others.

And an *Epiphonem*, or striking termination, at the end of a psalm, as in Ps. xxv. and xxxiv. ; which we find of use in explaining what has been thought to be a redundant verse in those alphabetical psalms : but when once we see it is an epiphonem. we no longer regard it as redundant. The epiphonem appears also in two other alphabetical psalms, x. and xxxvii. ; and from its thus occurring in four out of the eight alphabetical psalms, we may assume that it may be looked for generally in other psalms, as in Ps. xv., l., xcii., xciii., xcvi., cvii., cxi. and cxii. The epiphonem in many of the psalms forms an antiphon, as in xxxv.

Sometimes we meet with repeated *Collocations*, and *Alliterations*, as in Psalms xiii., xxix., xcvi., and cxviii.

Sometimes with a *Peripateia*, or sudden change of subject, as in Ps. vi., " Away from me all ye that work vanity ;" in Ps. xxviii., " Praised be the Lord," &c. ; in Ps. xliv. and lxxxix. " But now Thou hast cast off," &c.: in Ps. lvii., " My heart is fixed, O God," &c.; in Ps. cii., " But Thou, O Lord, shalt endure for ever ;" in Ps. cix., " But Thou, O Lord my God," &c.; and Ps. cxvi., " What return shall I make unto the Lord," &c.

And sometimes with an *Aposiopesis*, or suppression of part of the sentence : exhibiting itself sometimes with an abrupt beginning, as in Ps. lxx.—

. . . . O God, to deliver me :
Haste Thee, O God, to my help,

where the words " Haste Thee " are understood. " *Her* foundations are upon the holy hills ;" (Ps. lxxxvii. :) " Judah was *His* sanctuary ;" (Ps. cxiv. 2 ;) " I will give thanks unto *Thee* with my whole heart ;" Ps. (cxxxviii.;) and many other instances ; or by an imperfect termination, showing deep excitement or intense feeling, as, " My soul also is sore troubled : but, Lord, how long . . . . ? (vi. 3.) where the words " wilt Thou punish me " are understood ; " Unless I had been persuaded of the goodness of the Lord in the land of the living, I . . . . ." (Ps. xxvii. 13:) " Then may my right hand forget . . . ." (Ps. cxxxvii. 15,) where the words *how to play* are understood; and sometimes in the middle of a sentence ; as " God ! His way is perfect," (Ps. xviii. 30 ;) " For I said . . . . .lest they should rejoice over me," (Ps. xxxviii. 16,) where the words *Hear me*, are understood ; " I will sing psalms unto Thee upon a ten-stringed lute ; (here we are to insert the words— *Yea, it is GOD*) who giveth victory unto kings," (cxliv. 9, 10,) But the most remarkable instance occurs in Ps. lxxiii., from the beginning of which—". . . . but God is loving unto Israel, even unto such as are of a true heart. But I . . . . my feet were almost gone," it is evident tha' the psalmist had been previously musing on the prosperity of th' wicked in this life, and on his own forgetfulness of God. An instance of the rendering of an aposiopesis by our translators, occurs in Exod. xxxii. 32.[1]

Sometimes, and indeed constantly, we meet with an *Anadiplosis*, or *Epiploce*, the taking up in the beginning of a verse the last clause of the preceding verse, as in Ps. xxiv. 7—10.[2]

Frequently we observe an *Epanaphora*, or occurrence of some particular catchword, or burden to the psalm, as " The Lord " in Ps. xxxiv. and cvi. ; " iniquity " in Ps. li. ; " verily " in Ps. lxii. ; " lifting up " in Ps. lxxv. ; " remember " in Ps. lxxvii. ; "turn" in Ps. lxxx. ; " born " in Ps. lxxxvii. ; " mercy and truth " in Ps. lxxxix.; " works " in Ps. cxi. ; " keep " in Ps. cxxi. ; " peace " in Ps. cxxii. ; " eyes " in Ps. cxxiii. and " vanity " in Ps. cxxvii.

Very frequently we meet with a *Paronomasia*, or play upon

---

[1] For similar instances Dr. Hammond refers to Virgil's Æneid. i. 131 : and Hengstenberg to Gen. xxxi. 42. Another instance may be found in one of Wesley's hymns, beginning— " Depth of mercy " —

   " I have spilt His precious blood !
   " Trampled on the Son of God !
   " Filled with pangs unspeakable,
   " I ——— and yet am not in hell."

[2] This is so frequent in the " Songs of Degrees," or " Songs of the Going-up," that it has given birth to the latest theory respecting the title of these psalms. It is supposed that they acquire this name in consequence of the frequent occurrence of the epiploce; the subject of each psalm thus going on constantly from the beginning to the end. It is sufficient here to mention the fact, without entering into an argument on the subject, except to say that the *epiploce* is equally evident in other psalms, as in Ps. xxix. and cxxxvii. ; and that the name of "Songs of the Going-up" much more probably arose from the annual "going-up" to Jerusalem, a conjecture which is confirmed by one of these psalms, cxxii. 4, where the same word עלה *oloh, to go up*, is used :— " Thither the tribes *go up*."

words; but this can be seen only by an examination of the
original Hebrew. Thus in the conclusion of Ps. vi., "they shall
return ashamed," we have the same word spelt backward, יָשֻׁבוּ
and יֵבֹשׁוּ *jashubu* and *jeboshu*; in Ps. x. 16, in "committeth"
and "helper," we have *oze* and *ozar*; in Ps. xviii. 7, "the earth
trembled and was troubled," we have "*Vatigeas vatiraas haarez.*"
In verse 15 of the same psalm the same word is used for "hear"
and "obey"—"in hearing of me they shall obey me." The
same play upon words occurs in Ps. xv. 3 and xxviii. 3, where the
words "evil" and "neighbour" are introduced; in Ps. xxiv. 3, in
"rise up" and "place;" in Ps. xl. 5, in the words "see" and "fear;"
in Ps. lx. 4, in "banner" and "displayed;" the play upon which
word in the original we have imitated by altering them to "standard"
and "stand up;" in Ps. lxxiv. 4, in the words "ensign" and "sign,"
which we have also imitated; in Ps. lxxx. 16, in the word *bain*,
which signifies both "branch" and "son;" and in Ps. cxix. 130, in the
words "goeth forth" and the "simple." A number of other instances have been pointed out in Ps. cxxii.[1] A double paronomasia
occurs in Ps. xc., where we have the word *shenoh*, signifying both
year and *sleep* or *dream*; and the word *khalaph*, to change, signify-
in one place *changing for the better*, sprouting forth; and in the
other *changing for the worse*, withering; reminding us of the
paronomasia in Gen. xl. 13, 19, where Joseph foretells that Pharaoh
would *lift up* the head of the chief butler, and restore him; and
lift up the head of the chief baker, and hang him.

The last peculiarity that will be noticed is the occasional introduction of Acrostic or alphabetical arrangements, signifying the
Alpha and Omega of religion. The psalms so composed are Ps. ix. and
x., which together form one alphabet, xxv., xxxiv., xxxvii., cxi.
cxii., cxix., and cxlv. It has been supposed that this artificial
construction marks a decadence in poetic taste,[2] and that it affords a
proof of the later date of such psalms: but this assumption cannot
be supported; for five of these psalms bear the name of David.
But in addition to these eight psalms there are several others, the
number of verses of which correspond with the number of letters
of the alphabet, as Ps. xxxviii. and ciii., and there are others which
when written in the poetic form appear to consist of about twenty-
two verses, as xxvii., li., and lix.; all of which have David's name:[3]

[1] Jebb, i. 270.
[2] Such as the Hebrew doggrels (פיוטים) consisting of flippant acrostics,
remarkable only for an ingenious jingling of rhyme, which found their way
into the Jewish ritual during the Middle Ages.
[3] Of others, xxxiii. is between two which bear David's name, and lxxii. is
the psalm *to* or *by* Solomon.

so that there seems no authority for affirming that the alphabetical psalms were written in a later age. One of these, Ps. xxxviii., is remarkable in having the *Aleph* and *Tau*, the first and last letters of the alphabet, occurring together three times in the last two verses. It is in the words " Forsake me not," " Be not far," and "O Lord my salvation." In the same manner the double psalm, ix.—x., has the letter *Aleph* four times in the beginning, and the letter *Tau* three times at the conclusion. It is probably owing to the signification of the alphabetical arrangement of these psalms, and to the repeated occurrence of the first and last letters in these instances, that our Lord calls himself "*Alpha* and *Omega*," in the Book of Revelation.

From what has been adduced it must be evident that the Hebrew poetry was characterized by a rhythmical symmetry of great variety, and though divested of both rhyme and metre, that it possesses, even in a translation, a poetic character, which must have been much more apparent in its original form. But when we say that Hebrew poetry has no rhyme, we mean of course that there is no correspondence of sound between the last syllable or syllables of two successive lines : but it is not necessary that this correspondence should exist at the end of lines, it may exist in the beginning ; for rhyme is merely " an harmonical succession of sounds," a " word chiming with another word ;" and in Hebrew poetry we not only have words sounding alike, but we have the identical words and series of words occurring constantly : and it is evident that this correspondence, which how-ever is mere assonance and alliteration, is more visible to the eye when it takes place at the beginning of the line, than when it takes place at the end. From this it will appear that the word *Rhythmi-cal*, which we have adopted in the Title-page, is more appropriate than the word *metrical*, which is often used : for as Augustine says in his work *De Musica*, —" Omne metrum rhythmus, non omnis rhythmus etiam metrum est." The following examples will not, it is appre-hended—and many others might be cited—be considered to exhibit a mean appearance, even in an English dress :—

> The Lord is my light and my salvation :
>   Whom then shall I fear ?
> The Lord is the strength of my life :
>   Of whom then shall I be afraid ?
> When the wicked came upon me,
>   To eat up my flesh ;
> Even mine enemies and my foes,
>   They stumbled and fell.
> Though a host encamp against me,
>   Yet shall not my heart be afraid :
> Though war should rise against me,
>   Yet will I put my trust in Him.   (Ps. xxvii.)

[Haste Thee,] O God, to deliver me
Haste Thee, O Lord, to my help!
Let them be ashamed
And confounded together,
   That seek after my soul :
Let them be driven backward!
And put to confusion,
   That seek to do me evil.
Let them be desolate,
As a reward for their shame,
   That say—"Aha, aha!"
Let them be joyful
And glad in Thee, all they
   That seek after Thee :
Let them say alway—
"Let God be praised,"
   That love Thy salvation.   (Ps. lxx.)

The Lord is King! He is clothed with majesty!
The Lord is clothed with strength, wherewith He hath girded Himself!
The world is established, that it cannot be moved :
Thy throne was established of old :
   Thou art from everlasting!
⎰ The floods are risen, O Lord,
   The floods have lift up their voice,
⎱ The floods lift up their waves.
More excellent than the voice of many waters,
More excellent than the waves of the sea,
   Is Jehovah in the highest!
Thy testimonies are very sure !
Holiness becometh Thy house, O Lord, for evermore !   (Ps. xciii.)

While the Hebrew song does not appear mean either to eye or ear, in one respect it has a surpassing excellence even as compared with the classic poetry of Greece and Rome, which appealed only to the sight and hearing ; for it appeals to the sense and meaning of the words, instead of to the mere quantity : and as we rightly judge that only to be poetry which conveys a poetical sentiment poetically expressed ; and that to be mere verse or rhyme which is wanting in that characteristic ; so we must give Hebrew song, as exhibited in the Bible, the loftiest place in the realms of poetry ; from the sublimity of its sentiment, the purity of its morals, the fervour of its piety, the exultation of its joy, and the humility and pathos of its contrition ; and let it be remembered that though the words are the words of man, the sentiments which they express proceed from the inspiration of GOD.

It is much to be regretted that the version of the Psalms by Bardesanes has not come down to us.   Bardesanes is said to have

been a heretic and a Gnostic, but he was opposed to the grosser
vagaries of Gnosticism, for he wrote against them.   But with all his
errors, and taking his opponents' view of them, he was one of the
fathers of church music, for he lived so early as the second century.
Valentinus, another heretic, who lived a generation earlier, also
wrote a collection of psalms.   Bardesanes was succeeded by his son,
who so distinguished himself in church music that he obtained the
name of Harmonius.   Living in so early a period of the Church's
history, it would have been most interesting to us in these days if
their labours had been preserved to us.   Theological errors appear
to assume different phases at different epochs, without being reproduced; so that however much the works of these early writers may
have abounded in Gnostic absurdities, there would be little danger
of such delusions being engrafted in the minds of their readers in
the present day.   After a lapse of two centuries, the "heretic"
Bardesanes was followed by the orthodox Ephraem, whose Hymns
and Homilies are in our possession, and which are replete with
interest: but he wrote no psalms; so that we regret the more the
loss of those written by his predecessors.   Theodoret and Sozomen
inform us that Ephraem took the metre and music of Bardesanes
and Harmonius, and substituted his own words to them; so that it
is clear he appreciated their genius: indeed he acknowledged the
skill of Bardesanes, though he does not mention the name of
his son :—

> " In the resorts of Bardesanes
> " There are songs and melodies.
> " For seeing that young persons
> " Loved sweet music,
> " By the harmony of his songs
> " He corrupted their minds."

After reading the following notice of his psalms from a hostile
pen, it is the more to be regretted that we are not enabled to judge
of them for ourselves :—

> " For these things Bardesanes
> " Uttered in his writings.
> " He composed Odes,
> " And mingled them with music :
> " He harmonized Psalms,
> " And introduced measures :
> " By measures and balances
> " He divided words.
> " He thus concealed for the simple
> " The bitter with the sweet.
> " For the sickly do not prefer
> " Food which is wholesome."

" He sought to imitate David ;
" To adorn himself with his beauty ;
" So that he might be praised by the likeness.
" He therefore set in order
" Psalms one hundred and fifty ;
" But he deserted the truth of David,
" And imitated only his numbers."

ESSAY III.

THE ZION OF DAVID RESTORED TO DAVID.

LII.

THE ZION OF DAVID RESTORED TO DAVID.

(*Being a Note to Ps. xlviii. 2.*)

" (On) the sides of the north
" (Is) the City of the Great King."

THIS passage has presented great difficulties to some commentators, and led to great confusion. Some foreign theologians, as Hengstenberg, Hitzig, Ewald, and Capponi, recognizing the traditional position of Mount Zion, have attempted to explain the words, " (On) the sides of the north," by supposing that there is an indication here of the pagan belief that a mountain existed in the extreme north where the gods resided, forming a connecting link between heaven and earth; a belief thrown in the teeth of the king of Babylon by the spirits in Hades; (Is. xiv. 13;) others, more naturally, suppose that Mount Zion is described as being at the northern extremity of the hills in this region. But what was merely a difficulty in the minds of these foreign theologians, has become a cause of great confusion in the works of some English writers, who think that they can discover proofs in the sacred narrative that Mount Zion is no other than the Temple mount, or Mount Moriah, and that the City of David lay, as described in this psalm, to the north of it.

Josephus describes Jerusalem in his time as standing on four hills.

Zion, or the Acropolis, or the City of David, which in his time was called the Upper City, occupied the south west quarter; the portion of city chiefly covered with houses, and which often was especially called Jerusalem, but which in his time was called Acra, or the Lower City, occupied the north-west quarter; the Temple the south-east quarter ; and Bezetha, or the New City, the north-east quarter. But let us hear Josephus—" The city, which was fortified with three walls, except where encompassed with unapproachable ravines ; for in these parts there was but one wall—was built, *the one part facing the other*, (ἀντιπρόσωπος,) *on two hills*, (I. and II.,) *separated by an intervening valley*, at the brink of which on either side the houses terminated. Of these hills, that on which the Upper City stood, (I.) was by far the higher, and was *steeper throughout its extent*.[1] Accordingly, on account of (this, its steepness and) its strength, it was styled the Citadel by king David, the father of Solomon, who first built the Temple ; but by us it is called the Upper Market-place.[2] The other hill, (II.) which bears the name of Acra, and which sustained the Lower City, *sloped down on either side*. Over against this was a third hill, (III.) naturally lower than Acra, and separated from it formerly by *another* broad valley. Afterwards, however, the Asmoneans, when they were in power, filled up the valley in order to unite the city to the Temple ; (this has thence been called the Asmonean Valley ;) and they levelled the summit of Acra, (Josephus here refers to the citadel of that name,) and reduced its elevation, so that the Temple might

[1] The word ἰθύτερος is evidently antithetical to ἀμφίκυρτος, as applied to Acra immediately afterwards. While the last hill had a round top sloping down on all sides, the upper hill had almost precipitous sides : and while the upper hill is almost comparatively level, the hill of the Lower City, even at present, has a fall of 100 feet from the "Giant's Castle" (Tower of the Furnaces) towards the Damascus Gate, (Gate of Ephraim,) 72 feet to the Jaffa Gate, (Valley Gate,) and 172 feet to the north-east angle of Mount Zion ; but each of these points has been raised some 50 feet above the original levels, by the embankments of the Romans, the overthrowing of the walls, and the levelling of the ground ; so that this hill was well described by Josephus as *sloping down on both sides*. The level character of Mount Zion, on the contrary, is witnessed by Murray, who says—"On the summit of Zion towards its western brow there is a level tract, extending in length from the citadel to the 'Tomb of David,' about 600 yards, and in breadth from the city walls to the eastern side of the Armenian Convent, about 250 yards : a much larger space, however, was accessible for building purposes." (*Handbook*, p. 94.) The word ἰθύς signifies straight, direct, a straight line, a direct course, which may of course apply to steepness, as in *Od.* θ. 377, "They played with the ball upwards," *i.e.* throwing it perpendicularly. It may be mentioned that the usual translation of this passage "straighter, or more direct, in its length," *in longitudinem directior*, conveys no meaning ; for as the upper and lower cities were conterminous, and facing each other, and divided only by the Tyropœon ; how could one of them be described as "gibbous" (on plan), and the other as presenting a straight line of front ?

[2] We are not to suppose that this was a mere market-place for the Lower City : for Josephus has just called it the Upper City. But being a fortress, and one of considerable strength and extent, it was essential that it should be supplied with its own market-place. Comp. Jer. x. 17.

be higher than it. (Com. *Antiq.* xiii. 6, 7.) The valley known as the Tyropœon, which we mentioned as dividing the hills of the Upper and Lower City, (*and therefore not the same as the "broad valley" mentioned afterwards,*) reaches as far as the fountain which we call Siloah, (and therefore now divided the first and the third hills, as it had previously divided the first and the second hills,) whose waters are at once sweet and abundant. On the outside, the two hills (see Tacitus, *Hist.* v. 11,) on which the city stood, were surrounded by deep valleys ; and by reason of the precipices on either side there was no approach to them from any quarter. . . . . . As the city increased in population, it extended by degrees beyond the walls, till the parts adjoining the hill, north of the Temple, were filled up with houses, thus extending not a little beyond the old hills, so that a *fourth* hill (IV.) was covered with houses, called Bezetha. It lay over against Antonia, and was separated from it by a deep fosse, artificially formed, to cut off the foundations of Antonia from the hill, and so render them less easy of access, and to add to their elevation. Thus, the depth of the trench added greatly to the height of the towers. The newly-built quarter was called in our native tongue, Bezetha, which signifies Newtown." [1]

Nothing can be clearer than this description of Josephus ; and we thus see that the city was composed of four distinct parts, four distinct hills, or four distinct quarters, which it is impossible to confound together. That must be a false exposition which would place one of these hills upon the top of another.

Jebus then, or the city of the Jebusites, occupied quarters I. and II.—

Jerusalem, from the time of Solomon, when the Temple was built, to the time of Nehemiah, and until the "New City" was enclosed, occupied quarters I., II., and III.—

[1] *Bell.* v. 4. 1, 2.

But in Christian times this disposition has been questioned. Some, finding the church of the Holy Sepulchre in quarter II., affirm this to have been outside the city in the time of our Lord—

while others, from what we conceive to be a misapprehension as to certain passages in the Bible, affirm the city of Jerusalem in the time of Nehemiah to have consisted only of quarters I. and III.—

though from their believing Acra, the Lower City, the City of David, Antonia, and the Temple, all to have stood on Mount Moriah, which they hold to be identical with Mount Zion, they may be said to affirm that the city occupied but one quarter, and

one hill, in the time of David, and in the time of Nehemiah; Josephus, and everybody else, notwithstanding;[1] though subsequently, in the time of the Maccabees, and in the time of Josephus, the S.W. quarter had become an "Upper City," or "Citadel," or "Upper Market-place."

The real positions of Calvary and Golgotha are foreign to our present consideration; the subject having been already sufficiently discussed, not only by the advocates of the traditional sites, but in the most able and temperately written *Biblical Researches* of Professor Robinson; the remarkable work on the Holy Sepulchre by Mr. Fergusson, *An Essay on the Ancient Topography of Jerusalem*, 1847;[2] the views of which were subsequently embodied in Smith's

[1] "Acra was the ancient Zion, or the hill on which the Temple, the City of David, Paris, Acra, and Antonia stood." Smith's *Dict. of the Bible*, p. 1025a.
[2] Mr. Fergusson's theory was attacked by the *Edinburgh Review*, Oct. 1860, and the strictures answered by Mr. Fergusson in the *Athenæum*, and subsequently in his *Holy Sepulchre, and the Temple at Jerusalem*, 1865. The system

Dictionary of the Bible; the exhaustive treatise by Dr. Tobler, *Golgotha, seiner Kirchen und Klöster*, 1851; the two essays by the present writer, *On the alleged site of the Holy Sepulchre*, and *On the true site of Calvary*, in the Museum of Class. Antiq.—Longman, 1860, originally published in 1853; the article on "Jerusalem" by Horatius Bonar in the *Imperial Bible Dictionary*, 1864; and that by Dr. Kitto in his *Cycl. of Bibl. Lit.*, 3rd edition, 1870. We will therefore confine our attention to the modern theory, that Zion, the City of David, the Lower City, Gihon, Acra, and Antonia, all stood upon the Temple-hill. Let it not be supposed, however, that this is a wild and arbitrary fancy of these writers. We have seen that it is essentially opposed to the statement of Josephus; but there is no doubt they would not have attempted to establish such a theory in the face of this statement, did they not think that there is overpowering evidence in support of their position. Let us proceed then to examine this evidence, premising that these writers do not question the accuracy of Josephus, but merely dispute the interpretation of his statement. It is necessary here, however, to distinguish between the particular views of recent writers, as it will be seen that they differ in many points.

Smith's Dictionary of the Bible, 1860.—In this work the city of the Jebusites is placed in the western half of the city, and in the map of Jerusalem at a subsequent period it is called the "Upper Market-place:" but the name of "Zion" is given to the Temple-mount. "It cannot be disputed that from the time of Constantine downwards to the present day this name has been affixed to the western hill (south-western) on which the city of Jerusalem now stands, and in fact always has stood. Notwithstanding this, it seems equally certain that up to the time of the destruction of the city by Titus, the name was applied exclusively to the eastern hill, or that on which the Temple stood." (p. 1026.) The "City of David" is also shown to be on the Temple-mount. The "Upper City," taking in the north-west as well as the south-west quarters, is bounded by a Tyropœon running from the Damascus-gate, here called also the Valley of Gihon, on the eastern side of which valley therefore must have been Gihon. The "Lower City" of Josephus is shown to coincide with this valley, and the slopes on either side, although

has been further attacked with fourteen objections in the *Imperial Bible Dict.* 1864; and with twelve objections by Mr. Lewin, in his *Siege of Jerusalem.* It has been approved of in the *Dub. Univ. Mag.* Jan. 1848; and attacked again by the Comte de Vogüé, in his *Églises de la Terre Sainte*; and by Dr. Wolcott, in the American Edition of *Smith's Dict. of the Bible*, 1867–1870. Mr. Fergusson has defended himself in many lectures.

Josephus describes the Lower City, or Acra, as its name would signify, to be a *hill*, and indeed the second highest hill of Jerusalem. On the Temple-mount also are shown Antonia and Acra, and at a later date Golgotha and the Church of the Holy Sepulchre. This theory, in addition to historical and architectural evidence adduced by Mr. Fergusson, is supported by the fact of the monument of King Alexander being in this locality, (Jos. *Bell*, v. 7.3,) " so that certainly there were tombs hereabouts :" (p. 1031 :) though there is no proof from Josephus's words, that the monument was within the walls, and that it was not, like the generality of graves, at Jerusalem, cut out on the slope of the hill ; or, if it were within the walls, that it was other than a memorial monument, as the name μνῆμα, μνημεῖον, although commonly used for a grave, would signify. Goath also is placed in this locality, to give countenance to this theory : though there seems more reason to believe that it was to the south-west of the city. The " Armoury," the " Prison," the " Horse-gate," and the " Sepulchres of David," are also shown to be on the north of the Temple-area ; though, as we shall see, it is quite evident from Nehemiah, that they were to the south of it. The site of Hippicus is identified with the "Giant's Castle,"[1] thus thrusting the Tyropœon to the Damascus Gate, or Gate of Ephraim. The Temple is restricted to an area of 600 feet square to the south-west angle of the Temple-area : and certainly Mr. Fergusson, Mr. Lewin, and the other supporters of this position, adduce cogent arguments on its behalf, which we shall have to consider when we come to the Temple : while Dr. Lightfoot, in referring to the Talmud, states, that the former Temple differed but little from that of Herod.[2]

Thrupp, Antient Jerusalem, 1855.—Zion, the City of David, and the Lower City, are here all identified with the Temple-mount. "These arguments seem conclusively to prove that the antient hill of Zion, or the City of David, is not to be identified with the Zion of modern days, but with the eastern or Temple-hill." (p. 20.) Mr. Thrupp supposes, however, that in the time of the Maccabees the name of "Zion" was transferred to the south west quarter of the city. Identifying the Tyropœon with the valley proceeding from the Damascus-gate, he agrees with the writers of the Biblical Dictionary in making the whole western portion of the city the hill No. I. of Josephus : the Temple-mount becomes hill No. II. ; "The Akra of Josephus lay to the east of the valley, and is none other than the Temple-hill, the Zion of Scripture," (p. 35) ; " The

[1] See the argument for and against this in p. 336, note.
[2] *Prospect of the Temple*, x.

City of David occupied approximately the north-western part of the present Haram esh-Sherif," (p. 86); while the portion of the city north of the Temple-area is hill No. III., notwithstanding that Josephus says it was the *fourth* hill which stood north of the Temple : and this difficulty seems to have struck the author, for he has written Bezetha in large capitals extending not merely across this land, but covering even a portion of the Temple-area. With the Biblical Dictionary he makes his Tyropœon valley the line of Hezekiah's conduit, but identifies the Pool of Bethesda with the "Upper Pool ;" and from his position of the wall of Manasseh, which we are told was on the west of Gihon, it is evident that he considers that Gihon was only another name for Zion, or the City of David, or the Lower City. The fountain-head of Gihon he asserts to be in the neighbourhood of the Damascus-gate, or somewhere nearly due north of this, and that it was the scene of the anointing of King Solomon ; notwithstanding that the sacred narrative describes the event as taking place beneath the city. The Lower City is by this author reduced to its very smallest proportions ; and the Church of the Holy Sepulchre is of course far outside the walls ; while Goath takes the place of Gareb, so as to be near to Golgotha. Mr. Thrupp places the Temple at the south-west angle of the Haram platform, and altogether repudiates the name of Moriah, as applied to this hill. With these views Mr. Thrupp naturally rejects the opinion of those previous writers who, following Josephus, place Zion on the south-west quarter of the city : Other writers "have nearly all fallen into a *fundamental error* with respect to the position of the antient Zion. . . . Strange as it at first sight may appear that so important an error should have originated with the Jews themselves, it admits of the *clearest demonstration* that such is the case." (p. 12.) It is "a view respecting the position of Zion, so *completely opposed*, as will be presently shown, *to the indications of Scripture*." (p. 16.) "No modern travellers, so far as I have been able to find, have ever *produced the slightest evidence of any kind, in support of the view they have adopted*." (p. 20.)

Lewin, Siege of Jerusalem, 1863.—Mr. Lewin holds that the names "Zion" and the "City of David" were originally applied to the *whole* city of Jerusalem ; that the latter name was subsequently appropriated, as he says, "by popular belief," (query) to that portion of Ophel where he supposes "David's palace" to have stood ; and that eventually, in the time of the Maccabees, the name "Zion" was applied exclusively to the Temple-hill ; while the name of the "City of David" was transferred to the Acra or citadel built by Antiochus in the Lower City. Accordingly, throughout his book, he speaks of the south-west quarter of the city as "now called Sion," thereby intimating that it had no antient right to this especial designation; and yet, inconsistently enough, the name of Sion is given to it on his plan. "In the historical books of the Old Testament we meet with Sion in but few instances. The first is on the capture of Jebus by David, where it stands for Jerusalem generally. Again, Solomon 'brought up the ark of the covenant of the Lord out of the city of David which is Zion.' In this passage I suspect that the words 'which is Zion' have crept into the text from the mistaken gloss of some commentator who did not understand the passage 2 Sam. v. 7, where the stronghold of Zion is called the city of David, in the sense of Jerusalem as a whole. . . . The only other references to Sion in the historical books are 2 Kings xix. 21 and 31; in both these passages Sion is evidently used as synonymous with Jerusalem. In the prophetic or poetical books of the Old Testament Sion, or Zion, stands simply for Jerusalem." (p. 243.) He makes the south-western hill No. I., and Ophel No. II.,[1] notwithstanding that Josephus says that "the third hill (the Temple-mount) was naturally lower than Acra, (the second hill,) and parted formerly from the other by a broad valley;" while the Temple-hill is higher than Ophel, and has no valley separating it. He places the Upper Pool of Gihon at the top of the Valley of Hinnom, and fixes the "Lower Gihon" valley in the Tyropœon, where it is difficult to point out how the wall of Manasseh could have existed on its western side.

But the principal peculiarity of his book is that, like the Comte de Vogüé, M. de Sauley, and Krafft, he makes the third wall, built by Agrippa, identical with the limited area of the modern wall; relying principally upon Josephus saying that it went διὰ σπηλαίων βασιλικῶν, which royal caverns he connects with the "cotton cavern," or quarries to the east of the Damascus-gate. Dr. Porter, however, argues for the tombs called the "Tombs of the Kings" being the monuments of Helena; while he places the royal caverns, or Tombs of the Kings, 250 yards east by south, in an offset of the valley of Jehoshaphat.[2] This restricted area of the Third Wall is

---

[1] See his plan.

[2] "Its sides are rocky and precipitous, and almost filled with excavated tombs, many of them highly ornamented. May not these be the Royal caverns of Josephus? Both their appearance and situation favour the supposition. The natural course of a line of fortification would be along the rocky brow of the hill round which the Kidron sweeps to the south. Here may have stood the Tower of the Corner, near the Fuller's tomb. From hence

naturally opposed to Josephus, who gives the circuit of the wall as thirty-three stadia ;[1] to help out which dimension Mr. Lewin extends the southern wall of Zion down to the valley, thus doing away with the chief characteristic of Zion, its being girt about with inaccessible ravines. As a result of this the Assyrian Camp is placed in a confined nook where, according to Mr. Lewin's plan, it would have been impossible to accommodate the army of Titus, and where it would have been exposed on each side to the arrows of the besieged, which commanded a range of upwards of one stadium ;[2] and indeed, Josephus tells us that previous to his taking the third wall Titus encamped at the distance of two stadia from Psephinus, and two stadia from Hippicus.[3] This distance of two stadia would leave no room at all. The ground north of the present walls, which we have hitherto supposed to have been inclosed by Agrippa's wall, but which Mr. Lewin excludes, stating that no traces of the wall now exist, is, it is said by another writer, "covered with ruins and cisterns ; and bears evident traces of its having been once thickly peopled."[4] The Lower City is thus restricted to a small area, and the Holy Sepulchre falls without its lines. As the monument of King Alexander has been thought to countenance the position of the Sepulchre on the Temple-mount, so the monument of the High Priest John is made use of here to prove that the Church of the Holy Sepulchre was outside the walls. (p. 369.) But first, there is no proof that this monument was more than a cenotaph. Secondly, we think we shall be able to show that this portion of the city was inclosed so early as the time of King Manasseh. And thirdly, even if admitted to be a tomb, we know that tombs were sometimes formed within the

---

southward to the city scarcely a doubt can be entertained as to the course the wall followed. The brow of the hill above the Kidron forms such an admirable line of defence that no engineer could have overlooked it. And at a point on the steep bank, not far from the north-east angle of the city, are apparently the substructions of a tower." Murray's *Handbook of Syria*, 1868. p. 102.

[1] "Some discrepancy exists as to the circuit of the walls. The 'Syrian land-surveyor' gives it as twenty-seven stadia ; Josephus as thirty-three ; Timochares and Aristeas as forty ; while Hecataeus augments the measure to fifty stadia. The 'Syrian land-surveyor' lived in the time of Eusebius, at which period the greater portion of Bezetha had reverted into cornfields and olive groves ; and the remaining portion of the city, supposing the whole of Zion and Ophel to have been inclosed as formerly, would then differ only one stadium and a half from the twenty-seven stadia then given. The other dimensions probably included the suburbs of the city." *Mus. Class. Antiq.* p. 420.

[2] Strabo, p. 561.   [3] *Bell.* v. 3. 5.

[4] Williams, *Holy City*. Moreover Prof. Robinson shows traces of a northern wall on his plan.

city, as in the instances of Manasseh and Amon, who were "buried
in the garden of their own house." See also Ezek. xliii. 7. Pau-
sanias describes the tomb of Achilles and the sepulchre of Oxylus
in the agora at Elis; Arrian tells us that the tomb of Heropythus
was in the agora at Ephesus; Philostratus informs us that Diony-
sius the rhetorician was buried there; and Thucydides and Dio-
dorus relate that Themistocles was buried in the agora of Magnesia.
Thus we have abundant evidence that it was no uncommon thing
for people to be buried inside a city; and we have also seen that
the Jews were so. Dr. Pococke says "It was the ancient Eastern
custom to bury in their own houses or gardens."[1] And Dr. Lightfoot tells us that the children of Huldah were buried within the walls
of Jerusalem.[2] From Nehemiah's description of the walls, which
we shall presently consider, it is evident that the kings of Judah
were buried in the "king's garden," where David had one of his
houses; we find the tombs of Jerusalem not confined to any one
place, but on the slopes of every hill all round the city, in positions
admirably adapted for gardens; and thus we find also that Joseph
of Arimathæa, an "honourable man," a "rich man," was able to
have a sepulchre in a rock in his own garden, which was sufficiently large to have a "gardener" expressly employed in its
care.[3]

[1] _Descr. of the East_, ii. part i. p. 9.   [2] _Chorog._ Cent. 38.
[3] There is every reason to believe that this garden was in the Valley of
Tophet, which though rendered infamous from its sacrifices to Moloch, was
yet a "pleasant valley." The Dung Gate would seem to correspond with
the Porta Charonia of Athens, through which the condemned were led to
execution, and with the Esquiline Gate of Rome, or with the Porta Metia.
And if so, the original tradition of the Via Dolorosa being on Mount Zion
was doubtless the correct one. It probably led from the Prætorium, or
Palace of Herod, to this gate. It is remarkable that more than one traditional site has been changed from time to time. The Prætorium has been
changed from Herod's Palace, or the "Castle of David," to the Governor's
house, adjoining the Haram esh Sherif; the Via Dolorosa, or Via Crucis, was
changed in position in 1187, and again in the last quarter of the sixteenth
century; and the traditional site of St. Stephen's Martyrdom has been
changed four times, north, south, east, and west! The Empress Eudocia
built a large church over the authenticated spot in A.D. 460. Mr. Fergusson
says in the year 600 it was stated to be outside the Jaffa Gate, or to the _west_
of the city; in 695, it was found at the Coenaculum on Mount Zion, or
outside the _south_ wall of the city; during the Crusades, it was outside the
Damascus-gate, on the _north_ of the city; and since the fourteenth century
it has been established on the _east_ of the city. (_Essay on Anct. Top. of
Jer._ pp. 168, 169.) Eusebius, in A.D. 330, places Aceldama to the north
of Zion: Jerome, 70 years later, fixes it to the south, where it is still
shown. And as the Empress Helena thought she had complied with the
requirements of Acts i. 9—12 in building the Church of the Ascension on

Two objections lie against this restricted line of the Second and Third Walls. The Upper City being the Acropolis, the Lower City constituted the main portion of the inhabited city; and the Second Wall, as here drawn, would embrace far too small an area. And in like manner the Third Wall, from the terms used by Josephus —*extendens, protendens, in longum ductus*—evidently embraced a large area, which is confirmed also by the vicinity of the monuments of Helena, and by its being so much as thirty-three stadia in circuit. But it is contended by Mr. Lewin that Titus's wall of circumvallation being only thirty-nine stadia, which must have been two stadia at least from the walls in every direction, the Third Wall could not have been as much as thirty-three stadia. A glance at the map, however, will show that this presents no difficulty; for the Third Wall was destroyed when Titus formed his wall of circumvallation. It is also contended that as Scopus was so much as seven stadia from the walls, (*Bell.* v. 2. 3,) it is impossible that the Third Wall could have extended so far northward. Let us examine this. Jerusalem is separated both from the Mount of Olives and from Mount Scopus by the Valley of the Kedron: what we find, therefore, in one case, we may expect to find in the other. Now, the Mount of Olives measures by the Ordnance map four stadia from the Haram Wall; and Mount Scopus (Chérćfé, or El Mechärif, the *Observatory, or place whence one can see*[1]) measures nine stadia from the Second Wall. But Josephus tells us that the Mount of Olives was *six* stadia distant. (*B.* v. 2. 3.) Thus we find it half as much again as it measures on the map, owing to the double slope: consequently, we must allow at least one more stadium for these slopes in the upper part of the valley in calculating the real distance of Scopus by the road. This will make the real distance of Scopus ten stadia from the Second Wall; from which, if we deduct the

the *summit* of the Mount of Olives; when Luke xxiv. 50, 51 would have told her she was wrong, and that it was at the bottom : so, though she thought she had complied with the requirements of Scripture by building her church of the Resurrection, or church of the Holy Sepulchre, outside the walls of Ælia Capitolina, modern research has discovered that this position is within the line of the second wall as described by Nehemiah, and forming the wall of Jerusalem in the time of our Lord. But the subject of Calvary and Golgotha has been treated at length in our former articles in the *Mus. Class. Antiq.*, to which the reader is referred for the connection between the Dung Gate with the Valley of Hinnom, and Tophet ; (p. 455 ;) with Goath or Golgotha ; (p. 460 ;) and with Bethso, and the Gate of the Essenes ; (p. 462.)

[1] Ordnance Survey, △ 26863. The Mussulmans have placed a cairn, or heap of small stones there; because they say that it is the point from which Jerusalem and the Mosque of the Sakhra are first observed in coming from Nablous.

seven stadia distance from the Third Wall, we shall have three stadia as the amount of extension of the Third Wall beyond the Second Wall. Again, the monuments of Helena measure four stadia from the Damascus Gate on plan, which may represent say five stadia by the road: but Josephus says they were three stadia distant from the Third Wall. (*Antiq.* xx. 4. 3.) This will leave, therefore, an extension of two stadia of the Third Wall beyond the Second Wall. Thus the distance of seven stadia of Scopus, as mentioned by Josephus, instead of being an objection, is really a proof in favour of a northerly extension of the Third Wall.

Again, an argument against all reduced areas of the Second Wall, whether the object be to exclude the church of the Holy Sepulchre, or to make the Third Wall coincident with the present wall, lies in the fact that if the Second Wall were so restricted, Bezetha, or the New City, could not have been described by Josephus as north of Antonia; for it might more accurately have been described as north of the Upper City at one end, and of Antonia at the other. Another argument against the restricted area of the Second Wall lies in the fact that if it ran where these writers suppose, it would have been impossible for those on the wall to have heard the words of Rabshakeh when standing at the Upper Pool. (2 Kings xviii. 26, 28.) Mr. Lewin points out (pp. 158—160) some " remains of the Second Wall" in pretended line within the city, but from the plan which he gives it is evident that the wall is much too thin for a city wall; and moreover, it faces the wrong way! Other *supposed* "remains" had previously been pointed out by Mr. Williams, (pp. 286, 287, 2nd edit. suppl. 83,) Lord Nugent, (*Lands Classical and Sacred*, pp. 36—39,) and Schultz. (*Jer.* p. 60.) They consisted of a pier of a gateway, the crown of a circular arch, a colonnade of four or five columns ten feet apart, (!) and the spring-course of an arch. The remains were shown by Mr. Whiting (*Bibl. Sac.* v. 96) to be portions of the palace of the Knights of St. John: in which opinion Dr. Tobler unites. (*Das Ausland*, Jan. 20, 1848.)

Imperial Bible Dictionary, 1864. *Article on Jerusalem by Rev. Horatius Bonar.* Fortunately, this writer is opposed to the new position of Zion, and places it in the south-west quarter; but he does not confine it there; for owing to the extraordinary northern position of his Hippicus, which Josephus tells us was one of the *western towers*, his Zion is disproportionately extended, thereby thrusting Acra out of its natural position, and invading the greater part of what Josephus calls the fourth hill:—"But where was Hippicus? somewhere *northward*, as Josephus tells us; (*Bell.*

v. 4. 2;) not πρὸς ἕνσεν, but κατὰ βοῤῥᾶν: so that we must
look for it somewhere in the north-west quarter of the *city;*"
not on Zion merely, at the present *Kulat,* or "Castle of David,"
which is "at the *south*" of the city. (p. 886.) "Psephinus is
said to be at the north-west corner, and Hippicus at the *north* of
the city, where the old wall began, κατὰ βοῤῥᾶν, and the historian
could not possibly have intended 'north' to mean the present Jaffa
Gate, while he intended 'north-west' to mean the neighbourhood of
the Tombs of the Kings; the one nearly a mile from the other!
If 'north-west' means with him north-west in reference to the
whole city, as we know it does, 'north' must have a similar reference,
and cannot merely mean north of Zion, which the necessities of
some topographical theories require it to do, thereby making
'north' mean one thing in one page of Josephus, and another in
another." He then quotes Robinson with a note of astonishment,
—"The tower of Hippicus must be sought at the north-west of
Zion!" (p. 895.)

Now, in answer to this argument, we would mention first, that,
if Psephinus is said to be "north-west," and Hippicus "north,"
we ought naturally to place Hippicus to the *east* of Psephinus, and
on the *Third Wall,* which we know it was not: secondly, that it is
the writer, and no one else, who places Psephinus near to the
"Tombs of the Kings;" thirdly, that no one can read Josephus's
account (*Bell.* v. 4. 2) without perceiving that he describes Hippicus as being on the north side of the *First Wall,* which wall
enclosed Zion, or the Upper City; fourthly, that after speaking
of Hippicus as on the north of Zion, he adds—"But on the *west*
side, beginning at the same tower." (*Bell.* v. 4. 2); fifthly, that
the present Jaffa Gate is always described as the western gate of
the city, not the "south," as Mr. Bonar here calls it; and sixthly,
that Hippicus was one of the "Three Towers" forming part of
the Royal Palace, where the final attack was made, "on the *west*
side of the city," (*Bell.* vi. 8. 1,) when the panic-stricken Jews cried
out that "the whole *western* wall was overthrown." (vi. 8. 4.) By
what we think a false stress on the word κυκλούμενον, encircling,
surrounding, or enclosing—for Josephus uses the same word κύκλῳ
when describing the walls round the Temple, which we know
to be square—he makes the wall of Acra a half-circle. Again,
owing to his position of Hippicus, the author no doubt felt, in
endeavouring to trace Nehemiah's description of the walls, that
he had too great an extension of wall to go along before reaching
Siloam, and therefore took a "near cut" to the present Dung Gate,
(*ant.* Water Gate,) thinking it might have some traditional connection

with the ancient Dung Gate, which ought to be only 1,000 feet distant; but, like all *near cuts*, this has only led him into trouble, and he has been obliged to retrace his steps backwards, thus forming the line of the letter S, or rather of the figure 8, for he quite returns upon his steps; and when he at length reaches Hippicus a second time, he has to jump back again right across the city to the present Dung Gate, in order to complete the circuit of the walls by going round Ophel. By this position of Hippicus, he naturally makes the Tyropœon proceed from the Damascus Gate; a confirmation of which line is he thinks the very sharp angle (he erroneously calls it acute) which Hezekiah's aqueduct would take if it had proceeded from the Jaffa Gate, when it had to turn under the bridge. But the author's plan is here in error: for instead of being only thirty-nine feet from the south-west angle of the Temple-area, this bridge is shown in his plan as 300 feet distant. The bottom of the Tyropœon he calls the valley of Hinnom.

It is with great diffidence that the author ventures to differ from the conclusions of these writers on some points, men whose names are known as those of writers of great power and ability, and whose works are regarded as the latest authorities on the topography of Jerusalem. He trusts it will be found that in doing so he has not forgotten the respect due to these writers, and he takes this opportunity of acknowledging the great assistance he has derived from the perusal and study of their works. It is indeed from the importance he attaches to their labours that he has entered at such length into the consideration of their arguments, the exposition of which he trusts he has faithfully represented.

The arguments which have been adduced in favour of the new position of Zion and the City of David are:—

(i) The description of the taking of the city of the Jebusites by David, as given in 2 Sam. v., 1 Chron. xi., and Josephus, *Ant.* vii. 3. 1, 2;

(ii.) The water-course of Gihon having evidently entered the city from the north by the Damascus Gate, and therefore having Gihon and the City of David on the east of it;

(iii.) The position of the city of David and the sepulchres of David as described by Nehemiah;

(iv.) The forty-eighth psalm, where the city of the great king (Zion, or the City of David,) is said to be "on the sides of the north," *i.e.* to the north of the Temple;

(v.) Numerous passages in the Book of Maccabees, where the citadel in the Lower City is called the citadel in the City of David;

(vi.) Some minor arguments;

(vii.) and finally, a great number of passages in Scripture which speak of Mount Zion as the Temple-mount.

This is a goodly array of witnesses, and some others will be added; and if they be found true we do not wonder at the conclusion which is arrived at. Let us examine each of these proofs: and first as to the description of the taking of the city of the Jebusites.

(I.) Some of those who insist upon the change of site contend that it is evident from the words—" David took the stronghold of Zion: the same is the City of David;" "So David dwelt in the fort, (or 'castle,') and called it the City of David;" and from the more explicit description of Josephus,—that David took the *Lower City* with its stronghold, or castle, and that he called it the stronghold (or fort, or castle, for it is the same word in the original, *Metsoodoh*) of Zion, or the City of David; and that *after this* Joab took the Upper City.

Josephus has told us that the Upper City was "far higher" than the Lower City, and that except where it was defended only by one wall, it was "girt about with unapproachable ravines or valleys." Where these two valleys, the Valley of Kedron and the Valley of Hinnom, meet, the depth is more than 600 feet! A writer in "Smith's Dictionary of the Bible," says—" On the other three sides so steep is the fall of the ravines, so trench-like their character, and so close do they keep to the promontory at whose feet they run, as to leave on the beholder almost the impression of the ditch at the foot of a fortress, rather than of valleys formed by nature."[1] Josephus goes on to say—" On the outside the two hills on which the city stood" (he here speaks of hills I. and II. as one hill, and hill III. as another) " were surrounded by deep valleys; and by reason of the precipices on either side there was no approach to them from any quarter." With this agrees the description by Tacitus — "*Duos colles, immensum editos, claudebant muri, per artem obliqui, aut introrsus sinuati.*"[2] Josephus also expresses the same in another place :—" The valley before the walls was terrible." (*Bell.* i. 7. 1.) He then goes on to say—" Accordingly, on account of its (steepness and) strength it was styled the citadel of King David." There can be no doubt that this acropolis, or citadel of the Upper City, as described by Josephus, was what is called in the Bible narrative the "stronghold of Zion," the "fort," or "castle," and "City of David." But where would the propounders of the new theory place this stronghold? Not on the Lower hill which was "far lower" than the Upper City, but on the Temple hill, or third hill, which was still

[1] p. 985. [2] *Hist.* v. 11.

lower: for Josephus says it was "naturally lower than Acra" or the Lower City. Now independently of its being unreasonable to suppose that the lowest of all the hills of Jerusalem should be selected for a stronghold, we have no evidence throughout the whole of the Jewish history up to the time of Antiochus of any such detached stronghold, or fort, or castle, existing at Jerusalem ; and, what is more, we have Josephus's authority for saying that this third hill on which the stronghold, or fort, or castle, is supposed to have stood, did not form part of the city at this time ; for he says "the city . . . was built . . . on two hills." At this period the third hill constituted a farm in the occupation of a Jebusite who had been allowed to remain unmolested.

Let us now take the order of narration as given us in the Bible. And here we may make bold to say that there is not one person in a thousand who, on reading this narrative, did not, before this new theory was promulgated, suppose that David took Zion, or the Upper City, and called it after his name. Certainly Josephus understood it so : for after describing the steepness of the Upper City, he says, "Accordingly, on account of its strength it was called 'the Citadel' by King David."[1] It would appear from Judges i. 8, 21, that though Jerusalem had been taken twice previously, by the men of Judah, and by the men of Benjamin,[2] the Upper City had remained impregnable ; and it seems to have been on this account, and from the boastful confidence of the Jebusites, who tauntingly told David that the lame and the blind were sufficient to defend the walls, that he prided himself so much on having taken it. But it is argued that while David took the stronghold of Zion, Joab took this acropolis of the Jebusites. How are we to reconcile this ? We all know the danger which exists in putting a literal interpretation upon every passage in the Bible, instead of "comparing Scripture with Scripture." An example of this occurs in the accounts of the victory over the Edomites in the Valley of Salt, when 18,000 Edomites were slain. If we read 2 Sam. viii. 13, we are told that it was David who got this victory. But if we turn to the Introduction to Ps. lx. we see that it was not David, but Joab who gained the battle. But if we turn now to 1 Chron. xviii. 12 we see that it was not Joab, but his brother Abishai who gained the victory. While Abishai really won the battle, Joab, being commander-in-chief, was said to have won it, while David, being king, had all the glory of it. A similar in-

[1] See also *Antiq.* v. 3 § 1 : and what he says of the Upper City in *Bell.* i. 7 § 1 ; v. 4 § 2 ; v. 6 § 2 ; vi. 8 § 1.

[2] See also *Antiq.* v. 2 § 2, 5.

stance occurs in the account we have in 1 Sam. xvii. 54, where we are told that " David took the head of the Philistine, and brought it to Jerusalem; but he put his armour in his tent;" from which we might suppose that this took place immediately after his having slain Goliath; whereas it could not have occurred till eighteen years afterwards. So, in the instance before us, though Joab took the acropolis of the Jebusites, or as it was now called the stronghold of Zion, for it is one and the same thing, David had the glory of it, and called this stronghold or fastness after his own name. If any further doubt remains, on account of the order of narration, David appearing to have taken something, and Joab something else, let us turn to the thirty-eighth chapter of Isaiah, where we find the psalm which Hezekiah wrote when he had been sick, and was recovered of his sickness. This psalm occupies the greater part of the chapter, from v. 9 to v. 20, and it is not till towards the end of the psalm that we read the occasion of it, which occasion ought to have been narrated first—" For Isaiah had said, Let them take a lump of figs," &c. We find frequent examples of this involved order of narration in the Psalms of David. Thus, in Ps. xxx., the natural order would have been to begin with the sixth verse—

> In my prosperity I said, I shall never be removed ;
> Thou, Lord, of Thy goodness hast made my hill so strong :

instead of which we find the Psalmist begins with praise, and ends with praise. In the following psalm the natural order would have been to begin with the tenth verse—

> Have mercy upon me, O Lord, for I am in trouble,
> And mine eye is consumed for very heaviness :

instead of which the Psalmist begins and ends with an expression of trust in God. Similar instances will be found in the two following psalms, and many others. Let us take Ps. lxviii., which, were we to follow the natural order, should have begun with the seventh verse—

> O God, when Thou wentest forth before the people,

instead of which it begins more emphatically by quoting the words of Moses, which he used when the ark went forward, (Num. x. 35)—

> " Let God arise, and let His enemies be scattered.
> " Let them also that hate Him flee before Him."

With this key to the interpretation, we have no difficulty in understanding that though " Joab went first up," it was David who was said to have taken the castle or stronghold of Zion. A parallel instance occurs in 2 Sam. xii. 26—29 :—" And Joab fought against

Rabbah of the children of Ammon, and took the royal city. And Joab sent messengers to David, and said, I have fought against Rabbah, and have taken the city of waters. Now therefore gather the rest of the people together, and encamp against the city and take it; lest I take the city, and it be called after my name. And David . . . fought against it, and took it." The whole confusion would have been obviated had our translators rendered the Hebrew particle *for* instead of *and:*—" *For* David said on that day." The whole passage therefore is perfectly intelligible, and perfectly confirmatory of the position of Zion and the City of David:—" The Jebusites spake unto David, saying, ' Except thou take away the blind and the lame, thou shalt not come in hither,' thinking David could not come in thither. *Nevertheless, David took the stronghold of Zion:* the same is the City of David." (2 Sam. v.) We now turn to 1 Chron. xi. which supplies what is wanting in the first account—" *For* David said, Whosoever smiteth the Jebusites first, shall be chief and captain. So Joab the son of Zeruiah went first up, and was chief." There is not the slightest warranty for reading the passage in other than this its legitimate sense. Any contrary reading leads us to endless confusion; for we should not only get a castle where none existed, and a hill which was not yet enclosed, but by the word " nevertheless " it becomes evident, if the stronghold of Zion which David took was on the Temple-hill, then the Jebusites lived on that hill; for the word " nevertheless " proves that it was the stronghold of the Jebusites which David took. Immediately after mentioning the " City of David," the chronicler goes on, " And he built the city round about, even from Millo round about." This agrees with 2 Chron. xxxii. 5, where he speaks of " Millo in the city of David." What this Millo was which David and Solomon (1 Kings ix. 15, 24; xi. 27) built, and which Hezekiah repaired, is uncertain.[1] But though we have shown that the City of David was Mount Zion, and therefore, as everybody acknowledges, a part of the city of Jerusalem, Josephus asserts that the name applied to the whole of the city. (*Antiq.* vii. 3 § 2.) This, however, is a mistake of the Jewish historian; for 1 Kings viii. 1 is decisive. We there read, after a long description of the building and finishing of the Temple on Mount Moriah—" Then Solomon assembled the elders of Israel . . . unto King Solomon in Jerusalem, that they might bring up the ark of the covenant of the Lord out of the City of David, which is Zion." Here it is said that the ark of

---

[1] Millo signifies *filled-up*, or *fulness*. The Seventy have translated the word *a citadel.*

the Lord was brought from one part of the city to another; from the City of David, or Mount Zion, to the Temple-Mount: which proves that they were different places, and not one and the same, as now supposed.

(II.) The second argument adduced is the position of the "water-course of Gihon." In 2 Chron. xxxii. 30, Hezekiah is described as bringing down the water-course of Gihon by subterranean pipes (Ecclus. xlviii. 17) "to the west side of the City of David." It is asserted that there is no spring to the west of Jerusalem, but that there must have been one formerly to the north of the city outside the Damascus Gate. From Josephus' mention of a "Serpent's Pool" as connected with Herod's monuments and Scopus, it has been supposed that, as Scopus was to the north of the city, the Serpent's Pool also was to the north of the city, and therefore that a spring of water once existed in this locality; and it is this *sup-posed* spring and water-course entering the city by the Damascus gate, and running along the *supposed* northern extension of the Tyropœon, which is to *prove* that the City of David lay on the *east* side of this supposed line of water-course, and not on Mount Zion! But there is no authority for this supposition. It is true that Titus pitched his first camp at Scopus, at the safe distance of seven stadia from the city; here he placed two of his legions, while he placed a reserve force of one legion at a camp three stadia behind him. This ground was selected because it enabled him to view the city from an elevated position. But he had no idea of attacking from the north; he intended to attack towards the west, and he therefore levelled all the ground "from Scopus to Herod's monuments, which adjoined to the pool called the Serpent's Pool." (*Bell.* v. 3 § 2.) As we shall presently see, this attack was made near to the tower Hippicus, opposite to the monument of the High Priest John, adjoining which tower was the Valley Gate; and it is satisfactory to find that Nehemiah, when surveying the walls of the city, when he comes to the Valley Gate, says he went "even before the Dragon's Well," (ii. 13,) which is evidently the same as the Serpent's Pool of Josephus.

But the supposition of a water-spring north of the city, and consequent location of Gihon and the City of David on the north-east, is still further complicated by the account we have in 2 Chron. xxxiii. 14, where it is said, that Manasseh "built a wall *without* the City of David, on the west side of Gihon, in the valley." Surely it must be a hopeless endeavour to point out where this wall could be outside the City of David, and where the valley of Gihon could be, where Solomon *went down* to be anointed king, (1 Kings i. 38—45,) if the City of David formed part of the Temple mount. Great stress has been laid upon the fact that the "valley," which is mentioned in connection with Gihon, is called in the Hebrew *Nachal* or *Nokhal*, like the Kedron, a watered valley; whereas a dark ravine or glen, like the Valley of Hinnom, is called *Ge* or *Gai*. But the etymology of the words does not much help us; for if the Valley of Hinnom be a dry, dark ravine, the name of the Kedron is *dark*. And if, on the other hand, the Kedron be a watered valley, the name of Tophet, as it originally signified, would be a *pleasant valley*. With this agrees the name of Gihon itself, (*Gai-khoun*) a *valley of grace*, or favour; and of this valley the writer of the Book of Ecclesiasticus says— " He maketh the doctrine of knowledge appear as the light, and as Geon in the time of vintage." (xxiv. 27.) Neither can the Kedron be well called a watered valley, for it, as well as the Upper and Lower Pools, is quite dry in the summer months; indeed, a writer in the *Times*, April 30, 1874, says it "usually is without water during the whole year, and seldom runs for more than three or four days;"[1] moreover, it supplies no reservoirs, whereas the Valley of Gihon supplies two large reservoirs or pools. But as this Valley of Gihon has never been supposed to have been in the Valley of the Kedron—for water from it could not have entered the *west* side of the City of David—and as it could not have been in what is pointed out as the Asmonean Valley, (the Broad Valley, or Street of Ephraim,) for this is rather a depression than a valley, and certainly cannot be called a *watered* valley, and cannot be connected with Solomon's anointing; we have no choice but that of placing it in the Valley of Hinnom on the west of the city, whence, as we shall find reason to see, the principal water supply of the city was obtained, and where we have a valley of sufficient depth to answer all the requirements of the narrative connected with Solomon's anointing. That Gihon was to the north-west of the city appears, not only from its water-course being conducted to the west side of the city of David, but from the fact which we have seen that Manasseh " built a wall *without* the City of David, on the west side of Gihon, in the valley."[2]

[1] " We crossed the bridge over the brook Kedron, but there was not water in it, and, as I understood, never is, except occasionally in winter." Lewin, *Siege of Jer.* p. 141.

[2] That Gihon occupied this locality was the opinion of Pococke, Sandys, Doubdan, Mantegazze, Besson, Robinson, Paxton, Schultz, Fuhrer, Amico, Berggren, and Leeman; references to whose works will be seen in *J. us. Class. Antiq.* p. 349 note.

If we admit this position of Gihon, we must also admit the identity of the Upper and Lower Pools of the Valley of Hinnom with the Upper and Lower Pools of Gihon, of 2 Chron. xxxii. 2, 3, 4, 30; and Is. xxii. 9, 11. The Upper Pool, or rather the waters which fed the Upper Pool,[1] were conveyed into the city at the gate occupying the position of the present Jaffa Gate;[2] while the waters of the Lower Pool were conveyed by similar conduits within the Water Gate, beneath the Temple.

But water was not only brought into the city by the Valley Gate, to supply the Pool of Hezekiah, and other pools of the Lower City,

[1] These waters were obtained from the entire surface water of the country west of the city up to seven miles distance, though from the sinuosities of the hills the conduits must have been twelve miles in length. (Dr. Trail, *Josephus*.)

[2] Speaking of the Upper Pool in the Valley of Gihon, Dr. Robinson states that "in the winter-season it becomes full; and its waters are then conducted by a small rude aqueduct, or channel, to the vicinity of the Jaffa Gate, and so to the Pool of Hezekiah within the city." (*Bib. Res.* i. 352.) It is probable that the ancient conduit by which Hezekiah supplied his pool lies beneath the surface of the ground, and that the rude aqueduct here spoken of is of recent date. Antoninus of Placenza (A.D. 600) records that "on putting the ear to the ground on the side of Golgotha, you will hear the sound of running water." Old authors affirm that the fountain of the Upper Pool flowed by the place of Golgotha. (Reusner, *Alben Jerus.* fol. lxvii.; Korte, *Reise,* p. 183.) After speaking of the aqueduct which supplies the *Piscina del Calvario* (Pool of Hezekiah) from the Upper Pool, and which passes beneath the wall, Mariti says there are no traces of this aqueduct within the city, but "quanto poi ai condotti che possono essere sotto la città, crederei che questi fossero nella maggior parte scavati nella rocca, anche all' altezzo di un uomo, giacchè tali essempj non mancano in quelle parti." (Gio. Mariti, *Istoria dello stato presente della città di Gerusalemme,* i. 196.) Owing to neglect, the subterranean aqueduct which supplied the Pool of Hezekiah, is become obstructed, so that whereas in 1600 the pool was so full that there were only thirteen steps above the water, you now have to descend (in 1767) by forty-seven. This pool supplied the Pool of Bethesda, and the other pools of the city. (Mariti, *Istoria,* i. 207, 208.) Rabbi Joseph Schwarz writes: "A very deep cistern, the water of which is just like that of the spring of Siloah, and I think it therefore certain that the former aqueduct of Hezekiah is now below the surface of the ground in this direction. . . . . The learned Azulai mentions in ‘*The Names of the Great,*’ (fol. 30b,) that so late as the time of the Cabalist Rabbi Chayim Vital, who lived in 5340, (A.D. 1580,) one could hear near the Kallai, or David's Tower, a strong subterranean rushing of running water, which was represented as the ancient aqueduct of King Hezekiah." *Descr. Geogr. and Brief Hist. Sketch of Palestine,* translated by Leeser, 5610, (A.D. 1850,) p. 266. (*Mus. Class. Antiq.* p. 348, 349, 467.) Mr. Whitty, whose especial object it was to ascertain the means of supplying the town with water, appears to have discovered the ancient duct; for he speaks of a rock-cut duct, in length 790 yards. (*Proposed Water Supply and Sewerage for Jerus.* p. 70, 92, 125.) The model of Jerusalem which has been formed from the Ordnance Survey shows a fall of about twenty-five feet from the Upper Pool to the so-called Pool of Hezekiah.

but it was also conveyed into the Upper City, or City of David, as
described in the Book of Chronicles. For, on digging for the foundations of the Protestant church on Mount Zion, at a depth of about
thirty-five feet, the workmen came upon "an immense conduit, partly
hewn out of the solid rock ; and where this was not the case, it was
solidly built in even courses, and cemented on the face with a hard
coating of cement, about one inch thick, and was covered over with
large stones." After tracing 200 feet of it in length, the architect
writes—"There is no doubt on my own mind that they have been
used for the purpose of supplying the inhabitants with pure water ;
and this is proved by there being several apertures opening from
the streets at distant intervals : the aqueduct was nearly level,
the fall being so slight as to allow the water to remain level, so
that by means of a line and bucket water could be procured at
any time."[1]   This account is confirmed by Mr. Lewin, who
examined the conduit again after it had been closed up twenty-
one years.   He gives the depth at thirty-three feet, and explored
the same "two or three hundred feet" in an easterly direction, and
about a hundred and sixteen feet (117 ft. 6 in.) in a westerly course,
where it turned sharply to the left, (therefore a southerly direction,)
but "did not reach far when it was terminated by a wall built
across it."[2]

We shall see presently that Josephus also proves that the water
supply was brought into the city from its western side, and not its
northern. But before we show this, it is necessary that we establish
the position of the tower called Hippicus as one of the three
towers built by Herod. It is the general conviction that Hippicus
stood on the site of what is now called the castle of David ; and if
so, from Josephus beginning to describe the circuit of the first and
third walls from this tower, it must have occupied the north-west
angle of Mount Zion, at a spot due west and exactly opposite to
the Temple.[3]   A glance at the map will show, independently of the
evidence of actual facts which could be adduced, that while Mount
Zion was defended by precipitous ravines on the west, south and
east sides, this defence became less and less perfect on the northern
side as the Tyropœon approached its head towards the west :
though even here, where the valley of the Tyropœon was least
profound, we are told by Josephus that the cliff of the Upper City

[1] Bartlett, Walks about Jerusalem, p. 89, 90.
[2] Siege of Jerusalem, p. 207—208.
[3] The Ordnance Survey describes : "an escarpment of masonry surmounted
by a berme, or rounded top, on which is a solid mass of masonry similar to
that of the Wailing Place."

overlooking this valley was thirty cubits high. (*Bell.* v. 4 § 4.)
And in another place we are told that "the Upper City was so steep
that it could not possibly be taken without raising banks against
it," (vi. 8 § 1,) and this of course must refer to the northern side.
Mr. Lewin says "The depth of it opposite the Pool of Hezekiah
must have been very considerable: for while the pool is excavated
out of the rock, the *débris* in David Street (the Street of the
Valley Gate) reaches down from thirty to sixty feet."[1] The Cte de
Vogüé makes it thirty-three feet near the citadel. It was, however,
on account of this comparative weakness that Rabshakeh besieged the
city at this point, and that notwithstanding Herod's building these
three celebrated towers, it was at this same point that the city
was afterwards besieged by Cestius, and subsequently taken by
Titus. These three towers formed part of Herod's Palace, "inwardly thereto adjoining," (*Bell.* v. 4 § 4,) and on this account the
towers are called by Josephus the "Royal Towers." (*Bell.* ii.
17 § 8.)[2] Probably between two of these towers, or close to them,
was the Gate Gennath or the "Garden Gate," which led to the
beautiful gardens (v. 4 § 4) connected with the palace, and which
must have occupied a portion of that Gihon which was inclosed by
the wall of Manasseh. But that we may be quite clear respecting
these details, let us give the passages themselves. In 2 Kings
xviii. 17 we read that Rabshakeh and his host encamped at "the
conduit of the Upper Pool," which can only mean the Upper Pool
of Gihon. Cestius, after he had taken the outer wall, and had got
possession of Bezetha, "pitched his camp over against the Royal
Palace." (*Bell.* ii. 19 § 4.) Titus formed banks against the
"Upper City," which were "erected on the *west* side of the city,
over against the Royal Palace." (vi. 8 § 1.) And immediately
these banks and engines were completed, "a part of the wall was
battered down," and the Jews, panic-stricken, gave out that "the

---

[1] *Siege of Jerus.* p. 134. "The descent from the Jaffa Gate is at first very
steep, and the stones so well polished that you can with difficulty maintain
the perpendicular. The first street on the right hand is ascended by twelve
steps, and the first two or three lanes or streets on the left have a perceptible
rise, so that even at the present day there is a decided valley here if we
regard the ascent on the south, and something of a valley even as regards
the north." From the Governor's house "the depression of the valley from
the Jaffa Gate to the Temple was distinctly visible, and in ancient times the
hollow must have been infinitely greater." (p. 142.) Murray also makes the
same observation. (*Handbook*, p. 94.)

[2] This palace was the Praetorium, or Palace of Pontius Pilate, erroneously
placed by modern tradition at the N.W. angle of the Haram-esh-Sherif. For
the identification of the Praetorium, see the case well stated by Lewin, *Siege
of Jer.* p. 364—366.

whole *western* wall was overthrown ;" and thus the Romans
finally got possession of the Upper City, and consequently of all
Jerusalem, at the place where "the Three Towers" stood.
(vi. 8 § 4.) This is made still more clear by what Josephus tells
us of the monument of the High Priest John, and the Pool Amygdalon. This monument of the High Priest is mentioned in the
attacks on each wall—the outer, the second, and the old walls, and
from what is said of it it is evident that it must have been close to,
and therefore at about equal distance from each wall. " An important
point in the topography of Jerusalem as indicating the line of the
Second Wall, is the position of the High Priest John's monument.
Judging only from the first mention of this monument, it would
appear that it stood near the Outer or *Third* Wall ; for it marked the
spot where Titus attacked the Outer Wall. (*Bell.* v. 6 § 2.) Then,
further on, we are told that when Titus had taken the Outer Wall,
and was preparing to attack the Second Wall, Simon fortified the
walls from the point in the Second Wall opposite to the monument
of the High Priest John, round about to Hippicus, (v. 7 § 3,) thus
identifying the monument with the *Second* Wall : but afterwards,
when Titus had taken both the Outer and Second Walls, and laid
siege to the first wall, we read, that he planted two machines, one
at the Pool Amygdalon, (as the Pool of Hezekiah was then called,)
and the other nearer to Hippicus at John's monument ; (v. 9 § 2,
and v. 11 § 4 ;) [1] thus clearly proving that the monument was near
the *First* Wall. These perplexing accounts are satisfactorily explained when we consider the High Priest's monument to have
been situated about equi-distant from all three walls ; the walls
forming three sides of a square, and the monument standing in
the middle. The exact position may be determined from
Josephus ; for he states that the machine by the High Priest's
monument was thirty cubits only distant in a westerly direction from that which stood by the Pool Amygdalon.[2] (v. 11 § 4.) "

" But the determination of the High Priest's monument is useful,
not only in showing the point where Titus made his breach in the
Outer Wall ; it also enables us to fix with great precision the line of

---

[1] Josephus does not use the words nearer to Hippicus, but he implies this.
He first describes a bank opposite to Antonia, then one twenty cubits from
this ; then one "a great way off these, at the pool called Amygdalon," and
then the fourth, (which must necessarily have been still further westward,)
"about thirty cubits from it, and at the High Priest's monument."

[2] Horatius Bonar thinks it possible that the Amygdalon or *Almond Pool*
took its name originally from מִגְדָּל *Mighdol* a tower, the Tower-pool. (*Imp.
Bib. Dict.* p. 885.)

the Second Wall. It is very remarkable that all[1] attacks on the Upper City were made opposite to the three strong towers described by Josephus. . . . . . Here therefore must have stood the fourth machine, thirty cubits from which was the third machine by the Pool Amygdalon, the two machines being separated from each other by the line of Second Wall, and the Gate Gennath. Thus, then, by the High Priest's monument, we are enabled to prove, not only that the Second Wall lay to the west of the Pool of Hezekiah, or Amygdalon, but that an *outer* wall existed yet more to the west, occupying the position of the present modern wall, of the same antiquity as the other walls."[2] With the explanation above given, assisted by the plan, we shall be able to understand what Josephus says in the sixth chapter relative to Titus's first attack upon the city :—" Titus went round the city on the outside, with some chosen horsemen, and looked about for a proper place where he might make an impression upon the walls, but as he was in doubt where he could possibly make an attack on any side, for the place was no way accessible where the valleys were, and on the other (north) side the first wall appeared too strong to be taken by the engines, he thought it best to make his assault by the monument of John the High Priest : for there it was that the first fortification was lower, and the second was not joined to it : the builders neglecting to build the wall strong, where the new city was not much inhabited : here also was an easy passage to the Third Wall, through which he thought to take the Upper City." (v. 6 § 2.)

The careful consideration and comparison of all these passages cannot fail to enable us to fix the position of the Royal Palace, the Three Towers, and consequently of the tower Hippicus, which forms the basis and starting-point for the determination of the gates and walls of the city, as described by Nehemiah, which we shall next consider. At present we have only to add that the determi-

---

[1] The final and successful attack on the upper city was made on the west wall of the royal palace. (*Bell.* vi. 8 §1.)

[2] *Mus. Class. Antiq.* p. 426—428. The writer had previously shown that Titus took the outer wall, on the west of Gihon, close to the three towers, and opposite to the High Priest's monument : which of course gave him possession of the whole of the new city ; that he then attacked the second wall at a spot close to the same monument, but subsequently on the northern side ; and that when he had thus got possession of the Lower City, he destroyed the walls and towers, except the southern extremity of such walls and towers; (v. 8 § 2 ;) for these, as they united on to the Old Wall, the better enabled him to attack the Upper City ; and that after this he proceeded to attack the Upper City from opposite the same monument.

nation of this tower *westward of the pool called Amygdalon*, or
Hezekiah's pool, forms a striking confirmation of the fact that it
was at this point that Hezekiah brought in his water supply to the
city. Josephus, describing the Jews' preparations for the defence
of the Second Wall, says—"Simon's army also took for their share
the spot of ground which was near John's monument, and fortified
it as far as to that gate (the Valley Gate) where water was brought
in to the tower Hippicus." (v. 7 § 3.)[1]

(III.) We now come to the third argument, which is that the description of the walls and gates of the city, given us by Nehemiah,
proves that the "city of David" and the "sepulchres of David"
were to the north of the Temple. As Hippicus is the basis or
starting-point of Josephus' description, so the Valley Gate is the
basis or starting-point of Nehemiah's. Hippicus we have established; and the determination of this tower is of great assistance
to us in determining also the position of the Valley Gate. But
before we consider the order of the gates as given us by Nehemiah,
it is very important that we observe the natural requirements of
the place, as shown by its present gates and principal streets. The
three principal gates of the modern city are those leading to Jaffa,
Damascus, and Jericho : and gates must always have existed in the
same places. The ancient names of these gates were the Valley
Gate, the Gate of Ephraim, and the Sheep Gate. The ancient
streets, the names of which are mentioned in the Bible, were the
Street of the (Valley) Gate of the city, the Street of the Gate of
Ephraim, the East Street, the Street of the Water Gate, the

---

[1] This important fixing of the position of Hippicus and the Valley Gate
disposes of the theory brought forward in the *Dictionary of the Bible*,
that Hippicus stood on the spot marked in the accompanying plan as the
Tower of the Furnaces. The reasons alleged for this position are two-fold :
its being a "corner tower ;" and the remains of the tower at the north-west
of the present walls agreeing better in plan than the "Castle of David" with
the dimensions of Hippicus as described by Josephus. But, in the first place,
there is no proof that the tower in question is ever called a "corner tower ;"
and if it were, if it stood where is now the "Castle of David" it would have
been a most important corner tower of the Old Wall or the Upper City : and
secondly, we are not at all sure that either the "Castle of David," or the
north-west tower, are of this antiquity, though there is no doubt that their
materials are ancient. There are, however, two facts which quite confute
this theory :—one, that the three towers, of which Hippicus formed one,
were *westward of the Pool Amygdalon*, and only thirty cubits from it ; the
other, that water was brought into the city by the gate close to this tower,
which could not have been the case with the north-west tower of the present
city, which is one hundred feet higher up. The same argument operates, of
course, with still greater force against the theory of the *Imperial Bible
Dictionary*, that Hippicus was still more northward.

Bakers' Street, and the Street of the House of God. We must also notice preliminarily, as important land-marks, those passages in the Bible which refer to *opposite* portions of the city ; as the Fish Gate and the Second Gate (Zeph. i. 10) ; the Tower of Hananeel (sometimes itself called a corner gate, 2 Kings xiv. 13), and the Gate of the Corner (at Ophel) ;[1] Gareb and Goath,[2] or Goatha ; the Valley of the Dead Bodies (Hinnom) and the Horse Gate (Jer. xxxi. 38—40) ; Benjamin's Gate (the East Gate ?) and the First Gate (the Valley Gate) ; the Tower of Hananeel and the King's wine-presses. (Zech. xiv. 10.)

With these materials we can easily trace the walls and gates of the city, as existing in the time of Nehemiah, and described by him in his third chapter. He commences his description at the *Sheep Gate*, near which was the pool *Bethesda ;* (John v. 2 ;) from which gate he passes to the *Tower of Meah*, and the *Tower of Hananeel*, also called a corner tower, and which we know to have been at the *north-east* corner of the city, and being only 400 cubits distant from the Gate of Ephraim, (2 Kings xiv. 3,) must have been north-west of the Temple, and not in an extended line from the eastern face of the Temple area, where a wall was afterwards built by Agrippa, forming a part of the " New-town." After leaving this tower, he describes the *Fish Gate*,[3] which must have been very near to it ; the *Old Gate ;* and then, taking no notice of the Gate of Ephraim, possibly because he was describing the work of four different sets of builders, passes on to the *Throne of the Governor ;* the *Broad Wall ;*[4] the *other piece ;* the *Tower of the Furnaces* (called by the Turks the castle of Goliath), and thought by Adrichonius to be a beacon to night-wanderers. A letter from Jerusalem states—" We are now living in a house at the extreme north-west corner of the city, close to the remarkable ruins of the so-called Kalat-el-Jalud. From the upper room of this house there is a very fine view of the Moab mountains ; but that is not all : we have also a peep of the Dead Sea."[5] He next comes to the *Valley Gate*, opposite to which was the *Dragon's Well*, (Neh. ii. 13,) near the Upper Pool of Gihon.

The position of this gate forms the keystone to the whole arrangement of the walls. A distinguished advocate of the site of the Holy Sepulchre feels great difficulty as to the position of

---

[1] So Thrupp also : *Ant. Jer.* p. 79.

[2] The word Goath is said to signify a *violent death*. (Krafft, p. 158 ; Lewin, p. 367.)

[3] Fish appears to have been procured chiefly from Tyre. See Neh. xiii. 16.

[4] It was probably in this position that " the narrow streets led obliquely to the wall." (*B. J.* v. 8. 1.) And see plan. [5] *Impl. Bibl. Dict.* p. 887.

this gate: for he places it to the north, south, east, and west of
the city in so many different pages,[1] while the supporters of the
new theory of Mount Zion imagine the Valley Gate to be on the
south (one on the south-east) of what they call the modern Zion,
in positions overlooking the Valley of Hinnom, and between six
and seven hundred feet above it. The true position of the
Valley Gate is, as we have seen, near to Hippicus, and corresponded with the present Jaffa Gate. This gate took its name,
either from its being the only gate (with the exception of the
Water Gate) facing a valley, as Dr. Robinson argued; or else
from its communicating directly with the Valley of the Tyropœon.
This was one of the principal gates of the city; and, with the exception of the Dung Gate, the only western gate. "It was in the
Street of the (Valley) Gate that the princes and the priests assembled on the occasion of the dedication of the walls by Nehemiah;
and it was probably this same 'Street of the (Valley) Gate of the
city' where Hezekiah, after he had brought water into the city,
assembled the captains; (2 Chron. xxxii. 6;) and it is further
remarkable that Josephus begins his description at this same point.
(*Bell.* 5, 4 § 2.) It was probably from this circumstance, its natural
importance owing to its situation, that it acquired the name of the
First Gate; (Zech. xiv. 10:)"[2] and as we find mention of a
"Second Gate," (Zeph. i. 10,) it is possible that all the gates were
numbered: and that the gates of the Temple were also numbered;
for we find reference to "the Third Entry that is in the house of
the Lord." (Jer. xxxviii. 14.) In like manner it is probable that
all the towers were numbered: for we find Isaiah asking—"Where
is he that counted the towers?" (xxxiii. 18.) One other circumstance must be mentioned, which is in itself conclusive as to this
position of the Valley Gate. It is that on the occasion of the
dedication of the walls by Nehemiah, he assembled the Priests,
and the Levites, and the singers, and the Princes of Judah, together, and divided them in two companies; of which one went
on the right hand, and the other on the left; with orders to meet at
the Temple to complete the rites of consecration. It was important
therefore that they should start at some point which should be
about equidistant either way from the Temple. Such a point was
the western gateway of the city, the Valley Gate. Occupying the
position of the present Jaffa Gate, it was exactly opposite to the
Temple; and the company would assemble in its spacious street

[1] See *Mus. Class. Antiq.* p. 421, 422.
[2] *Ib.* p. 411. See also p. 414 for the opinions of Offerhaus, Rosenmüller,
Thenius and Leeman.

before defiling to the right and left. It need not be pointed out
that were the Valley Gate—for it was from this gate they started—
to have been on the south or south-east of Zion, this requirement
would not be answered. We may be quite sure then that the Valley Gate stood on the spot pointed out in the accompanying map.

We will now proceed with Nehemiah's description. At the
distance of 1,000 cubits from the Valley Gate stood the *Dung
Gate*, which was in number the *Second Gate*, (Zeph. i. 10,) and
which was also called the *Gate Harsith*, or the *Gate of Potsherds :*
(Jer. xix. 2 :) improperly translated in our Bibles, the "East
Gate." In Josephus's time the locality was still called Bethso,
(*Beth-Tsouoh*) the *place of filth*, and the gate, the Gate of the
Essenes. (*Bell.* v. 4. 2.) He next describes the *Fountain Gate*, so
called from being opposite to the Fountain of Siloam, to which
steps in the rock appear to lead down ;[1] the *wall of the Pool of
Siloah*, (*En Rogel*,[2]) *by the king's garden*. That the king's gardens
were in this position seems evident from the fact that gardens still
exist in this locality. "At the mouth of the Tyropœon the fountain of Siloam flows winter and summer with a refreshing and
plentiful stream, pouring fertility and luxuriance over the vineyards and gardens that reach from it down some way along the
valley of Jehoshaphat. In this little Elysium are grown, even at
the present day, the vegetables for the supply of the Jerusalem
market, and here are the pleasure-grounds to which, in summer, the
inhabitants of the sultry city repair at eventide, to sip their coffee,
and smoke their narghileh."[3] That the king's garden was in this
locality, and not to the south of Ophel, at the meeting of the two
valleys, as generally thought, is evident from 2 Kings xxv. 4, and
Jer. xxxix. 4, and lii. 7, where we read of the "king's garden"
before mention is made of the "way betwixt the two walls." In
this garden David appears to have built a summer-palace ; for
in his account of the dedication of the walls, Nehemiah, on coming
to the spot, speaks of "the going up of the wall *above* the house
of David, even unto the Water Gate." (xii. 37.) While the wall
here is described as *above* the house of David, a little further on,
where he describes Ophel, he speaks of the "king's *high* house ; "
as though contrasting this upper house on Ophel with the lower
house in the valley of Siloam. That David had other houses
besides that on Mount Zion, appears from 1 Chron. xv. 1, "and
David made him houses in the city of David." He next mentions
the *stairs that go down to* (from) *the City of David;* and the *place*

¹ Krafft, *Jerus.*   ² Jos. *Antiq.* vii. 14. 4 ; ix. 10. 4.
³ Lewin, *Siege of Jer.* p. 251; quoting De Saulcy and Schultz.

over against the Sepulchres of David. The words *over against* would imply that the sepulchres were outside the walls, adjoining the king's garden, having the stairs from the City of David between them : and this for other reasons is extremely probable. (See p. 320.) Dr. Thenius places them in this position.[1] They were thus immediately outside the Water Gate on the west side, and seen therefore, like the tombs in most ancient cities, by " all that went in at the gate of the city." The next objects mentioned are the *Pool that was made;* and the *house of the mighty.* Here appears to have been the *Water Gate,* which we know from Nehemiah xii. 37, was a gate in the outer wall ; but which, like the Gate of Ephraim, is not here mentioned, though the " place over against the Water Gate, towards the east," is mentioned in the 26th verse. Nehemiah twice mentions the " Street that was before the Water Gate." (viii. 1. 3.)[2] In 2 Kings xxv. 4 and Jer. lii. 7, it is spoken of as the " gate between the two walls, which is by the king's garden ;" and in Jer. xxxix. 4, as " by the king's garden, by the gate betwixt the two walls." A stream of water which has been discovered at " Wilson's arch," must have flowed through this gateway, and it led out to the three pools. On the other hand, a subterranean duct was brought through this gateway from Solomon's Pools at Etam, upwards of twelve miles distant, which supplied the cisterns beneath the Temple, and the " reservoir[3] betwixt the two walls, for the water of the old pools." (Is. xxii. 11.) He then describes the *piece over against the going up to the Armoury, at the turning of the wall.* The Armoury built by David—" The tower of David builded for an armoury, wherein there hung a thousand bucklers, all shields of mighty men," (*Song of Sol.* iv. 4,) has been confused with the Armoury afterwards built on the Temple-mount. It is probable that David's armoury occupied the position of Hippicus : and that this Hippicus was the armoury in which Simon, who held the upper city at the siege by Titus, stored his engines of war, which had been taken from Cestius and from the tower of Antonia. (*Bell.* v. 6. 3.) And it is somewhat singular that the present " castle of David," which now occupies the site, also served as an armoury. Some years ago a chamber was discovered in the thickness of the wall, full of bows and arrows, several of the latter of which the author took away with him. The Armoury of the Temple-mount, (Neh. iii. 19,) was built by Solomon in the

[1] *Das vorexelische Jerusalem, und dessen Tempel*, taf. i.
[2] There appears to have been a Water Gate connected with the Temple, on its southern side.
[3] מקוה, *Mikveh*, a *gathering of water* : translated " ditch " in our Bibles.

House of the Forest of Lebanon : (Is. xxii. 8 ; 1 Kings vii. 2 :)
and in it he hung up three hundred shields of beaten gold.
(1 Kings x. 17 : see also 2 Chron. xxxii. 5.) It seems probable
from 2 Kings xi. 10, and Jos. *Antiq.* ix. 7. 2, that David's armour
was afterwards removed to the armoury built by Solomon for the
Temple. The words *at the turning of the wall,* (*Mikzoah,*) is
pointed out by Psalmanazar and Villalpandus, as signifying a *re-
entering or internal angle :* and the same term appears in 2 Chron.
xxvi. 9, where we are told that Uzziah built a strong tower at this
spot. He then describes the piece over against the *houses of
Eliashib the High Priest, of Benjamin and Hashub,* and *of Azariah ;*
the *turning of the wall, even the corner.* Here appears to have
been a *corner gate.* (Jer. xxxi. 38.) After this is the *Tower which
lieth out from the king's high house.* We have already spoken of
David's summer palace in the gardens below, as distinguished from
this upper palace built by Solomon. This latter consisted of
several houses—the house for Pharaoh's daughter, the house of the
Forest of Lebanon, and others. If connected with Beth-Millo, or
" the house of Millo which goeth down to Silla," (2 Kings xii. 20,)
and if, as Mr. Lewin thinks,[1] Silla and Mesilla (1 Chron. xvi. 16)
were identical, this palace would appear to have been connected on
the western side of Ophel with the Valley of Siloam ; while, from
the " tower which lieth out " it would appear to have extended right
across Ophel to its eastern side. That it was below the Temple,
and on its southern side, and immediately adjoining it, is evident
from Ezek. xliii. 7 ; 2 Kings xi. 5, 6, 19 ; and 2 Chron. xxiii. 5 ;
and from the accounts we have of *going-up* from the king's house
to the Temple, (2 Chron. viii. 11 ; ix. 4 ; Jer. xxvi. 10,) and of
going down from the Temple to the king's house. (2 Kings xi. 19 ;
Jer. xxii. 1 ; xxxvi. 12.) Nehemiah goes on to say that the king's
house was by the *Court of the Prison :* consequently the Prison
could not have been, as has been supposed, to the north of the
Temple. Indeed this position, close to the king's house, is confirmed by Jer. xxxii. 2. Here again the *Prison Gate* is not mentioned, though it is described in the twelfth chapter. The next
piece was built by the Nethinims who dwelt in *Ophel,* unto the
place *over against the Water Gate, towards the east.* He then
describes another tower *that lieth out ;* the place *over against the
great tower that lieth out ;* and the wall of *Ophel.*[2] This wall of
Ophel has been discovered by the Exploration Society :—" The

[1] *Siege of Jer.* p. 266.
[2] Ophel signifies strong, a stronghold, or tower ; (2 Kings, v. 24 ; Is. xxxii.
14 ; Mich. iv. 8 ;) but its signification here is a hill or mount.

Eastern wall (of the Haram-enclosure) is prolonged beyond the southern face, and continues in the general direction of Siloam, with all the solidity and antiquity which characterize its known portions." It is 14 feet thick, and 700 feet long, and 40 to 60 feet beneath the surface, and has "*several towers projecting from the wall, one of which is very remarkable, as it projects more than any of the rest*, standing upon scarped rock. It is also remarkable that many of the stones in this wall are polished, reminding one of the 'polished corners of the Temple.'" He next describes the *Horse Gate*, which he says was rebuilt *by the Priests*. We are therefore now close to the Temple platform. This was the gateway "by which horses came into the king's house." (2 Kings xi. 16; 2 Chron. xxiii. 15.) We are therefore still on the south side of the Temple. Here also the Hippodrome appears to have been built in later times, and which Josephus says was to the south of the Temple; (*Bell.* ii. 3. 1 ;) and the spot is marked by the Mahometan tradition attached to the vaults under the south-east angle of the Haram enclosure, which they call "Solomon's Stables :" and Mr. Lewin adduces many solid arguments in support of this supposition.[1] We now arrive at the Temple : but the Temple is not mentioned : and instead of this we read of the houses of the priests, each of them repairing the wall against his house, *every one over against his house*, and particular mention is made of the wall repaired by *Zadok*, the son of Immer, *over against his house*. From this it seems evident that the Temple of Solomon, repaired by Zerubbabel, did not extend to the eastern wall of the platform, but was separated from it by the houses of the priests ; and that this land was subsequently taken in by Herod, when he rebuilt and enlarged the Temple.[2] We now come to the *East Gate*, which is not to be confounded with the "beautiful gate of the Temple," Nicanor, which was the principal gate, and faced the east, and which is so frequently referred to by Ezekiel, and which Josephus tells us was of Corinthian brass, which far excelled those which were only covered with silver and gold, and that the two doors were thirty cubits high. The sanctity of this gate no doubt gave rise to the Jewish and Mahometan tradition that the golden gateway, which is a walled-up gateway on the eastern side of the present Haram-enclosure, will not be opened till Christ comes to judge the world. The East Gate of the city appears to be identical with the "*High Gate of Benjamin*, which was by the House of the Lord," (Jer. xx. 2,) and on its northern side. (Ezek. ix. 2.) The East Gate gave name to the street leading up to it, (2 Chron. xxix. 4,) having shops on each side.

[1] *Siege of Jer.* p. 484, 485. [2] See Note at end of this Essay.

He then mentions the names of several contributors together with the Nethinims and merchants, the place over against the Gate *Miphkad*, (an internal gate,)[1] and the *going up of the corner;* from which place the goldsmiths and the merchants rebuilt the wall up to the *Sheep Gate.*

The reader who has followed this description will not have failed to see that there are several landmarks fixing the description as it goes along:—The Sheep Gate, determined by the pool Bethesda; the Gate of Ephraim by the present Gate of Damascus; the Tower of Hananeel by the distance of 400 cubits from the Gate of Ephraim, and by its being a corner gate; the Valley Gate by the present Jaffa Gate; the Dung Gate by its distance of 1,000 cubits from the Valley Gate, and from the connection between its name Harsith and Bethso and the Valley of Tophet; the Fountain Gate, and "the wall of the pool of Siloah" by the King's Garden, by the Pool of Siloam, or En Rogel, and by the gardens which still exist in this locality; the Water Gate by the Pools and reservoirs and conduits in the vicinity, and by its being at a re-entering angle of the wall; the walls of Ophel by the promontory or spur of the Temple hill towards the south, and by the remark-able correspondence with the Scripture narrative which we have in the account given to us by the Exploration Society of the *towers lying out;* the Horse Gate by its traditions; and finally the East Gate by its proximity to the Temple. From all this confirmatory evidence we can now point to Nehemiah's description of "*the stairs that go down to (from) the City of David,*" and "*the place over against the Sepulchres of David,*" as proving that the City of David, or Mount Zion, ever occupied the same place which is now pointed out; and consequently that this supposed "proof" of their being on the north-side of the Temple-mount falls to the ground.

Nehemiah's description of the dedication of the wall in his twelfth chapter is useful to us in supplying the omissions in the former account: for he here mentions the *Gate of Ephraim*, the *Water Gate*, and the *Prison Gate*, which he had omitted before; while he now omits several other points which he had mentioned previously: but one thing fortunately he mentions with more particularity: in speaking of the *Stairs of the City of David*, he adds the words, "*at the going up of the wall*, above the house of David, *even unto the Water Gate:*" thus showing that the City of David must have been on the left hand as he approached the Water Gate. The two companies divided at the Valley Gate, (the

---

[1] Possibly a gate in the wall connecting the northern side of Zion with the western portions of the Temple.

name of which however he does not here mention,) one company, headed by Nehemiah, passing the Tower of the Furnaces, the Broad Wall, the *Gate of Ephraim*, the Old Gate, the Fish Gate, the Towers of Hananeel and Meah, the Sheep Gate, and so on, without mentioning other names, till they arrive at the *Prison Gate*: while the other, headed by Ezra, pass the Dung Gate, the Fountain Gate, the Stairs of the City of David, *at the going up of the wall*, above the house of David, even unto the *Water Gate*. The two companies therefore on arriving at the Prison and Water Gates, would meet together, and ascending to the House of the Lord by the grand southern approach would enter the Temple probably by the gate Huldah. It was this southern approach leading from Solomon's palace that appears to be alluded to in 2 Chron. ix. 4, where we read, among the works which he executed, and other wonders which excited the astonishment of the Queen of Sheba, of "his ascent by which he went up into the House of the Lord." The gateway is considerably above the level of the ground on the Ophel side, and it must therefore have been approached by a grand flight of steps. It will give some idea of what this grand ascent must have been, when we recollect that there is a difference of level of 90 feet between Ophel and the Temple-area.

It may be desirable, here, to give Josephus's account of the circuit of the walls, premising that he speaks of each separately. The first wall enclosed Zion, the sacred area. "Of the three walls the *most ancient* was impregnable, as much on account of the ravines, and the hills which rose above them, as from the addition to the natural strength of the place caused by the defences carried out by David, Solomon, and subsequent kings, who bestowed great labour and expense in this work. Beginning at the north, at the tower Hippicus, and extending to the Xystus, and joining the Curia, it terminated at the western portico of the Temple. But on the west side, beginning at the same tower, and extending to the part called Bethso, and to the Gate of the Essenes,[1] and then at the south bending towards the Fountain of Siloam, and then again in the east bending towards the Pool of Solomon, and stretching out to that place called Ophla, it joined the eastern portico of the Temple. The *Second Wall* had its beginning at the gate called Gennath, belonging to the first wall. It enclosed only the northern quarter of the town, and extended to Antonia. The *Third Wall* had its beginning at the tower Hippicus, from which

[1] Solinus says that the Essenes inhabited the most inland parts of Judæa, towards the west. (*Lib.* xxxviii.)

it went towards the north as far as the tower Psephinus, and then
passing over against the monuments of Helena, and stretching out
a great way by the Tombs of the Kings, (*Royal caves,*) and bending
at the corner tower near the Fuller's Monument, joined the old
wall at the Valley of the Kedron. It was Agrippa who built this
wall, to enclose the parts of the city which were previously unpro-
tected." (*Bell.* v. 1. 2.) The reader can here consult the account
of Titus's wall of circumvallation. (v. 12. 2.) The *Great Wall*
is mentioned in v. 6. 1 ; it appears to have gone across from the
southern slopes of Zion to the point of Ophel, thus enclosing the
Pool of Siloam. It was probably built by Agrippa. The wall
of *Ophel* was built by Jotham (2 Chron. xxvii. 3) and Manasseh ;
the latter of whom built the western wall of Gihon ; (2 Chron.
xxxiii. 11 ;) while Hezekiah built a small portion of wall near the
Gate of Ephraim. (2 Chron. xxv. 23, and xxxii. 5.)

In addition to the gates of the Outer Wall there were, of course,
many gates in the internal walls : one of these, Miphkad, has been
already referred to ; another was the Middle Gate, (Jer. xxxix. 6,)
which of course had its street leading to it. Josephus, in his description of the siege, frequently refers to gates between the different
portions of the city. The "gate of Joshua the governor of the
city" (2 Kings xxiii. 8) was probably another name for one of the
gates of the city. The Temple also had several gates. A double
and a treble gate exist in the southern platform wall. The principal entrance was towards the east, which had a "broad place" in
front of it. (Esdras i. 9, 38.) There was a gate on the northern
side, and four gates on the western, three of which have been discovered, and which bear the names of Robinson, Barclay, and
Wilson. The first and last are remarkable, not only from their
exhibiting the remains of arches, but from their forming viaducts
of communication across the street of the Water Gate or Valley of
the Tyropœon. The northern one, Wilson's, is a double causeway,
presenting roads of 21 feet and 23 feet in width, communicating
with the Lower City, Acra. These might lead to the "Street of
the House of God," unless this street formed the approach from
Ophel at the south of the Temple. Josephus thus describes these
gates : "In the western quarter of the enclosures of the Temple
there were four gates : the first led to the king's palace, (the Asmonean palace on Mount Zion,) and to a passage over the intermediate valley ;[1] two more led to the suburbs of the city ; and the

[1] "The bridge which once connected the Palace with the Temple must
have had an elevation above the ravine of the Tyropœon of no less than 200
feet." (Murray's *Handbook*, p. 111.)

last led to the other city, where the road descended down into the valley by a great number of steps, and thence up again by the ascent." (*Antiq.* xv. 11. 5.) Other gates of the Temple were "the Gate of Sur," and the Gate behind the guard, or "the Gate of the guard to the king's house," and "the Gate of the foundation." (2 Kings xi. 6, 19 ; 2 Chron. xxiii. 5.)

(IV.) The next argument adduced is founded on the passage in the Psalm before us—

> " (On) the sides of the north
> " (Is) the city of the GREAT KING."

We have already seen in the introductory remarks to this Essay that these words have led some foreign theologians to consider that the expression has merely a metaphorical explanation, while some English writers insist upon a literal interpretation, and take the passage to assert positively that Mount Zion and the City of David stood to the north of the Temple-mount. Several of the arguments in support of this allegation we have already considered ; and we have found no reason for doubting that Mount Zion and the City of David ever stood on the spot hitherto appropriated to them. While Mount Zion was considered an impregnable fortress, insomuch that Pompey is described as saying that " the walls were so firm that it would be hard to overcome them, and the valley before the walls was terrible ; " (*Bell.* i. 7. 1 ;) Acra, or the Lower City, occupying the Christian and greater portion of the Mahometan quarter of the present city, was a hill sloping down on all three sides, and therefore admirably adapted for the private habitations of the citizens. While on the one hand, the local term of " Mount Zion " is most frequently made to embrace the whole city ; so on the other hand the general name of " Jerusalem " is frequently, especially by Josephus, restricted to this habitable portion of the city. While Mount Moriah was hallowed by the Temple of the Lord, and Mount Zion hallowed, " because the place is holy whereunto the ark of the Lord hath come," (2 Chron. viii. 11,) Jerusalem, or the Lower City, was looked upon as the city of God's people. The Psalmist, then, in composing this psalm, is not thinking of David and his stronghold, which he called the City of David ; he is thinking of Jerusalem as the city of God's people, and therefore a " holy city." (Cp. Neh. xi. 1. and many other passages in the Bible :) he is not thinking of David, the great king of Israel and Judah, but of GOD, THE GREAT KING OVER ALL THE EARTH, (xlvii. 2,) THE GREAT KING ABOVE ALL GODS, (xcv. 3.) And it is thus our Lord applies it—" Neither by Jerusalem, for it is the city of the

Great King." (Mat. v. 35.) The Psalmist says—" Beautiful for
elevation, the joy of the whole earth, is the mountain of Zion."
Whether he is speaking here of Mount Zion only, or of the entire
city is immaterial : though there is no doubt he is speaking of the
entire city, as he does in the second antiphon,—" Let the Mount
Zion rejoice, and the daughters (other cities) of Judah be glad : "
and again immediately afterwards, " Walk about Zion ; go round
about her ; and tell the towers thereof. Mark well her bulwarks,
behold her *palaces*," &c. He then says—" On the north side
is the city of the GREAT KING." That is, on the north side is the
habitable part of the city, the city of God's people. " God as a
sure refuge is known in her palaces." This interpretation is confirmed by the proem—" In the city of our God," and by the antiphon—" In the city of the Lord of hosts, in the city of our God."
This psalm therefore gives no authority for the recent hypothesis
respecting the position of Mount Zion.

(V.) The next argument adduced is that afforded by the Book of
Maccabees : and here it must be acknowledged that this evidence is
very extraordinary. So long as Mount Zion retained the Ark of
God, its glory was confined to it : but on the removal of the Ark to
Mount Moriah, the glory of Mount Zion was transferred to the
Temple-mount, or given to the whole city, as in Ps. xxxiii. 20,
" Zion, the city of our solemnities," and Ps. cxxxiii. 3, " Like as
the dew of Hermon, which fell upon the mountains of Zion," thus
including all the mountains or quarters of the city. Occasionally,
however, but very rarely, after this period is the name of Zion
limited to the ancient acropolis. One instance is in the Book
of Micah, (iii. 12,) quoted also by Jeremiah, (xxvi. 18,) where the
three quarters of the city are named :—" Zion shall be ploughed as
a field, and Jerusalem shall become heaps, and the mountain of the
house as the high places of the forest." [1] Another, which is similar,

[1] This remarkable prophecy has been wonderfully fulfilled. One half of
the ancient Zion is not included in the modern walls, and was ploughed up
as a common field : in Jerusalem, or the Lower City, there is an accumulation
of forty feet of soil over the ancient level : and with regard to the mountain
of the house we read in 1 Mac. iv. 38—"They saw the Sanctuary desolate,
and the altar profaned, and the gates burned up, and shrubs growing in the
courts as in a forest, or in one of the mountains." But the ploughed fields
were not confined to the outside of the modern wall. The Bordeaux Pilgrim,
who beheld Jerusalem in the year 333, says—" But inside, within the wall of
Sion, is seen the place where David had his palace, and the seven synagogues
which were there, one only of which remains, but the rest are ploughed and
sown, as said the prophet Isaiah." *Itin. Hieros.* (The Pilgrim mistook the
name of the prophet.) Even in the present day we are told there are
" ploughed fields inside the western and northern walls . . . . . The south

is in Zech. viii. 3—"Thus saith the Lord: I am returned unto
Zion; and will dwell in the midst of Jerusalem; and Jerusalem
shall be called a city of truth; and the Mountain of the Lord of
hosts the holy mountain."[1]   Another is in Isaiah, (ii. 3,) which is
repeated by Micah, (iv. 2,)—"And many people shall go and say,
Come ye, and let us go up to the Mountain of the Lord, to the
house of the God of Jacob; and He will teach us of His ways, and
we will walk in His paths: for out of Zion shall go forth the law;
and the word of the Lord from Jerusalem."   In Joel ii. 15-17,

hill has been ploughed up for we know not how many centuries; and at this
day is covered with corn, vegetables, especially cauliflowers of enormous size."
(*Impl. Bib. Dict.* p. 881, 884.)

As regards the second portion of the prophecy, we have already noticed
how the ancient valleys have been filled in, and the general level of the city
raised, so that we have now to dig down from forty to sixty feet to the
ancient foundations.   This has been caused partly by the repeated destructions of the city, after which "the city was builded on its own heap,"
(Jer. xxx. 18,) but partly also by the filthy habits of the people.   Dr. Robinson, indeed, states that of all oriental cities which he had seen, "Jerusalem,
after Cairo, is the cleanest:" (*Bib. Res.* i. 222:) but other travellers say that
this is only outside show.   "Habitations which have a very respectable
appearance as seen from the street, are often found, upon entering them, to
be little better than heaps of ruins.   Nothing of this would be suspected
from the general appearance of the city, as seen from without, nor from
anything that meets the eye in the streets.   If one room tumbles about his
ears, the occupant removes into another, and permits rubbish and vermin to
accumulate as they will in the deserted halls: and when the edifice becomes
untenantable, he seeks another a little less ruinous, leaving the wreck to a
smaller, or more wretched family; or more probably to a goatherd and his
flock."   (Kitto, *Cycl. Bib. Lit.* 3rd Edit. p. 538.)   "There seems to be a
law *against* carrying away any filth beyond the walls.   The consequence is
that the most pestiferous exhalations arise from the action of a powerful sun
upon one vast dung-heap, and fevers of course are generated."   (Lewin, *Siege
of Jer.* p. 196.)   With this agrees the author's personal experience, not only
of fever at Jerusalem, but as to the reports that he heard, that it was no
uncommon thing for the occupier to devote one room of his house to filth of
every description; and when that was full, to select another!   Yet however
filthy a Jerusalem Jew may be, he compares favourably with the Jew of the
Steppes of Russia: and the author looks back with horror on what he suffered
when travelling there before roads were formed, or railways thought of.   He
is afraid to say at how many paces a Russian Jew may be smelt!   And so
Dr. Schweinfurth—"To one who has travelled by 'Russian posts' the worst
trials and wants in Africa are child's play."   (*Times,* Aug. 4, 1874.)   A letter
from Jerusalem, dated April 9th, 1874, which appeared in the *Times* April
30th, says—"There is reason to fear that the ground will soon exhale miasma
in this unsewered city, whose streets are ever reeking with filth, and strewed
with offal, and mouldering carcases, and that fever will consummate what
cold and privation have already commenced."

[1] And yet Mr. Thrupp adduces this text to show that Zion is the Temple-
mount.   *Ant. Jer.* p 21.

the three quarters of the then city appear to be represented in
"Zion," the "people," and the "priests":—"Blow the trumpet in
Zion, sanctify a fast, call a solemn assembly. Gather the *people*,
sanctify the congregation, assemble the elders, gather the children
and those that suck the breasts; let the bridegroom go forth of his
chamber, and the bride out of her closet. Let the *priests*, the
ministers of the Lord, weep," &c. While in Micah iv. 7, 8,
Mount Zion takes back its old name of the "stronghold of Zion";
—"The Lord shall reign over them in *Mount Zion*, from hence-
forth even for ever. And thou, O tower of the flock, the *stronghold* of the daughter of *Zion*, unto thee shall it come, even the first
dominion; the kingdom shall come to the daughter of *Jerusalem*."
Again, in Jer. x. 17, Zion, or the Upper City, though not mentioned by name, is evidently referred to:—"Gather up thy wares
out of the land, O inhabitant of the fortress;" and in Jer. xxi. 13
Zion and Jerusalem appear to be referred to; the one as being the
rock or fortress, the other as sheltering the inhabitants below:—
"Behold, I am against thee, O inhabitant of the valley, and rock
of the plain." In every other instance "Zion," when not applied
to the Temple-mount, is put, by *Synecdoche*, for the whole city; as
"Her foundations are upon the holy hills:" not one hill, but all
three hills—Zion, Jerusalem, and the Temple-mount. But in
the time of the Maccabees the name Zion was again limited to
the mount so-called, as in 1 Mac. iv. 60; vi. 48, 62; x. 11. It
is unnecessary to quote the passages at length, for one of the
advocates of the change of site acknowledges that "the modern
Zion is identical with the Zion of the Maccabees:"[1] though a
subsequent writer[2] denies this. Indeed, it cannot be conceived
that the acropolis of the Jebusites, which was so famous in the
time of David, and which, under the name of the Upper City,
was the most important, and last stronghold in the time of Titus,
and which was finally taken, not by force, but by the destruction
of provisions by the besieged themselves, could have been utterly
neglected, as some of these writers would have us suppose, during
the long wars of the Maccabees. In one of these passages (1 Mac.
iv. 60, 61) we read—"At that time also they builded up the
Mount Sion with high walls and strong towers round about, lest the
Gentiles should come and tread it down, as they had done before;
and they set there a garrison to keep it. And he fortified Bethsura
to preserve it." Our reference Bibles connect this passage with
1 Mac. i. 31, which mentions the destruction of the city by

[1] Thrupp, *Ant. Jer.* pp. 14, 15, 20.
[2] Lewin, *Siege of Jer.* pp. 249, 322.

Antiochus :—" .Andwhen he had taken the spoils of the city, he
set it on fire, and pulled down the houses and walls thereof on
every side."   And that it does refer to the *city*, including of
course the Upper City, or Mount Zion, is evident not merely from
the fact that the outer Temple-enclosure had no towers, but from
the manner in which Josephus records this restoration of the
walls:—" Judas also rebuilt the walls round about the *city*, and
reared towers of great height against the incursions of enemies, and
set guards therein.   He also fortified the city Bethsura :" &c.
(*Antiq.* xii. 7. 7 :) thus identifying " Mount Sion " of the Book of
Maccabees with the "city," and not with the Temple-mount.   In
another passage also, (ch. x.,) where the refortifying of the city by
Jonathan is described, we are justified in asserting that it is the
city, and of course the Upper City, or Mount Zion, more especially,
and not the Temple-mount, which is referred to.   In verses 10 and
11 we read—" This done, Jonathan settled himself in Jerusalem,
and began to build and repair the *city*.   And he commanded the
workmen to build the walls and the Mount Sion round about with
great stones for fortification."   This reparation of the fortifications
of the city is referred to again in verses 44 and 45, where Demetrius
offered to pay the expenses of " the building and repairing of the
works of the Sanctuary," and " the building of the walls of Jerusalem, and the fortifying thereof round about :" the fortifications
here mentioned clearly referring to Mount Zion, as opposed to the
Temple-mount.

But it was different with the name of the "City of David."
We have seen that David called Zion the " City of David."   In
2 Sam. vi. 12, 16, we find that he removed the ark of God there,
and did so with great rejoicing and ceremony.   Afterwards, when
the farm of Araunah was purchased, and the Temple built there, we
read that Solomon assembled all the elders of the people " that they
might bring up the ark of the covenant of the Lord out of the
City of David, which is Zion ;" (1 Kings viii. 1 ;) thus showing
that the City of David, or Zion, was a different part of the city to
the Temple-mount.   We have seen that the City of David was
referred to, and its site determined, by the notice we have of
Hezekiah's supply of water to Jerusalem, and of Manasseh's wall
outside the city : and we find the name preserved throughout the
time of all the kings of Judah ; for we read of each one of them,
with few exceptions, that he was " buried in the City of David."
Of one of these, Ahab, we read that he was not buried in Zion,
" but they buried him in the city, even in Jerusalem," (2 Chron.
xxviii. 27,) thus showing that the name of Jerusalem was specially

given to the Lower City ; and also showing that the "sepulchres of the Kings of Israel " were outside the walls, and not within the city. The name "City of David " was still preserved after the captivity ; for we have seen that Nehemiah points out the " City of David," and the "Sepulchres of David." But a great change had taken place in the time of the Maccabees. During this period of trouble and disaster, while the Maccabees held possession of Mount Zion and the Temple, the more worthless inhabitants abjured their religion, and joined the Macedonians in erecting a strong castle or fortress in Acra, over-looking and so threatening the Temple. This fortress has been placed by recent writers to the *north* of Antonia, and on the north west angle of the Haram-esh-sherif : but there are two facts which show that it must have been to the west of Antonia : first, its name proves that it must have been in the Acra or Lower Town of Josephus : and, secondly, we are told that the Xystus, or "Gymnasium," (2 Mac. iv. 12,) which we know to have adjoined the bridge, and which was built in the time of Antiochus Epiphanes, was underneath the Acra or "Acropolis." (2 Mac. iv. 12.)[1] This they called, perhaps in bravado, the "City of David."[2] The first account we have of this fortress is—"Then builded they *the City of David* with a great and strong wall, and with mighty towers, and made it a stronghold for them :" (i. 33 :) and it is spoken of in the same manner in other passages—"The host that was in Jerusalem, in the City of David ;" (ii. 31 ;) "they also that were in the City of David in Jerusalem had made themselves a tower." (xiv. 36.) And that this is not to be interpreted as one of the quarters of the city is evident from its being afterwards constantly referred to as a "fortress," or " tower," or "castle." (iv. 2, 41 ; vi. 18; x. 6—9 ; xi. 41 ; xii. 36 ; xiii. 21 ; xiv. 36 ; 2 Mac. iv. 12 ; v. 5.) It is called "The Tower in Jerusalem," (vi. 26 ; x. 32 ; xi. 20—23 ; xiii. 49—51 ; xv. 28.) It will be observed that it is never described as the tower, or fortress, or castle, *in* the City of David ; but always as the tower &c. in Jerusalem. Where the name City of David is mentioned it always appears to be the name of the fortress, not the name of the quarter in which it stood. Thus then the Book of Maccabees which describes a castle or tower which it calls " The City of David," cannot be taken as an authority for

[1] Either this "acropolis" is the Acra, or Mount Zion. In either case it proves its position on the western side of the Temple-area.

[2] Lewin, also—" With this view he erected the celebrated Acra, or Citadel, called the City of David." (*Siege of Jer.* p. 319.)

determining the position of the original "City of David, which is Zion," the impregnable acropolis of the Jebusites, and the Upper City of Josephus.

(VI.) An argument has been brought forward by one advocate of this theory, that the Temple-mount was not Moriah, and if not Mount Moriah, it must have been Mount Zion. "It will be generally allowed that the original city of Jerusalem stood on the western hill; and it is in the nature of things that any new part which was added to the city afterwards, would be distinguished by a special name; and if the Temple-mount was not called Zion, what then was it called? Some persons will perhaps answer, Moriah. I shall have occasion to show hereafter that Moriah was the name of a tract of country, and not of a single hill; meanwhile, it is sufficient for our present purpose to observe, that the name of Moriah never once occurs either in the strictly historical Books of Samuel and Kings, or throughout the whole of the Psalms and Prophets, ... and although we read that 'Solomon began to build the house of the Lord at Jerusalem in Mount Moriah, where the Lord appeared unto David, his father,' (2 Chron. iii. 1,) yet there is no ground for supposing that the name Moriah is even here restricted to any single hill: the Hebrew word *hor*, which we render 'mount,' is constantly used in the Old Testament, as for instance in the phrase 'Mount Ephraim,' to denote the whole of a mountainous district. . . . . . It has too generally escaped notice, that the name Moriah is clearly employed in the Book of Genesis not as the designation of a single hill, but of a whole district or tract of country."[1]

Now, without entering into the etymological meaning of the word Moriah in the Book of Genesis, which would evidently limit it to one particular mountain, and without examining how the word *hor* is applied in other instances, it is sufficient for our purpose to show, not only that the word *Mount* in Chronicles is *Hor*, and not *Horeem*, but that this same word *Hor* is applied in this forty-eighth psalm both to Zion, and the Temple-mount—"the mountain of his holiness." ' Now, there was only one Mount Zion—though in one instance where Zion is used collectively for the whole city, (Ps. cxxxiii. 3,) we read of the "mountains of Zion"—as certainly there was but one holy Temple-mount, or "mountain of his holiness;" and consequently there can be no reason for refusing to admit that the word in Chronicles has this limited meaning also: and if this hill was Mount Moriah, then it could not have been Mount Zion. But although this hill was Mount Moriah, it was not generally called by that name; but it was called, as we have seen

[1] Thrupp, *Ant. Jer.* 25, 43.

above in the forty-eighth psalm, the "holy hill," or "holy mountain," or "mountain of his holiness." We find these terms running all through the Psalms and the Prophets; and we find them still preserved in the time of the Maccabees, (1 Mac. xi. 37,) and by the writer of the Book of Wisdom. (ix. 8.) It is also called the "mountain of the Lord," (Is. ii. 3 ; xxx. 29 ; Micah iv. 2 ; Zech. viii. 3,) and the "mountain of the house," (Micah iii. 12,) and the "mountain of the Temple." (1 Mac. xvi. 20.)

Another argument is that Zion must have been on Ophel, beneath the Temple area, because the act of *ascending* is always spoken of when proceeding from one to the other :—"The City of David denotes the new part added and fortified by David, afterwards called the Low Town, or Acra, and more particularly that part of it which we may designate as the Outer Low Town, on Ophel, where David's palace stood. (?) Thus 'Solomon brought the daughter of Pharaoh into the city of David, until he had made an end of building his own house, and the House of the Lord, and the wall of Jerusalem round about;' (1 Kings iii. 1 ;) 'and Solomon *brought up* the daughter of Pharaoh out of the city of David unto the house that he had built for her.' (ix. 24 ; 2 Chron. viii. 11.) Here the daughter of Pharaoh is not *brought down* from the High Town, but is *brought up* from the Low Town on Ophel. . . . . Again, Solomon ' *brought up* the ark of the covenant of the Lord out of the City of David which is Zion.' (1 Kings viii. 1.)"[1] Now, the whole force of this argument falls to the ground when we show that the word עלה, *oloh*, "to ascend," which is used in all these passages, does not always have the absolute sense here given to it. We use the same word in a conventional manner in our own language :— we talk of going up to London, of up-trains and down-trains, of a son's being well brought up, of his going up to the university, of his going up for examination, of his going up for a degree : so of this word in the Hebrew, Gesenius says—"Persons are said to *go up*, to *ascend*, not only upon a mountain, wall, roof, bed ; but also in other less obvious relations, *e.g.* (a) from a lower region to a higher ; (β) of those who go into deserts, since these were often on hills and mountains ; also to a place of judgment. Yet perhaps the sanctuary and place of judgment were regarded as *heights also in a sacred and moral sense, which would accord better with some passages*, as Numb. xvi. 12, 14 ; Ruth iv. 1. So too, where Joseph is said to go up to the court of Pharaoh, Gen. xlvi. 31. Compare ܐܣܠܩ, ἀναβαίνω, of those who go up to the metropolis," &c., &c. But in addition to this, how can we give a literal signification to the phrase of *bringing-up* as applied to Ophel, which was the lowest

[1] Lewin, *Siege of Jer.* p. 241, 243.

A A

portion of the whole city? Again, when, as we have just seen, the author places David's palace on Ophel, and Solomon's palace also in the same locality, (p. 267,268,) how can he give a literal and absolute signification to the words *bring up* when applied to moving from one to the other? "And Solomon brought up the daughter of Pharaoh out of the City of David unto the house that he had built for her." And further, how, if these two palaces occupied the same site, on Ophel, are we to explain the reason why Solomon removed the daughter of Pharaoh from one place to another?—"For he said—My wife shall not dwell in the house of David king of Israel, because the places are holy whereunto the ark of the Lord hath come." (2 Ch. viii. 11.) This evidently refers to two distinct portions of the city : and thus we see that the bringing up, or going up, naturally refers to the solemnity with which the holy Temple would be approached, or the ceremony which would take place in entering a palace for the first time, with processions, and music, and singing, and great state : and when we consider the hilly nature of the ground, we shall see that even if the act referred to starting from the Upper City, the highest quarter of the whole city, the procession would have first to descend into the valley and then ascend to the Temple area, and as this would constitute the most important part of the ceremony, it would be spoken of as though it constituted the whole. In addition to the instances mentioned by Gesenius many other passages might be adduced, showing that no literal significance can be attached to this word :—"a red heifer . . . upon which never *came (up)* yoke ;" (Num. xix. 2 ;) "no razor shall *come (up)* on his head ;" (Judg. xiii. 5 ; 1 Sam. i. 11.;) " If so be the king's wrath *arise ;*" (2 Sam. xi. 20 ;) and Jehoash "*went (up)* away from Jerusalem ; (2 Kings xii. 18 ; and this notwithstanding that Jerusalem is 3,000 feet above the sea ;) "600 shekels of beaten gold *went (up)* to one target ;" " 300 shekels of gold *went (up)* to one shield ;" (2 Chron. ix. 15, 16 ;) "the wrath of the Lord *arose* against his people ;" (2 Chron. xxxvi. 16:) " like as a shock of corn *cometh (up)* in his season ;" (Job v. 26 ;) "The wrath of God *came (up)* upon them ;" (Ps. lxxviii. 31 ;) " And she *brought up* one of her whelps ;" (Ezek xix. 3 ;) " ye are *taken up* in the lips of talkers." (Ezek. xxxvi. 3.) The same word is constantly used for *offering* sacrifice.[1]

Another argument is brought forward by Dr. Kitto, who, quoting Isaac Taylor's saying that in making what at first appears so simple a thing as a plan of Jerusalem, one must

[1] Again, if the word *oloh* has this absolute sense, how is it that it is not used in 1 Kings iii. 1—" Solomon *brought* her into the City of David"?

"take position after position upon battle-field, and prepare to
defend every inch of that position," says—"It is possible, however, and this is the design of the present article, to survey the
battle-field as spectators, and even to reconnoitre it minutely as
engineers, without taking a position as combatants."[1] It has,
however, been often found on such occasions, that it is impossible to resist entering the *mêlée;* and accordingly, Dr. Kitto,
starting from the assumed, though false, position, that Acra was
a part of the Temple-mount, contends that the "other side,"
which Josephus says the fourth western gate of the Temple gave
access to, (*Ant.* xv. 11. 5,) "would be the Upper City, in distinction from the Lower, which was more closely identified with
the Temple." (p. 528.) This, however, is clearly a mistake. If
the first gate led to the king's palace in the Upper City, the fourth
gate which led to the "other city," must have led to Acra, and
this corresponds perfectly with Josephus's description of the four
hills of the city, (*Bell.* v. 4. 1, 2,) and with the "broad valley"
which he says separated Acra from the Temple-mount, or Third
hill. This situation of Acra, or the Lower City, is moreover confirmed by another passage of Josephus, where he describes the four
towers erected by John; one of which was at the N.W. angle of
the Temple, "over against the Lower City." (*Bell.* iv. 9. 12 : v. 1. 3.)

(VII.) Finally, it has been attempted to prove that Zion must
have been on the Temple-mount, by adducing a number of passages
from the Bible in which Zion is, exclusively, spoken of as holy in
the sight of God :—"There are also numberless passages in which
Zion is spoken of as a Holy Place, in such terms as are never
applied to Jerusalem, and which can only be understood as applied
to the Holy Temple-mount. Such expressions, for instance, as
Ps. ii. 6; lxxxvii. 2; cxxxii. 13; Is. lx. 14; Jer. xxxi. 6;
Zech. viii. 3; Joel iii. 17, 21, and many others."[2] Now, of these
instances,[3] certainly none of them but the third and last can be

[1] *Cyc. Bib. Lit.* 3rd Edit. p. 525.   [2] *Dict. of the Bible.*
[3] Another advocate adduces many more, as Ps. ii. 6; ix. 11, 14; xiv. 7; xx.
2; l. 2; liii. 6; lxv. 1; lxviii. 16; lxxvi. 2; lxxviii. 68; lxxxiv. 7;
lxxxvii. 2; xcix. 2; cx. 2; cxvi. 9; cxxxviii. 5; cxxxii. 12—14; cxxxiv. 3;
cxxxv. 21; cxxxvii. 3, 4; Is. ii. 2, 3; viii. 18; x. 12; xii. 6; xiv. 32;
xviii. 7; xxiv. 23; xxviii. 16; xxxi. 9; xxxiii. 20; lx. 14; Jer. i. 5; l. 28;
li. 10; Lam. i. 4; ii. 4, 6; Joel ii. 1; iii. 17, 21; Micah iv. 1, 2, 7;
Zech. viii. 3. (Thrupp, *Ant. Jer.*) We give these for the reader's investigation; though we believe them all to be misquotations so far as the fact is
concerned: and indeed if, as these advocates believe, "the stronghold of
Zion, or of the City of David, occupied the highest part of the hill, to the
north of the Temple, and so commanded the Temple," or what was formerly
the threshing-floor of Araunah the Jebusite, the several parts of the city would
be jumbled together in as great confusion as the "holy places" are in the

limited to the Temple mount. It is the whole city which is
esteemed holy in the sight of God; and so far from Jerusalem, or
the habitable part of the city being excluded, there are numerous
instances in which holiness is attributed to it in particular: such
as—"For Jerusalem's sake, which I have chosen," "In Jerusalem
will I put my name," "The God of Jerusalem," "The God of
Israel, whose habitation is in Jerusalem," "Jerusalem, the holy
city," "I will pay my vows in the midst of thee, O Jerusalem,"
"The Lord dwelleth at Jerusalem," "The Lord of hosts shall reign
in Jerusalem," "Put on thy beautiful garments, O Jerusalem, the
holy city," "Jerusalem, the throne of the Lord," and the whole
of the hundred and twenty-second Psalm, besides two instances
in the New Testament, Matt. iv. 5; xxvii. 53; God looking upon
the inhabitants of the city as "The holy people, the redeemed of
the Lord." (Is. lxii. 12.) See also pp. 346, 347.

Having thus considered the various arguments which have been
adduced in favour of a change of site, we find that each of such arguments—the history of the first taking of Zion by David; the
account of Hezekiah's water-course of Gihon; the description of the
walls by Nehemiah; the expressions in the forty-eighth Psalm;
the expressions in the Book of Maccabees; and various other passages of Scripture—only confirms instead of opposes, the position
of Zion in the south-western quarter of the present city. We see
then no reason for rejecting the assertion of Josephus, according to
whom the city was divided into four quarters or hills—the Upper
City; Acra, or the Lower City; Mount Moriah, or the Temple-
mount; and Bezetha, or the New City: and we may rest convinced
that the first quarter or Upper City of Josephus, was Mount Zion,
or the City of David.

<hr/>

church of the Holy Sepulchre. Take for example one of these instances,
Joel ii. 1—"Blow ye the trumpet in Zion: and sound an alarm in my holy
mountain." Why should we suppose that Zion here signifies the holy
mountain or Temple-mount, from this contiguity of reference, any more than
that Zion in the following chapter signifies Jerusalem, or the Lower City,
because they are mentioned together in the same verse?—"The Lord also
shall roar out of Zion: and utter his voice from Jerusalem." (Joel iii. 16.)
For if the first passage proves Zion and the Temple-mount to be identical,
the second must naturally prove that Zion and Jerusalem are so also. Indeed,
so far are these texts of Scripture from proving the case supposed, that it is
a curious fact that while the writer in the *Dictionary of the Bible*, and
Mr. Thrupp bring forward a long list of quotations to prove that "Zion" in
the Bible always represents the Temple-mount, in distinction to Jerusalem;
another writer, Mr. Lewin, brings forward most of these very same passages
to prove that "Sion and Jerusalem are constantly employed as convertible
terms; i.e. they both denote the same city;" (p. 244;) "Sion and Jerusalem
are synonyms for one and the same city;" (p. 245;) "Sion and Jerusalem
are positively asserted to be identical." (p. 246.)

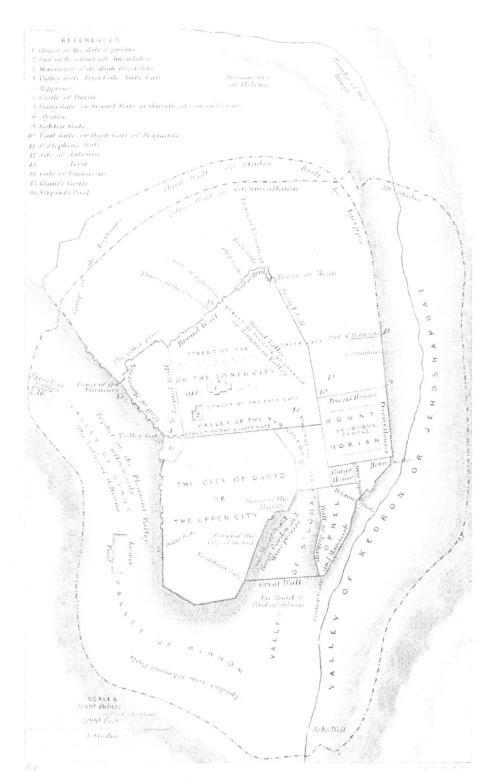

JERUSALEM

NOTE

ON THE TEMPLE-AREA.

WITH the object in the foregoing Essay of restoring the Zion of David to David, we found it necessary to study the account given us by Nehemiah of the rebuilding and repairing of the walls in his time; which account could only be made intelligible by a plan. But on executing this, and arriving at the Temple, we found ourselves in great perplexity as to the position and extent of the Temple-area: and it therefore became necessary, in order to complete the plan, to investigate the subject of the Temple-site. Unlike the site of the Holy Sepulchre, the Temple-site is fortunately unconnected with theological controversy: the difficulty here is purely a topographical one: how to interpret the confused historical evidence, to compare it with what we now find existing; and to reconcile the Temple-area as described by Josephus with the platform of the Haram-esh-Sherif, as we now find it.

The Temple of Solomon was 600 feet square: whereas the Haram-esh-Sherif is 922 by 1,530 feet: that is to say, the Haram-esh-Sherif would nearly contain four temples of Solomon within its area. In what part of the Haram, then, did the Temple of Solomon stand? This is the great difficulty: and writers have attempted to meet it in a variety of ways, with great research and ingenuity. Prof. Robinson, Krafft, Kiepert, Dr. Barclay, and Dr. Porter place the Temple-area in the southern half of the Haram; Mr. Williams in the northern half; Mr. Fergusson, Mr. Thrupp, and Mr. Lewin place it at the south-western angle of the Haram; Mr. Williams, the Comte de Vogüé, Dr. Porter, and the writer in the *Edinburgh Review*, (Jan. 1873,) connect the altar of the Jewish Temple with the rock Sakrah;[1] while the Comte de Vogüé, M. de

---

[1] It is right to observe that Dr. Porter says—"In the centre of the roof is a cylindrical aperture through the whole thickness of the rock: and beneath

Saulcy, and the writer in the *Edin. Rev.* appropriate the whole
Haram-area to the Temple. Arguments will be found of great
force on behalf of each of these theories : and in listening to these
arguments we are tempted to embrace each in turn, were it not
that the arguments we listened to in one, form an objection to all
the rest ; and we are thus led to see the difficulties of the case.
Thus, Mr. Williams places his Temple to the north, because we are
told that Cestius's army attacked it "from the northern quarter ;
but the Jews beat them off from the cloisters ;" (*Bell.* ii. 19. 5 ;)
and that when Titus afterwards attacked it from the same place,
"John and his faction defended the wall from the Tower of
Antonia, and from the northern cloister of the Temple." (v. 7. 3.)
The southern portion he supposes to have been formed by Justinian for the erection of his church. Mr. Fergusson and others
place it at the south-western angle, which is the only square angle
of the Haram, and where, they say, the ground is solid, and thus
separated from the vaults to the south-east, called Solomon's
Stables ; while the writer in the *Edin. Rev.* discovers that the
Sakrah is immediately in a straight line with the gate Huldah ;
that the eastern face of the raised mosque-platform of the Sakrah
is exactly in a line with the meridian ; that the line of axis of the
Temple, from west to east, is within a degree of the line of sunrise
on the day on which the Temple of Solomon is supposed (in the
Talmud) to have been founded ; and, curiously enough, that the
northern, western, and southern sides of the present Haram exactly
make up the six stadia mentioned by Josephus as the circuit of
Herod's Temple. In addition to this, he fancies that all the steps
and doorways of this mosque-platform correspond with the traditional sites of the Jewish temple, as described in the Talmud.
With these arguments in favour of, and the objections which
necessarily result from each of these theories, it is naturally with
great diffidence that we propose any fresh theory. Let us, however, examine the evidence before us.

To begin with the platform. Solomon's Temple was only 600
feet square ; Herod's twice as large ; while the Haram is nearly
twice as large again. It is evident, therefore, that unless we suppose "twice as large" meant *very much larger*, the platform must
have been, subsequently to Herod's time, enlarged by Hadrian,
Justinian, or someone else. In support, however, of the present
length, we find on the foundation stones of its eastern wall,

it we observe a small slab of marble covering a deep cavity, to which Moslems
give the name, "The Well of Spirits." Murray's *Handbook of Syria*, 1868,
p. 117.

masons' marks in the Phœnician character, both at the extreme
south of this wall, and at the extreme north : and we naturally call
to mind Hiram and the Phœnician workmen employed by Solomon.
We shall have something to say of these marks presently. Of the
whole platform only the south-west angle is square : but of this
also we shall have to speak. And now for the historical evidence.
We begin, of course, with the account we have in the twenty-
fourth chapter of the Second Book of Samuel, where we find a
threshing-floor mentioned. The rock Sakrah is too limited for
this purpose : neither is it flat. But on the north side of it is a
comparatively level space of 110 feet with a fall of only 10 feet ;
being a slope of 1 in 11 : on the south side we find a space twice
as large of exactly the same slope, and being thus of larger area,
and facing the south, it would naturally be chosen in preference as
a threshing-floor. But even this area is limited ; and thus we find
it said—"At first the plain at the top was hardly sufficient for the
Holy House and the altar ; for the ground about it was very un-
even, and like a precipice : but when King Solomon had built a
wall to it on the east side, there was then added one cloister founded
on a bank cast up for it : and on the other parts the house stood
naked." (B. v. 5. 1.) That Solomon built cloisters on all four
sides, and that each side measured one stadium, or 600 feet, in
length, is evident from Josephus, who in describing the events of
Solomon's reign, says—"He also built beyond the priests' court
an outer court, the figure of which was that of a quadrangle, and
erected for it great and broad cloisters. . . . He filled up great
valleys with earth, which on account of their immense depth
could not be looked at, when you bended down to see them,
without pain ; and he elevated the ground 400 cubits (in length)
raising it to a level with the top of the mountain . . . . and he
encompassed this also with a double row of cloisters." (Ant. viii.
3. 9.) In Book xv. ch. 11, Josephus has got to the time of Herod,
and in § 3 he is describing his works : but in the middle of this
description he refers to what Solomon had done before him :—
"This hill it was which Solomon encompassed with a wall," &c.,
and presently afterwards we read what still appears to refer to
Solomon :—"This hill was walled all round, and in compass four
stadia." In Book xx. ch. 9, he is describing the works of Agrippa,
and in § 7 we read :—"This eastern cloister belonged to the outer
court, and it was situated in a deep valley, and had walls that
reached 400 cubits (in length). This was the work of King Solomon." Thus there is no doubt but that Solomon's Temple was a
square of 400 cubits, or 600 feet. So far with regard to Solomon.

"But in future ages the people added new banks, and the hill became a larger plain. They then broke down the wall on the north side, and took in as much as sufficed afterwards for the compass of the entire Temple; and when they had built walls on three sides of the Temple round about, (west, south, and east,) from the bottom of the hill, and had performed a work that was greater than could be hoped for, in which long years were spent by them, and all their sacred treasures were exhausted, though replenished by those tributes which were sent to God from the whole habitable world, they then encompassed the upper courts with cloisters, as they did also the lowest (court of the) Temple.[1] . . . . The cloisters were in breadth 30 cubits, while the *entire compass* was by measure, *including the tower of Antonia, six stadia.*" (*Bell.* v. 5. 1, 2.) In *Antiq.* xv. 11. 3, it is said to be Herod who "encompassed the entire Temple with very large cloisters, and laid out larger sums of money upon them than had been done before:" and in *Bell* .i. 21. 1, we are told that "Herod rebuilt the Temple, and encompassed a piece of land about it with a wall, which land was *twice as large as that before enclosed.* The expenses he laid out upon it were vastly large also; and the riches about it unspeakable: a sign of which you have in the great cloisters that were erected about the Temple, and the citadel which was on its north side. *The cloisters he built from the foundation.*" In *Antiq.* xv. 11. 5, where Herod's buildings are described, the southern or Royal cloister is described as "reaching in length from the east valley to the west: for it was impossible it could reach any further."[2] Lastly, in *Bell.* vi. 5. 4, the historian says, "*When Antonia was destroyed, their Temple had become four-square,*[3] thus fulfilling the prediction that 'Then should their city be taken, as well as their Holy House, when once their Temple should become four-square.'"

With these materials it does not seem difficult to determine the position, size, and proportions of Herod's Temple. It was twice

[1] Here follows a description of the foundations, in which Josephus may well be excused for exaggeration in some particulars: as when he says that the walls were raised 300 cubits, and in some places more; when "it has been calculated that in filling up these valleys 90 to 100 feet each, not less than 70,000,000 cubic feet of earth or rubbish would be required to fill up this enormous space: that is to say, a solid cube of earth as high as St. Paul's and 400 feet square." *Our Work in Palestine,* p. 130.

[2] It is here said to be 400 cubits: but this probably refers to Solomon's work.

[3] It is not necessary to suppose that the whole of Antonia stood within the Temple-square: though it is certain from this that part of it did so. In *Bell.* v. 5. 8 we are told that it was situated at the corner of two cloisters of the Temple, of that on the west, and that on the north.

as large as Solomon's; the circuit of its cloisters including Antonia was six stadia; and when Antonia was destroyed it was four-square. A square of six stadia in circuit would be a square of a stadium and a half on each side, or 900 feet. The actual width of the southern end of the present Haram is 922 feet, which may be deemed sufficiently near. On the eastern side of the present Haram we find a break of two feet in the masonry at 907 feet from the south-east angle, which is nearer still. We thus have a square, or thereabouts, of six stadia in circumference. A square of four stadia in circumference contains 360,000 square feet, which doubled would be 720,000; while a square of six stadia in circumference would contain 810,000, or rather more than double. This calculation may be deemed to sufficiently answer the requirements.

Herod, then, rebuilt his Temple round Solomon's Temple; extending the embankments *on three sides*, (the west, south, and east,) with retaining walls, surmounting the south and west banks and the northern side with cloisters; and carrying out all these works, as a wise builder, before he commenced pulling down the old cloisters. He then pulled down and rebuilt the Temple itself built by Zerubbabel: but all these gigantic operations occupied 18,000 workmen, we are told, for the space of more than one lifetime; so that sixty-five years afterwards, when the works were said to be completed, (*Antiq.* xx. 9,)[1] the eastern cloister of Solomon's Temple had not been pulled down and rebuilt; and Agrippa refused to undertake the work on account of its cost. This cloister is frequently spoken of in the New Testament as "Solomon's porch."[2]

It has been mentioned that Phœnician marks, in red ochre, have been discovered at the extreme northern as well as at the extreme southern end of the eastern wall of Haram, thereby leading us to infer that Solomon's platform was co-extensive with the present Haram; but the northern marks occur on what is called "the tower," a projection of the wall of about two feet at the north-east angle of the platform, part of which *extends for about* 160 *feet beyond the north-east angle:*[3] thereby showing that this wall, or

[1] In St. John, ii. 6, we read—"Forty and six years was this Temple in building." It was begun in the eighteenth year of Herod's reign, or sixteen years before the time of our Lord, who was thirty years old when he uttered these words: but it was not completed till the time of Agrippa, A.D. 19.

[2] John x. 23; Acts, iii. 11; v. 12.

[3] (Letter, May 31, 1869.) "We struck the Sanctuary wall about 18 feet south of north-west angle, and at a depth of 42 feet below the surface. We

so-called "tower" on which these marks occur, had nothing to do with Solomon's Temple, but that it must have formed a portion of the Third Wall, which was built by Agrippa: and we may readily suppose that if Phœnicia was celebrated for its workmen in the time of David and Solomon, it might have been equally celebrated in the time of Agrippa.

It has been mentioned also that the south-west angle is the only right angle of the Haram: but an examination of the map of levels will show why the south-east angle was naturally drawn in. Even now it is forty feet deeper than the south-west angle: but had the southern end of platform been made equal to the northern in breadth, the foundations would have had to go forty feet deeper still: a sufficient reason for drawing in the width at this point. The inclination of present northern line is probably owing to the inclination of the pool Bethesda.

Though Solomon's Temple was only 600 feet square, while Herod's was 900 feet square, it is possible that even in Solomon's time this extra portion of ground was covered and enclosed, though not included in the Temple-enclosure; for in *Ant.* xv. 11. 3 we are told that "He also built a wall below, beginning at the bottom, which was encompassed by a deep valley :" and this extra portion of ground may have been appropriated to the priests' residences, and thus account for the fact that in Nehemiah's description of the

___

then turned north, and ran along the Sanctuary wall for 26 feet without finding any angle similar to that above. . . . . *It was some time before I could believe that we had really passed to the north of the north-east angle: but there can be no doubt of it:* and that the ancient wall below the surface runs several feet to the north of the north-east angle, without any break of any kind   If the portions above ground are *in situ* it would appear that this angle is a portion of an ancient tower reaching above the old city wall."

(Letter, Aug. 18, 1869.) "We have now made further progress at this angle, and have settled several points of considerable interest :—

"1. We find that 'the tower' at the north-east angle of the Sanctuary *forms part of the main east wall,* and at near its base the wall and tower are flush, or in one line.

"3. The wall is 110 feet below ground: and the total height is 150 feet

"5. Some characters in red paint have been found on the bottom stones of the Haram wall, under the southern end of the tower.

"6. It appears probable that the four courses of drafted stones of this tower which appear above ground, are *in situ.*

"8. For the first 48 feet above rock it is one wall . . . . The wall throughout the distance has a battu, caused by each course receding 4½ inches from that below it. The portion forming the wall continuing to recede to 7 inches, while that forming the tower only recedes 1½ inch : so that at 70 feet from the bottom the projection is nearly 2 feet." (Captain Wilson and Captain Warren, *Recovery of Jerusalem.* 1871.)

walls he makes no mention of the Temple, but speaks only of the houses of the priests.

Connected with the Temple was the Tower of Antonia. That it was at the north-west angle of the Temple is clear ; for it communicated both with the western and northern cloisters. (*Bell.* v. 5. 8 ; vi. 2. 9.) But it does not equally appear certain whether it extended to the north-east of the Temple ; for we are told that when Cestius attacked the northern parts of the Temple, the Jews "drove them off from the cloisters." (ii. 19. 5.) Again, when Titus besieged the city, the Jews defended the wall "from the tower of Antonia and from the northern cloister of the Temple :" (v. 7. 3 :) thus leading us to suppose that the cloisters of the Temple stood upon the northern wall. On the other hand, Antonia is described constantly as lying on the north of the Temple, (*Ant.* xv. 11. 4 ; *Bell.* i. 5. 4 and 21. 1) as though it occupied the entire northern side. Again, Bezetha, or the New City, is described as "lying over against the tower Antonia," (*Bell.* v. 4. 2, and 5. 8,) without mentioning the Temple. But one passage is so positive, that we are forced to admit that Antonia must have extended right across the Temple-mount, and covered the Temple on its northern side. It is on the occasion of Titus's attack on the Temple :—"There were now four great banks raised, one of which was at the Tower of Antonia, *over against the middle of the pool Struthius.* Another was cast up at the distance of about twenty cubits." (v. 11. 4.) This passage is most important, for it not only proves that Antonia extended right across the Temple-mount, but that the present northern wall of the Haram area could not have existed in the time of Titus ; for as he placed his battering-rams *between* the pool Struthius and the wall, we must suppose a considerable space to be thus left free. Two other things follow : one that the "pool of Bethesda" was always a pool, and not a fosse ; the other, that the fosse existed south of the pool of Bethesda. The Haram, therefore, does not coincide with the Temple-mount, as it existed in the time of Titus. The attack was made on the curtain-wall ; and this explains how the Jews were enabled to build an inner wall to oppose the Romans, when they succeeded in breaking through the outer wall. (vi. 1. 4.) The breach, however, was made, and subsequently widened, (vi. 2. 1, 7,) so as to admit the whole of the army : but we find that the Tower of Antonia was still standing, and that it was used by Titus as a fortress from which to attack the Temple. (vi. 1. 4, 7, 8 ; and 2. 5, 6.) We thus see that though the whole area lying to the north of the Temple was called the Tower of Antonia, the *keep*, or Tower of Antonia itself, stood on the south-

west corner, and within the enclosure of the Temple ; and that the
remainder of the area constituted its courtyard, affording ample
space for "courts, and places for bathing, and broad spaces for
camps." (*Bell.* v. 5. 8.) The tower, or keep, had towers at each
of its corners, that on the south-east angle being twenty-five feet
higher than the others. This tower possibly stood on the Sakrah.

THE TEMPLE AREA.

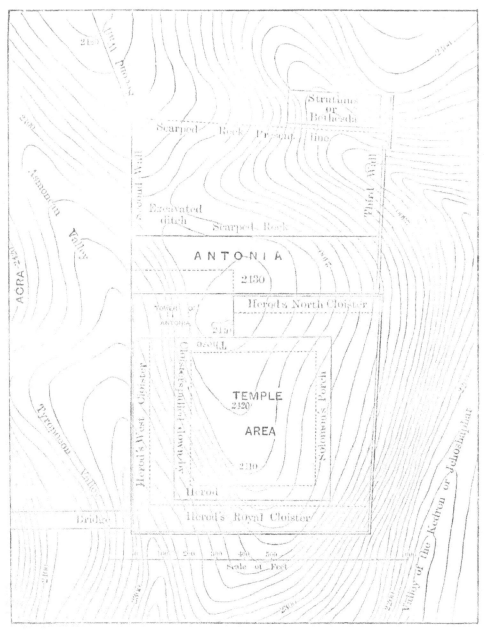

From Plan of Levels, published by the Palestine Exploration Society—
"Our Work in Palestine." 1873.

CORRIGENDA.

Page 6, *line* 13, add :—The alternate recitation by verse, instead of by antiphon, shows itself to be wrong in many instances where a verse is recited by the Minister, which should be recited by the people. Among other instances see the antiphons xlii. 7, 15; xlvi. 7, 11 ; li. 5, 9 ; lxvii. 3, 5 ; lxxiv. 11, 19, 23 ; lxxx. 3, 7, 19 ; lxxxvi. 13, 17 ; and lxxxviii. 9, 13.

Page 46, *line* 17, should not be indented.

Page 88, *note* 2. For "forty" read fourteen.

Page 103, *line* 2. For "Schechem" read Shechem.

Page 251. At end of last line but three add—Ps. lx. Superscription, where it is said that "*Joab* returned, and smote of Edom in the Valley of Salt twelve thousand." For had the compiler inserted this superscription from the history, he would, had he taken it from 1 Chron. xviii. 12, have inserted the name Abishai, instead of Joab : or had he taken it from 2 Sam. viii. 13, he would have inserted the name David. So also of the super-scription of

LONDON:
R. CLAY, SONS, AND TAYLOR, PRINTERS,
BREAD STREET HILL.

GENERAL LIST OF WORKS

PUBLISHED BY

Messrs. LONGMANS, GREEN, and CO.

PATERNOSTER ROW, LONDON.

————◦○◦——

History, Politics, Historical Memoirs, &c.

JOURNAL of the REIGNS of KING GEORGE IV. and KING WILLIAM IV. By the late CHARLES C. F. GREVILLE, Esq. Clerk of the Council to those Sovereigns. Edited by HENRY REEVE, Registrar of the Privy Council. 3 vols. 8vo. 36s.

RECOLLECTIONS and SUGGESTIONS of PUBLIC LIFE, 1813-1873. By JOHN Earl RUSSELL. 1 vol. 8vo. [*Nearly ready.*

The HISTORY of ENGLAND from the Fall of Wolsey to the Defeat of the Spanish Armada. By JAMES ANTHONY FROUDE, M.A. late Fellow of Exeter College, Oxford.

> LIBRARY EDITION, Twelve Volumes, 8vo. price £8. 18s.
> CABINET EDITION, Twelve Volumes, crown 8vo. price 72s.

The ENGLISH in IRELAND in the EIGHTEENTH CENTURY. By JAMES ANTHONY FROUDE, M.A. late Fellow of Exeter College, Oxford. 3 vols. 8vo. price 48s.

ESTIMATES of the ENGLISH KINGS from WILLIAM the CON-QUEROR to GEORGE III. By J. LANGTON SANFORD. Crown 8vo. 12s. 6d.

The HISTORY of ENGLAND from the Accession of James II. By Lord MACAULAY.

> STUDENT'S EDITION, 2 vols. crown 8vo. 12s.
> PEOPLE'S EDITION, 4 vols. crown 8vo. 16s.
> CABINET EDITION, 8 vols. post 8vo. 48s.
> LIBRARY EDITION, 5 vols. 8vo. £4.

LORD MACAULAY'S WORKS. Complete and Uniform Library Edition. Edited by his Sister, Lady TREVELYAN. 8 vols. 8vo. with Portrait price £5. 5s. cloth, or £8. 8s. bound in tree-calf by Rivière.

On PARLIAMENTARY GOVERNMENT in ENGLAND; its Origin, Development, and Practical Operation. By ALPHEUS TODD, Librarian of the Legislative Assembly of Canada. 2 vols. 8vo. price £1. 17s.

The CONSTITUTIONAL HISTORY of ENGLAND, since the Accession of George III. 1760—1860. By Sir THOMAS ERSKINE MAY, C.B. The Fourth Edition, thoroughly revised. 3 vols. crown 8vo. price 18s.

DEMOCRACY in EUROPE; a History. By Sir THOMAS ERSKINE MAY, K.C.B. 2 vols. 8vo. [*In the press.*

A

The ENGLISH GOVERNMENT and CONSTITUTION from Henry
VII. to the Present Time. By JOHN Earl RUSSELL, K.G. Fcp. 8vo. 3s. 6d.

The OXFORD REFORMERS — John Colet, Erasmus, and Thomas
More : being a History of their Fellow-work. By FREDERIC SEEBOHM.
Second Edition, enlarged. 8vo. 14s.

LECTURES on the HISTORY of ENGLAND, from the Earliest Times
to the Death of King Edward II. By WILLIAM LONGMAN, F.S.A. With Maps
and Illustrations. 8vo. 15s.

The HISTORY of the LIFE and TIMES of EDWARD the THIRD.
By WILLIAM LONGMAN, F.S.A. With 9 Maps, 8 Plates, and 16 Woodcuts.
2 vols. 8vo. 28s.

INTRODUCTORY LECTURES on MODERN HISTORY. Delivered
in Lent Term, 1842 ; with the Inaugural Lecture delivered in December 1841.
By the Rev. THOMAS ARNOLD, D.D. 8vo. price 7s. 6d.

WATERLOO LECTURES ; a Study of the Campaign of 1815. By
Colonel CHARLES C. CHESNEY, R.E. Third Edition. 8vo. with Map, 10s. 6d.

HISTORY of ENGLAND under the DUKE of BUCKINGHAM and
CHARLES the FIRST, 1624-1628. By SAMUEL RAWSON GARDINER, late
Student of Ch. Ch. 2 vols. 8vo.   [In the press.

The SIXTH ORIENTAL MONARCHY ; or, the Geography, History,
and Antiquities of Parthia. By GEORGE RAWLINSON, M.A. Professor of Ancient
History in the University of Oxford. Maps and Illustrations. 8vo. 16s.

The SEVENTH GREAT ORIENTAL MONARCHY ; or, a History of
the Sassanians : with Notices, Geographical and Antiquarian. By G. RAWLINSON,
M.A. Professor of Ancient History in the University of Oxford. 8vo. with Maps
and Illustrations.   [In the press.

A HISTORY of GREECE. By the Rev. GEORGE W. COX, M.A. late
Scholar of Trinity College, Oxford. VOLS. I. & II. (to the Close of the Peloponnesian War) 8vo. with Maps and Plans, 36s.

The HISTORY OF GREECE. By Rev. CONNOP THIRLWALL, D.D. late
Bishop of St. David's. 8 vols. fcp. 8vo. 28s.

GREEK HISTORY from Themistocles to Alexander, in a Series of
Lives from Plutarch. Revised and arranged by A. H. CLOUGH. New Edition.
Fcp. with 44 Woodcuts, 6s.

The TALE of the GREAT PERSIAN WAR, from the Histories of
Herodotus. By GEORGE W. COX, M.A. New Edition. Fcp. 3s. 6d.

The HISTORY of ROME. By WILLIAM IHNE. VOLS. I. and II.
8vo. price 30s. VOLS. III. and IV. preparing for publication.

HISTORY of the ROMANS under the EMPIRE. By the Very Rev.
C. MERIVALE, D.C.L. Dean of Ely. 8 vols. post 8vo. 48s.

The FALL of the ROMAN REPUBLIC ; a Short History of the Last
Century of the Commonwealth. By the same Author. 12mo. 7s. 6d.

The STUDENT'S MANUAL of the HISTORY of INDIA, from the
Earliest Period to the Present. By Colonel MEADOWS TAYLOR, M.R.A.S
M.R.I.A. Second Thousand. Crown 8vo. with Maps, 7s. 6d.

The HISTORY of INDIA, from the Earliest Period to the close of Lord
Dalhousie's Administration. By J. C. MARSHMAN. 3 vols. crown 8vo. 22s. 6d.

INDIAN POLITY; a View of the System of Administration in India. By Lieutenant-Colonel GEORGE CHESNEY, Fellow of the University of Calcutta. New Edition, revised; with Map. 8vo. price 21s.

The **IMPERIAL** and **COLONIAL CONSTITUTIONS** of the BRITANNIC EMPIRE, including INDIAN INSTITUTIONS. By Sir EDWARD CREASY, M.A. With 6 Maps. 8vo. price 15s.

The **HISTORY of PERSIA and its PRESENT POLITICAL SITUATION**; with Abstracts of all Treaties and Conventions between Persia and England, and of the Convention with Baron Reuter. By CLEMENTS R. MARKHAM, C.B. F.R.S. 8vo. with Map, 21s.

REALITIES of IRISH LIFE. By W. STEUART TRENCH, late Land Agent in Ireland to the Marquess of Lansdowne, the Marquess of Bath, and Lord Digby. Cheaper Edition. Crown 8vo. price 2s. 6d.

CRITICAL and HISTORICAL ESSAYS contributed to the *Edinburgh Review*. By the Right Hon. LORD MACAULAY.

   CHEAP EDITION, authorised and complete. Crown 8vo. 3s. 6d.

CABINET EDITION, 4 vols. post 8vo. 24s. | LIBRARY EDITION, 3 vols. 8vo. 36s.
PEOPLE'S EDITION, 2 vols. crown 8vo. 8s. | STUDENT'S EDITION, 1 vol. cr. 8vo. 6s.

HISTORY of EUROPEAN MORALS, from Augustus to Charlemagne By W. E. H. LECKY, M.A. Second Edition. 2 vols. 8vo. price 28s.

HISTORY of the RISE and INFLUENCE of the SPIRIT of RATIONALISM in EUROPE. By W. E. H. LECKY, M.A. Cabinet Edition, being the Fourth. 2 vols. crown 8vo. price 16s.

The **HISTORY of PHILOSOPHY**, from Thales to Comte. By GEORGE HENRY LEWES. Fourth Edition. 2 vols. 8vo. 32s.

The **HISTORY of the PELOPONNESIAN WAR.** By THUCYDIDES. Translated by R. CRAWLEY, Fellow of Worcester College, Oxford. 8vo. 21s.

The **MYTHOLOGY of the ARYAN NATIONS.** By GEORGE W. COX, M.A. late Scholar of Trinity College, Oxford. 2 vols. 8vo. 28s.

HISTORY of CIVILISATION in England and France, Spain and Scotland. By HENRY THOMAS BUCKLE. New Edition of the entire Work, with a complete INDEX. 3 vols. crown 8vo. 24s.

SKETCH of the HISTORY of the CHURCH of ENGLAND to the Revolution of 1688. By the Right Rev. T. V. SHORT, D.D. Lord Bishop of St. Asaph. Eighth Edition. Crown 8vo. 7s. 6d.

HISTORY of the EARLY CHURCH, from the First Preaching of the Gospel to the Council of Nicæa, A.D. 325. By Miss SEWELL. Fcp. 8vo. 4s. 6d.

MAUNDER'S HISTORICAL TREASURY; General Introductory Outlines of Universal History, and a series of Separate Histories. Latest Edition, revised by the Rev. G. W. COX, M.A. Fcp. 8vo. 6s. cloth, or 10s. calf.

CATES' and WOODWARD'S ENCYCLOPÆDIA of CHRONOLOGY, HISTORICAL and BIOGRAPHICAL; comprising the Dates of all the Great Events of History, including Treaties, Alliances, Wars, Battles, &c.; Incidents in the Lives of Eminent Men and their Works, Scientific and Geographical Discoveries, Mechanical Inventions, and Social Improvements. 8vo. price 42s.

The **FRENCH REVOLUTION and FIRST EMPIRE**; an Historical Sketch. By WILLIAM O'CONNOR MORRIS, sometime Scholar of Oriel College, Oxford. With 2 Coloured Maps. Post 8vo. 7s. 6d.

The **HISTORICAL GEOGRAPHY of EUROPE.** By E. A. FREEMAN, D.C.L. late Fellow of Trinity College, Oxford. 8vo. Maps. *[In the press.*

A 2

EPOCHS of HISTORY: a Series of Books treating of the History of England and Europe at successive Epochs subsequent to the Christian Era. Edited by EDWARD E. MORRIS, M.A. of Lincoln College, Oxford. The three following are now ready:—

The Era of the Protestant Revolution. By F. SEEBOHM. With 4 Maps and 12 Diagrams. Fcp. 8vo. 2s. 6d.

The Crusades. By the Rev. G. W. COX, M.A. late Scholar of Trinity College, Oxford. With Coloured Map. Fcp. 8vo. 2s. 6d.

The Thirty Years' War, 1618–1648. By SAMUEL RAWSON GARDINER, late Student of Christ Church. With Coloured Map. Fcp. 8vo. 2s. 6d.

The Houses of Lancaster and York; with the Conquest and Loss of France. By JAMES GAIRDNER, of the Public Record Office. With Maps. Fcp. 8vo. 2s. 6d.

Edward the Third. By the Rev. W. WARBURTON, M.A. late Fellow of All Souls College, Oxford. With Maps. Fcp. 8vo. 2s. 6d.

Biographical Works.

AUTOBIOGRAPHY. By JOHN STUART MILL. 8vo. price 7s. 6d.

The LIFE of NAPOLEON III. derived from State Records, Unpublished Family Correspondence, and Personal Testimony. By BLANCHARD JERROLD. In Four Volumes. Vol. I. with 3 Portraits engraved on Steel and 9 Facsimiles. 8vo. price 18s. Vol. II. is in the press.

LIFE and CORRESPONDENCE of RICHARD WHATELY, D.D. Late Archbishop of Dublin. By E. JANE WHATELY. New Edition. in 1 vol. crown 8vo. [In the press.

LIFE and LETTERS of Sir GILBERT ELLIOT, First EARL of MINTO. Edited by the COUNTESS of MINTO. 3 vols. 8vo. 31s. 6d.

MEMOIR of THOMAS FIRST LORD DENMAN, formerly Lord Chief Justice of England. By Sir JOSEPH ARNOULD, B.A., K.B. late Judge of the High Court of Bombay. With 2 Portraits. 2 vols. 8vo. 32s.

ESSAYS in MODERN MILITARY BIOGRAPHY. By CHARLES CORNWALLIS CHESNEY, Lieutenant-Colonel in the Royal Engineers. 8vo. 12s. 6d.

ISAAC CASAUBON. 1559–1614. By MARK PATTISON, Rector of Lincoln College, Oxford. 8vo. [In the press.

BIOGRAPHICAL and CRITICAL ESSAYS, reprinted from Reviews, with Additions and Corrections. Second Edition of the Second Series. By A HAYWARD, Q.C. 2 vols. 8vo. price 28s. THIRD SERIES, in 1 vol. 8vo. price 14s.

The LIFE of LLOYD, FIRST LORD KENYON, LORD CHIEF JUSTICE of ENGLAND. By the Hon. GEORGE T. KENYON, M.A. of Ch. Ch. Oxford. With Portraits. 8vo. price 14s.

MEMOIR of GEORGE EDWARD LYNCH COTTON, D.D. Bishop of Calcutta and Metropolitan. With Selections from his Journals and Correspondence. Edited by Mrs. COTTON. Crown 8vo. 7s. 6d.

LIFE of ALEXANDER VON HUMBOLDT. Compiled in Commemoration of the Centenary of his Birth, and edited by Professor KARL BRUHNS; translated by JANE and CAROLINE LASSELL, with 3 Portraits. 2 vols. 8vo. 36s.

LORD GEORGE BENTINCK; a Political Biography. By the Right Hon. BENJAMIN DISRAELI, M.P. Crown 8vo. price 6s.

The LIFE OF ISAMBARD KINGDOM BRUNEL, Civil Engineer. By ISAMBARD BRUNEL, B.C.L. With Portrait, Plates, and Woodcuts. 8vo. 21s.

RECOLLECTIONS of PAST LIFE. By Sir HENRY HOLLAND, Bart. M.D. F.R.S. late Physician-in-Ordinary to the Queen. Third Edition. Post 8vo. price 10s. 6d.

The LIFE and LETTERS of the Rev. SYDNEY SMITH. Edited by his Daughter, Lady HOLLAND, and Mrs. AUSTIN. Crown 8vo. price 2s. 6d.

LEADERS of PUBLIC OPINION in IRELAND; Swift, Flood, Grattan, and O'Connell. By W. E. H. LECKY, M.A. New Edition, revised and enlarged. Crown 8vo. price 7s. 6d.

DICTIONARY of GENERAL BIOGRAPHY; containing Concise Memoirs and Notices of the most Eminent Persons of all Countries, from the Earliest Ages to the Present Time. Edited by W. L. R. CATES. 8vo. 21s.

LIFE of the DUKE of WELLINGTON. By the Rev. G. R. GLEIG, M.A. Popular Edition, carefully revised; with copious Additions. Crown 8vo. with Portrait, 5s.

FELIX MENDELSSOHN'S LETTERS from *Italy and Switzerland*, and *Letters from 1833 to 1847*, translated by Lady WALLACE. New Edition, with Portrait. 2 vols. crown 8vo. 5s. each.

MEMOIRS of SIR HENRY HAVELOCK, K.C.B. By JOHN CLARK MARSHMAN. Cabinet Edition, with Portrait. Crown 8vo. price 3s. 6d.

VICISSITUDES of FAMILIES. By Sir J. BERNARD BURKE, C.B. Ulster King of Arms. New Edition, remodelled and enlarged. 2 vols. crown 8vo. 21s.

The RISE of GREAT FAMILIES, other Essays and Stories. By Sir J. BERNARD BURKE, C.B. Ulster King of Arms. Crown 8vo. price 12s. 6d.

ESSAYS in ECCLESIASTICAL BIOGRAPHY. By the Right Hon. Sir J. STEPHEN, LL.D. Cabinet Edition. Crown 8vo. 7s. 6d.

MAUNDER'S BIOGRAPHICAL TREASURY. Latest Edition, reconstructed, thoroughly revised, and in great part rewritten; with 1,000 additional Memoirs and Notices, by W. L. R. CATES. Fcp. 8vo. 6s. cloth; 10s. calf.

LETTERS and LIFE of FRANCIS BACON, including all his Occasional Works. Collected and edited, with a Commentary, by J. SPEDDING, Trin. Coll. Cantab. Complete in 7 vols. 8vo. £4. 4s.

Criticism, Philosophy, Polity, &c.

A SYSTEMATIC VIEW of the SCIENCE of JURISPRUDENCE. By SHELDON AMOS, M.A. Professor of Jurisprudence to the Inns of Court, London. 8vo. price 18s.

A PRIMER of the ENGLISH CONSTITUTION and GOVERNMENT. By SHELDON AMOS, M.A. Professor of Jurisprudence to the Inns of Court. New Edition, revised. Post 8vo. [*In the press.*

The INSTITUTES of JUSTINIAN; with English Introduction, Translation and Notes. By T. C. SANDARS, M.A. Sixth Edition. 8vo. 18s.

SOCRATES and the SOCRATIC SCHOOLS. Translated from the German of Dr. E. ZELLER, with the Author's approval, by the Rev. OSWALD J. REICHEL, M.A. Crown 8vo. 8s, 6d.

The STOICS, EPICUREANS, and SCEPTICS. Translated from the German of Dr. E. ZELLER, with the Author's approval, by OSWALD J. REICHEL, M.A. Crown 8vo. price 14s.

The ETHICS of ARISTOTLE, illustrated with Essays and Notes, By Sir A. GRANT, Bart. M.A. LL.D. Third Edition, revised and partly rewritten.   [In the press.

The POLITICS of ARISTOTLE; Greek Text, with English Notes. By RICHARD CONGREVE, M.A. New Edition, revised. 8vo. 18s.

The NICOMACHEAN ETHICS of ARISTOTLE newly translated into English. By R. WILLIAMS, B.A. Fellow and late Lecturer of Merton College, and sometime Student of Christ Church, Oxford. 8vo. 12s.

ELEMENTS of LOGIC. By R. WHATELY, D.D. late Archbishop of Dublin. New Edition. 8vo. 10s. 6d. crown 8vo. 4s. 6d.

Elements of Rhetoric. By the same Author. New Edition. 8vo. 10s. 6d. crown 8vo. 4s. 6d.

English Synonymes. By E. JANE WHATELY. Edited by Archbishop WHATELY. Fifth Edition. Fcp. 8vo. price 3s.

DEMOCRACY in AMERICA. By ALEXIS DE TOCQUEVILLE. Translated by HENRY REEVE, C.B., D.C.L., Corresponding Member of the Institute of France. New Edition, in two vols. post 8vo.   [In the press.

POLITICAL PROBLEMS. Reprinted chiefly from the *Fortnightly Review*, revised, and with New Essays. By FREDERIC HARRISON, of Lincoln's Inn. 1 vol. 8vo.   [In the press.

THE SYSTEM of POSITIVE POLITY, or TREATISE upon SOCIOLOGY. of AUGUSTE COMTE, Author of the System of Positive Philosophy. Translated from the Paris Edition of 1851–1854, and furnished with Analytical Tables of Contents. In Four Volumes, 8vo. to be published separately :—   [In the press,

VOL. I. The General View of Positive Polity and its Philosophical Basis. Translated by J. H. BRIDGES, M.B.

VOL. II. The Social Statics, or the Abstract Laws of Human Order. Translated by F. HARRISON, M.A.

VOL. III. The Social Dynamics, or the General Laws of Human Progress (the Philosophy of History). Translated by E. S. BEESLY, M.A.

VOL. IV. The Synthesis of the Future of Mankind. Translated by R. CONGREVE, M.A.

BACON'S ESSAYS with ANNOTATIONS. By R. WHATELY, D.D. late Archbishop of Dublin. New Edition, 8vo. price 10s. 6d.

LORD BACON'S WORKS, collected and edited by J. SPEDDING, M.A. R. L. ELLIS, M.A. and D. D. HEATH. 7 vols. 8vo. price £3. 13s. 6d.

ESSAYS CRITICAL and NARRATIVE. By WILLIAM FORSYTH, Q.C. LL.D. M.P. for Marylebone; Author of 'The Life of Cicero,' &c. 8vo. 16s.

The SUBJECTION of WOMEN. By JOHN STUART MILL. New Edition. Post 8vo. 5s.

On REPRESENTATIVE GOVERNMENT. By JOHN STUART MILL. Crown 8vo. price 2s.

On LIBERTY. By JOHN STUART MILL. New Edition. Post 8vo. 7s. 6d. Crown 8vo. price 1s. 4d.

PRINCIPLES of POLITICAL ECONOMY. By the same Author. Seventh Edition. 2 vols. 8vo. 30s. Or in 1 vol. crown 8vo. price 5s.

ESSAYS on SOME UNSETTLED QUESTIONS of POLITICAL ECONOMY. By JOHN STUART MILL. Second Edition. 8vo. 6s. 6d.

UTILITARIANISM. By JOHN STUART MILL. New Edition. 8vo. 5s.

DISSERTATIONS and DISCUSSIONS, POLITICAL, PHILOSOPHI- CAL, and HISTORICAL. By JOHN STUART MILL. 3 vols. 8vo. 36s.

EXAMINATION of Sir. W. HAMILTON'S PHILOSOPHY, and of the Principal Philosophical Questions discussed in his Writings. By JOHN STUART MILL. Fourth Edition. 8vo. 16s.

An OUTLINE of the NECESSARY LAWS of THOUGHT; a Treatise on Pure and Applied Logic. By the Most Rev. W. THOMSON, Lord Archbishop of York, D.D. F.R.S. Ninth Thousand. Crown 8vo. price 5s. 6d.

PRINCIPLES of ECONOMICAL PHILOSOPHY. By HENRY DUNNING MACLEOD, M.A. Barrister-at-Law. Second Edition. In Two Volumes. VOL. I. 8vo. price 15s.

A SYSTEM of LOGIC, RATIOCINATIVE and INDUCTIVE. By JOHN STUART MILL. Eighth Edition. Two vols. 8vo. 25s.

The ELECTION of REPRESENTATIVES, Parliamentary and Muni- cipal; a Treatise. By THOMAS HARE, Barrister-at-Law. Crown 8vo. 7s.

SPEECHES of the RIGHT HON. LORD MACAULAY, corrected by Himself. People's Edition, crown 8vo. 3s. 6d.

Lord Macaulay's Speeches on Parliamentary Reform in 1831 and 1832. 16mo. 1s.

FAMILIES of SPEECH : Four Lectures delivered before the Royal Institution of Great Britain. By the Rev. F. W. FARRAR, D.D. F.R.S. New Edition. Crown 8vo. 3s. 6d.

CHAPTERS on LANGUAGE. By the Rev. F. W. FARRAR, D.D. F.R.S. New Edition. Crown 8vo. 5s.

A DICTIONARY of the ENGLISH LANGUAGE. By R. G. LATHAM, M.A. M.D. F.R.S. Founded on the Dictionary of Dr. SAMUEL JOHNSON, as edited by the Rev. H. J. TODD, with numerous Emendations and Additions. In Four Volumes, 4to. price £7.

A PRACTICAL ENGLISH DICTIONARY, on the Plan of White's English-Latin and Latin-English Dictionaries. By JOHN T. WHITE, D.D. Oxon. and T. C. DONKIN, M.A. Assistant-Master, King Edward's Grammar School, Birmingham. Post 8vo. [In the press.

THESAURUS of ENGLISH WORDS and PHRASES, classified and arranged so as to facilitate the Expression of Ideas, and assist in Literary Composition. By P. M. ROGET, M.D. New Edition. Crown 8vo. 10s. 6d.

LECTURES on the SCIENCE of LANGUAGE. By F. Max Müller,
M.A. &c. Seventh Edition. 2 vols. crown 8vo. 16s.

MANUAL of ENGLISH LITERATURE, Historical and Critical. By
Thomas Arnold, M.A. New Edition. Crown 8vo. 7s. 6d.

SOUTHEY'S DOCTOR, complete in One Volume. Edited by the Rev.
J. W. Warter, B.D. Square crown 8vo. 12s. 6d.

HISTORICAL and CRITICAL COMMENTARY on the OLD TESTA-
MENT; with a New Translation. By M. M. Kalisch, Ph.D. Vol. I. *Genesis*,
8vo. 18s. or adapted for the General Reader, 12s. Vol. II. *Exodus*, 15s. or
adapted for the General Reader, 12s. Vol. III. *Leviticus*, Part I. 15s. or
adapted for the General Reader, 8s. Vol. IV. *Leviticus*, Part II. 15s. or
adapted for the General Reader, 8s.

A DICTIONARY of ROMAN and GREEK ANTIQUITIES, with
about Two Thousand Engravings on Wood from Ancient Originals, illustrative
of the Industrial Arts and Social Life of the Greeks and Romans. By A. Rich,
B.A. Third Edition, revised and improved. Crown 8vo. price 7s. 6d.

A LATIN-ENGLISH DICTIONARY. By John T. White, D.D.
Oxon. and J. E. Riddle, M.A. Oxon. Revised Edition. 2 vols. 4to. 42s.

WHITE'S COLLEGE LATIN-ENGLISH DICTIONARY (Intermediate
Size), abridged for the use of University Students from the Parent Work (as
above). Medium 8vo. 18s.

WHITE'S JUNIOR STUDENT'S COMPLETE LATIN-ENGLISH and
ENGLISH-LATIN DICTIONARY. New Edition. Square 12mo. price 12s.

Separately { The ENGLISH-LATIN DICTIONARY, price 5s. 6d.
{ The LATIN-ENGLISH DICTIONARY, price 7s. 6d.

A LATIN-ENGLISH DICTIONARY, adapted for the Use of Middle-
Class Schools. By John T. White, D.D. Oxon. Square fcp. 8vo. price 3s.

An ENGLISH-GREEK LEXICON, containing all the Greek Words
used by Writers of good authority. By C. D. Yonge, B.A. New Edition.
4to. price 21s.

Mr. YONGE'S NEW LEXICON, English and Greek, abridged from
his larger work (as above). Revised Edition. Square 12mo. price 8s. 6d.

A GREEK-ENGLISH LEXICON. Compiled by H. G. Liddell. D.D.
Dean of Christ Church, and R. Scott, D.D. Dean of Rochester. Sixth Edition.
Crown 4to. price 36s.

A Lexicon, Greek and English, abridged from Liddell and Scott's
Greek-English Lexicon. Fourteenth Edition. Square 12mo. 7s. 6d.

A SANSKRIT-ENGLISH DICTIONARY, the Sanskrit words printed
both in the original Devanagari and in Roman Letters. Compiled by T.
Benfey, Prof. in the Univ. of Göttingen. 8vo. 52s. 6d.

A PRACTICAL DICTIONARY of the FRENCH and ENGLISH LAN-
GUAGES. By L. Contanseau. Revised Edition. Post 8vo. 10s. 6d.

Contanseau's Pocket Dictionary, French and English, abridged from
the above by the Author. New Edition, revised. Square 18mo. 3s. 6d.

NEW PRACTICAL DICTIONARY of the GERMAN LANGUAGE;
German-English and English-German. By the Rev. W. L. Blackley, M.A
and Dr. Carl Martin Friedländer. Post 8vo. 7s. 6d.

The MASTERY of LANGUAGES; or, the Art of Speaking Foreign
Tongues Idiomatically. By THOMAS PRENDERGAST. 8vo. 6s.

Miscellaneous Works and Popular Metaphysics.

ESSAYS on FREETHINKING and PLAIN-SPEAKING. By LESLIE
STEPHEN. Crown 8vo. 10s. 6d.

THE MISCELLANEOUS WORKS of THOMAS ARNOLD, D.D.
Late Head Master of Rugby School and Regius Professor of Modern History in
the University of Oxford, collected and republished. 8vo. 7s. 6d.

MISCELLANEOUS and POSTHUMOUS WORKS of the Late HENRY
THOMAS BUCKLE. Edited, with a Biographical Notice, by HELEN TAYLOR.
3 vols. 8vo. price 52s. 6d.

MISCELLANEOUS WRITINGS of JOHN CONINGTON, M.A. late
Corpus Professor of Latin in the University of Oxford. Edited by J. A.
SYMONDS, M.A. With a Memoir by H. J. S. SMITH, M.A. 2 vols. 8vo. 28s.

ESSAYS, CRITICAL and BIOGRAPHICAL. Contributed to the
Edinburgh Review. By HENRY ROGERS. New Edition, with Additions. 2 vols.
crown 8vo. price 12s.

ESSAYS on some THEOLOGICAL CONTROVERSIES of the TIME.
Contributed chiefly to the Edinburgh Review. By HENRY ROGERS. New
Edition, with Additions. Crown 8vo. price 6s.

LANDSCAPES, CHURCHES, and MORALITIES. By A. K. H. B.
Crown 8vo. price 3s. 6d.

Recreations of a Country Parson. By A. K. H. B. FIRST and
SECOND SERIES, crown 8vo. 3s. 6d. each.

The Common-place Philosopher in Town and Country. By A. K. H. B.
Crown 8vo. price 3s. 6d.

Leisure Hours in Town; Essays Consolatory, Æsthetical, Moral,
Social, and Domestic. By A. K. H. B. Crown 8vo. 3s. 6d.

The Autumn Holidays of a Country Parson; Essays contributed to
Fraser's Magazine, &c. By A. K. H. B. Crown 8vo. 3s. 6d.

Seaside Musings on Sundays and Week-Days. By A. K. H. B.
Crown 8vo. price 3s. 6d.

The Graver Thoughts of a Country Parson. By A. K. H. B. FIRST
and SECOND SERIES, crown 8vo. 3s. 6d. each.

Critical Essays of a Country Parson, selected from Essays contributed to Fraser's Magazine. By A. K. H. B. Crown 8vo. 3s. 6d.

Sunday Afternoons at the Parish Church of a Scottish University
City. By A. K. H. B. Crown 8vo. 3s. 6d.

Lessons of Middle Age; with some Account of various Cities and
Men. By A. K. H. B. Crown 8vo. 3s. 6d.

Counsel and Comfort spoken from a City Pulpit. By A. K. H. B.
Crown 8vo. price 3s. 6d.

CHANGED ASPECTS of UNCHANGED TRUTHS; Memorials of St.
Andrews Sundays. By A. K. H. B. Crown 8vo. 3s. 6d.

Present-day Thoughts; Memorials of St. Andrews Sundays. By
A. K. H. B. Crown 8vo. 3s. 6d.

SHORT STUDIES on GREAT SUBJECTS. By JAMES ANTHONY
FROUDE, M.A. late Fellow of Exeter Coll. Oxford. 2 vols. crown 8vo. price 12s.

LORD MACAULAY'S MISCELLANEOUS WRITINGS :—
LIBRARY EDITION. 2 vols. 8vo. Portrait, 21s.
PEOPLE'S EDITION. 1 vol. crown 8vo. 4s. 6d.

LORD MACAULAY'S MISCELLANEOUS WRITINGS and SPEECHES.
STUDENT'S EDITION, in crown 8vo. price 6s.

The Rev. SYDNEY SMITH'S ESSAYS contributed to the Edinburgh
Review. Authorised Edition, complete in 1 vol. Crown 8vo. price 2s. 6d.

The Rev. SYDNEY SMITH'S MISCELLANEOUS WORKS; including
his Contributions to the *Edinburgh Review*. Crown 8vo. 6s.

The Wit and Wisdom of the Rev. Sydney Smith ; a Selection of
the most memorable Passages in his Writings and Conversation. 16mo. 3s. 6d.

The ECLIPSE of FAITH; or, a Visit to a Religious Sceptic. By
HENRY ROGERS. Latest Edition. Fcp. 8vo. price 5s.

Defence of the Eclipse of Faith, by its Author ; a rejoinder to Dr.
Newman's *Reply*. Latest Edition. Fcp 8vo. price 3s. 6d.

CHIPS from a GERMAN WORKSHOP; Essays on the Science of
Religion, and on Mythology, Traditions, and Customs. By F. MAX MÜLLER,
M.A. &c. Second Edition. 3 vols. 8vo. £2.

ANALYSIS of the PHENOMENA of the HUMAN MIND. By
JAMES MILL. A New Edition, with Notes, Illustrative and Critical, by
ALEXANDER BAIN, ANDREW FINDLATER, and GEORGE GROTE. Edited, with
additional Notes, by JOHN STUART MILL. 2 vols. 8vo. price 28s.

An INTRODUCTION to MENTAL PHILOSOPHY, on the Inductive
Method. By J. D. MORELL, M.A. LL.D. 8vo. 12s.

ELEMENTS of PSYCHOLOGY, containing the Analysis of the
Intellectual Powers. By J. D. MORELL, M.A. LL.D. Post 8vo. 7s. 6d.

The SECRET of HEGEL; being the Hegelian System in Origin,
Principle, Form, and Matter. By J. H. STIRLING, LL.D. 2 vols. 8vo. 28s.

SIR WILLIAM HAMILTON ; being the Philosophy of Perception : an
Analysis. By J. H. STIRLING, LL.D. 8vo. 5s.

The SENSES and the INTELLECT. By ALEXANDER BAIN, M.D.
Professor of Logic in the University of Aberdeen. Third Edition. 8vo. 15s.

MENTAL and MORAL SCIENCE: a Compendium of Psychology
and Ethics. By the same Author. Third Edition. Crown 8vo. 10s. 6d. Or
separately : PART I. *Mental Science*, 6s. 6d. PART II. *Moral Science*, 4s. 6d.

LOGIC, DEDUCTIVE and INDUCTIVE. By the same Author. In
Two PARTS, crown 8vo. 10s. 6d. Each Part may be had separately :—
PART I. *Deduction*, 4s. PART II. *Induction*, 6s. 6d.

The PHILOSOPHY of NECESSITY ; or, Natural Law as applicable to Mental, Moral, and Social Science. By CHARLES BRAY. 8vo. 9s.

On FORCE, its MENTAL and MORAL CORRELATES. By the same Author. 8vo. 5s.

A MANUAL of ANTHROPOLOGY, or SCIENCE of MAN, based on Modern Research. By CHARLES BRAY. Crown 8vo. price 6s.

A PHRENOLOGIST AMONGST the TODAS, or the Study of a Primi- tive Tribe in South India ; History, Character, Customs, Religion, Infanticide, Polyandry, Language. By W. E. MARSHALL, Lieutenant-Colonel B.S.C. With 26 Illustrations. 8vo 21s.

A TREATISE of HUMAN NATURE, being an Attempt to Introduce the Experimental Method of Reasoning into Moral Subjects ; followed by Dia- logues concerning Natural Religion. By DAVID HUME. Edited, with Notes, &c. by T. H. GREEN, Fellow and Tutor, Ball. Coll. and T. H. GROSE, Fellow and Tutor, Queen's Coll. Oxford. 2 vols. 8vo. 28s.

ESSAYS MORAL, POLITICAL, and LITERARY. By DAVID HUME. By the same Editors. 2 vols. 8vo. price 28s.

UEBERWEG'S SYSTEM of LOGIC and HISTORY of LOGICAL DOCTRINES. Translated, with Notes and Appendices, by T. M. LINDSAY, M.A. F.R.S.E. 8vo. price 16s.

A BUDGET of PARADOXES. By AUGUSTUS DE MORGAN, F.R.A.S. and C.P.S. 8vo. 15s.

Astronomy, Meteorology, Popular Geography, &c.

BRINKLEY'S ASTRONOMY. Revised and partly re-written, with Additional Chapters, and an Appendix of Questions for Examination. By J. W. STUBBS, D.D. Fellow and Tutor of Trinity College, Dublin, and F. BRÜNNOW, Ph.D. Astronomer Royal of Ireland. Crown 8vo. price 6s.

OUTLINES of ASTRONOMY. By Sir J. F. W. HERSCHEL, Bart. M.A. Latest Edition, with Plates and Diagrams. Square crown 8vo. 12s.

ESSAYS on ASTRONOMY, a Series of Papers on Planets and Meteors, the Sun and Sun-surrounding Space, Stars and Star-Cloudlets ; with a Dissertation on the approaching Transit of Venus. By RICHARD A. PROCTOR, B.A. With 10 Plates and 24 Woodcuts. 8vo. 12s.

THE TRANSITS of VENUS ; a Popular Account of Past and Coming Transits, from the first observed by Horrocks A.D. 1639 to the Transit of A.D. 2112. By R. A. PROCTOR, B.A. Cantab. With 20 Plates and numerous Woodcuts. Crown 8vo. [Nearly ready.

The UNIVERSE and the COMING TRANSITS : Presenting Re- searches into and New Views respecting the Constitution of the Heavens ; together with an Investigation of the Conditions of the Coming Transits of Venus. By R. A. PROCTOR, B.A. With 22 Charts and 22 Woodcuts. 8vo. 16s.

The MOON ; her Motions, Aspect, Scenery, and Physical Condition. By R. A. PROCTOR, B.A. With Plates, Charts, Woodcuts, and Three Lunar Photographs. Crown 8vo. 15s.

The SUN; RULER, LIGHT, FIRE, and LIFE of the PLANETARY
SYSTEM. By R. A. PROCTOR, B.A. Second Edition, with 10 Plates (7 coloured) and 107 Figures on Wood. Crown 8vo. 14s.

OTHER WORLDS THAN OURS; the Plurality of Worlds Studied
under the Light of Recent Scientific Researches. By R. A. PROCTOR, B.A. Third Edition, with 14 Illustrations. Crown 8vo. 10s. 6d.

The ORBS AROUND US; a Series of Familiar Essays on the Moon
and Planets, Meteors and Comets, the Sun and Coloured Pairs of Stars. By R. A. PROCTOR, B.A. Crown 8vo. price 7s. 6d.

SATURN and its SYSTEM. By R. A. PROCTOR, B.A. 8vo. with 14
Plates, 14s.

SCHELLEN'S SPECTRUM ANALYSIS, in its application to Terres-
trial Substances and the Physical Constitution of the Heavenly Bodies. Translated by JANE and C. LASSELL; edited, with Notes, by W. HUGGINS, LL.D. F.R.S. With 13 Plates (6 coloured) and 223 Woodcuts. 8vo. price 28s.

A NEW STAR ATLAS, for the Library, the School, and the Observatory,
in Twelve Circular Maps (with Two Index Plates). Intended as a Companion to 'Webb's Celestial Objects for Common Telescopes.' With a Letterpress Introduction on the Study of the Stars, illustrated by 9 Diagrams. By R. A. PROCTOR, B.A. Crown 8vo. 5s.

CELESTIAL OBJECTS for COMMON TELESCOPES. By the Rev.
T. W. WEBB, M.A. F.R.A.S. Third Edition, revised and enlarged; with Maps, Plate, and Woodcuts. Crown 8vo. price 7s. 6d.

AIR and RAIN; the Beginnings of a Chemical Climatology. By
ROBERT ANGUS SMITH, Ph.D. F.R.S. F.C.S. With 8 Illustrations. 8vo. 24s.

NAUTICAL SURVEYING, an INTRODUCTION to the PRACTICAL
and THEORETICAL STUDY of. By J. K. LAUGHTON, M.A. Small 8vo. 6s.

MAGNETISM and DEVIATION of the COMPASS. For the Use of
Students in Navigation and Science Schools. By J. MERRIFIELD, LL.D. 18mo. 1s. 6d.

DOVE'S LAW of STORMS, considered in connexion with the Ordinary
Movements of the Atmosphere. Translated by R. H. SCOTT, M.A. 8vo. 10s. 6d.

KEITH JOHNSTON'S GENERAL DICTIONARY of GEOGRAPHY,
Descriptive, Physical, Statistical, and Historical; forming a complete Gazetteer of the World. New Edition, revised and corrected to the Present Date by the Author's Son, KEITH JOHNSTON, F.R.G.S. 1 vol. 8vo. [Nearly ready.

The POST OFFICE GAZETTEER of the UNITED KINGDOM. Being
a Complete Dictionary of all Cities, Towns, Villages, and of the Principal Gentlemen's Seats, in Great Britain and Ireland; Referred to the nearest Post Town, Railway and Telegraph Station: with Natural Features and Objects of Note. By J. A. SHARP. 1 vol. 8vo. of about 1,500 pages. [In the press.

The PUBLIC SCHOOLS ATLAS of MODERN GEOGRAPHY. In
31 Maps, exhibiting clearly the more important Physical Features of the Countries delineated, and Noting all the Chief Places of Historical, Commercial, or Social Interest. Edited, with an Introduction, by the Rev. G. BUTLER, M.A. Imp. 4to. price 3s. 6d. sewed, or 5s. cloth.

The PUBLIC SCHOOLS MANUAL of MODERN GEOGRAPHY. By
the Rev. GEORGE BUTLER, M.A. Principal of Liverpool College; Editor of 'The Public Schools Atlas of Modern Geography.'   [In preparation.

The **PUBLIC SCHOOLS ATLAS of ANCIENT GEOGRAPHY** Edited,
with an Introduction on the Study of Ancient Geography, by the Rev. GEORGE
BUTLER, M.A. Principal of Liverpool College. Imperial Quarto.
[*In preparation.*

A **MANUAL of GEOGRAPHY**, Physical, Industrial, and Political.
By W. HUGHES, F.R.G.S. With 6 Maps. Fcp. 7s. 6d.

MAUNDER'S TREASURY of GEOGRAPHY, Physical, Historical,
Descriptive, and Political. Edited by W. HUGHES, F.R.G.S. Revised Edition,
with 7 Maps and 16 Plates. Fcp. 6s. cloth, or 10s. bound in calf.

Natural History and Popular Science.

TEXT-BOOKS of SCIENCE, MECHANICAL and PHYSICAL,
adapted for the use of Artisans and of Students in Public and Science Schools.
Edited by T. M. GOODEVE, M.A. and C. W. MERRIFIELD, F.R.S.

> ANDERSON'S Strength of Materials, small 8vo. 3s. 6d.
> ARMSTRONG'S Organic Chemistry, 3s. 6d.
> BLOXAM'S Metals, 3s. 6d.
> GOODEVE'S Elements of Mechanism, 3s. 6d.
> —————— Principles of Mechanics, 3s. 6d.
> GRIFFIN'S Algebra and Trigonometry, 3s. 6d. Notes, 3s. 6d.
> JENKIN'S Electricity and Magnetism, 3s. 6d.
> MAXWELL'S Theory of Heat, 3s. 6d.
> MERRIFIELD'S Technical Arithmetic and Mensuration, 3s. 6d. Key, 3s. 6d.
> MILLER'S Inorganic Chemistry, 3s. 6d.
> SHELLEY'S Workshop Appliances, 3s. 6d.
> THORPE'S Quantitative Chemical Analysis, 4s. 6d.
> THORPE & MUIR'S Qualitative Analysis, 3s. 6d.
> WATSON'S Plane and Solid Geometry, 3s. 6d.
>
> *,* Other Text-Books in active preparation.

ELEMENTARY TREATISE on PHYSICS, Experimental and Applied.
Translated and edited from GANOT'S *Éléments de Physique* by E. ATKINSON,
Ph.D. F.C.S. New Edition, revised and enlarged; with a Coloured Plate and
726 Woodcuts. Post 8vo. 15s.

NATURAL PHILOSOPHY for GENERAL READERS and YOUNG
PERSONS; being a Course of Physics divested of Mathematical Formulæ
expressed in the language of daily life. Translated from GANOT'S *Cours de
Physique* and by E. ATKINSON, Ph.D. F.C.S. Crown 8vo. with 404 Woodcuts,
price 7s. 6d.

HELMHOLTZ'S POPULAR LECTURES on SCIENTIFIC SUBJECTS.
Translated by E. ATKINSON, Ph.D. F.C.S. Professor of Experimental Science,
Staff College. With an Introduction by Professor TYNDALL. 8vo. with nume-
rous Woodcuts, price 12s. 6d.

SOUND: a Course of Eight Lectures delivered at the Royal Institution
of Great Britain. By JOHN TYNDALL, LL.D. D.C.L. F.R.S. New Edition,
with 169 Woodcuts. Crown 8vo. 9s.

HEAT a MODE of MOTION. By JOHN TYNDALL, LL.D. D.C.L.
F.R.S. Fourth Edition. Crown 8vo. with Woodcuts, 10s. 6d.

CONTRIBUTIONS to MOLECULAR PHYSICS in the DOMAIN of RADIANT HEAT. By J. Tyndall, LL.D. D.C.L. F.R.S. With 2 Plates and 31 Woodcuts. 8vo. 16s.

RESEARCHES on DIAMAGNETISM and MAGNE-CRYSTALLIC ACTION; including the Question of Diamagnetic Polarity. By J. Tyndall, M.D. D.C.L. F.R.S. With 6 plates and many Woodcuts. 8vo. 14s.

NOTES of a COURSE of SEVEN LECTURES on ELECTRICAL PHENOMENA and THEORIES, delivered at the Royal Institution, A.D. 1870. By John Tyndall, LL.D., D.C.L., F.R.S. Crown 8vo. 1s. sewed; 1s. 6d. cloth.

A TREATISE on MAGNETISM, General and Terrestrial. By Humphrey Lloyd, D.D., D.C.L., Provost of Trinity College, Dublin. 8vo. price 10s. 6d.

ELEMENTARY TREATISE on the WAVE-THEORY of LIGHT. By Humphrey Lloyd, D.D. D.C.L. Provost of Trinity College, Dublin. Third Edition, revised and enlarged. 8vo. price 10s. 6d.

LECTURES on LIGHT delivered in the United States of America in the Years 1872 and 1873. By John Tyndall, LL.D. D.C.L. F.R.S. With Frontispiece and Diagrams. Crown 8vo. price 7s. 6d.

NOTES of a COURSE of NINE LECTURES on LIGHT delivered at the Royal Institution, A.D. 1869. By John Tyndall, LL.D. D.C.L. F.R.S. Crown 8vo. price 1s. sewed, or 1s. 6d. cloth.

ADDRESS delivered before the British Association assembled at Belfast; with Additions and a Preface. By John Tyndall, F.R.S. President. 8vo. price 3s.

FRAGMENTS of SCIENCE. By John Tyndall, LL.D. D.C.L. F.R.S. Third Edition. 8vo. price 14s.

LIGHT SCIENCE for LEISURE HOURS; a Series of Familiar Essays on Scientific Subjects, Natural Phenomena, &c. By R. A. Proctor, B.A. First and Second Series. Crown 8vo. 7s. 6d. each.

The CORRELATION of PHYSICAL FORCES. By the Hon. Sir W. R. Grove, M.A. F.R.S. one of the Judges of the Court of Common Pleas. Sixth Edition, with other Contributions to Science. 8vo. price 15s.

Professor OWEN'S LECTURES on the COMPARATIVE ANATOMY and Physiology of the Invertebrate Animals. Second Edition, with 235 Woodcuts. 8vo. 21s.

The COMPARATIVE ANATOMY and PHYSIOLOGY of the VERTE- BRATE ANIMALS. By Richard Owen, F.R.S. D.C.L. With 1,472 Woodcuts. 3 vols. 8vo. £3. 13s. 6d.

PRINCIPLES of ANIMAL MECHANICS. By the Rev. S. Haughton, F.R.S. Fellow of Trin. Coll. Dubl. M.D. Dubl. and D.C.L. Oxon. Second Edition, with 111 Figures on Wood. 8vo. 21s.

ROCKS CLASSIFIED and DESCRIBED. By Bernhard Von Cotta. English Edition, by P. H. Lawrence; with English, German, and French Synonymes. Post 8vo. 14s.

The ANCIENT STONE IMPLEMENTS, WEAPONS, and ORNA- MENTS of GREAT BRITAIN. By John Evans, F.R.S. F.S.A. With 2 Plates and 476 Woodcuts. 8vo. price 28s.

PRIMÆVAL WORLD of SWITZERLAND. By Professor OSWALD HEER, of the University of Zurich. Translated by W. S. DALLAS, F.L.S., and edited by JAMES HEYWOOD, M.A., F.R.S. 2 vols. 8vo. with numerous Illustrations. [In the press.

The ORIGIN of CIVILISATION and the PRIMITIVE CONDITION of MAN: Mental and Social Condition of Savages. By Sir JOHN LUBBOCK, Bart. M.P. F.R.S. Third Edition, revised, with Woodcuts. [Nearly ready.

BIBLE ANIMALS; being a Description of every Living Creature mentioned in the Scriptures, from the Ape to the Coral. By the Rev. J. G. WOOD, M.A. F.L.S. With about 100 Vignettes on Wood. 8vo. 21s.

HOMES WITHOUT HANDS; a Description of the Habitations of Animals, classed according to their Principle of Construction. By the Rev. J. G. WOOD, M.A. F.L.S. With about 140 Vignettes on Wood. 8vo. 21s.

INSECTS AT HOME; a Popular Account of British Insects, their Structure, Habits, and Transformations. By the Rev. J. G. WOOD, M.A. F.L.S. With upwards of 700 Illustrations. 8vo. price 21s.

INSECTS ABROAD; a Popular Account of Foreign Insects, their Structure, Habits, and Transformations. By J. G. WOOD, M.A. F.L.S. Printed and illustrated uniformly with 'Insects at Home.' 8vo. price 21s.

STRANGE DWELLINGS; a description of the Habitations of Animals, abridged from 'Homes without Hands.' By the Rev. J. G. WOOD, M.A. F.L.S. With about 60 Woodcut Illustrations. Crown 8vo. price 7s. 6d.

OUT of DOORS; a Selection of original Articles on Practical Natural History. By the Rev. J. G. WOOD, M.A. F.L.S. With Eleven Illustrations from Original Designs engraved on Wood by G. Pearson. Crown 8vo. price 7s. 6d.

A FAMILIAR HISTORY of BIRDS. By E. STANLEY, D.D. F.R.S. late Lord Bishop of Norwich. Seventh Edition, with Woodcuts. Fcp. 3s. 6d.

FROM JANUARY to DECEMBER; a Book for Children. Second Edition. 8vo. 3s. 6d.

The SEA and its LIVING WONDERS. By Dr. GEORGE HARTWIG. Latest revised Edition. 8vo. with many Illustrations, 10s. 6d.

The TROPICAL WORLD. By Dr. GEORGE HARTWIG. With above 160 Illustrations. Latest revised Edition. 8vo. price 10s. 6d.

The SUBTERRANEAN WORLD. By Dr. GEORGE HARTWIG. With 3 Maps and about 80 Woodcuts, including 8 full size of page. 8vo. price 21s.

THE AERIAL WORLD. By Dr. GEORGE HARTWIG. With 8 Chromoxylographs and 60 Illustrations engraved on Wood. 8vo. price 21s.

The POLAR WORLD, a Popular Description of Man and Nature in the Arctic and Antarctic Regions of the Globe. By Dr. GEORGE HARTWIG. With 8 Chromoxylographs, 3 Maps, and 85 Woodcuts. 8vo. 10s. 6d.

KIRBY and SPENCE'S INTRODUCTION to ENTOMOLOGY, or Elements of the Natural History of Insects. 7th Edition. Crown 8vo. 5s.

MAUNDER'S TREASURY of NATURAL HISTORY, or Popular Dictionary of Birds, Beasts, Fishes, Reptiles, Insects, and Creeping Things. With above 900 Woodcuts. Fcp. 8vo. price 6s. cloth, or 10s. bound in calf.

MAUNDER'S SCIENTIFIC and LITERARY TREASURY. New Edition, thoroughly revised and in great part rewritten, with above 1,000 new Articles, by J. Y. JOHNSON. Fcp. 8vo. 6s. cloth, or 10s. calf.

**HANDBOOK of HARDY TREES, SHRUBS, and HERBACEOUS
PLANTS,** containing Descriptions, Native Countries, &c. of a Selection of the
Best Species in Cultivation; together with Cultural Details, Comparative
Hardiness, Suitability for Particular Positions, &c. By W. B. HEMSLEY. Based on
DECAISNE and NAUDIN's *Manuel de l'Amateur des Jardins,* and including the 264
Original Woodcuts. Medium 8vo. 21s.

A GENERAL SYSTEM of BOTANY DESCRIPTIVE and ANALYTICAL.
I. Outlines of Organography, Anatomy, and Physiology; II. Descriptions and
Illustrations of the Orders. By E. LE MAOUT, and J. DECAISNE, Members of
the Institute of France. Translated by Mrs. HOOKER. The Orders arranged
after the Method followed in the Universities and Schools of Great Britain, its
Colonies, America, and India; with an Appendix on the Natural Method, and
other Additions, by J. D. HOOKER, F.R.S. &c. Director of the Royal Botanical
Gardens, Kew. With 5,500 Woodcuts. Imperial 8vo. price 52s. 6d.

The TREASURY of BOTANY, or Popular Dictionary of the Vegetable
Kingdom; including a Glossary of Botanical Terms. Edited by J. LINDLEY,
F.R.S. and T. MOORE, F.L.S. assisted by eminent Contributors. With 274
Woodcuts and 20 Steel Plates. Two Parts, fcp. 8vo. 12s. cloth, or 20s. calf.

The ELEMENTS of BOTANY for FAMILIES and SCHOOLS.
Tenth Edition, revised by THOMAS MOORE, F.L.S. Fcp. with 154 Woodcuts, 2s. 6d.

The ROSE AMATEUR'S GUIDE. By THOMAS RIVERS. Fourteenth
Edition. Fcp. 8vo. 4s.

LOUDON'S ENCYCLOPÆDIA of PLANTS; comprising the Specific
Character, Description, Culture, History, &c. of all the Plants found in
Great Britain. With upwards of 12,000 Woodcuts. 8vo. 42s.

A DICTIONARY of SCIENCE, LITERATURE, and ART. Fourth
Edition, re-edited by W. T. BRANDE (the original Author), and GEORGE W.
COX, M.A., assisted by contributors of eminent Scientific and Literary
Acquirements. 3 vols. medium 8vo. price 63s. cloth.

Chemistry and *Physiology.*

A DICTIONARY of CHEMISTRY and the Allied Branches of other
Sciences. By HENRY WATTS, F.R.S. assisted by eminent Contributors.
6 vols. medium 8vo. price £8. 14s. 6d. SECOND SUPPLEMENT *in the Press.*

ELEMENTS of CHEMISTRY, Theoretical and Practical. By W. ALLEN
MILLER, M.D. late Prof. of Chemistry, King's Coll. London. New
Edition. 3 vols. 8vo. £3. PART I. CHEMICAL PHYSICS, 15s. PART II.
INORGANIC CHEMISTRY, 21s. PART III. ORGANIC CHEMISTRY, 24s.

A Course of Practical Chemistry, for the use of Medical Students.
By W. ODLING, F.R.S. New Edition, with 70 Woodcuts. Crown 8vo. 7s. 6d.

A MANUAL of CHEMICAL PHYSIOLOGY, including its Points of
Contact with Pathology. By J. L. W. THUDICHUM, M.D. With Woodcuts.
8vo. price 7s. 6d.

**SELECT METHODS in CHEMICAL ANALYSIS, chiefly INOR-
GANIC.** By WILLIAM CROOKES, F.R.S. With 22 Woodcuts. Crown 8vo.
price 12s. 6d.

A PRACTICAL HANDBOOK of DYEING and CALICO PRINTING.
By WILLIAM CROOKES, F.R.S. With 11 Page Plates, 40 Specimens of Dyed and
Printed Fabrics, and 36 Woodcuts. 8vo. 42s.

OUTLINES of PHYSIOLOGY, Human and Comparative. By JOHN
MARSHALL, F.R.C.S. Surgeon to the University College Hospital. 2 vols.
crown 8vo. with 122 Woodcuts, 32s.

PHYSIOLOGICAL ANATOMY and PHYSIOLOGY of MAN. By the
late R. B. TODD, M.D. F.R.S. and W. BOWMAN, F.R.S. of King's College.
With numerous Illustrations. Vol. II. 8vo. 25s.

Vol. I. New Edition by Dr. LIONEL S. BEALE, F.R.S. in course of publication, with many Illustrations. PARTS I. and II. price 7s. 6d. each.

The Fine Arts, and Illustrated Editions.

A DICTIONARY of ARTISTS of the ENGLISH SCHOOL: Painters,
Sculptors, Architects, Engravers, and Ornamentists; with Notices of their Lives
and Works. By S. REDGRAVE. 8vo. 16s.

The THREE CATHEDRALS DEDICATED to ST. PAUL, in LONDON:
their History from the Foundation of the First Building in the Sixth Century
to the Proposals for the Adornment of the Present Cathedral. By WILLIAM
LONGMAN, F.A.S. With numerous Illustrations. Square crown 8vo. 21s.

IN FAIRYLAND; Pictures from the Elf-World. By RICHARD
DOYLE. With a Poem by W. ALLINGHAM. With Sixteen Plates, containing
Thirty-six Designs printed in Colours. Second Edition. Folio, price 15s.

ALBERT DURER, HIS LIFE and WORKS; including Auto-
biographical Papers and Complete Catalogues. By WILLIAM B. SCOTT.
With Six Etchings by the Author, and other Illustrations. 8vo. 16s.

The NEW TESTAMENT, illustrated with Wood Engravings after the
Early Masters, chiefly of the Italian School. Crown 4to. 63s. cloth, gilt top;
or £5 5s. elegantly bound in morocco.

LYRA GERMANICA; the Christian Year and the Christian Life.
Translated by CATHERINE WINKWORTH. With about 325 Woodcut Illustrations
by J. LEIGHTON, F.S.A. and other Artists. 2 vols. 4to. price 42s.

The LIFE of MAN SYMBOLISED by the MONTHS of the YEAR.
Text selected by R. PIGOT; Illustrations on Wood from Original Designs
J. LEIGHTON, F.S.A. 4to. 42s.

SACRED and LEGENDARY ART. By MRS. JAMESON.

Legends of the Saints and Martyrs. New Edition, with 19
Etchings and 187 Woodcuts. 2 vols. square crown 8vo. 31s. 6d.

Legends of the Monastic Orders. New Edition, with 11 Etchings
and 88 Woodcuts. 1 vol. square crown 8vo. 21s.

Legends of the Madonna. New Edition, with 27 Etchings and
165 Woodcuts. 1 vol. square crown 8vo. 21s.

The History of Our Lord, with that of his Types and Precursors.
Completed by Lady EASTLAKE. Revised Edition, with 31 Etchings and
281 Woodcuts. 2 vols. square crown 8vo. 42s.

B

DAEDALUS; or, the Causes and Principles of the Excellence of Greek Sculpture. By EDWARD FALKENER, Member of the Academy of Bologna, and of the Archæological Institutes of Rome and Berlin. With Woodcuts, Photographs, and Chromolithographs. Royal 8vo. 42s.

FALKENER'S MUSEUM of CLASSICAL ANTIQUITIES; a Series of Essays on Ancient Art. New Edition, complete in One Volume, with many Illustrations. Royal 8vo. price 12s.

The Useful Arts, Manufactures, &c.

HISTORY of the GOTHIC REVIVAL; an Attempt to shew how far the taste for Mediæval Architecture was retained in England during the last two centuries, and has been re-developed in the present. By C. L. EAST-LAKE, Architect. With 48 Illustrations. Imperial 8vo. 31s. 6d.

GWILT'S ENCYCLOPÆDIA of ARCHITECTURE, with above 1,600 Engravings on Wood. Fifth Edition, revised and enlarged by WYATT PAPWORTH. 8vo. 52s. 6d.

A MANUAL of ARCHITECTURE: being a Concise History and Explanation of the principal Styles of European Architecture, Ancient, Mediæval, and Renaissance; with a Glossary of Technical Terms. By THOMAS MITCHELL. Crown 8vo. with 150 Woodcuts. 10s. 6d.

HINTS on HOUSEHOLD TASTE in FURNITURE, UPHOLSTERY, and other Details. By CHARLES L. EASTLAKE, Architect. New Edition, with about 90 Illustrations. Square crown 8vo. 14s.

PRINCIPLES of MECHANISM, designed for the Use of Students in the Universities, and for Engineering Students generally. By R. WILLIS, M.A. F.R.S. &c. Jacksonian Professor in the University of Cambridge. Second Edition, enlarged; with 374 Woodcuts. 8vo. 18s.

GEOMETRIC TURNING: comprising a Description of Plant's New Geometric Chuck, with directions for its use, and a series of Patterns cut by it, with Explanations. By H. S. SAVORY. With numerous Woodcuts. 8vo. 21s.

LATHES and TURNING, Simple, Mechanical, and Ornamental. By W. HENRY NORTHCOTT. With about 240 Illustrations. 8vo. 18s.

PERSPECTIVE; or, the Art of Drawing what One Sees. Explained and adapted to the use of those Sketching from Nature. By Lieut. W. H. COLLINS, R.E. F.R.A.S. With 37 Woodcuts. Crown 8vo. price 5s.

INDUSTRIAL CHEMISTRY; a Manual for Manufacturers and for use in Colleges or Technical Schools. Being a Translation of Professors Stohmann and Engler's German Edition of PAYEN's *Précis de Chimie Industrielle*, by Dr. J. D. BARRY. Edited and supplemented by B. H. PAUL, Ph.D. 8vo. with Plates and Woodcuts. [*In the press.*

URE'S DICTIONARY of ARTS, MANUFACTURES, and MINES. Sixth Edition, re-written and enlarged by ROBERT HUNT, F.R.S. assisted by numerous Contributors eminent in Science and the Arts, and familiar with Manufactures. With above 2,000 Woodcuts. 3 vols. medium 8vo. £4 14s. 6d.

HANDBOOK of PRACTICAL TELEGRAPHY. By R. S. CULLEY Memb. Inst. C.E. Engineer-in-Chief of Telegraphs to the Post Office. Sixth Edition, with 144 Woodcuts and 5 Plates. 8vo. price 16s.

The ENGINEER'S HANDBOOK; explaining the Principles which should guide the Young Engineer in the Construction of Machinery, with the necessary Rules, Proportions, and Tables. By C. S. LOWNDES. Post 8vo. 5s.

ENCYCLOPÆDIA of CIVIL ENGINEERING, Historical, Theoretical, and Practical. By E. CRESY, C.E. With above 3,000 Woodcuts. 8vo. 42s.

The STRAINS IN TRUSSES computed by means of Diagrams; with 20 Examples drawn to Scale. By F. A. RANKEN, M.A. C.E. With 35 Diagrams. Square crown 8vo. 6s. 6d.

TREATISE on MILLS and MILLWORK. By Sir W. FAIRBAIRN, Bart. F.R.S. New Edition, with 18 Plates and 322 Woodcuts. 2 vols. 8vo. 32s.

USEFUL INFORMATION for ENGINEERS. By Sir W. FAIRBAIRN, Bart. F.R.S. Revised Edition, with Illustrations. 3 vols. crown 8vo. price 31s. 6d.

The APPLICATION of CAST and WROUGHT IRON to Building Purposes. By Sir W. FAIRBAIRN, Bart. F.R.S. Fourth Edition, enlarged; with 6 Plates and 118 Woodcuts. 8vo. price 16s.

GUNS and STEEL; Miscellaneous Papers on Mechanical Subjects. By Sir JOSEPH WHITWORTH, Bart. C.E. Royal 8vo. with Illustrations, 7s. 6d.

A TREATISE on the STEAM ENGINE, in its various Applications to Mines, Mills, Steam Navigation, Railways, and Agriculture. By J. BOURNE, C.E. Eighth Edition; with Portrait, 37 Plates, and 546 Woodcuts. 4to. 42s.

CATECHISM of the STEAM ENGINE, in its various Applications to Mines, Mills, Steam Navigation, Railways, and Agriculture. By the same Author. With 89 Woodcuts. Fcp. 8vo. 6s.

HANDBOOK of the STEAM ENGINE. By the same Author, forming a KEY to the Catechism of the Steam Engine, with 67 Woodcuts. Fcp. 9s.

BOURNE'S RECENT IMPROVEMENTS in the STEAM ENGINE in its various applications to Mines, Mills, Steam Navigation, Railways, and Agriculture. By JOHN BOURNE, C.E. New Edition, with 124 Woodcuts. Fcp. 8vo. 6s.

HANDBOOK to the MINERALOGY of CORNWALL and DEVON; with Instructions for their Discrimination, and copious Tablets of Localities. By J. H. COLLINS, F.G.S. With 10 Plates. 8vo. 6s.

PRACTICAL TREATISE on METALLURGY, adapted from the last German Edition of Professor KERL's *Metallurgy* by W. CROOKES, F.R.S. &c. and E. BÖHRIG, Ph.D. M.E. With 625 Woodcuts. 3 vols. 8vo. price £4 19s.

MITCHELL'S MANUAL of PRACTICAL ASSAYING. Fourth Edition, for the most part rewritten, with all the recent Discoveries incorporated, by W. CROOKES, F.R.S. With 199 Woodcuts. 8vo. 31s. 6d.

LOUDON'S ENCYCLOPÆDIA of AGRICULTURE: comprising the Laying-out, Improvement, and Management of Landed Property, and the Cultivation and Economy of Agricultural Produce. With 1,100 Woodcuts. 8vo. 21s.

Loudon's Encyclopædia of Gardening: comprising the Theory and Practice of Horticulture, Floriculture, Arboriculture, and Landscape Gardening. With 1,000 Woodcuts. 8vo. 21s.

Religious and Moral Works.

SERMONS; Including Two Sermons on the Interpretation of Prophecy, and an Essay on the Right Interpretation and Understanding of the Scriptures. By the late Rev. THOMAS ARNOLD, D.D. 3 vols. 8vo. price 24s.

CHRISTIAN LIFE, its COURSE, its HINDRANCES, and its HELPS; Sermons preached mostly in the Chapel of Rugby School. By the late Rev. THOMAS ARNOLD, D.D. 8vo. 7s. 6d.

CHRISTIAN LIFE, its HOPES, its FEARS, and its CLOSE; Sermons preached mostly in the Chapel of Rugby School. By the late Rev. THOMAS ARNOLD, D.D. 8vo. 7s. 6d.

SERMONS chiefly on the INTERPRETATION of SCRIPTURE. By the late Rev. THOMAS ARNOLD, D.D. 8vo. price 7s. 6d.

SERMONS preached in the Chapel of Rugby School; with an Address before Confirmation. By the late Rev. THOMAS ARNOLD, D.D. Fcp. 8vo. price 3s. 6d.

THREE ESSAYS on RELIGION: Nature; the Utility of Religion; Theism. By JOHN STUART MILL. 8vo. price 10s. 6d.

INTRODUCTION to the SCIENCE of RELIGION. Four Lectures delivered at the Royal Institution; with Two Essays on False Analogies and the Philosophy of Mythology. By F. MAX MÜLLER, M.A. Crown 8vo. 10s. 6d.

SUPERNATURAL RELIGION; an Inquiry into the Reality of Divine Revelation. Third Edition, revised. 2 vols. 8vo. 24s.

ESSAYS on the HISTORY of the CHRISTIAN RELIGION. By JOHN Earl RUSSELL. Cabinet Edition, revised. Fcp. 8vo. price 3s. 6d.

The NEW BIBLE COMMENTARY, by Bishops and other Clergy of the Anglican Church, critically examined by the Right Rev. J. W. COLENSO, D.D. Bishop of Natal. 8vo. price 25s.

REASONS of FAITH; or, the ORDER of the Christian Argument Developed and Explained. By the Rev. G. S. DREW, M.A. Second Edition, revised and enlarged. Fcp. 8vo. price 6s.

SYNONYMS of the OLD TESTAMENT, their BEARING on CHRIS-TIAN FAITH and PRACTICE. By the Rev. R. B. GIRDLESTONE, M.A. 8vo. 15s.

An INTRODUCTION to the THEOLOGY of the CHURCH of ENGLAND, in an Exposition of the Thirty-nine Articles. By the Rev. T. P. BOULTBEE, LL.D. New Edition, Fcp. 8vo. price 6s.

SERMONS for the TIMES preached in St. Paul's Cathedral and elsewhere. By the Rev. THOMAS GRIFFITH, M.A. Crown 8vo. 6s.

An EXPOSITION of the 39 ARTICLES, Historical and Doctrinal. By E. HAROLD BROWNE, D.D. Lord Bishop of Winchester. New Edit. 8vo. 16s.

The LIFE and EPISTLES of ST. PAUL. By the Rev. W. J. CONYBEARE, M.A., and the Very Rev. J. S. HOWSON, D.D. Dean of Chester:—
LIBRARY EDITION, with all the Original Illustrations, Maps, Landscapes on Steel, Woodcuts, &c. 2 vols. 4to. 48s.
INTERMEDIATE EDITION, with a Selection of Maps, Plates, and Woodcuts. 2 vols. square crown 8vo. 21s.
STUDENT'S EDITION, revised and condensed, with 46 Illustrations and Maps. 1 vol. crown 8vo. price 9s.

The **VOYAGE** and **SHIPWRECK** of **ST. PAUL**; with Dissertations on the Life and Writings of St. Luke and the Ships and Navigation of the Ancients. By JAMES SMITH, F.R.S. Third Edition. Crown 8vo. 10s. 6d.

COMMENTARY on the **EPISTLE** to the **ROMANS**. By the Rev. W. A. O'CONOR, B.A. Crown 8vo. price 3s. 6d.

The **EPISTLE** to the **HEBREWS**; with Analytical Introduction and Notes. By the Rev. W. A. O'CONOR, B.A. Crown 8vo. price 4s. 6d.

A **CRITICAL** and **GRAMMATICAL COMMENTARY** on **ST. PAUL'S** Epistles. By C. J. ELLICOTT, D.D. Lord Bishop of Gloucester and Bristol. 8vo.

Galatians, Fourth Edition, 8s. 6d.

Ephesians, Fourth Edition, 8s. 6d.

Pastoral Epistles, Fourth Edition, 10s. 6d.

Philippians, Colossians, and Philemon, Third Edition, 10s. 6d.

Thessalonians, Third Edition, 7s. 6d.

HISTORICAL LECTURES on the **LIFE** of **OUR LORD**. By C. J. ELLICOTT, D.D. Bishop of Gloucester and Bristol. Fifth Edition. 8vo. 12s.

EVIDENCE of the **TRUTH** of the **CHRISTIAN RELIGION** derived from the Literal Fulfilment of Prophecy. By ALEXANDER KEITH, D.D. 37th Edition, with Plates, in square 8vo. 12s. 6d.; 39th Edition, in post 8vo. 6s.

The **HISTORY** and **LITERATURE** of the **ISRAELITES**, according to the Old Testament and the Apocrypha. By C. DE ROTHSCHILD and A. DE ROTHSCHILD. Second Edition, revised. 2 vols. post 8vo. with Two Maps, price 12s. 6d. Abridged Edition, in 1 vol. fcp. 8vo. price 3s. 6d.

An **INTRODUCTION** to the **STUDY** of the **NEW TESTAMENT**, Critical, Exegetical, and Theological. By the Rev. S. DAVIDSON, D.D. LL.D. 2 vols. 8vo. 30s.

HISTORY of **ISRAEL**. By H. EWALD, Prof. of the Univ. of Göttingen. Translated by J. E. CARPENTER, M.A., with a Preface by RUSSELL MARTINEAU, M.A. 5 vols. 8vo. 63s.

The **TREASURY** of **BIBLE KNOWLEDGE**; being a Dictionary of the Books, Persons, Places, Events, and other matters of which mention is made in Holy Scripture. By Rev. J. AYRE, M.A. With Maps, 16 Plates, and numerous Woodcuts. Fcp. 8vo. price 6s. cloth, or 10s. neatly bound in calf.

LECTURES on the **PENTATEUCH** and the **MOABITE STONE**. By the Right Rev. J. W. COLENSO, D.D. Bishop of Natal. 8vo. 12s.

The **PENTATEUCH** and **BOOK** of **JOSHUA CRITICALLY EXAMINED**. By the Right Rev. J. W. COLENSO, D.D. Bishop of Natal. Crown 8vo. 6s.

THOUGHTS for the **AGE**. By ELIZABETH M. SEWELL, Author of 'Amy Herbert,' &c. New Edition, revised. Fcp. 8vo. price 3s. 6d.

PASSING THOUGHTS on **RELIGION**. By Miss SEWELL. Fcp. 8vo. 3s. 6d.

SELF-EXAMINATION before **CONFIRMATION**. By Miss SEWELL. 32mo. price 1s. 6d.

READINGS for a **MONTH** preparatory to **CONFIRMATION**, from Writers of the Early and English Church. By Miss SEWELL. Fcp. 4s.

READINGS for **EVERY DAY** in **LENT**, compiled from the Writings of Bishop JEREMY TAYLOR. By Miss SEWELL. Fcp. 5s.

PREPARATION for the **HOLY COMMUNION**; the Devotions chiefly from the Works of JEREMY TAYLOR. By Miss SEWELL. 32mo. 3s.

THOUGHTS for the **HOLY WEEK** for Young Persons. By Miss SEWELL. New Edition. Fcp. 8vo. 2s.

PRINCIPLES of **EDUCATION** Drawn from Nature and Revelation, and applied to Female Education in the Upper Classes. By Miss SEWELL. 2 vols. fcp. 8vo. 12s. 6d.

LYRA GERMANICA, Hymns translated from the German by Miss C. WINKWORTH. FIRST and SECOND SERIES, price 3s. 6d. each.

SPIRITUAL SONGS for the **SUNDAYS** and **HOLIDAYS** throughout the Year. By J. S. B. MONSELL, LL.D. Fcp. 8vo. 4s. 6d.

ENDEAVOURS after the **CHRISTIAN LIFE**: Discourses. By the Rev. J. MARTINEAU, LL.D. Fifth Edition, carefully revised. Crown 8vo. 7s. 6d.

HYMNS of **PRAISE** and **PRAYER**, collected and edited by the Rev. J. MARTINEAU, LL.D. Crown 8vo. 4s. 6d.

WHATELY'S INTRODUCTORY LESSONS on the **CHRISTIAN** Evidences. 18mo. 6d.

BISHOP JEREMY TAYLOR'S ENTIRE WORKS. With Life by BISHOP HEBER. Revised and corrected by the Rev. C. P. EDEN. Complete in Ten Volumes, 8vo. cloth, price £5. 5s.

Travels, Voyages, &c.

EIGHT YEARS in **CEYLON.** By Sir SAMUEL W. BAKER, M.A. F.R.G.S. New Edition, with Illustrations engraved on Wood, by G. Pearson. Crown 8vo. 7s. 6d.

The RIFLE and the HOUND in CEYLON. By Sir SAMUEL W. BAKER, M.A. F.R.G.S. New Edition, with Illustrations engraved on Wood by G. Pearson. Crown 8vo. 7s. 6d.

MEETING the SUN; a Journey all round the World through Egypt, China, Japan, and California. By WILLIAM SIMPSON, F.R.G.S. With 48 Heliotypes and Wood Engravings from Drawings by the Author. Medium 8vo. 24s.

UNTRODDEN PEAKS and UNFREQUENTED VALLEYS; a Midsummer Ramble among the Dolomites. By AMELIA B. EDWARDS. With a Map and 27 Wood Engravings. Medium 8vo. 21s.

The DOLOMITE MOUNTAINS; Excursions through Tyrol, Carinthia, Carniola, and Friuli, 1861-1863. By J. GILBERT and G. C. CHURCHILL, F.R.G.S. With numerous Illustrations. Square crown 8vo. 21s.

The VALLEYS of TIROL; their Traditions and Customs, and how to Visit them. By Miss R. H. BUSK, Author of 'The Folk-Lore of Rome,' &c. With Maps and Frontispiece. Crown 8vo. 12s. 6d.

HOURS of EXERCISE in the ALPS. By JOHN TYNDALL, LL.D. D.C.L. F.R.S. Third Edition, with 7 Woodcuts by E. Whymper. Crown 8vo. price 12s. 6d.

The ALPINE CLUB MAP of SWITZERLAND, with parts of the Neighbouring Countries, on the Scale of Four Miles to an Inch. Edited by R. C. NICHOLS, F.S.A. F.R.G.S. In Four Sheets, price 42s. or mounted in a case, 52s. 6d. Each Sheet may be had separately, price 12s. or mounted in a case, 15s.

MAP of the CHAIN of MONT BLANC, from an Actual Survey in 1863–1864. By ADAMS-REILLY, F.R.G.S. M.A.C. Published under the Authority of the Alpine Club. In Chromolithography on extra stout drawing-paper 28in. × 17in. price 10s. or mounted on canvas in a folding case, 12s. 6d.

TRAVELS in the CENTRAL CAUCASUS and BASHAN. Including Visits to Ararat and Tabreez and Ascents of Kazbek and Elbruz. By D. W. FRESHFIELD. Square crown 8vo. with Maps, &c. 18s.

PAU and the PYRENEES. By Count HENRY RUSSELL, Member of the Alpine Club, &c. With 2 Maps. Fcp. 8vo. price 5s.

HOW to SEE NORWAY. By Captain J. R. CAMPBELL. With Map and 5 Woodcuts. Fcp. 8vo. price 5s.

GUIDE to the PYRENEES, for the use of Mountaineers. By CHARLES PACKE. With Map and Illustrations. Crown 8vo. 7s. 6d.

The ALPINE GUIDE. By JOHN BALL, M.R.I.A. late President of the Alpine Club. 3 vols. post 8vo. Thoroughly Revised Editions, with Maps and Illustrations:—I. *Western Alps*, 6s. 6d. II. *Central Alps*, 7s. 6d. III. *Eastern Alps*, 10s. 6d.

Introduction on Alpine Travelling in General, and on the Geology of the Alps, price 1s. Each of the Three Volumes or Parts of the *Alpine Guide* may be had with this INTRODUCTION prefixed, price 1s. extra.

VISITS to REMARKABLE PLACES: Old Halls, Battle-Fields, and Stones Illustrative of Striking Passages in English History and Poetry. By WILLIAM HOWITT. 2 vols. square crown 8vo. with Woodcuts, 25s.

The RURAL LIFE of ENGLAND. By the same Author. With Woodcuts by Bewick and Williams. Medium 8vo. 12s. 6d.

Works of Fiction.

WHISPERS from FAIRYLAND. By the Rt. Hon. E. H. KNATCH-BULL-HUGESSEN, M.P. Author of 'Stories for my Children,' 'Moonshine,' 'Queer Folk,' &c. With Nine Illustrations from Original Designs engraved on Wood by G. Pearson. Crown 8vo. price 6s.

ELENA, an Italian Tale. By L. N. COMYN, Author of 'Atherstone Priory.' 2 vols. post 8vo. 14s.

CENTULLE, a Tale of Pau. By DENYS SHYNE LAWLOR, Author of 'Pilgrimages in the Pyrenees and Landes. Post 8vo. 10s. 6d.

LADY WILLOUGHBY'S DIARY, 1635—1663; Charles the First, the Protectorate, and the Restoration. Reproduced in the Style of the Period to which the Diary relates. Crown 8vo. price 7s. 6d.

TALES of the TEUTONIC LANDS. By the Rev. G. W. Cox, M.A. and E. H. Jones. Crown 8vo. 10s. 6d.

The FOLK-LORE of ROME, collected by Word of Mouth from the People. By Miss R. H. Busk, Author of 'Patrañas,' &c. Crown 8vo. 12s. 6d.

NOVELS and TALES. By the Right Hon. B. Disraeli, M.P. Cabinet Edition, complete in Ten Volumes, crown 8vo. price £3.

Lothair, 6s.	Henrietta Temple, 6s.
Coningsby, 6s.	Contarini Fleming, &c. 6s.
Sybil, 6s.	Alroy, Ixion, &c. 6s.
Tancred, 6s.	The Young Duke, &c. 6s.
Venetia, 6s.	Vivian Grey, 6s.

The MODERN NOVELIST'S LIBRARY. Each Work, in crown 8vo. complete in a Single Volume :—

Atherstone Priory, 2s. boards ; 2s. 6d. cloth.
Melville's Gladiators, 2s boards ; 2s. 6d. cloth.
———— Good for Nothing, 2s. boards ; 2s. 6d. cloth.
———— Holmby House, 2s. boards ; 2s. 6d. cloth.
———— Interpreter, 2s. boards ; 2s. 6d. cloth.
———— Kate Coventry, 2s. boards ; 2s. 6d. cloth.
———— Queen's Maries, 2s. boards ; 2s. 6d. cloth.
———— Digby Grand, 2s. boards ; 2s. 6d. cloth.
———— General Bounce, 2s. boards ; 2s. 6d. cloth.
Trollope's Warden, 1s. 6d. boards ; 2s. cloth.
———— Barchester Towers, 2s. boards ; 2s. 6d. cloth.
Bramley-Moore's Six Sisters of the Valleys, 2s. boards ; 2s. 6d. cloth.
The Burgomaster's Family, 2s. boards ; 2s. 6d. cloth.

CABINET EDITION of STORIES and TALES by Miss Sewell :—

Amy Herbert, 2s. 6d.	Ivors, 2s. 6d.
Gertrude, 2s. 6d.	Katharine Ashton, 2s. 6d.
The Earl's Daughter, 2s. 6d.	Margaret Percival, 3s. 6d.
Experience of Life, 2s. 6d.	Laneton Parsonage, 3s. 6d.
Cleve Hall, 2s. 6d.	Ursula, 3s. 6d.

CYLLENE; or, the Fall of Paganism. By Henry Sneyd, M.A. University College, Oxford. 2 vols. post 8vo. price 14s.

BECKER'S GALLUS; or, Roman Scenes of the Time of Augustus : with Notes and Excursuses. New Edition. Post 8vo. 7s. 6d.

BECKER'S CHARICLES: a Tale illustrative of Private Life among the Ancient Greeks : with Notes and Excursuses. New Edition. Post 8vo. 7s. 6d.

TALES of ANCIENT GREECE. By George W. Cox, M.A. late Scholar of Trin. Coll. Oxon. Crown 8vo. price 6s. 6d.

Poetry and The Drama.

FAUST: a Dramatic Poem. By Goethe. Translated into English Prose, with Notes, by A. Hayward. Ninth Edition. Fcp. 8vo. price 3s.

MOORE'S IRISH MELODIES, Maclise's Edition, with 161 Steel Plates from Original Drawings. Super-royal 8vo. 31s. 6d.

Miniature Edition of Moore's Irish Melodies, with Maclise's Designs (as above) reduced in Lithography. Imp. 16mo. 10s. 6d.

BALLADS and LYRICS of OLD FRANCE; with other Poems. By A. LANG, Fellow of Merton College, Oxford. Square fcp. 8vo. price 5s.

MOORE'S LALLA ROOKH. Tenniel's Edition, with 68 Wood Engravings from Original Drawings and other Illustrations. Fcp. 4to. 21s.

SOUTHEY'S POETICAL WORKS, with the Author's last Corrections and copyright Additions. Medium 8vo. with Portrait and Vignette, 14s.

LAYS of ANCIENT ROME; with IVRY and the ARMADA. By the Right Hon. Lord MACAULAY. 16mo. 3s. 6d.

LORD MACAULAY'S LAYS of ANCIENT ROME. With 90 Illustrations on Wood, from the Antique, from Drawings by G. SCHARF. Fcp. 4to. 21s.

Miniature Edition of Lord Macaulay's Lays of Ancient Rome, with the Illustrations (as above) reduced in Lithography. Imp. 16mo. 10s. 6d.

The ÆNEID of VIRGIL Translated into English Verse. By JOHN CONINGTON, M.A. New Edition. Crown 8vo. 9s.

HORATII OPERA. Library Edition, with Marginal References and English Notes. Edited by the Rev. J. E. YONGE. 8vo. 21s.

The LYCIDAS and EPITAPHIUM DAMONIS of MILTON. Edited, with Notes and Introduction (including a Reprint of the rare Latin Version of the Lycidas, by W. Hogg, 1694), by C. S. JERRAM, M.A. Crown 8vo. 3s. 6d.

BOWDLER'S FAMILY SHAKSPEARE, cheaper Genuine Editions. Medium 8vo. large type, with 36 Woodcuts, price 14s. Cabinet Edition, with the same ILLUSTRATIONS, 6 vols. fcp. 8vo. price 21s.

POEMS. By JEAN INGELOW. 2 vols. fcp. 8vo. price 10s.
FIRST SERIES, containing 'DIVIDED,' 'The STAR'S MONUMENT,' &c. Sixteenth Thousand. Fcp. 8vo. price 5s.
SECOND SERIES, 'A STORY of DOOM,' 'GLADYS and her ISLAND,' &c. Fifth Thousand. Fcp. 8vo. price 5s.

POEMS by Jean Ingelow. FIRST SERIES, with nearly 100 Illustrations, engraved on Wood by Dalziel Brothers. Fcp. 4to. 21s.

Rural Sports, &c.

DOWN the ROAD; Or, Reminiscences of a Gentleman Coachman. By C. T. S. BIRCH REYNARDSON. With Twelve Chromolithographic Illustrations from Original Paintings by H. Alken. Medium 8vo. [Nearly ready.

The DEAD SHOT; or, Sportsman's Complete Guide: a Treatise on the Use of the Gun, Dog-breaking, Pigeon-shooting, &c. By MARKSMAN. Revised Edition. Fcp. 8vo. with Plates, 5s.

ENCYCLOPÆDIA of RURAL SPORTS; a complete Account, Historical, Practical, and Descriptive, of Hunting, Shooting, Fishing, Racing, and all other Rural and Athletic Sports and Pastimes. By D. P. BLAINE. With above 600 Woodcuts (20 from Designs by JOHN LEECH). 8vo. 21s.

The FLY-FISHER'S ENTOMOLOGY. By ALFRED RONALDS. With
coloured Representations of the Natural and Artificial Insect. Sixth Edition,
with 20 coloured Plates. 8vo. 14s.

A BOOK on ANGLING; a complete Treatise on the Art of Angling
in every branch. By FRANCIS FRANCIS. New Edition, with Portrait and 15
other Plates, plain and coloured. Post 8vo. 15s.

WILCOCKS'S SEA-FISHERMAN; comprising the Chief Methods of
Hook and Line Fishing, a Glance at Nets, and Remarks on Boats and Boating.
New Edition, with 80 Woodcuts. Post 8vo. 12s. 6d.

HORSES and STABLES. By Colonel F. FITZWYGRAM, XV. the King's
Hussars. With Twenty-four Plates of Illustrations, containing very numerous
Figures engraved on Wood. 8vo. 10s. 6d.

The HORSE'S FOOT, and HOW to KEEP it SOUND. By W.
MILES, Esq. Ninth Edition, with Illustrations. Imperial 8vo. 12s. 6d.

A PLAIN TREATISE on HORSE-SHOEING. By W. MILES, Esq.
Sixth Edition. Post 8vo. with Illustrations, 2s. 6d.

STABLES and STABLE-FITTINGS. By W. MILES, ESQ. Imp. 8vo.
with 13 Plates, 15s.

REMARKS on HORSES' TEETH, addressed to Purchasers. By W.
MILES, Esq. Post 8vo. 1s. 6d.

A TREATISE on HORSE-SHOEING and LAMENESS. By JOSEPH
GAMGEE, Veterinary Surgeon. 8vo. with 55 Woodcuts, price 10s. 6d.

The HORSE: with a Treatise on Draught. By WILLIAM YOUATT.
New Edition, revised and enlarged. 8vo. with numerous Woodcuts, 12s. 6d.

The DOG. By WILLIAM YOUATT. 8vo. with numerous Woodcuts, 6s.

The DOG in HEALTH and DISEASE. By STONEHENGE. With 70
Wood Engravings. Square crown 8vo. 7s. 6d.

The GREYHOUND. By STONEHENGE. Revised Edition, with 24
Portraits of Greyhounds. Square crown 8vo. 10s. 6d.

The OX; his Diseases and their Treatment: with an Essay on Parturi-
tion in the Cow. By J. R. DOBSON. Crown 8vo. with Illustrations, 7s. 6d.

Works of Utility and General Information.

The THEORY and PRACTICE of BANKING. By H. D. MACLEOD,
M.A. Barrister-at-Law. Second Edition, entirely remodelled. 2 vols. 8vo. 30s.

M'CULLOCH'S DICTIONARY, Practical, Theoretical, and Historical,
of Commerce and Commercial Navigation. New and revised Edition. 8vo. 63s.

The CABINET LAWYER; a Popular Digest of the Laws of England,
Civil, Criminal, and Constitutional: intended for Practical Use and General
Information. Twenty-fourth Edition. Fcp. 8vo. price 9s.

BLACKSTONE ECONOMISED, a Compendium of the Laws of England to the Present time, in Four Books, each embracing the Legal Principles and Practical Information contained in their respective volumes of Blackstone, supplemented by Subsequent Statutory Enactments, Important Legal Decisions, &c. By D. M. Aird, Barrister-at-Law. Revised Edition. Post 8vo. 7s. 6d.

PEWTNER'S COMPREHENSIVE SPECIFIER; a Guide to the Practical Specification of every kind of Building-Artificers' Work, with Forms of Conditions and Agreements. Edited by W. Young. Crown 8vo. 6s.

COLLIERIES and COLLIERS; a Handbook of the Law and Leading Cases relating thereto. By J. C. Fowler. Third Edition. Fcp. 8vo. 7s. 6d.

HINTS to MOTHERS on the MANAGEMENT of their HEALTH during the Period of Pregnancy and in the Lying-in Room. By the late Thomas Bull, M.D. Fcp. 8vo. 5s.

The MATERNAL MANAGEMENT of CHILDREN in HEALTH and Disease. By the late Thomas Bull, M.D. Fcp. 8vo. 5s.

The THEORY of the MODERN SCIENTIFIC GAME of WHIST. By William Pole, F.R.S. Fifth Edition, enlarged. Fcp. 8vo. 2s. 6d.

CHESS OPENINGS. By F. W. Longman, Balliol College, Oxford. Second Edition revised. Fcp. 8vo. 2s. 6d.

THREE HUNDRED ORIGINAL CHESS PROBLEMS and STUDIES. By James Pierce, M.A. and W. T. Pierce. With numerous Diagrams. Square fcp. 8vo. 7s. 6d. Supplement, price 2s. 6d.

A PRACTICAL TREATISE on BREWING; with Formulæ for Public Brewers, and Instructions for Private Families. By W. Black. 8vo. 10s. 6d.

MODERN COOKERY for PRIVATE FAMILIES, reduced to a System of Easy Practice in a Series of carefully-tested Receipts. By Eliza Acton. Newly revised and enlarged; with 8 Plates and 150 Woodcuts. Fcp. 8vo. 6s.

MAUNDER'S TREASURY of KNOWLEDGE and LIBRARY of Reference; comprising an English Dictionary and Grammar, Universal Gazetteer, Classical Dictionary, Chronology, Law Dictionary, a synopsis of the Peerage useful Tables, &c. Revised Edition. Fcp. 8vo. 6s. cloth, or 10s. calf.

Knowledge for the Young.

The STEPPING-STONE to KNOWLEDGE; or upwards of 700 Questions and Answers on Miscellaneous Subjects, adapted to the capacity of Infant minds. 18mo. 1s.

SECOND SERIES of the STEPPING-STONE to KNOWLEDGE: Containing upwards of 800 Questions and Answers on Miscellaneous Subjects not contained in the First Series. 18mo. 1s.

The STEPPING-STONE to GEOGRAPHY: Containing several Hundred Questions and Answers on Geographical Subjects. 18mo. 1s

The **STEPPING-STONE** to **ENGLISH HISTORY**; Questions and Answers on the History of England. 18mo. 1s.

The **STEPPING-STONE** to **BIBLE KNOWLEDGE**; Questions and Answers on the Old and New Testaments. 18mo. 1s.

The **STEPPING-STONE** to **BIOGRAPHY**; Questions and Answers on the Lives of Eminent Men and Women. 18mo. 1s.

The **STEPPING-STONE** to **IRISH HISTORY**: Containing several Hundred Questions and Answers on the History of Ireland. 18mo. 1s.

The **STEPPING-STONE** to **FRENCH HISTORY**: Containing several Hundred Questions and Answers on the History of France. 18mo. 1s.

The **STEPPING-STONE** to **ROMAN HISTORY**: Containing several Hundred Questions and Answers on the History of Rome. 18mo. 1s.

The **STEPPING-STONE** to **GRECIAN HISTORY**: Containing several Hundred Questions and Answers on the History of Greece. 18mo. 1s.

The **STEPPING-STONE** to **ENGLISH GRAMMAR**: Containing several Hundred Questions and Answers on English Grammar. 18mo. 1s.

The **STEPPING-STONE** to **FRENCH PRONUNCIATION and CONVERSATION**: Containing several Hundred Questions and Answers. 18mo. 1s.

The **STEPPING-STONE** to **ASTRONOMY**: Containing several Hundred familiar Questions and Answers on the Earth and the Solar and Stellar Systems. 18mo. 1s.

The **STEPPING-STONE** to **MUSIC**: Containing several Hundred Questions on the Science; also a short History of Music. 18mo. 1s.

The **STEPPING-STONE** to **NATURAL HISTORY**: VERTEBRATE OR BACK-BONED ANIMALS. PART I. *Mammalia*; PART II. *Birds, Reptiles, Fishes.* 18mo. 1s. each Part.

THE **STEPPING-STONE** to **ARCHITECTURE**; Questions and Answers explaining the Principles and Progress of Architecture from the Earliest Times. With 100 Woodcuts. 18mo. 1s.

INDEX.

Spottiswoode & Co., Printers, New-street Square, London.